# STREAMS OF COURAGE

## SPIES OF THE CIVIL WAR
### BOOK FOUR

## SANDRA MERVILLE HART

WILD HEART
BOOKS

Cover design by: Carpe Librum Book Design

Author is represented by Hartline Literary Agency

ISBN-13: 978-1-942265-90-0

*"Be strong and courageous. Do not be afraid or terrified because of them, for the Lord your God goes with you; he will never leave you nor forsake you."*
Deuteronomy 31:6 (NIV)

*Lovingly dedicated to my dad,*
*Who had the courage to stand on his convictions.*
*Though he lived a humble life,*
*His love and compassion changed the world*
*For those who loved him.*

*And to my mom,*
*Who, though small in stature compared to her adoring husband,*
*Was a tower of strength for him*
*And for all who loved her.*

# CHAPTER 1

*U*nbelievable. Mississippi had voted to secede from the Union.

Ashburn Mitchell reeled from the catastrophe. He'd held onto hope after strongly Unionist Vicksburg had voted the previous month to send two co-operationalist delegates to Jackson for the Mississippi State Convention.

It was all for naught.

"You going to say something?" William Sanderson, Junior, Ashburn's best buddy, had ridden from his father's plantation two miles outside the city to Ash's saddle shop to deliver the unfortunate news.

"I fear this vote ensures there will be a fight between the North and South." A fight Ash never wanted. He limped to his work bench. How could this have happened after all the fervor among Vicksburg's citizens to remain in the Union? He leaned an elbow on his knee, his suddenly throbbing head resting on his palm.

Willie joined him, folding his tall, thin frame onto the

1

bench. "That's what Pa figures. I didn't want to secede either. We've got too much to lose. But the vote wasn't even close. The die is cast."

No, it couldn't be. Ash couldn't accept the fact that they'd lost the vote. "What are they saying around town?" He'd heard nothing since he worked alone and no customers had visited his saddle shop that day.

"It's pretty quiet." Willie peered out the door, always opened except on the coldest of days. "Heard they celebrated the vote with fireworks in Jackson. Shot off cannons too."

Cannons that soon enough would be used in war.

Ash could barely swallow past the lump in his throat.

"I don't feel much like celebrating." Willie's shoulders slumped.

"You going to accept this?" After their latest conversation about it at an annual Christmas ball, where Ash waltzed with the lovely Julia Dodd, he'd been comforted to learn that he and his friend agreed on the matter, despite the fact that slave labor harvested the cotton on Willie's plantation.

"Mississippi's my home," Willie said. "I'll abide by the convention's decision."

"I'm not ready to do that." Ash's heart plummeted. He hated to think that he and his best friend would land on different sides of the conflict. He'd have wagered that nothing could separate them.

"You're not saying you'd turn your back on the South." Willie rose slowly, staring at him through narrowed brown eyes.

"Mississippi is my home too." He understood Willie's reasoning. It wasn't in Ash to raise a weapon against his state.

"Glad we got that settled." Stiffness eased from Willie's shoulders.

Did they settle it? Ash stared down at his leg. His old injury might keep him from becoming a Union soldier, but he wasn't about to serve the Confederacy—of that he was determined.

～

*EARLY FEBRUARY, 1861*

"*A*re you certain?" Texas had seceded as well? Julia Dodd's fingers tightened around her lace-trimmed handkerchief.

Carlton Murphy, her beau, had made this unplanned visit to deliver the triumphant news to her personally.

"Of course, though I don't expect you to understand the importance." The stocky man of twenty-two stepped to the wide hearth in her mother's elegant parlor and stared down into a crackling fire on the cold winter's afternoon. "You see, our great state of Mississippi didn't let grass grow under its feet after South Carolina lit the way. Florida, Alabama, Georgia, and Louisiana followed our example last month."

Carlton loved to tell her what she'd already learned in the local newspapers. When she, Mama, and her brother, Eddie, had visited Carlton's family's cotton plantation ten miles from the city, she'd noticed the same superior attitude in Mr. Murphy toward his wife.

Julia's beau had made it clear in their six-month courtship that he didn't respect her intellect. Still, Mama had high hopes that Julia would marry Carlton and enjoy a life of luxury.

"We can whip those Yankees good now, sure enough, but it won't hurt to have the rest of our fellow Southern states join us." Carlton slammed a fist into his open palm.

A war. That would be a nightmare. At least she and her mother were in agreement on their Unionist support, a fact that they'd kept hidden from Carlton. "Perhaps there won't be any battles."

"Northerners would be wise to allow us to start our own country in peace." His blond mustache twitched. "But if it comes to it, I'll join the army and fight for our beloved state. No red-blooded Mississippian will take such threats sitting down."

Julia leaned against her armchair's cushioned back. She hadn't considered the possibility that her beau would fight for the South. She'd figured nothing beyond his frequent trips to New Orleans to see to his father's business interests there would keep him from his family's plantation.

"That surprises you. No need for you to worry. I'll be fine. No doubt your tatting will keep you busy."

Heat blazed in her cheeks. Did he consider her a mindless simpleton with no opinions to call her own? "I continue to hold my Unionist views, which I've long held."

There. That ought to end this courtship. *Sorry, Mother.* But she couldn't bear another moment of being courted by this man.

Carlton brushed off her words with a flick of his wrist. "No, you don't. That changed when our state seceded."

"Mr. Murphy, I assure you, I know my own mind." Standing, she met his piercing eyes.

Raindrops pounded against the shutters, the only sound in the tense silence spreading between them.

"No matter," he said. "We simply won't talk about such things in public."

"I'll talk about them wherever I please." A rash claim she immediately regretted. It was a sore topic around town. Tensions were growing these days. It was wiser not to enter the arguments on the side of the North—as Ash Mitchell was wont to do.

Carlton crossed the room, stopping an arm's length from her. "What don't you understand?" He spoke slowly. "I'll explain everything."

"Don't trouble yourself." She doubted he grasped anything

beyond what his father spouted. What had made her think she could entertain a marriage proposal from him? She must thank God most particularly in her prayers tonight that the man had never hinted at marriage.

"It's my duty." He reached for her hand.

She dodged him. "Consider yourself relieved of duty." She stepped to the window, where raindrops slid down the pane. "I regret we won't be able to entertain you for supper, after all." Mama had invited him to dine with them, but now that Julia's decision to end the courtship was made, she couldn't be rid of him soon enough. And yes, he would be fine. She'd never seen any indication of a special regard for her.

As if she'd marry a man who didn't support the Union. She should have seen this coming. His plantation was run using slave labor.

His shoulders stiffened. "My decision to fight distresses you. Put it from your mind. One battle is all that's required to end the turmoil between our countries."

That view, shared by many Southerners, seemed optimistic to Julia.

Carlton continued. "There's obviously a misunderstanding between us. Let's sit together and discuss the matter until you're comfortable."

Julia turned to face him. "I already comprehend the situation."

"I don't understand why you're acting this way." His brow furrowed. "Surely, you don't want me riding in the rain."

He'd be inside his snug carriage while his driver endured the weather.

"I'm sorry, Carlton." He didn't comprehend her delicate hints, so she must speak plainly. "I've decided we won't suit."

The words seemed to register slowly. His cheeks turned scarlet. "Do you realize what you're tossing aside? I stand to inherit seven thousand acres."

That was the part of Carlton that appealed most to her mother.

No, it was unjust to assume so.

"Our three-story stone mansion will be mine. As my wife, it could be yours." His brown eyes pierced through her. "If I walk out that door, you won't be able to *beg* me to return."

"I regret—"

"It's too late for apologies." He held up his hand. His normally jovial face was stiff as a mask.

"I'll fetch your coat and hat." She left to gather them from the front closet.

How Julia missed their butler, who could have handled this awkward situation with grace. Unfortunately, Mama had decided they could no longer afford his salary after Papa died.

She returned to the parlor with Carlton's things, which he snatched from her hands before storming out the front door and stalking toward the stable behind their home.

"Julia?" Mama descended the steps with barely a sound and peered into the parlor. "Where's Carlton?"

"He's gone, Mama." Relief settled on Julia's spirit. She'd agreed to the courtship merely to please her parent, but she'd taken as much as she could stand. "He won't be back."

"Oh, Julia. What have you done?" Mama rolled her eyes heavenward.

"He's not the man for me."

"Then who is?"

She didn't know, what with all the local men supporting the South in this foolhardy war. But then, there was Ash Mitchell...

Unfortunately, Mama had higher expectations for her than a saddler.

# CHAPTER 2

*Mid-March, 1861*

"Why, Ash, what a pleasant surprise." Julia pushed the front door wider as she glanced at the empty porch behind him. He came alone? He'd never come uninvited without Willie and her friend Savannah in tow. Willie and Savannah, who'd been childhood friends, had been courting for a couple of years. "Please, won't you come inside? Such a blustery day."

"Indeed." He stepped into the hall, holding his hat. "Though it's often so in the winter on our bluff."

"Please come into the parlor. Mama and Eddie are out this afternoon." She led him to comfortable cushioned chairs arranged before a cozy fire. What had prompted Ash Mitchell to call on a Saturday afternoon? Of course, he was as welcome as any of her friends, for she'd known him since childhood.

"Forgive the interruption." Still holding his hat, he waited until she sat to take the chair opposite.

"Not at all." She waved her hand. "I'm just tatting some lace to pass away the dreary afternoon. Will you take refreshment?"

"No, thank you." He set his felt hat on a round table beside him. "I came to ask if I might escort you and your family to church in the morning."

That was unexpected yet welcome. She hadn't visited with him since dancing with him at Savannah's annual Christmas ball, one she'd attended with Carlton. "Why, that would be lovely." They didn't attend the same church, so this invitation indicated Ash's interest in her. "You may be aware that my courtship with Carlton ended a month ago."

"I saw him leave rather...abruptly." Hazel eyes met hers. "Waited for him to return these past weeks. Can't say I was sorry he didn't come back."

"It was my choice. But it hasn't been long enough that I'm ready to court anyone yet." She didn't want to make another mistake.

"I'll wait, then, as long you give me a chance when you're ready."

He couldn't have said anything that pleased her more. "If you will be content to escort me to church for now..." Julia didn't want to close the door on a possible courtship.

His countenance lightened. "I'd like that."

"Well, then, I will see you tomorrow." She rose and extended her hand.

He clasped it between his. "Until tomorrow."

After he left, Julia sat before the fire, full of wonder. She'd been to many events since girlhood where Ash was also a guest. They'd established a friendship. Could it be more?

"Julia?"

She gave a start. How had Mama entered the house with her noisy little brother without Julia hearing them?

"Whatever can you be doing?" Mama sat in the seat Ash had vacated a half hour before and began to peel off her gloves.

"Ash Mitchell stopped by. He's walking with us to tomorrow's services."

"A saddler, Julia?" Mama's frown marred her nearly flawless complexion. "Set your sights higher, my dear."

Her face tightened. "It's simply an escort to church." This saddler had twice the integrity as Carlton. That mattered more to her.

∼

*LATE APRIL, 1861*

"*T*here's still a chance to reunite the North and South without bloodshed." As he stood outside a busy cigar store in Vicksburg on a cloudy spring afternoon, Ash's voice rose with emotion as he pleaded with a group of the city's businessmen.

"The time for talking has passed." A gray-haired man tapped his cane against the sidewalk.

"One good battle will decide the thing." A grocer stroked his full black beard. "The North will then agree to our states' rights."

"I fear it won't be that easy." Ash pinched the bridge of his nose. He'd received the same responses last week with a different group. "Let's stop this madness before it escalates to shedding Southern men's blood."

"We're Mississippians first." The middle-aged bookbinder crossed his arms.

"We stand with Mississippi." A newspaper reporter raised his fist. "Right, fellas?"

Several cheers went up.

"Ain't you for Mississippi, Ash?" A menacing tone from the back of the group.

Ash peered around the grocer's broad shoulders into the steely eyes of a foundry worker. "Always." Yet his state had left the Union. He couldn't support that decision.

"Best stay that way." This from a burly man in his thirties who worked for the brickyard. "You ain't a Unionist, right?" His eyes narrowed.

The atmosphere turned frosty in an instant. "What if I was?" Ash straightened his shoulders.

"That'd be mighty uncomfortable for you. Maybe for your family, if they feel the same way. Don't you have a new girl?" The brickyard worker's tone was almost pleasant.

The hair stiffened on the back of Ash's neck. Was he being watched?

"Mind your words." This warning came from the foundry worker. "Iffen you know what's good for you."

The cigar store owner patted his shoulder as the group broke up. Ash might have one fellow townsman in agreement.

Ash looked over his shoulder on the way back to his shop. No one seemed to be following him. When he reached his shop, he peered at his home next door. All seemed to be well. He'd watch to make certain it stayed that way.

He had no more than picked up a buckle for a harness when booted footsteps scuffed outside his open door. When he spotted the bricklayer and foundry worker with a gunsmith, blood rushed through his veins. "Howdy, fellas. You all here to order a saddle?"

They stepped inside. He recognized all of them but didn't know their names.

"Nope. We don't do business with traitors." The deep voice of the gunsmith fit his solid frame.

"I'm not a traitor." The men all had at least a dozen years on him. Outweighed him. These were the vigilantes he'd heard had been threatening Unionists.

"You're at least a Union sympathizer." The gunsmith circled him. "And that's enough to earn you this visit. We don't want no talk of supporting the Union." Quick as a snake strike, he punched Ash in the stomach.

The blow sent Ash reeling. His shoulder struck his wooden workbench, the pain warring with that in his midsection.

"Keep your yapper shut"—the gunsmith spoke standing over him—"or the next time, we won't be so friendly." He stalked out, followed by the foundry worker.

The bricklayer stopped in the doorway. "Be grateful we're not dragging you to jail. Take this as a warning."

Ash slumped against his workbench. He'd be more careful in the future. To protect himself, his family, and now...Julia.

~

WEDNESDAY, MAY 22, 1861

*A* shadow crossed over Ash as he pumped the well's handle, and he looked up to see Willie approaching. "What brings you to town? You here to have supper with Savannah?"

"Been here all day. I'll stop over at Savannah's when I leave here." Willie's customary grin was missing. "You about done for the day?"

"Yup." Water spurted over Ash's grimy hands. He lathered lye soap over them as he studied his friend. Odd that he wore work pants and a wool shirt without a coat. The plantation owner's son was dressed more like a saddler. Something was up. "Want to talk in the house or shop?"

"Shop." Willie folded his arms. "Selling many saddles?"

"Business has picked up this spring." Ash rinsed his hands.

"You courting Julia Dodd?"

"Just escorted her to church so far." He'd suffered through watching her court three other men the past two years. Mrs. Dodd had always been rather frosty toward him, and he'd taken the hint. This time, he'd best try his hand before someone snatched the beautiful Julia from him forever.

"'Bout time." Willie kicked at a clump of dirt. "Savannah and I planned outings for all of us every time Julia ended a courtship." Their families, Luke, and his girl, Felicity, were often included in those outings.

Their mutual friend, Luke, had been courting Julia's friend over a year. "That was on purpose?" He swiped wet hands on his pants.

"Savannah figured you'd eventually notice Julia."

"Oh, I did, and I'd have asked her to court sooner except that she was always courting or getting over someone." Shaking his head, he put his hands on his hips. "I guess I owe you a thank you. I doubt Julia would have consented to my escort to church without all those picnics, fishing parties, and drives to the country."

"You're welcome." He slid his boot across the dirt. Back again. "Got something to say."

"Let's step inside." Ash led the way to his shop. When they were seated on his workbench, he asked, "What's on your mind?"

"I mustered into the army." His jaw set. "Signed up with the Jeff Davis Guards."

Ash rubbed the back of his neck. He knew Willie had decided to support their state, but to become a Confederate soldier? A slap on the face would have been more welcome.

"Been drilling to prepare to fight and riding home every night." Willie pushed up his sleeves.

Ash knew about the companies forming in Vicksburg—and had avoided the officers pressuring men to join the army for months. Some companies had left for war in early spring. "I... don't know what to say." His heart hammered against his chest. Though Willie had warned him his loyalty was to the South, it was still a blow.

"Maybe you should have figured I'd join the fight." Willie looked at him squarely.

"You've been in town for drills and never stopped by?"

"Training lasts hours. Savannah's proud of me but expects me to stop by every evening."

Made sense she wanted to see her beau. But he and Ash had been friends since childhood, despite the fact Ash wasn't in the same social class. "You could stay here. Mama's got fresh sheets in the spare bedroom."

"Mama's having a hard time with my decision. Wants me home as much as possible. Our company heads out Monday."

"So soon?"

"Since the Fort Sumpter incident, the Union's been gathering regiments in Washington City. We must be ready to meet them." He stood and looked down at Ash. "Come with us."

Ash pushed up from the bench and strode to the open window.

"Luke mustered in today," Willie said. "He's telling Felicity tonight."

Luke too? The three of them had been buddies for years. He and Willie were twenty, Luke a year younger. He'd believed Luke loyal to the Union. Ash rested his forehead against the window jamb. The war was about to change their lives forever.

Willie's footsteps sounded on the wood floor as he crossed toward Ash. "None of us have ever been to Virginia. Can you imagine it? What a lark it will be."

"Men die in battle."

"Pshaw." Willie waved his hand. "Everyone knows this whole thing will blow over with one battle. Sure hope we get there in time."

"I can't do it." This wasn't the time to speak of differing loyalties, but Ash felt the need to explain himself. "Too much holds me here." Being the sole support for his family paled as a reason when compared to his desire that the country remain whole, united.

"More than what's waiting for me here?"

Footsteps sounded on the stone steps between the saddle shop and his house. His mother poked her head inside. "Willie, how good to see you." The petite woman beamed at him. "Supper's ready. Want to dine with us?"

"Evening, Mrs. Mitchell." He gave her a polite nod and crossed to the door. "I have to get to Savannah's. Thank you kindly, though, for the invitation."

"We look forward to seeing you again when you can stay longer."

"Yes, ma'am." Willie looked back at Ash. "Think about what I said."

Mama watched him go, straightening her apron over her plump form. "What's happened?"

He explained, and as he did, her expression turned grave.

Friends on opposite side of the conflict.

It wasn't supposed to happen this way.

~

"*D*on't tug at my hair so, Julia." Wincing, Mama covered the blond ringlets on at the nape of her neck. "I've a mind to ask Daisy to try her hand with the curling tongs. Surely, she wouldn't pull my hair out."

"Sorry, Mama. I guess I'm distracted about tonight's party." Julia wrapped the last curl in heated tongs, though their maid could do no worse than her fumbling fingers. She didn't often style her mother's hair, who customarily wore a chignon covered in a snood.

Ashburn Mitchell would arrive in just over an hour with his mother and oldest sister to escort them all to the last hurrah before their mutual friends, Willie and Luke, left for Richmond.

"I hope you don't view Ash's escort to this evening's festivities as the beginning of a courtship, Julia." Mama's blue eyes, reflected in the oval mirror over her vanity table, studied her.

"Why not? He's a fine gentleman. Surely, there can be no objection." He'd been driving her family to Sunday church services and staying for lunch this spring. Though they'd danced together at other balls, this was the first one they'd attend together.

"Have a care for your place in society. A saddler with one small shop that must also support his mother and sisters can't provide for you in the manner in which you were raised. I believe you'll soon come to your senses."

Her mother hadn't been obsessed with their place in society before Julia's father died in a hunting accident in 1858. Mama had changed and not for the better. Her greatest concern these days centered around money, not her family. Mama had been pushing her toward wealthy suitors. So far, Ash suited Julia better than anyone who'd called on her.

Mama sighed. "And now, I shall have to spend the evening with Louisa Mitchell."

"Ash said his mother is looking forward to furthering your acquaintance."

"To raise her own standing in society." Mama groaned.

That seemed unfair. Mrs. Mitchell might be a gossip, but she had been nothing but kind to Julia. Besides, Julia's friendship with the wealthy Savannah Adair had elevated Mama's status to become friends with Mrs. Adair. The families had often attended events with Willie and Ash. Lately, that had expanded to include Luke, who courted Julia's friend, Felicity.

"Too bad about Carlton. You'd have a life of luxury on his plantation."

Julia bit back her frustration. She hadn't seen him since their courtship ended. "He wasn't right for me."

"You're nineteen. You were born when I was that age." She

met Julia's eyes in the mirror. "There will surely be wealthy bachelors at the ball."

"I won't marry a Confederate soldier. You share those sentiments."

"Please, lower your voice."

"Sorry." Julia's gaze darted to the large bedroom window, open to relieve the early-evening heat. Thankfully, no one but her nine-year-old brother, Eddie, was in the garden by the veranda. She didn't know the loyalties of their hired house workers. Until she was certain of them, she'd refrain from speaking her opinions in their hearing.

"Emma Balfour hinted how shameful it is for strong young men to stay home while those more courageous fight battles for them." Mama's lips pursed. "Why, I scarcely knew what to say since I'd just explained that Ash was your escort to the party."

Julia stiffened. "Ash is as courageous as any of them." Did his limp prevent him from becoming a soldier? He'd been vocal about his Union support until disagreements on the subject led to arrests. She imagined his opinion hadn't changed, though they'd never spoken of it. She placed the tongs on the stove across the spacious room with its elegant cherry furniture and returned to remove brown papers from her mother's curls.

"Folks believe an able-bodied twenty-year-old man ought to fight."

At her mother's words, paper crunched in Julia's hand. As strong as her Union loyalties were, she couldn't bear the thought of Ash joining the Union army and taking up arms against their neighbors.

But Ash didn't need folks spreading rumors that he was a coward, as he'd been branded by Emma Balfour.

Alone in her room a few minutes later, she donned a beautiful off-the-shoulder peach silk trimmed with slightly darker ribbon.

The gossip about Ash's lack of courage concerned her.

She'd warn him what was being said so that he didn't defend himself by spouting Unionist views at a party celebrating Confederate troops.

~

*a*sh stepped into the Adairs' elegant parlor converted into a ballroom with a radiant Julia at his side, their families following. Musicians tuned their instruments as soldiers mingled with smiling ladies. Five circular rows of glowing candles in the chandelier lent a romantic ambience, or was that due to the beautiful woman in peach that glided across the room at his side? Ash feared the cheaper fabric of his best black coat, gray waistcoat, and trousers seemed out of place next to Julia's gown. Yet she didn't seem to notice. Was she as happy as he to attend this first dance together?

Once their mothers were settled in chairs lining the dance floor, the music started. Ash raised an eyebrow at Daphne. His youngest sister had pleaded to come until their mother agreed. Both his sisters were invited to dance the quadrille by soldiers who'd be on their way to Virginia tomorrow. At fifteen, Caroline was ready for such entertainment. Daphne was two years younger, and Ash couldn't like her dancing with grown men.

"Don't fret, Ash." His mother waved away his concern. "Daphne won't waltz, and she's to return to me after every set. I daresay these soldiers will dance with every girl here before the night is over."

"I agree, Louise. Such an air of celebration." Martha Dodd, Julia's mother, scanned the crowd.

"I'll dance if you do." His mother patted Mrs. Dodd's arm, who shifted away.

Mama had been lonely since his father passed. Her only surviving brother, Uncle Clark, lived in Texas. She craved friendship. The hurt in his mother's eyes at Mrs.

Dodd's rebuff scalded him. Surely, if Julia's mother was pleased that he escorted her daughter, she'd be more approachable.

"Son, you two go on," Mama said. "Remember to spend time with Willie and Luke."

The very thing he was eager to do—besides waltz with Julia. His heart had skipped a beat when she descended the stairs at her home, her peach dress swaying like a bell. Her brown eyes had held his as he drank in her shoulder-length golden curls swept back from her face in combs.

He reached for Julia's hand as the quadrille continued. Pink infused her cheeks. What a mesmerizing vision of loveliness. He recalled their mothers watched them. "Ladies, may I fetch you some refreshments first?"

"Not right now." His mother waved her ivory fan over her face. "My, it's warm this evening."

"Enjoy your dance." Mrs. Dodd shooed them away.

Ash offered his arm.

Taking it, Julia inclined her head toward the dancers.

The next dance wasn't a waltz. Grimacing, Ash shifted directions and led them toward the chairs facing the dance floor.

Julia's look expressed her surprise.

Releasing her hand, he faced her. "I should have warned you."

"Yes?" Her eyebrows rose.

"The only dance I can manage with this bum leg is a waltz." Ash's face burned to confess his inadequacy.

"How glad I am, then, that my favorite dance is the waltz." A smile curved her lips. "You will not mind when I dance with others?"

His relief at her gracious acceptance invited his own. "Of course not. Save me some waltzes?"

"I shall." Her smile wavered as she peered around them

before lowering her voice. "Actually, I hoped for a moment alone."

"Let's step outside." Their courtship was so new, he didn't know if her serious expression meant bad news.

~

*W*ith her hand again resting comfortably on Ash's muscular arm, Julia peered around Savannah's veranda for a quiet corner on the hot evening. The sun sank toward the trees on the horizon, casting orange rays on the gardens and orchards behind the mansion, a breathtaking sight. Gray-haired women in animated conversation had claimed most of the seats. Men of all ages, many of them wearing soldiers' uniforms, puffed at cigars. She employed her fan to dislodge the smoke that hung over the space.

"How about there?" Ash nodded toward an intricate white metal loveseat in the grass, a dozen paces from the crowded veranda. It faced a fragrant peach orchard.

"That will be perfect." Close enough to the house to raise no eyebrows, yet far enough away that she could speak without being overheard.

Once they were seated, she took a breath. "There's no easy way to say this."

He stiffened. "Go on."

"It's been suggested that you're not going to war with Willie because of cowardice."

"I was afraid of that." He flushed. "No one has said it to me directly." Hazel eyes searched hers, then fell away.

"I don't feel that way, Ash."

He glanced at her. "It's not that I'm afraid."

"I believe you." Didn't she? Was it more his limp, which worsened as the day progressed, keeping him from the fight, or did Unionist views demand he stay clear of mustering into the

Confederate army? Too risky to ask at a party honoring the Jeff Davis Guards leaving in the morning.

"That means a great deal." But his gaze was on the closest fruit tree.

"Everyone's celebrating," she said, "yet tension lies just under the surface. Keep a cool head if someone speaks ill toward you tonight." There. She'd warned him.

Mama already cast a wary eye on him. Their courtship needed to be given the opportunity to blossom.

"I will." He didn't look at her as he stood.

"Ash?" She clasped the hand he extended to her. Held onto his strength after she stood beside him. "Don't let one woman's opinion destroy your confidence."

"Reckon that depends on the woman." His hazel eyes lightened with his smile. "There are some women whose opinion matters to me very much, indeed."

Her breath caught in her throat. That special look, those words, came too soon. She needed to ease from friendship into courtship with Ash. "Your mother's opinion matters a lot to me, too," she teased to lighten the moment.

Ash laughed. "Shall we return for our waltz?"

"Let's do." Everything was so comfortable with Ash. Was it because they had been friends for years?

～

*A*sh hadn't missed that Julia had stared at his bum leg. Coupled with the gossip about his cowardice, her appraisal filled him with shame. What had he done that Julia felt she must warn him to keep a cool head? Those three men who knocked him down last month had made it clear they were watching. Yes, he was learning to choose his words carefully.

But now, Julia's gloved hand on his arm felt as if it belonged there.

The opening strains of a waltz floated over the conversation and laughter as they stepped through the door. "May I have this dance, Miss Dodd?"

"You may, Mr. Mitchell." She curtsied.

Holding her hand, he led her onto the shiny hardwood floor. "Have I told you how lovely you look tonight?"

Ash loved the blush infusing Julia's beautiful face as they waltzed across the Adairs' parlor. His slow steps were too measured for his liking, yet Julia followed his lead with graceful ease.

Her brown eyes sparkled under flickering candlelight from the chandelier. "I don't mind hearing it again."

He laughed. Dancing as a couple was as he'd dreamed it would be. She seemed content with his stumbling, nervous steps. He relaxed. Even his limp ceased to matter.

Ash twirled her around as the song ended, her hoopskirt swaying into a couple beside them. He inclined his head at the lovely woman in blue. "My apologies, Felicity. My fault entirely. Luke, I intended to seek you out." He held out his hand.

"Aye. A fortuitous bumble, for sure." Grinning, the tall, auburn-haired soldier grasped his hand in a firm handshake.

Ash chuckled. "It's a little noisy. Shall we step outside?"

The girls led the way, complimenting one another's gowns.

Outside, a dozen soldiers and townsmen talked in small groups. Lanterns on round tables were already lit as the sun sank toward the horizon. Vibrant silk and satin gowns complemented gray uniforms and black jackets.

Julia turned to Ash. "Let's stroll among the peach grove."

"A stroll it is." A short one. Ash knew Julia's love of dancing and didn't aim to keep her from it, even if he couldn't fill her dance card.

They climbed steps in the beautifully terraced yard with a fragrant orchard on the left and a flower garden that included roses, daylilies, and aromatic sweet olive on the right.

Imbedded stones created a path on each level with stone stairs leading to each successive level. They walked four abreast, ladies in the middle, as the path widened.

"Savannah won't mind if we steal a ripe peach, will she?" Luke eyed the full, sweet-scented trees.

"Speaking for myself, I say, steal away." Savannah, her white-gloved hand tucked in Willie's arm, closed the distance between them and their friends. Looped blond braids skimmed the shoulders of her pink silk gown as her brown eyes twinkled up at her beau. "See, we have surprised them, Willie, as we meant to do."

"It's a wonder, all right, that you could be quiet long enough to accomplish the feat." Grinning, the tall blond man ducked from her playful swat.

Ash chuckled, then sobered. This was the last time all of them would be together for many weeks, perhaps months. Would they return changed? Or at all?

# CHAPTER 3

Felicity's brave smile and Savannah's forced gaiety didn't mask their heartbreak.

Julia hoped to distract them. "Let's stroll among the plum trees. They won't tempt us since the fruit ripens later this summer."

"I can't eat a bite, anyway," Felicity said.

"I feel the same way." Savannah turned to the men munching on peaches. "We're going to walk a bit farther."

"Don't go far." Ash studied the pink and yellow horizon. "It's already dusk."

"We'll be but a moment." She hooked arms with Julia and Felicity and led the way.

"Not even your last Christmas ball was this well-attended." Julia ducked under a low-hanging branch.

"My parents honor Willie's sacrifice—and Luke's." Savannah's glance darted at Felicity. "There are several parties this evening, or there'd be more in attendance."

"Thank you for including Luke." Scarlet tinged Felicity's cheeks. A profusion of blond ringlets hid the nape of her neck as she lowered her gaze to the stone path. "My aunt and uncle felt...well, we're all happy that Luke is an honored guest."

Some families, like Felicity's, didn't have the means for such a celebration. Her parents had died two years before, shortly after her sixteenth birthday.

"It's our privilege and pleasure." Savannah's pink slippers skimmed over a protruding root in the path. "I'm proud of Willie for defending our dear state."

Stiffening, Julia unhooked arms with her. What could she say without exposing her opposing views? "It requires great courage to become a soldier."

"Truly." Savannah's steps slowed in the gathering darkness. "Willie's father believes it pure cowardice for able-bodied men to stay home in comfort while others fight their battles for them."

The back of Julia's neck heated at the scathing remark directed at Ash.

"Who's that?" Felicity stopped and peered through the trees toward the flowers planted along the black wrought-iron fence banking the sidewalk. "Julia, is that Daphne, Ash's sister, with that man?"

A flash of yellow confirmed it. Julia was disappointed that the thirteen-year-old had allowed a soldier to lure her from the dance floor. Mama was searching for an excuse to erect barriers to Julia's courtship with Ash. She mustn't learn of this. "Let's rescue her."

They marched out of the fragrant plum orchard toward the garden as the young man bent to pick a snapdragon bloom.

"I'll thank you not to pick flowers from my mother's garden, sir." Savannah held out her hand for the purple bloom. "Bouquets fill the parlors and dining room. I'm certain if you apply to my mother at the end of the evening, she will give you your choice from one of them."

"My apologies, Miss Adair." Gas streetlamps illuminated

the young soldier's red face. "I simply wanted a flower for Miss Mitchell to remember me by." His ears stood out under his kepi as he glanced at Daphne, nearly as scarlet as he. "Since me won't be here after tomorrow."

He seemed to add that last bit to raise their sympathy. A fair number of Irish citizens had the same red hair and blue eyes. Julia had seen him around Vicksburg but didn't know him. He looked to be a couple of years younger than herself, barely old enough to enlist. Julia stepped forward. "You know Miss Adair. Our friend is Miss Felicity Danielson. My name is Julia Dodd. Daphne is the *thirteen-year-old* sister of my beau, Ashburn Mitchell." She blushed, as it was the first time she'd claimed him as her beau.

The man's Adam's apple bobbed.

"May we have the pleasure of knowing your name, sir?" Savannah raised a haughty brow.

"Patrick O'Sullivan." He raised his kepi and then, as if not knowing what to do with the cap, pressed it against his chest. "Pleasure to make your acquaintances. I thought Daphne only a couple of years younger than meself. That's eighteen I'll be come January."

"Perhaps you mistook her for her sister Caroline, who *is* fifteen." Julia turned to Daphne, whose brown braids had been pinned into a chignon. "Why did you leave the dance floor?"

"We started talking about the pretty flowers." Daphne studied the snapdragon in Savannah's hand. "He offered to pick me one from the garden, that's all."

Savannah gave it to her.

It seemed innocent enough, yet escaping with a man could lead to a scandal should the gossips get wind of it. Mama could pounce on the situation as a reason to end Julia's courtship. "Your poor mother is likely wondering where you are," Julia said. The girl wasn't defiant. She truly didn't seem to understand she'd taken a chance in trusting a boy none of them knew. "Let's find her." At Daphne's nod, Julia turned back to the boy, who seemed happier now that his girl had the flower in her possession. "Mr. O'Sullivan, I suggest you confine your conversations with impressionable young girls…"

Daphne's dark brows lowered.

"And young ladies," she added, "to the ballroom and the refreshment room in the future."

"Aye, that is, me will do that very thing, Miss Dodd."

She gave him a nod, concerned only with delivering Daphne to Mrs. Mitchell without Mama discovering the reason.

Mr. O'Sullivan was halfway to the house when he turned back. "Daphne? If me train leaves without me laying eyes on ye again, think of me whenever ye see a snapdragon in bloom."

The sweet innocence of the request touched Julia.

"I will." Daphne brushed the flower against her cheek. "Godspeed."

This man might not come home from war.

So many of them might not come home.

This conflict could be much worse than anyone imagined.

She'd lost too many loved ones to face the uncertain future calmly. Thankfully, her brother, Eddie, was only nine.

Ash must stay out of the army. She couldn't risk falling in love and losing him. She must protect her heart until she understood his intentions about the war.

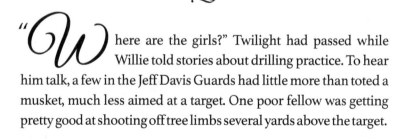

"Where are the girls?" Twilight had passed while Willie told stories about drilling practice. To hear him talk, a few in the Jeff Davis Guards had little more than toted a musket, much less aimed at a target. One poor fellow was getting pretty good at shooting off tree limbs several yards above the target.

Ash's friend must be stretching the truth a bit but, oh, how cleansing to his spirit to laugh with this pair. But where had Julia gone?

"Me spotted them with your little sister walking quick-paced toward the house." Luke peered ahead.

"Daphne?"

"Aye."

That girl. Daphne's actions often preceded thought. "We've been gone too long. Let's head back." At least his youngest sister was safe with Julia and the others. Ash would deal with that later. "This may be our last private talk for months. You ready for this?"

Luke, the tallest of the three at six feet, quirked an eyebrow at Willie.

"Wish you'd come with us." Willie kicked a stone in the path. "Change your mind, Ash. We'll see new places. Maybe fight a battle, if we're lucky."

A battle Ash never desired. But no one wanted to reason together any longer—the price of years of name-calling, escalating disagreements, even violence in many parts of the North and South.

Willy clapped him on the back harder than necessary. "It will be the adventure of a lifetime."

No one was close—a good thing because Ash hadn't expected Willie to renew his arguments on the very eve of his departure. He'd expected him to hint at the fear underlying his humor, the worry about difficult tasks ahead, his sorrow at leaving Savannah and his family.

No, that wasn't Willie's way. Jokes. Making people laugh. He rarely shared his deepest thoughts.

They neared the veranda, dark and shadowy now in dim lantern light. The band inside played a quadrille.

"Is your limp the problem?" Willie glanced down at the

slight dragging motion of Ash's left leg, always more pronounced by evening.

"That limp ain't keeping you from your duty, is it, Mitchell?"

Ash's head jerked at the censure in Rob Riley's voice. Rob, dressed as a soldier, leaned against a well-laden peach tree. Almost as if he'd hidden there in wait. He flicked cigar ashes in their direction.

Ash halted, as did his friends beside him. His body tensed.

Luke folded his arms.

"My reasons are my own business."

Julia had asked him to keep a cool head. Ash could only be thankful that no one on the crowded veranda several yards away appeared to pay them any mind.

"We're making it our business."

At the sound of a second voice, Ash's gaze darted to the other side of the path.

Tom Kelly stepped from a tree's spreading shadows. "You'll not find us hiding behind our mother's skirts."

The hair on the back of Ash's neck stood up. The nerve. These men barely knew him yet stood in judgment. His fist clenched at his side. Remembering Julia's request, he concentrated on keeping it there and not using it to wipe away Tom's sneer.

"Nay," Rob said. "Me believes ole Tom here's got the right of it." It was too dark to see Rob's expression clearly, but the derisive tone said it all.

"Watch yourselves." Ash had been publicly silent about his allegiance since last month's attack from the vigilante group. Silence protected his family and Julia. But how much insult should a man take?

Tom's mocking laughter thickened the tension.

"Ye know what, Tom?" Rob tossed down his cigar.

"What?" Tom responded.

"I reckon he's just plain yellow-bellied." Rob ground the cigar under his heel.

Blood rushed up Ash's face, burning hotter than a cannon-ball. He stepped closer. "I take exception to name-calling, Rob. Perhaps we should step out on the street."

Tom held up his hand. "No need for that."

One stride brought Luke beside Ash. "A man's reasons for joining the army be wide and varied, Rob." Muscles in his arms bulged under his gray uniform as he rested his hands on his hips. "Same for putting off the mustering in for another day."

Willie widened his stance at Ash's other side, his jaw set. "You don't have a beef with my friend for staying in the city, do you, Rob? Because I don't."

Taking a half step back, Rob shot a wary glance at Tom. "Meant no harm, fellas. Ash, I was only joking."

Ash knew better. In another setting, Rob might be nursing a black eye. But Julia's mother fairly itched to find fault with him. He'd not supply the ammunition. "No harm done."

"Lots of celebrations this evening." Willie's grin seemed a little forced. "Maybe you fellas were invited to another one."

"Aye. That's me next destination." Rob gave a slight nod. "Got a party at a friend's house to attend."

Willie's shoulders relaxed. "Then I'll see you in the morning."

The pair ambled away. Likely, their pride prevented a hurried pace more in line with their shameful accusations.

Music still drifted on the breeze. Laughter, conversations, and dancing had never paused.

The name-calling was enough to prompt Ash to fight for the Union. Except he couldn't risk killing Willie or Luke or a myriad of fellow Mississippians. "Thanks for supporting me."

His buddies had witnessed two Confederate soldiers—as they now were—branding him a coward. Were there others who believed the lie? For it wasn't true...but it felt true because he couldn't prove it through military service.

"Always." Luke clapped him on the shoulder.

"Pay them no mind." Willie gave him a nod. "Let's find our girls. Something tells me I'll miss Savannah more than I ever dreamed."

"The band's playing a waltz." Ash forced a grin. "Julia's saving them for me."

That four people heard the shameful accusations was two too many. As far as he knew, the most important person hadn't witnessed the altercation.

Julia.

~

Savannah and Felicity had been invited to dance a quadrille nearly as soon as they entered the ballroom with Daphne. Julia refused on her own and Daphne's behalf until she could find Mrs. Mitchell. Nearly every chair lining the dance floor was vacant. Soldiers outnumbered women at the party, and every female who wanted to dance—and some who might prefer a quiet visit with friends—were dancing.

Scanning the room, Julia kept her arm entwined with Daphne's. Good. Mama was dancing with an officer. Mrs. Mitchell, fanning herself, peered anxiously at the crush of dancers.

"Daphne, please ask your mother to join us on the veranda."

Waiting by the door, Julia breathed a sigh of relief as dancers blocked her view of her mother. She prayed they'd be outside before the song ended.

Mrs. Mitchell followed Daphne.

A man with a red mustache approached Julia. "May I have the pleasure of this dance, miss?"

"My apologies, sir. I must speak with someone on an important matter." At the disappointment in the husky soldier's face, Julia regretted her refusal. "Perhaps later." Though not a waltz. She'd save as many waltzes as possible for Ash—and not only because he was her escort.

"I shall look forward to it." He bowed slightly and moved away.

"Julia, is there a problem?" Mrs. Mitchell spoke from behind her fan.

"Let's step outside." Julia led the way to a secluded area in the darkness. She quickly explained what happened. "Unfortunately, this is the kind of situation that would cause my mother concern."

"Understood. What with Ash—"

"Exactly." Perhaps Ash's mother did comprehend that Martha Dodd wasn't pleased with their courtship. Julia hated to hurt her by alluding to it.

Taking a deep breath, Mrs. Mitchell turned to Daphne. "Young lady, we can talk about what happened later. The party is over for us all. We must find your sister. Do you know where Ash is, Julia?"

"He was strolling in the orchard with Willie and Luke."

"Will you mind sending him to me while I fetch Caroline? I think it best if you pass on my regrets to your mother. She's danced every dance. I don't like to bother her. You understand." Her face flushed as her gaze lowered to her fan.

"I do, indeed. Perhaps we can have you over for a meal soon." They'd never invited just the Mitchells to supper. Julia determined to approach her mother to issue the invitation.

"Oh, I'd love that above all things." Some of the tension left her shoulders. "Daphne, help me find Caroline."

Julia touched Mrs. Mitchell's arm. "I'll send Ash to you."

Where was he? Likely still with Luke and Willie. How he'd miss them. No one could make Ash laugh like Willie. And

31

Luke's own sense of humor fed off Willie's. Every party or dinner or picnic she'd attended in their company had contained plenty of laughter.

She stepped onto the dimly lit veranda and scanned the groups of men, women, and couples. She didn't see him, but she'd wait here rather than venture away from the crowd.

Two soldiers came from the orchard, quickening their pace as they rounded the side of the house. Shadows hid their faces. Something about them made her uneasy.

"Julia."

She spun around. "Ash. I wondered if you were still on your stroll."

"Just ended. Luke and Willy are already inside." His face appeared flushed in the flickering lantern light. "We came back to dance with our girls."

"That must wait. Your mother needs you to take them home." She gave him a brief explanation.

"My apologies." He looked around them with his brow knit. "How long have you stood there?"

"Perhaps ten minutes." And he hadn't given her his usual lazy smile. "Ash, are you all right?"

"Fine as a frog hair." He clasped her hand. "Let me escort you inside and then I'll find my family."

Watching Ash lead his family outside after she said her goodbyes, Julia couldn't help hoping the band played a string of waltzes upon his return.

# CHAPTER 4

*J*ulia smiled up at her beau as they waltzed. Her gloved hand was clasped in his strong one. "Did you have a good talk with Willie and Luke?" His stilted, hesitant step ceased to matter in the thrill of being held in his arms.

"Willie regaled us with mishaps from the company's drills." He chuckled. "The fellow knows how to tell a story."

"Then...is something else bothering you?" Perhaps she had imagined his uneasiness. Or perhaps he shared her own turmoil at the unrest in their country. Truthfully, it was difficult to celebrate her friends and neighbors heading east to fight a war she didn't want. Her prayers that the two sides reach a peaceful resolution had come to naught.

He hesitated. "For now, I just want to enjoy this dance with you."

Julia nodded. She scanned the dwindling crowd. A dozen or so soldiers stood by a line of vacant chairs, chuckling as if they hadn't a care. She supposed their bravery was to be honored, but, oh, what a shame this conflict had come to pass. To pray that the North was victorious meant that these men lost the battle. Willie and Luke were good men, as were most Southern soldiers. She wished them long, prosperous lives. Still, she prayed for a united country and an end to slavery.

The song ended, shaking her from her melancholy.

"Thank you for the dance, Julia."

His reluctance to release her brought her hope for their future. "My apologies for my distraction."

"I share it." His brow furrowed. "This evening has been a mixture of celebration and..." He glanced at a group of soldiers and clamped his mouth shut.

"Turmoil?" she whispered.

"Exactly."

They stared at one another.

Julia tried to guess the thoughts swirling behind his troubled hazel eyes. "I feel it too." As far as she knew, he'd stopped speaking out in support of the Union. Perhaps that was for the best because some sought to squelch such talk with violence.

Mama joined them, interrupting her thoughts. "Where did Louise go with the girls?" She scanned the room.

"Daphne's unaccustomed to late hours." Ash spoke quickly. "Mama sent her regrets for leaving without saying goodbye."

"You danced all evening, Mama." Julia didn't allow Mama's curiosity to dwell on the Mitchell ladies' quick exit. "I was happy to see it."

"Yes, it was almost like balls of my youth." A faraway look in her eyes made her appear younger than her thirty-eight years. "I was much sought after at my parents' balls."

"A true Southern belle." For a moment, she envisioned her mother as she had been before Julia's father died. Seemingly carefree. Happily in love with her husband. Interested in the activities of her daughter and son.

"Yes, well, those days are past." Mama lifted her chin. "Shall we find our hostess?"

Indeed, those days were long past. Would the carefree days of Julia's youth soon become a memory as well?

~

*A*fter escorting Julia and Mrs. Dodd home, Ash went to his two-story clapboard home on Second North Street to change into comfortable trousers and boots. Willie had asked him and Luke to walk in the city with him after the party, and they soon arrived, both in uniform.

The three men set off on foot after one o'clock. They'd been friends since boyhood, ever since Ash and Luke had saved Willie from drowning in the Mississippi. Ash dove in to save him, and so did another boy. They both pulled him to the riverbank. It was the day they met Luke. That experience had bonded them for life.

Thousands of stars cast dim shadows on the streets. They exchanged greetings with several groups of merrymakers who, like Willie and Luke, would be on a train in a few hours. Otherwise, houses and businesses were dark. Ash kept a watch for Rob or Tom, whose families were his customers but whom he otherwise barely knew.

The jail they passed likely held suspected Unionists, courtesy of the vigilante committee that roamed the streets at night. No sign of the group that had assaulted Ash.

Tension built in his gut as he followed Willie down the hill past Greek Revival homes hidden by hedges toward the heart of the city built on the bluffs. Luke sauntered along on Willie's other side. These two were Union folk four months before. Perhaps they could still be convinced to revert to those old loyalties. He still had some time, didn't he?

A subdued Willie reminded them of things they'd done at locations they passed. They stopped to survey the new courthouse's stucco façade, which had become a landmark. Its four-faced clock showed half past one. They had an hour or so at most before they'd have to return home, and Will wanted to admire the city and the murky waters of the Mississippi from its columned cupola.

"Why don't we head to the Sky Parlor?" The barren hilltop two squares from the waterfront should be deserted at this hour, making it a perfect place to confront his friends.

The others agreed. They climbed a long flight of wooden stairs up a hillside. Ash's leg throbbed from the long day. He looked longingly at the rugged drive for horses and wheeled vehicles that circled the hill. If only they had headed out on horseback.

"Let's sit a spell." Ash lowered himself to the grass on the hill's edge, allowing his aching left leg to rest on the downward slope. Tonight, they had the popular destination for wealthy families to themselves. "We don't have much time, and I've got something to say."

"What's this about?" Willie sat and drew his knees to his chest.

"Just a few months ago, we all supported the Union. Now you're wearing Confederate uniforms. Something doesn't tally out." Ash glanced between the friends on either side of him. "I'm asking you to reconsider."

Willy stood and glared down at him. "How can you ask it of us?"

Ash steeled himself against his friend's anger. "Lower your voice. Don't want our words carrying clear to the river."

"Mississippi's decision is my decision." Willie turned to stare out at the murky waters. "I'll not go back on it."

"Fair enough." Ash's heart sank. "Luke?"

"Me's mustered into the army, Ash. Can't alter it at this late juncture."

Ash didn't believe Luke's deeply felt loyalties had changed.

"No doubt, there'd be shame in it for you. But it's worth it not to betray your allegiance."

"More shame than not fighting at all?" Willie wheeled to face him.

Ash pushed himself to his feet. He hadn't expected Willie to suggest Ash was a coward.

"You're staying home," Willie said, "where it's safe."

Ash stiffened. It was a jab below the belt.

Luke stood, raising and lowering his hands. "No one here's got any reason to feel shame."

"You're a fine one to speak of betrayal." Willie poked a finger at Ash's chest. "Some town folk might even call *you* a traitor."

Ash's pulse sped. Must he prove his courage to everyone?

"Ye don't mean that, Willie." Luke laid a hand on his shoulder. "Say so."

Willie's brows lowered as he glared at Ash. "*I* don't consider you a traitor."

A chill settled over Ash's heart. It wasn't an apology. The war had come between them already. "Brave men follow their convictions."

Luke turned away.

"Not much can change your mind once you're set on something. If folks were to discover how you feel, the vigilante committee would make things mighty hot for you." Willie stared at him in the dim starlight.

"They already have." Ash touched his stomach where he'd been punched. "It's the reason I've stopped joining the public discussions."

"I'll not tell a soul, but have a care. Those fellas will run you out of town."

"Agreed." Ash regretted the ill feeling he'd caused between them. They had once been as close as brothers. "I hope you understand that I had to ask."

"Seems like you don't respect my decision." Willie crossed his arms.

"Not at all. I misspoke." It was too late. He should have kept his pleas to himself.

Willie studied the ground. "I gotta get back home, fellas. Ash, you coming to the morning church service?"

"Wouldn't miss it." The Catholic church planned a special service for the soldiers. The company would leave afterward. "Julia's joining me."

"I'll see you there." His running footsteps clopped against the wood stairs.

Ash sighed. "He must be pretty mad."

"Hurt, more likely." Luke crossed his arms. "He's scared."

"You're joking." His friend had been fearless through all their childhood scrapes.

"It's bad dreams he's been having. Aye, nightmares that happen in a new land, yet not in battle."

Typical nerves when heading to war?

"Me started thinking about Joseph in the Bible. His dreams that made no sense but came true." Luke looked at Ash squarely. "Me mustered in the next day."

"To watch over him?"

"Aye. Me loyalties to the Union didn't change, Ash. Neither did me loyalties to Willie."

"'There is a friend who sticketh closer than a brother.' That's in Proverbs somewhere." Ash clapped him on the shoulder. "That's you, my friend."

"Ye also. Willie's father is sending George with him whether he wants to go or not. Doubt anyone asked." He sighed. "Can't feel good about it meself. Regardless, George is a good man. Willie trusts him. I believe George will also keep watch over him."

George had been serving Willie for years. They'd grown up together, played together until Willie's father made George his son's slave. Then their relationship changed. Willie had grown up with a plantation full of servants and didn't seem to question the system that had always been part of his life. His acceptance chafed like a burr in Ash's boot. Ash's father had hated slavery and raised him to feel the same. Even less wealthy neighbors employed slave labor. That made Ash's family a minority among Vicksburg citizens, though Julia's family paid their domestic staff as well, part of his attraction to her.

The faint sound of the river lapping against the ships on the wharf failed to soothe Ash. "Wonder why Willie told you about the nightmares and not me."

"'Tis my opinion he planned to tell you tonight. Ready to head back?" The clock bell rang three times.

Ash rubbed his aching leg. It started to stiffen in the night's chill. Didn't bode well for the walk home, nearly all uphill. "You go on. I'll see you in the morning."

"Your leg?" Luke studied him in the dim moonlight.

"Don't want to slow you down." His pride smarted to admit it. Feared it made him less of a man in his friend's eyes. And Julia's.

"It's not a burden to walk with my Unionist friend."

*Friend.*

That sure sounded good. "And I with mine."

Luke gave a firm nod. "Aye. Ye not be the only one too stubborn to change his mind."

"What about firing on Union troops?"

"I'll aim for the trees."

Could it be as simple as that?

Not for him. Ash must find another way to support the Union.

# CHAPTER 5

$S$upported by a crutch, Ash waited with a heavy heart beside Julia in the Catholic church's grassy yard the following morning as soldiers and their families exited the service. After a special mass, Father LeRay had consecrated and blessed the flag of the Jeff Davis Guards. Who knew the future of soldiers who followed that flag into battle? God alone.

It was impossible to know everyone in a city of forty-five hundred, yet Ash recognized most of the uniformed men who filed out. This might be the last time he saw some of these neighbors. Tenderhearted Julia wasn't the only one to employ a handkerchief on damp cheeks.

Conversation resumed when families and friends congregated in the yard. Mothers gave final instructions. Fathers checked knapsacks and bags in wagons and carriages to ensure all was in order. Tearful young ladies held onto the arms of their beaus while younger siblings clamored for their brothers' attention.

"Do you want to join Luke or Willie?" Julia asked.

"I'll give Willie this time with his family." It seemed best after the way they'd parted. "Let's make our way to Luke. My guess is, he misses his parents more today than usual."

"I imagine so." Julia accepted his free arm.

Ash gritted his teeth that his crutch made a thumping noise with each step.

"Is your leg painful this morning?"

"It's fine." Was she embarrassed by his crutch? It was temporary. A day or two at most.

"Good."

He didn't miss her frown, which disappeared as they reached their friends. He'd leave the crutch behind next time.

They joined a solemn Luke and ashen Felicity. Soldiers stirred as the crowd began to move down the hill.

"You walking to the depot?" Luke scanned the soldiers and families sharing a mixture of pride, laughter, and tears.

"Wouldn't miss it," Ash said. "Where are your bags and your musket?"

"In Willie's landau." He chuckled. "Look there. Tom Kelly's carrying a bouquet on the blade of his bayonet."

Both the soldiers and the citizens needed this celebratory atmosphere to bolster their courage for the looming separation.

"There are more up ahead." Felicity indicated the variety of floral bouquets men waved while the now-exuberant crowd headed toward Pearl Street. "Makes me wish I had picked you roses."

"Ye are rose enough for me." Luke caressed her hand clutching his. "And the only one me will ever need."

Blushing, Felicity rested her head against his shoulder.

Ash prayed that his courtship with Julia reached the same level of trust as Luke's with Felicity. Julia's previous courtship had lasted only a matter of months.

As loud hurrahs from the boisterous crowd increased in intensity, conversation became impossible. Wagons, carriages, and other vehicles that followed with soldiers' bags and possessions on the cobblestone streets couldn't be heard above the noise.

Ash's crutch pounded against the cobblestone as he made his careful way down the hill in the jostling crowd. Wouldn't do to stumble. Any noise the wood made in striking the stone was drowned out by cheers of shopkeepers standing on the sidewalks outside their businesses. For that mercy, he was thankful.

All too soon, they were on Pearl Street approaching the long station at the corner of Depot Street. Shouting continued as the throng filled the street, the station yard, and even neighboring properties of small homes and businesses.

"Where's Willie?" He couldn't allow his friend to leave without saying goodbye, especially after the harsh words that had passed between them. At nearly six feet, Ash was taller than most, a helpful trait for scanning the crowd of uniformed soldiers.

"He promised to find me," Luke said. "We'll stay together on the journey."

"Good." Ash had a feeling that statement was almost a vow. Luke was a steady friend, indeed.

"Ash, old boy." Willie, with a firm hold on Savannah's hand, clapped him on the shoulder. "Been looking for you. Didn't want to leave without saying goodbye. And there you are, Luke. Felicity. Julia. How good of you to see us off." He tilted the rim of his beaver hat toward the ladies before turning to Luke again. "We'll board soon."

"How about our bags?"

"George is seeing to them." Willie waved off his concern. "He'll bring our muskets so we'll have them on the train."

Savannah eyed Ash's crutch. Her lips pursed.

Heat rose in Ash's neck at her disdain. Did she believe he'd brought it today as if to excuse his decision to remain in Vicksburg? He almost wished he'd said his farewells last night.

"All aboard!" The conductor's booming voice pierced the noise, bringing on a frenzy of hugs and handshakes.

Ash extended his hand to Willie. "Godspeed, my friend. May the Good Lord guide your steps."

"And yours. Write me?" Willie pumped Ash's hand.

"I will. And I'll want to hear about all your adventures."

"You will." Willie gave him a searching look and then gave Julia a hug.

At least Willie hadn't closed the door on their friendship. "Luke." Ash held out his hand. It was clasped in a firm grip. He clapped him on the shoulder. "I'll miss you, my friend. I'll write you too. Let me know what's happening." He leaned closer. "Watch over Willie. And yourself."

"Aye." Luke nodded.

"Godspeed. I'm praying for you both."

Luke exchanged a few words with Julia and then hugged her.

Ash put his arm around Julia's shoulder and stepped back to give the couples what little privacy an excited and proud crowd could afford. He looked down and caught her dabbing her eyes with a handkerchief. "Are you weeping?"

"It's just...the unknown."

"Yes." He drew her close for a hug. It was the first time he'd held her in his arms other than dancing. She was such a strong, compassionate woman. It was difficult *not* to be overcome with emotion at this farewell.

Soldiers filed onto the cars amidst cheers and tears.

A tall, muscular black man holding two muskets and three knapsacks was ready when Willie ended his embrace with Savannah. George was one of a dozen or so slaves who were heading toward war, not to fight but in service to a soldier or officer.

It wasn't fair, not in Ash's eyes, and he prayed for an end to slavery. Would the war bring an end to the abomination?

"Thank you, George." Willie accepted a musket and one of the knapsacks. "Glad you'll be with me."

"Much obliged, George." Luke took his musket and bag.

"I'll just go find my place." George headed to the back of the train.

"See you at the next stop." Willie turned to Luke. "We'd best get going."

"You'll be back in two or three months. Remember your family plans a birthday celebration in September for you." Savannah gave her beau a confident smile. "It won't take long for you to whoop up on those Yankees."

A few cheers went up at Savannah's words.

Grinning, Willie tipped his hat at her and then mounted the nearest car.

A tear fell down Felicity's cheek. Luke wiped it away and gave her a final kiss before following Willie.

Ash watched for their faces to appear at an open window. "There they are."

He followed the girls to stand in front of their window.

"Look what someone gave me." Willie stuck his bayonet through the window. A bouquet of red roses dangled from it.

Savannah giggled. "Keep them there as the train leaves."

The whistle blew twice. Wheels creaked forward. Black smoke hovered over the yard.

Ash raised his hand in final farewell. Luke and Willie returned the gesture. The train chugged along the tracks with Willie's bouquet swinging from the window.

Red petals wafted toward the ground like teardrops from heaven.

Ash leaned heavily on his crutch as smoke enveloped the cars. He did respect Willie's decision. He'd make that clear in his first letter. Opposing viewpoints mustn't destroy their friendship.

~

*J*ulia fought back a shudder as the caboose disappeared from sight. The loss of too many family members had birthed a fear in her of losing other loved ones.

Ash's brooding stare was fixed upon the empty tracks.

She'd thank God most fervently tonight that her beau wasn't among the departing soldiers. Actually, she rather depended upon his limp to keep him close to home and safe.

"They're gone." Felicity spoke softly, gripping Savannah's hand.

Julia turned to her friends. "Ladies, I do hope you're free to join me the next few hours. I'd like to buy you both lunch at the Washington Hotel." It was a splurge from the meager quarterly allowance her mother always doled out with a reminder that a wealthy husband could provide the comforts of luxury.

Ash couldn't provide them, but that didn't bother her. Julia's father had surely made allowances for her in his will. Her wealthy grandfather must have provided for her too. Mama had never shared the details. "Ash, I'll see myself home."

"Enjoy yourselves. Shall I escort you to church on Wednesday evening?"

"Please come for supper first." Ash had accompanied her to Wednesday services for a month, dining with her family twice.

His eyes brightened. "I accept your kind invitation. Thank you. Good day, ladies." He raised his bowler hat with a smile for all of them and then turned on his heel.

Julia watched him hurry away, his crutch thudding against the sidewalk. If he used it more often, no one would badger him about enlisting.

"Why do you suppose Ash is suddenly using his crutch?" Savannah's brown eyes narrowed as his steps slowed.

Did Julia detect a note of censure? "Our boys decided to

explore the town one last time after your party last night. Between that and the dancing, he taxed it. Want to do a little shopping? It's early for lunch."

"I want Mademoiselle Cognaisse to design me a dress to wear for Willie's return."

Neither of the others had ever owned a dress fashioned by the dressmaker of Parisian-inspired gowns. Julia looked forward to admiring the satins and silks while Savannah selected her fabric.

They all opened their parasols for the stroll, their hoop-skirts forcing several feet of distance between them and those following toward the main area of town.

"Luke said it was after four when he arrived home." Red rimmed Felicity's blue eyes. "Sure would like to have been a hoot owl in the nearest tree to hear their conversation."

"Why?" Savannah's looped blond braids swung as she looked at Felicity.

"Don't you think men have secrets the same as women?" Felicity raised her palms. Her blond ringlets brushed against the high collar of her green print cotton dress.

"Not Willie." Savannah burst into giggles. "That man never had a thought in his head he didn't tell somebody."

"He does seem rather an open book." Julia laughed.

"Let's stop by Clarke's Literary Depot after lunch." Felicity's pace quickened.

Though Julia was happy to distract them for the difficult first hours, her mind wandered back to her courtship with Ash.

It had been lovely that the two of them had attended the party as a couple—as though they were three couples finally instead of two with friends tagging along. Mama kept pushing her toward wealthy bachelors, ones with slaves. Ash paid his staff and seemed to abhor slavery as much as she did.

If they were ever alone, she might be able to confirm that they were of the same belief.

~

*a* stoop-shouldered customer stopped by for his saddle at seven o'clock the following morning.

Ash put down the stack of orders that he'd been organizing. His business had escalated with his skills. There wasn't enough money to hire another man to share the work load, as he'd wanted to do for a year. His goal to expand the saddle shop must wait because providing for his family came first. Perhaps Luke would need a job after the war ended.

"Good morning, Mr. Robinson. Always bright and early." Good, he'd have time to stock up on leather today. Mr. Routeledge, the best tanner this side of Jackson, lived between Bolton and Clinton.

"Don't see no reason to waste daylight." The old man peered behind Ash's broad shoulders. "Got my saddle done?"

"I do, indeed." Mr. Robinson was one of a handful of customers who didn't spare a minute talking about recent news. It was always business with him. Ash led him to the gleaming saddle displayed on a divider half the room's size. "What do you think?"

"Duke here is the one who has to like it. We already know he does because you measured it on him last week." He pushed his bowler hat back on his head, revealing a bald spot. His fingers traveled over the length of the saddle.

Ash waited while Mr. Robinson examined it. Most folks just picked up their saddles and left. A pit grew in his stomach as seconds stretched to minutes.

"That's good work, son." He gave a satisfied nod. "As good as any your papa made for me."

"Thank you, sir." Ash's chest expanded. Boy, did that feel good. This was one customer not given to flattery.

All his long hours to take the family business to more customers were finally paying off. His repeat customers appreciated his craftsmanship. Hopefully, this news somehow reached Mrs. Dodd's ears.

"Don't let that praise go to your head."

Ash chuckled. "No, sir." Still, he'd remember the praise when his spirits were low.

The saddle fit perfectly on the man's mount, filling Ash with a sense of accomplishment.

"Now I left you a little extra under that edging iron yonder. It ain't no accident. My thanks for having it done on time." He shook Ash's hand.

"Much obliged." After Mr. Robinson left, Ash found five dollars more than the saddle's price on the bench.

Caroline entered the open door while he was stowing away the money in the metal cash box. "Mama's keeping breakfast warm for you."

"Thanks." Both he and his sisters had inherited their father's brown hair and hazel eyes. In contrast to the bun she wore at the dance, today Caroline wore her customary braids. "I'll eat before heading to the tanner's."

"Why did you take that old thing out of the closet?" Caroline pointed at the crutch resting against a support beam with the same disdain he'd seen on Savannah's face.

"Leg's bothering me some, is all." Yawning, he rubbed at the ache.

"Well, put it back as soon as you can. You walk funny with it." Quick steps took her toward their house fifty yards distant.

He followed, leaning on the uncomfortable wooden crutch. How he hated the weakness it represented. It would be relegated to the attic as soon as he could manage without it again.

After breakfast, he headed out on Apple Blossom with Rosebud—his father had allowed his sisters to name the horses —to haul back the leather, a trek he'd made many times.

Trees shaded part of his thirty-mile journey. The fragrance of fresh peaches had him longing to help himself to the low-hanging fruit. He rode past without giving into temptation. As his father had taught him, he didn't know the owner and didn't have permission to take the man's property. His father had been a good man, and he'd instilled his values in his son. Those deep-seated beliefs were the reason Ash would not turn his back on the Union, no matter how much his neighbors—and friends—pushed him.

What if his customers learned his true loyalties? There'd be many who'd spurn his saddle shop. His family would suffer ridicule. He'd lose business. As the sole support of his family, it was a cost he couldn't afford.

Yet he couldn't do *nothing* in support of the Union. This bum leg prevented him joining the Union army. No long marches for him. So what could he do?

Ash might not be thrilled that Willie was fighting for the Confederacy, yet his friend followed the strength of his convictions. He had to admire that. Willie had shown more courage than Ash.

*Lord, guide my path. Help me find a way to serve the Union from Vicksburg.*

Two hours later, the Routeledge homestead came into view. The two-story stone house was set apart by forests from neighboring properties. A spacious corral with two mares, a filly, and a stallion grazing inside bordered a large barn. Clucking chickens ate grain in the area outside the open barn doors.

Ash dismounted and led his horses to a water trough shaded by the barn outside the fence. His mares, their reins looped over the post, took a long drink.

A red-haired man, rubbing his hands with a rag, stepped outside. "Ash, it's good to see you." He shook his hand in a firm grip.

"And you, Mr. Routeledge." Ash leaned an elbow on the corral fence. Spongy grass beneath his feet cushioned his leg. He'd purposely left his crutch behind, though the ache in his leg made him regret it. Almost, for he'd not come to rely on it again, as he had as a boy. "How's business?"

"I got a few irons in the pot." Green eyes probed his face as if hinting at a deeper meaning.

Secrets abounded these days.

"You here about more pig leather?" Mr. Routeledge folded his arms.

"Yes, sir. Thought it best to stock up."

"Smart idea. Let me show you what ain't already spoken for." There was a wider streak of gray in the widower's hair than had been there in April.

Ash followed him into the barn. The selection for saddle leather was as excellent, as he'd come to expect. He puchased ten. "Wish I could buy more."

"Give your horses a good rubdown and oats from that pail over there." He pointed to a shelf on the inside wall.

"Much obliged." Offering to feed a visitor's horses was the neighborly thing to do. "I brought a lunch big enough for sharing."

The widower grinned. "I'll add cold lemonade to it. Come into the house when you're done." He went inside and closed the door behind him, likely to keep the chickens from following him.

Did the tanner support the Union? Ash finished caring for his horses and then retrieved the saddlebag containing lunch.

Eyes closed and hands folded in prayer, Mr. Routeledge sat at the dining table on the right side of the spacious sitting room. "Join me." He pointed to a high-backed chair opposite his. The round table was set with silverware on napkins, plates, and glasses of lemonade. Condensation ran down a pewter pitcher in the middle.

"Don't mind if I do." Sitting, Ash divided the sandwiches, apples, and cookies onto the plates. Usually, folks waited to bless the food after everyone was seated. Perhaps the widower had lived alone too long.

"Let's ask the Lord to bless this food."

More confused than ever, Ash bowed his head. His host's simple prayer, as if he was picking up with the Lord on an earlier conversation, moved Ash.

"What's the news in Vicksburg?" Mr. Routeledge took a huge bite of his ham sandwich.

Between bites, Ash talked about the Jeff Davis Guards leaving the day before. "Another company, the Volunteer Southrons, leave tomorrow. Dr. Morris Emanuel is giving a dinner in their honor tonight. There will be music and dancing." Dr. Emanuel was druggist and the president of the Southern Railroad. Though Ash's family hadn't been invited, it was said that over two hundred were attending. His mother chafed at the snub.

"You taking your girl? Miss Dodd, right?"

"That's right, but we're not going. Julia decided against it because we attended the Adairs' ball on Sunday." Though Ash knew several soldiers leaving tomorrow, none were close friends.

"Lots of happenings in Vicksburg these days."

"Difficult to keep up with all the news."

"But I'll bet your customers like to chew the fat with you."

Ash grinned. "Some are quite the chatterboxes, I must say."

"Same here." Mr. Routeledge peeled an apple in a long strip. "I like it that way. Gets lonesome without my Harriet. She passed eleven years ago, and I still miss her. That's why I never pass up a chance for conversation."

"I still miss my pa." Ash spoke quietly. "He died in 1858, and there are still moments I wish I could ask his advice." Like with the current unrest sweeping the country.

"Horace was a good man." He bit into the apple with a

crunch and swallowed the bite. "Skilled saddle maker. We were of an age. I considered him a friend."

"He spoke highly of you. Said you were a man I could trust." Ash studied his companion's peaceful demeanor. "That's especially important these days."

"That it is." The widower raised a bushy eyebrow. "Something on your mind?"

Dare he be so bold? Papa had trusted him. "Rough to be a Unionist. You know something about that?"

Green eyes held his stare. "Sure enough."

So he'd guessed the man's loyalties correctly. "Looking for a way to serve the Union without mustering in."

Mr. Routeledge grunted.

"You find a way?" Ash shoved the last bite of his sandwich in his mouth and waited.

"It's dangerous for anyone in Mississippi to support the Union, much less put actions behind that support."

"Agreed. Our Vicksburg jail held several men whose only crime was Northern loyalties, but doing nothing is eating at me."

"Can you keep secrets?" His host's watchful gaze didn't leave his face as he munched on an oatmeal cookie.

Ash's heartbeat quickened. "I can."

"Good. Because you'll need discretion and courage by the bucket loads before all this is done. Now, as to how you can help..."

# CHAPTER 6

*J*ulia patted her linen handkerchief against her forehead after stepping inside her home on Tuesday afternoon. She'd finally found Eddie climbing trees along Cherry Street near his friend George's home. Her brother had become entirely too independent in the past months. Mama wasn't concerned, leaving it to Julia to monitor his activities. She'd reminded her brother to be home in an hour to wash up for supper.

"Julia, is that you?" Mama called from the front parlor.

"Yes, I'm here." Julia retrieved her fan from a long table in the entry hall. Gleaming wooden steps led to the second floor near the center, wide doors were opened to the spacious formal dining room, and a long narrow hall led to the kitchen and Papa's library, where she needed to clean next. They really required more than one maid for the spacious house. Daisy took on the basic cleaning jobs, and Julia did the special jobs, sometimes with her mother's help.

Julia entered the comfortable parlor on the left, with its mauve and green furniture arranged in groups about the room. She sank onto a mauve chair opposite where her mother lounged on a sofa facing the large fireplace. "What did Dr. Alison say about your cough?"

"He's not concerned since it's been under control for months." Wisps of blond hair that had escaped from her chignon stirred in the breeze from her silk fan.

"Good." Relief filled Julia. She'd lost too many family members to feel easy about her mother's sporadic respiratory illness.

"Dr. Alison mentioned that his nephew down in Grand Gulf is still a bachelor."

Julia rolled her eyes behind her fan. "That's some thirty miles away."

Mama coughed into a handkerchief. "Granted, that's too far for courtship. With so many of our young men headed to war, I despaired of finding you an eligible young man, so it's good to know not everyone is running off to war."

Julia fought back her irritation. "Ash is here. He's courting me."

"You can't be serious about him." Mama snapped her fan closed. "His income is not of our social standing."

"I like him." They enjoyed each other's company, and when they weren't together, she longed to be with him. That had never happened with anyone else. "Besides, you married Papa when he wasn't in your social class."

Mama's lips tightened. "You don't know what it's like to alter your lifestyle so completely. I married your father, a simple druggist, because I loved him. It changed my life forever."

Julia didn't doubt it. Mama's father had been a wealthy plantation owner near Charleston, South Carolina.

"My family was displeased with my marriage," she added, "though my father liked Harrison. That's probably why he didn't remove me from his will." Her gaze moved toward the flapping curtains, as if seeing into a window of the past. "I struggled to adjust to cooking meals and cleaning house. I failed. I was accustomed to having everything done for me and didn't even realize it."

Julia had never heard her mother speak so openly of those early struggles and didn't dare interrupt this rare opportunity to learn her family history.

"Harrison finally hired a cook. Later, a maid came three days a week. I watched her to learn what to do. Then you came along. And Juanita and then poor little Walter, who never drew a breath. I mourn them still."

Tears lodged in Julia's throat. She'd been only three when Juanita got pneumonia. She'd prayed for her little sister, but no one allowed her near Juanita. It had only scared her more, pushed her into a cocoon of loneliness that magnified when Juanita died before her first birthday.

Julia had never seen Walter, just his casket being lowered into the ground beside her sister. Both her parents stopped talking much, stopped playing with Julia for a long time after Walter's funeral. Things would have been so different for all of them had her siblings lived. Eddie had been a breath of fresh air for all of them.

Mama hadn't mentioned them in a long time. Julia's grief for them wasn't as buried as she'd imagined, since the mere mention of them ignited her loss all over again.

"Then your pa died. Part of my heart lies in the cemetery with all three of them."

"Mine too." It was scant comfort that Papa was with them now, watching over them in heaven.

Mama stood and walked to the window. "Harrison left us in debt. I sold the business to pay them and then wrote Father, who paid the mortgage. He sent more money than I needed and started sending me a quarterly allowance. But it wasn't enough."

Ah. Understanding dawned. Mama had lost her security when she married Julia's father. That he left her in debt further explained why she spiraled like a lost child when he died.

"I suggested Father make that allowance permanent, to write it into his will because my brothers wouldn't have continued it. A good thing, too, for he died within months of making the change. That allowance dies with me unless Eddie hasn't reached his majority, else it goes directly to him until he reaches the age of twenty-one."

Where did Julia figure into any of this? Mama had inherited one thousand plantation acres from her father, which she'd leave to Eddie. And the remaining allowance also went directly to Eddie upon their mother's death.

Mama turned to face Julia. "Your pa left this Vicksburg property to me with the stipulation that upon my death Eddie inherits it. I'm certain he intended that to safeguard the inheritance in case I remarried."

Eddie was the important child. Of course, Julia had realized that years before. Why did it hurt so much to hear Mama say it aloud?

"That's why it's imperative that you marry well." Mama's blue gaze hardened. "Ash inherited his father's shop. That helps. I'm pleased that his skills are touted about the city. It shows greater promise under Ash's leadership than his father's, but his business must increase. It's not enough to comfortably care for you, his mama, his sisters, and the children you'll have. That house isn't big enough either. He'll have to expand it or build a bigger one. That requires more money than he currently has."

A chill settled in the pit of her stomach. Papa had left nothing of value for Julia's future? Both her parents cared more for Eddie's future than Julia's.

*J*ulia was still reeling from the news the following evening at supper with Ash. That the wealthy grandfather she'd never known hadn't seen fit to leave her a dowry was a disappointment. Yet to have her father fail to provide for his only surviving daughter slashed at her self-worth. Why did her parents set such store on Eddie alone?

She picked at her peach pie as Ash and Eddie dominated the conversation. Mama watched their guest as they ate in the cozy family dining room before church. The formal dining room, with its gleaming cherry wood furnishings, was large enough to serve twenty. Julia imagined Ash preferred this table for six complemented by green wallpaper with threads of tiny yellow daylilies, her favorite flower, running through it, just as she did. An arrangement of them served as the table's center-piece, lending a faint lemony aroma to the room.

"Then George picked up the snapping turtle from the log" —Eddie's brown eyes twinkled with mischief—"and we chased Lottie and Mary Beth all the way back to Jackson Road."

Ash chuckled. "Did the turtle draw back inside its shell?"

"Yep. Them girls don't know nothin', or they'd have known it couldn't bite while it was hiding." Eddie speared a bite of pie. "Serves them right. No girls are allowed, and we told them so."

"You were playing up near City Hospital?" Julia frowned at him. The hospital was several squares from their home. Many strangers had been coming to town the past few months, and she liked him closer to home.

"That's where our hideout is." Blond hair standing straight up at his crown gave Eddie an impish look. "You didn't like us playing at the Old Brickyard, so we had to move it. But that's fine. We like this spot better because we built a little shack with branches and stones."

Julia looked at her mother. Instead of support, she found her mother giving Eddie an indulgent smile. Of course. Mama wasn't about to chastise her son, his father's heir. No, it was more like her to spoil him.

In fact, Mama left most of her responsibilities on Julia's shoulders. She hadn't been like this when Julia's father was alive. Something changed in Martha Dodd when her husband was accidentally shot while hunting. Even when her lung ailment was under control, she seemed content for her daughter to shoulder household duties and the care of her son.

"Too easy to get hurt at the brickyard." Ash lent his support as he finished his pie.

"Exactly. And the hospital's too far away for your hideout." Julia wiped the corners of her mouth with the napkin.

"Just make certain to tell us where you're going first." Mama pushed her untouched dessert to the side. "I don't believe I'll go to church this evening."

"Then I don't have to go either, right, Mama?" Eddie's back straightened.

"I suppose not." Turning her head, Mama coughed into an embroidered handkerchief. "Julia, you and Ash will have to walk. Silas asked for today off instead of tomorrow."

Julia had expected Ash to drive his buggy tonight, but he'd limped up without it. "I don't mind walking." She looked at her beau.

"Fine with me."

Julia didn't like her brother missing church, but her mother had already passed down her decision. On the other hand, this might give her an opportunity to discern Ash's loyalties. "Eddie, do you have schoolwork due in the morning?"

"Just to practice my sums."

"Then I suggest you finish them immediately."

Eddie frowned, then brightened. "By the time I'm done, the fireflies will be out."

Ash laughed. "I like that attitude. You're looking on the positive side." He ruffled the boy's hair, making it stand up even more. "It's always best to get work done before play. Then it doesn't weigh on you."

Mama gave Ash a nod of approval.

"I'll do it now." Eddie ran from the room.

"I'll read a book in the parlor." Mama waved a fan over her face, stirring such a breeze that it cooled Julia. "I may send for Dr. Alison tomorrow. My supply of pills is dwindling."

"Are you all right, Mama?" Her mother was in good health when her bronchitis was controlled by her medicine. The condition seemed to worsen when the wind stirred up dust on the bluff, which happened all summer. "Shall we stay home with you?"

"No, go on. I'm rather fatigued." She led the way down the hall toward the front of the house. "I'm not accustomed to dancing, I suppose." She smiled rather wistfully. "Our soldiers made us all feel like belles of the ball the other evening, didn't they?"

"Indeed." Julia couldn't help thinking some of those soldiers might never come home. *Not Willie or Luke, please, God. I can't take another loss.*

~

*I*t was sheer joy to listen to Julia's soprano voice at his side during the worship, but Ash's thoughts swirled around Mr. Routeledge's shocking admission. And his invitation—which Ash had readily agreed to.

Only he couldn't tell anyone. Not even Julia.

He glanced at her rapt face, her fan swaying back and forth to stir the air as she listened to Pastor Woodman read from the Good Book. Ash shifted to benefit from the slight breeze and settled back to listen to the comforting words of Psalms Twenty-three. Every window and door was open to coax in a breeze.

They stepped outside at the end of the service, the sun setting beneath the tall trees. It was a relief to leave the hot building and talk with friends in the yard.

There were no other men his age, so Ash stood beside Julia when she joined two of her friends.

"Julia, I'm sorry you missed the dinner at Dr. Emanuel's home last evening." Dora Wilkes placed a gloved hand on the high neck of her blue print dress. "Of course, you were invited?"

The probing question from the auburn-haired beauty alerted Ash to listen for information useful to the Union.

"We were. We had attended Savannah's ball on Sunday evening, and Mama felt it best to decline this one."

"Over half of the two hundred guests were officers and soldiers from the Volunteer Southrons. Brave men, all." A dreamy look glowed in Dora's blue eyes. "I danced every dance."

"As did I." Eleanor Finch smiled. The brunette had been a friend of Julia's since childhood. "Julia, there were so many in attendance that I truly didn't realize you weren't there."

"Small wonder." Julia smiled. "I'm certain the soldiers felt honored."

Not inclined to join the conversation, Ash gazed around. The church yard had emptied, and the sun had sunk over the horizon.

"It was sad to see them mount the train bound for Meridian this morning," Dora said.

Ash turned back. He'd neglected to tell Mr. Routeledge that destination, a mistake he'd rectify. Confederate troop numbers and movements were valuable information to the Union army.

"Our numbers of young men have sadly dwindled this spring." Dora gave Ash a steely glance.

"For a cause near and dear to our hearts. One can only be proud of the bravery of our young men." Eleanor shot Ash a look of scorn. "At least, most of them."

A cold sweat broke out on Ash's forehead. Truly, women seemed more outspoken than men about his perceived lack of courage. "Ladies, if I may." He took a step forward. The situation had escalated to the point where he'd be the coward they accused him of if he remained silent now. "We are a country at war. Sacrifices at all fronts have been—and will continue to be —made by all. Please know there are many ways to serve one's country."

"Perhaps." Dora shifted the conversation to sewing clothing for the soldiers in support of the cause. Julia seemed interested in helping.

The young women didn't need to know the country he referred to lay above the Mason-Dixon, or that he'd discovered a way to live in Vicksburg while serving the Union.

~

"*T*here's no need to hurry." Julia, hampered by the folds of her dress dragging behind her, could barely keep up with Ash's long strides on the paved sidewalk. "Full darkness has not yet fallen."

"My apologies." His steps slowed as they put distance between themselves and the church yard.

"Something on your mind? Perhaps I can help." Julia peeked up at Ash's contrite face. Though the businesses they passed were closed, a number of folks still moved about the city sidewalk well past dusk. Not the best time to discover Ash's allegiance, at least not directly.

"Only business." He spoke quickly without meeting her gaze.

That comment smacked of her former beau's superior attitude. "Of course. My intellect is too inferior for me to understand, is that it?" Her hand slid from his arm. She had thought him different. Perhaps Mama was right—she should look for a wealthier beau, one able to support her where her father had failed her.

"Not at all." He halted at the street corner and turned to face her. "Your intelligence, faith, and compassion are traits I value most about you." He spoke softly, looking down at her with earnestness in his hazel eyes.

She was touched by the compliments, the likes of which she'd never heard from another suitor. "Thank you."

A stranger tipped his hat as he passed. Another couple approached the street corner. She'd have to wait for another occasion to discover what troubled him—and whether his Union loyalties stood firm.

"Would you like to view the river from the courthouse cupola?" He offered his arm.

She rested her gloved hand on his muscular forearm— another difference from Carlton, who likely hadn't worked a day in his life. The city landmark was one of her favorite destinations, but his limp was more pronounced than normal, reason enough to stroll directly to her house. "Maybe next time."

"If you're certain."

Streetlamps illuminated the sidewalk. "I'd rather make certain my mother's cough hasn't worsened." Dr. Alison had assured them Mama's bronchitis could be controlled by medicine, and that did indeed seem to be the case. However, there was always that niggling of worry in the back of Julia's mind.

"Say, you're not worried about her, are you?"

"I worry these bouts will worsen." There. She'd admitted it aloud.

More than any danger posed by the war, Julia feared losing the people she loved. She'd been three when her baby sister, Juanita, took ill. Julia had played with her and helped her walk while grasping furniture. She'd also been the one to notice Juanita's hands were burning hot. Mama had called the doctor and took her to the nursery while Julia cried for her sister. Mama never let her inside the nursery, but Julia had whimpered against the door. But Juanita died without Julia ever seeing her again.

When her little brother Walter was stillborn two years after Juanita's death, it brought the sorrow of losing her back. Even Eddie hadn't been expected to live as a baby. Julia's grandparents—her father's parents—died shortly after Walter, but losing her adored father had nearly destroyed her family. Mama's world had crashed around her, taking Julia and Eddie tumbling with her.

Ever since, Julia had clung to those she loved, with a fear just under the surface that she'd lose another person if she didn't keep them safe.

Her father had been a druggist. Had he lived, he would have made his wife a concoction that worked better that Dr. Alison's —perhaps even cured Mother.

One of the myriad reasons she wished her dear papa were still alive. Yet her greatest reason for wishing to talk to him hadn't even been a consideration last week. Why had he betrayed her? Mama had always been partial to Eddie, but Julia had believed Papa loved her.

"The wind's been stirring dust on the bluff for the past month." He patted her hand. "Maybe something else is the true culprit."

"Dr. Alison mentioned that exposure to smoke can trigger it." While no one smoked cigars in any homes to prevent fires, Silas, their gardener and chauffeur, did enjoy a cigar now and then. "I'll ask Silas to smoke away from our veranda."

"Couldn't hurt." Ash frowned. "Your mother did stand on the Adairs' smoky veranda for a long while."

"You're right. I'll talk to the doctor tomorrow." Her three-story brick home loomed ahead in the darkness.

"May I take you for a drive on Saturday afternoon?"

"Yes, I'd love that." Before her feelings became more engaged, she must learn his opinions of the war. She wouldn't stand for any surprises such as Carlton had delivered the day their courtship ended.

If she was to continue fighting Mama to continue this relationship, Ash needed to give her solid ground to stand upon.

# CHAPTER 7

"*H*ow about a drive in the country?" Julia settled against the leather seat in Ash's buggy under cloudy skies on Saturday. Her relationship with Mama had been strained since she'd learned that her mother had gone to great lengths to protect Eddie's inheritance and done nothing about hers. She glanced up at her escort, handsome in a blue coat, gray-striped vest, and gray cravat. He seemed so strong. Solid. Dependable. Just what she needed right now.

Or was he? She was determined to discover the truth. The forested setting outside the city afforded privacy for their discussion.

Ash peered at the gray clouds. "We'd best not go far."

Within ten minutes, they were passing a farm outside Vicksburg, where a barefoot boy led cows toward a wide barn.

"It's good that your mother is improved." Ash glanced at her.

"Yes." Mama's health had improved enough that she was back to needling her about Ash's dismal prospects.

"Is something troubling you?" He guided his horse around a rut at the edge of the lane.

"As a matter of fact, there is." Julia straightened. "I need to ask about your loyalties."

His body tensed as he halted the buggy.

"You were a Union man when Mississippi seceded." Her knees grazed his leg as she turned toward him. "What about now?"

"My allegiance has not changed." His chin lifted. "And yours?"

She closed her eyes a moment, so great was her relief. "I'm a Unionist."

The atmosphere between them relaxed.

"I'm glad. Now you understand why I can't muster into the Confederate army."

"It might be best to use your crutch now and then so folks won't question your reasons for staying home."

Ash shifted in his seat. "Likely won't do that."

She studied the firm line of his jaw. Best not push it, though that crutch would make things easier for him. "Is your family Unionist?"

He grunted. "Daphne's more concerned with her friends and school. She can't be bothered with such things. I'm not certain about Mama. Papa's views influenced me and Caroline. That's not likely to change."

"It's good to know *everyone's* not against us." *Us.* That sounded good. And right.

"Sure can seem that way." Ash squinted up into the trees. "It's difficult when…"

"Good friends disagree on important loyalties?" She smoothed a curl that had fallen free of its comb.

"Exactly." His mouth formed a firm line. "I regret something I said to Willie."

"You can pen an apology."

He turned to her, his leg touching the folds of her gown. "I will."

"Savannah is...outspoken about her Southern support." Her vexation with her friend melted as his gaze fastened on her finger twisting the errant curl.

"Indeed." He looked into her eyes.

Julia laid her hand upon his muscular arm. She'd never felt so close to him. They'd finally spoken of situations that mattered.

His fingers caressed her hand. "Julia, I..."

"Yes?" She tilted her chin, inviting his kiss. Their first one.

Ash cupped her face and gave her a gentle kiss. When she didn't move away, he gave her another.

She smiled up at him.

He glanced at the gray sky peeking from the dense tree cover. "I'd best turn back, or we'll get caught in the rain."

"All right." Rain might threaten, but she doubted it would destroy her sunny mood. She shifted forward while Ash turned the buggy around.

His lips had been warm and soft, not cold as a dead fish like Carlton's.

In fact, Ash was superior in every way to her former beau.

~

The next two weeks were busy for Ash. Besides his work at the saddle shop, he'd escorted Julia to church and to the Washington Hotel for supper. He'd held her in his arms and kissed her on her porch. She was every bit a lady, and he was still amazed that she'd given him a second glance.

Willie's stiff parting from him at the train depot that last day stuck like a chicken bone in his craw. Ash hadn't realized how closely held Willie's ties to the Confederacy were until that last night. It weighed on him.

His friends had been gone nearly three weeks when the first

letters from Virginia arrived, one from Luke and the other from Willie. Ash tore open Willie's letter. He complained of long drills. Daily chores such as chopping wood, fetching water, or taking care of the horses left his body sore every night.

No mention of their argument.

But that was on Ash. He'd pen an apology, making it clear that he respected Willie's decision. He'd been rash to bring it up on the eve of his friends' departure.

A group of soldiers passed by. One of them observed to his companions that this was his first visit to Vicksburg. Where were they from?

Ash bought a paper from a newsboy outside the post office and pretended to scan it while listening to the men talking on a nearby street corner. They were from Louisiana. Ash listened long enough to learn they were headed to Richmond. Then he sallied toward the restaurants on Washington Street to get an idea how many troops were here. Yep, that's where the bulk of them were, gorging themselves of fine Mississippi cooking. Ash counted seventy-four soldiers milling about the streets and in the restaurants. They were leaving on the morning train.

Ash would go with them as far as Bolton, where he'd stop and give the information to Mr. Routeledge.

～

Julia was happy to see Savannah and her mother in her parlor, where her mother had tea served, as she did for guests every Thursday afternoon. After they visited for a few minutes, Julia invited Savannah to walk in the garden with her.

"Thank you for inviting me for a stroll," Savannah said once they were outside. "I'm in need of exercise." She rested a dainty white parasol against her shoulder with a sigh. "I haven't been riding since Willie left."

"You must miss him." Julia led the way toward her orchard of peach, apple, plum, and pear trees. It was half the size of Savannah's yet sufficient for her family's needs.

"It's the knowing he's not around that's difficult." Savannah's peaches-and-cream complexion had a tinge of red from the day's heat. "Willie spent the weekdays learning how to run his cotton plantation and came to town on Saturdays. And, of course, for church services on Sunday. I've had one letter from him in two weeks, but he warned me he won't write often. It was the same when he was away at school."

"Have you written him yet?"

"Three times." She laughed. "I wrote the first one after we finished our shopping excursion that first day."

Julia laughed. "I'd have done the same."

"*If* Ash had gone with them."

Julia's smile died. "Right." This was the third time Savannah had referred to Ash's decision to remain home since Willie left.

"Has his leg healed?" Savannah brushed nonexistent dust from her dress without meeting Julia's eyes. "He didn't have his crutch with him at church."

"He doesn't complain." Julia didn't want to hear anything else against Ash. Mama already said enough. Of course, Mama would be displeased if a rift developed between Savannah and Julia. Mama wouldn't want anything to jeopardize her friendship with the wealthier Adair family. "Have you seen Felicity lately?"

Her shoulders relaxed. "Not since our outing. She was so heartbroken at saying goodbye to Luke. Doesn't she realize this thing will be over by the end of summer?"

"We all pray it is so." It seemed optimistic to Julia.

"Even if it's six months, Felicity shouldn't take on so. Seeing her tears made me determined to send Willie off with a smile. That's how I want him to remember me until he sees me again."

"I admire your strength." Julia smiled. Savannah had a

strong personality. It wasn't only her beauty that drew all eyes to her when she entered the room.

"Thank you, dear friend." She entwined her arm with Julia's. "I have an idea. Shall we visit Felicity this afternoon? Mrs. Cummings likely has her sewing for our soldiers."

"Perhaps." Sewing societies had been started all over the city to provide for Confederate soldiers.

"Seamstresses are paid for their services. Volunteers offer their services for free. Felicity may appreciate assistance." Savannah released Julia's arm and held up her hands. "These fingers have never threaded a needle. Do you believe I can learn?"

Julia laughed. This was the Savannah she had grown up with and dearly loved. "Of course. You can do anything you set your mind to do."

"Do you know something funny? I believe you." Her eyes brightened. "Do you want to join a sewing group around town or work with Felicity?"

"I haven't had a chance to sew for the soldiers yet. I'd rather see if Felicity requires help." As much help as she would be free to give. Unlike Savannah, Julia spent a portion of her week on household chores. "Let's walk over and see."

~

*A*sh arrived at Mr. Routeledge's home midafternoon on Monday. They had worked out a plan where he'd purchase enough leather for two saddles each time, his ostensible reason for coming.

The widower stepped from the barn, which housed both his workshop and his animals. "Ash, I didn't expect you today." He extended his hand to shake.

"Good afternoon." This was the first time Ash had been back since agreeing to the mission. "I've got—"

Mr. Routeledge gave an almost imperceptible shake of his head. "I reckon you need some more leather. I've got a fine sampling for you to choose from. Give your horse water and hay. I'll be in the barn."

Heat emanated from Ash's face. Obviously, he'd already erred, and he'd done little more than dismount.

It might take a few times to get comfortable with the routine. He quickly took care of Rosebud and then carried his saddlebag to the barn.

The tanner glanced up from a pile of skins. "Didn't see anyone outside, did you?"

Ash swallowed. "Didn't look." Boy, did he have a lot to learn. Maybe he wasn't cut out for spying, after all.

"Go back and give your horse a handful of oats. Scan the surroundings without seeming to do so."

Ash did and then returned. "Nothing out of the way."

"Good." He still spoke in low tones. "I reckon you should refer to me as Jim. Routeledge is a mouthful."

"Agreed." Ash glanced at the open barn doorway. "I'm not certain what I did wrong."

"There may come a day when my home is watched." His green eyes lost their twinkle. "There's no reason to believe that's happening now, but it may come. We must begin as we mean to go on."

"I will." He marveled that the humble man had thought so far ahead. He gave the information about the Louisiana troops passing through Vicksburg. He took the newspapers from his bag and held them out. "I've saved these for you since we last spoke."

"Very good." He paged through them. "Just bring papers from the current week next time. Look at this." He tapped an article Ash had read. "'Agents for all imaginable kinds of merchandise, patents, medicines, books, newspapers, etc., may

SANDRA MERVILLE HART

be acting as emissaries and spies.'" He looked up. "Ash, they're talking about you and me."

It was as if the bite of winter cold swept through Ash. He'd thought of this as a mission. His neighbors saw him as an enemy—or would if they knew of his activities. If the vigilante group learned he was a spy, a beating was the least they'd do to him.

"You must be ever on your guard."

His chest tightened. "An earlier article prompted all individuals capable of pulling a trigger to be on duty in some capacity." Others had made similar statements in his hearing. "I've never lived anywhere but Vicksburg, yet even friends would scorn me if they knew."

"Times have changed." Jim sighed. "I've lived on this land all my life. It tears my heart to go against my neighbors and friends. I just can't go along with leaving the Union. It's a mistake. I fear we'll all pay a grave price."

The hair stiffened on the back of Ash's neck. The words seemed almost prophetic. "I don't wish that on anyone."

"These are hard days. No matter which side a person falls on, remember that we all do the best we can."

Ash reckoned that was true. "Serving as a Union spy in Mississippi comes at a price."

"That's the truth."

Ash wiped sweat from his brow. "The vigilantes used threats and jail to scare folks into silence on mere suspicion that they are Unionists. What will they do to spies?"

"If they find proof of spying, prison is a certainty."

Ash had never been able to abide being locked inside, not since his pa accidently locked him in the shop as a boy. Still, the cause was worth the risk.

The widower looked away. "That punishment will almost certainly escalate."

Hanging for treason. Prison didn't sound so bad when compared to death.

Ash wandered to the open barn door. He rested his hand against the wood as he scanned the horizon. This was his chance to do something significant. Though his limp was detrimental on long marches, it didn't hinder him from spying. This was his chance to live courageously, even if no one knew.

He turned to face a truly courageous man, one he'd try to emulate. "I'll return when I have more news."

"Good to hear." Jim gestured the pile of leather. "Select what you need, and you can be on your way after a glass of lemonade."

"Don't mind if I do." Even with all he'd learned, Ash's heart felt curiously lighter.

A spy. Savannah's scorn just lost its sting.

What would Julia think of him, if she knew? Would she be proud?

# CHAPTER 8

*J*ulia could scarcely believe the satisfaction she found in sewing for the soldiers during the next week. Even though they fought for the South, they still needed clothes. Felicity had indeed been sewing soldier uniforms when she and Savannah visited the seamstress shop.

Savannah had asked for a sewing lesson from Felicity. Mrs. Cummings, once she understood the young lady's motive was to volunteer her services for their dear, brave men, allowed the lesson. Much hilarity had ensued, yet Savannah had proven herself a worthy student.

Julia needed no lessons to sew jackets, trousers, and blouses in the shop cluttered with bolts of fabric, clothes pinned and ready to sew, and some cut and ready to be pinned. Her mother had taught her to sew and mend at an early age. Volunteering last Friday had been so rewarding that she'd gone back the next Monday and was preparing to return to the seamstress shop on the last Friday of June.

She found her mother in the upstairs parlor. "I'm leaving. Eddie's playing with his friends at their clubhouse by the hospital. He's promised to stay there or here while I'm gone. He'll return by noon for lunch."

"His appetite will likely see to that." Mama set aside her knitting. "Let's talk before you go."

Sitting, Julia bit back a sigh. Mama knew she wanted to leave by ten o'clock. "Do you feel all right?"

"Why must you assume everything is about my health?" Mama snapped.

"Sorry." Her mother was in a foul mood.

"Have you given any thought to courting someone else?"

"No." Julia rubbed her suddenly throbbing temples. "I'm quite content with Ash. Don't you like him?"

"He's pleasant enough. That's not the point. I don't want you to live in drudgery."

"Ash employs a cook and a maid, same as us." Julia lifted her chin. "I already do special cleaning jobs here that Daisy can't get to. How will it be different?"

"He can't give you the luxuries I give, that your father gave."

"Perhaps I don't need them. Apparently, Papa didn't think so, or he'd have provided for my future." She couldn't keep the bitterness from seeping into her voice.

"Don't you disrespect your father to me, young lady."

Julia turned away. She was supposed to accept such cavalier treatment from her father without emotion?

"Ash isn't the man for you. Another gentleman of your social standing will come along. Be prepared."

Julia stood. It was best not to try and reason with Mama in this mood. "I'll be home around four."

Her headache increased with her hurried pace to the seamstress shop. Mama wasn't giving up as she'd hoped. She was so certain that Ash couldn't support his family and the one he'd have with Julia if they married that it gave her pause. She should earn an income and lose her reliance on Mama. If Ash proposed, that income would augment his earnings.

She must make her own way, but how? Mama would never stand for her to get a job in a shop.

~

On Monday morning, the first day of July, Ash fit pigskin around an iron shape, arranging what would be a saddle over the padding, his least favorite task.

Footsteps on the stone path leading from his house on the adjoining property were a welcome distraction.

Mama held a stack of letters as she entered the open doorway. "Son, Caroline stopped at the post office on her way back from the grocery."

"Anything of interest?"

"I'm not certain a bill from my seamstress can be termed as such, but it must be paid regardless." She handed the open page to him.

He whistled at the total. It was the highest one in months.

She twisted an envelope in her hands. "You recall the Adair Ball in May? This bill of sale is for our gowns. I hope it's not too dear."

"No, you and my sisters need new clothes now and then." Paying it would set him back weeks. His mother's own father hadn't left her any money, though Uncle Clark had the good fortune to own a Texas ranch.

"I wanted us to look our best at the first event we attended with Julia and Martha."

Ash nodded. "Mrs. Dodd notices everything." It kept him on his toes.

"Exactly."

"Just keep me informed on expenditures." Surely, this would be the last dressmaker bill for a while. "The shop has expenses too. Supplies and tools must be purchased from time to time."

"Seems you could do a better job stocking up than you do, maybe at a discount." She folded her arms, the remaining letters flapping in the breeze against the sleeve of her blue summer dress. "Why, you've been to the tanner's house three times in the last month."

She'd noticed? She had never cared what he did in the saddle shop. "I buy pigskin when I know I need it." Delivering news he'd discovered to Mr. Routeledge wasn't something she'd care to know. "I'll go again soon."

"Please, take the train next time and leave us the horses for the buggy."

That explained why she'd noticed his absence. "I'll do that." It was actually a sound suggestion. The Routeledge homestead was an easy two-mile walk from the depot in Bolton. "Are those letters for me?"

She nodded. "Worry over our account nearly made me forget them. One from Willie and another from Luke." She handed him the mail.

"Now that's a welcome sight. Thank you."

"Lunch will be ready in an hour," she called over her shoulder as she left.

Ash would have to guard against doing anything to throw off his mother's routine. She had supported the Union early in the year when that had been all the talk and easily switched to support Mississippi when that had been the pervasive mood. She mustn't learn of his reports to Mr. Routeledge.

Seeking distraction for that worry, he picked up the letters.

Willie's attitude was lighthearted, giving Ash hope that their rift might be mended through correspondence. He'd apologized in his first letter. *Thanks for checking on Savannah for me. She wrote me that you and Julia visited her after church. As you said, it was her idea to sew for us soldiers. You were right—it was the first time she picked up a needle and thread at the same time! Still, she assures me that she's grown quite adept at the task and hopes one of the shirts she's made will find its way to me. Just between the two of us, I'd be more apt to hope for one of Felicity's shirts. She's the seamstress, after all. I greatly fear something sewn by Savannah will fall apart with the first washing.*

Chuckling, Ash opened Luke's letter. As he expected, it was longer and more informative.

*One thing I've learned in the army is how quickly things can change.*

*As you know, the Jeff Davis Guards and many other companies from Mississippi signed up to serve as soldiers until the end of the war. (May God grant that time be short.) We arrived in Virginia as a single company and were soon combined with others to become the First Battalion Mississippi Volunteers. Major William Brandon, who leads us, fought in the Mexican-American War. Me expected a younger fellow at the helm, for he's sixty if he's a day. However, I'm grateful for his experience, for there's but a smattering of that among the rest of us.*

*There are quite a number of requests for transfers among the many previously independent companies like us. Me imagines we will settle soon enough. For now, a fellow sitting around the campfire eating bacon with you in the evening may camp with another regiment the next night.*

*Please continue to keep an eye on Felicity for me. She claims to be so busy at the seamstress shop that she is fast asleep as soon as her head touches the pillow. Me suspects tears for me absence blot that pillow before sleep claims her. Make no mistake, she is a strong woman. Let no man say otherwise. It's simply that me leaving came as an unwelcome surprise. Never fear, she'll get her land legs under her in time. Until then, tis grateful I am for the friendship you and Julia and Savannah show her at every opportunity.*

Ash tapped the letter against his chin. Luke's assessment of Felicity's state of mind was an accurate one. How well he must know her to sense that from her letters, which Ash guessed to be bright and cheery.

Ash was getting to know Julia better and hoped their courtship blossomed into the kind of love his friends felt for their girls. He needed more time with Julia to make those feelings grow and time to grow his business to a level acceptable to Mrs. Dodd. How long would she wait?

His gaze fell on the dress bill. The needs of his family factored into his responsibilities.

He'd run an ad for his saddle shop. That might afford him new customers, but he'd have less time for Julia and for his spying.

〜

*T*wo days later, Ash strode home at dusk from Julia's house. They'd fallen into a pattern over the last month of dining together before Silas drove Mrs. Dodd, Eddie, Julia, and Ash in the family's landau to Wednesday evening church services. His own family attended a different church, the one they'd attended since his boyhood.

When Eddie squirmed through a long service, Ash had been sympathetic. His own boyhood hadn't been so long ago that he didn't remember a desire to play in the sun during sermons.

After the service, the two of them had chased fireflies in the churchyard while Julia and her mother caught up with friends. It had been quite a pleasant evening.

Tomorrow was Independence Day. With soldiers off at war and the country in turmoil, many in Vicksburg, Ash included, preferred to buckle down and work rather than attend the picnics that usually marked the day. Five orders for saddles had come in the previous week, promising income that would help replenish what had been paid to his mother's seamstress. He had one order ahead of those that should be completed on Friday. His newspaper ad had brought in three new customers that morning, so it had been money well spent.

By the time he approached Second North Street, where his home and shop were located, it was dark. He was well accustomed to walking the streets of Vicksburg after sundown, but there was an eerie silence tonight.

And then he heard something that had his heart thumping harder.

Heavy footsteps approached behind him. Vigilantes? His heartbeat quickened and he turned.

Three burly men carried lanterns. Not the same three as before. Ash recognized them as townspeople. Two had been his customers, yet Ash didn't like the menacing look on one face, that of Kyle Murphy. The Irish stove maker was nearly twice Ash's age. In fact, all three men were.

"Evening, folks." Ash maintained a friendly tone. "Just headed home from church. It's a little late, but if one of you wants to order a saddle—"

"Didn't come for no saddle." Bart Brown, a carriage maker, barked the words.

"Fine with me. I'd rather discuss orders in daylight hours." Why was no one else on the street? It was barely past nine. "Is there something I can do for you fellows?"

"Yeah, there is." Mr. Murphy's lantern scraped against the pavement as he set it down. "Suppose you explain why you didn't muster into the army with your buddies."

The hair stood up on the back of Ash's neck. These men were part of the vigilante group. They considered him a coward —or worse, a Unionist. A traitor.

Ash widened his stance. "I'm the sole support for my mother and sisters."

"So are a lot of other men." Eli Brickner had been a friend of Ash's father's.

The unfriendly tone sliced through Ash. How his father would grieve if he knew of this confrontation by one of his childhood friends. "Mr. Brickner, you know how hard I've worked to bring my saddle shop back to my father's standards."

"Our state needs defending. All able-bodied young men need to answer duty's call." Mr. Murphy curled a beefy hand into a fist. "Can't hide behind that limp."

Would this come to blows? His gaze flicked in every direction. Would anyone come to his aid if he called out?

"You a Unionist?" Mr. Brown crossed his arms, the lantern swinging from his right hand.

"What do you take me for? Why, I'm as loyal as any of you." Loyal to the North. He prayed to God they never discovered it.

"I ain't so sure." Mr. Murphy spat on the sidewalk by Ash's boot.

"I say we give him a little time in jail to think on things." Mr. Brown grabbed Ash's arm and jerked him so close that Ash smelled whiskey on his breath.

Ash's instinct was to fight, but that would escalate the situation—and he couldn't win against three men who outweighed him.

He squared his shoulders and focused on his father's old friend. "Sir, you know me. You know my family. Do you abide this treatment?" To the others, he added, "If you have evidence against me, bring it. Otherwise, I'll thank you to let me go home to my family."

Mr. Brickner gave him a long look, and Ash held his gaze, unwavering. Finally, the older man said, "We're done here, fellas."

Mr. Brown tightened his grip on Ash's upper arm. "We've done arrested men for less cause."

"I believe him." Mr. Brickner turned back down the hill toward town as if the matter were settled. "Let him go."

Mr. Brown shoved Ash so hard he smashed against a lamp-post two yards distant.

Refusing to cry out, he grabbed the post to steady himself.

"You just gonna take his word for it?" Mr. Murphy eyed Ash.

Mr. Brickner stopped. Turned back. "I knew his pa. A good man. Southern through and through." Mr. Brickner jerked his head toward the city. "We've other places to go."

"What if you're wrong?" Brown demanded.

Mr. Brickner turned toward Ash. "Then we come back. And we won't be so friendly next time."

# CHAPTER 9

*F*elicity's sewing machine stopped. "Do you believe the rumors?"

"I-I'm not sure." Julia shuddered at the apprehension in her friend's voice. She shifted in her chair by the window, her favorite spot to sew at the seamstress shop. It was Friday, July nineteenth, and there had been talk that a big battle must happen soon in Virginia. "Newspapers report of skirmishes in Virginia."

"I've read those articles, from all six of our city's newspapers." Felicity pushed wisps of blond curls behind her ear. "Minor clashes, reportedly."

"I pray it remains that way." Julia tucked her needle into the trouser seam she'd been stitching the past hour. Desiring a Union victory equally as much as *not* wanting her soldier friends and neighbors to be wounded or killed, her heart was torn. It was a dilemma she and Ash shared, though lately, he'd been busy at the shop, and she'd been chasing her little brother around the city.

Eddie was even more adventurous this summer than last— and she'd found it a chore to keep up with him then too. If only

Mama enforced simple rules. Julia could only be thankful for her mother's continued good health. Dr. Alison had cautioned her to avoid cigar smoke. Doing that and closing the windows on the worst of dusty days seemed to have done the trick.

"My prayer has been that this turmoil will be resolved without bloodshed." Felicity stared at the coat still in the sewing machine.

"Too late for that. Many believe one big battle will end this sad chapter in our history."

"Do you?" Felicity stared at her.

"Ash doesn't." Fostering false hope wasn't an act of friendship. "I know little of battles and yet...I feel difficult days are ahead." Julia held out her hands, palms up. "I don't know what that means for Vicksburg—or Willie and Luke."

"I don't either." Felicity pushed herself to her feet and leaned against the metal sewing machine stand, head bowed.

Was she praying? Or struggling for control?

"Thanks for your honesty," her friend finally said. "I needed confirmation that my fear is rooted in more than a woman for her beau." She straightened. There was a determined glint in her blue eyes that had been missing for weeks. "It's nearly noon. Mrs. Cummings is fitting the Faulkner twins for dresses and expects to be out until two. She left sandwiches and lemonade for us in the kitchen. Are you hungry?"

If her friend needed a change of topic, Julia was happy to oblige. "I'd welcome a break." Hands pressed against her lower back, she stood. "I don't know how you sew five days a week, hour after hour."

"It's my job." Felicity led the way down a short hall to the kitchen. "Uncle Charles and Aunt Mae don't charge me room and board, but I won't ask them to pay my personal expenses."

Her friend was likely saving for her future family. Julia seated herself in front of one of the linen-covered plates at the round table. "I'm glad you didn't decide to live with one of your siblings after your parents passed." They had died as result of a stagecoach accident in 1859. "Yet you must miss them terribly."

"None of my siblings was in a position to care for me." Felicity removed a red-and-white checked towel from a roasted beef sandwich, hard-boiled egg, and apple quarters. She settled on the opposite side of the table. "Will you pray for our meal?"

Julia bowed and asked the blessing. "How are you coping with Luke away?"

"He has commanded a lion's share of my thoughts." Blushing, she reached for an apple quarter. "I know he loves me. He won't propose until he's in a stable financial position, which Uncle Charles appreciates."

"I suspected as much." Surprising to hear Felicity speak of money matters. She'd always been close-lipped about her finances. Perhaps Savannah's presence had governed her reticence. Savannah had never worried about where her next meal was coming from. Slaves prepared her meals and took care of household chores, as in many homes in Vicksburg. Julia was thankful her papa had believed in paying a fair wage for a day's work.

Too bad he hadn't believed in providing for his unmarried daughter in the event of an untimely death.

~

One of Ash's customers, Matthew Boswell, stopped at the shop to see if his saddle was ready on Tuesday, July twenty-third. Ash showed him the progress he'd made and assured him it would be ready the following afternoon.

"Did you hear about the battle at Manassas?" Matt lit a cigar, his eyes barely visible under the wide brim of his hat.

"Battle?" Ash nearly dropped a mallet. He set it down and joined the man ten years his senior who was smoking outside the open door. "A big one? Not a skirmish?"

"Biggest yet." Matt offered him a cigar from his pocket, which he refused. "Happened Sunday. Our army won." He shook hands with Ash in shared congratulations.

Ash's senses reeled. The Confederates won.

"As we always knew we would." He chuckled. "Them Yankees hightailed it out of there after just a few hours of fighting."

The Union lost. Ash struggled to absorb that reality. "Were there many casualties?"

"It's early yet. What's said is that it was a great slaughter for both sides."

A tragedy. Thousands might be dead, yet his customer stood here acting happy as could be. Ash leaned against the sturdy brick wall, thankful for the support. "Details are exaggerated even in the small skirmishes." Were Willie and Luke safe?

Matt shook ashes off his cigar. "What's certain is General Beauregard led us to a resounding victory. Got his horse shot out from under him while he was at it. That didn't stop him."

"Brave man." Ash had to respect the general's courage. Losing a horse like that could discombobulate a man.

"It's said Manassas is an important railroad junction."

"Must be why we need to hold it." Thank goodness his voice didn't shake like his insides did at the terrible news.

"This is that one battle we've waited for." Matt clapped him on the back. "We gave them Yankees what for. They may surrender before the week is up."

That sobered Ash more than anything else he'd learned.

After Matt left to spread the news, Ash checked his pocket watch. Nearly noon. He'd tell his mother and sisters what had happened and then see what he could learn in town. There were always folks who wanted to talk, especially if they figured one was as happy as they were at the turn of events.

If he learned something significant, Ash would report to

Jim. He'd be up late tonight and arise before dawn to finish the saddle he'd promised tomorrow afternoon.

Troop movements around this first big battle was important news.

~

*A*sh rode to the Routeledge homestead that afternoon. Bouts of rain had brought a pleasant coolness.

"Ash, well met." Jim waved to him from the barn door. "I'm just closing up for the day, but I can sell a skin or two."

"Much obliged." He'd learned better than to speak military news in the open. Therefore, he was surprised when Jim talked about the battle while Ash gave Apple Blossom water, oats, and then a rubdown.

Once inside the barn, Ash wasted no time. "I've learned that new Tennessee regiments—the First, Third, and Eleventh— have been training at Camp Cheatham. At least the First has left that location and arrived at Manassas Sunday night after the battle, according to the father of one of the soldiers."

"Good work. You didn't write any of this on paper?"

"Didn't feel the need. I remember significant details."

"A wise choice, Ash. Not carrying concealed messages may save you from prison someday."

Reason enough to memorize everything.

Jim tapped his mouth with his index finger. "Let's put your memory to the test."

"What do you propose?"

"Next time you come, write down everything you want to report. Speak from memory, and I'll read it as you say it."

Seemed like a reasonable plan. Jim needed to trust he could remember details. "I'd best get back. I've got a customer coming for a saddle tomorrow." He started for the door.

"Aren't you forgetting something, son?"

Ash turned back.

"Pigskins."

His face heated. Someone might have noticed the omission. Certainly, his mother would. "Thanks for the reminder."

Outside, hooves pounded the dirt road.

Jim stiffened. "This could be more news. It's safer if you don't know one another. Pick out a skin while I take this fellow inside the house. Stay in the shadows, and keep your back turned to protect both of us. Pay me later."

Ash's heartbeat quickened. He strode to the back of the barn. Taking the top piece of leather to a horse stall, he bent over it as if to ascertain the quality. He remained there while the tanner gave a hearty greeting. The stranger's answer was muffled, as if he'd received a similar warning as Ash.

Booted steps led to the stone walk. The front door closed with a decisive snap.

Ash gave Jim a minute to draw the man away from the window. Then, hurrying to the corral, he tied the pigskin to his saddle. Within a minute, he rode through the forest, shielding himself from sight.

# CHAPTER 10

News from Manassas, Richmond, and even New York had been arriving all week. A report that Union General Irvin McDowell had been seriously wounded ended up being false. Thankfully, the number of Manassas fatalities on both sides were significantly fewer than first reported. Still, Ash agonized over his spying, fearful that some tidbit he'd passed on to Jim's network of spies had placed his friends in dangers. That fear kept him tossing and turning in his bed to the wee hours.

A walk to the post office on Friday finally bore fruit—two letters from Virginia. He strode toward home, in a hurry to read his friends' version of the day.

Townspeople stopped him on the corner, telling him what they knew and asking for updates. They were fairly well informed. Ash didn't have anything to add. It was comforting not to hide anything from fellow citizens. The war was only three months old, and he was already tired of secrets.

Once home, he hurried to his bedroom on the second floor. Dropping to the green cushioned armchair beside an open window, he reached for the first letter, this one from Willy.

*Well, we missed it. Oh, we were ordered to Manassas. You can imagine how we gripped our muskets on the train ride. Some men sang battle songs. Some prayed. Some got awful quiet...like Luke. Me, I just wanted to join the fight.*

*The battle was well in hand by the time we arrived. I came all the way to Virginia as a soldier and never even loaded my weapon. Of all the rotten luck. The Confederacy whopped up on the Yankees so well that they ran for their lives. Ash, you would have thought their trousers were afire!*

*The funny thing is that senators—Federal government officials, mind you!—brought their families from Washington City to see the show. They had their picnic baskets all laid out on blankets in a grassy field as though they were watching a play or something. I heard tell that it wasn't just the senators but other prominent society folks as well. Didn't someone tell them that there'd be bullets flying in every direction? Shot and shell from cannons? I'm still scratching my head over that one, Ash. At least we Southerners have more sense than that.*

*What's truly comical about the whole situation is that when the Yankees made a mad dash back to their capital, those spectators were shocked as could be. Pretty soon, fleeing soldiers shared the road with carriages, landaus, wagons, and horseback riders, all fighting over the country lane.*

*I talked with fellows who saw it all, and I'm telling you as it was told to me.*

Ash couldn't help laughing at the picture Willie painted.

*The best part for our army—besides winning—was picking up the new rifles that Union soldiers dropped on the battlefield in their mad retreat. Everyone in our company has a new rifle, a blessing indeed.*

*We also got canteens, bedrolls, knapsacks, socks, blouses, and trousers. I found a letter one fellow wrote to his sweetheart in a*

*knapsack. Think I'll mail that one for him myself, since I don't
know if he was wounded or killed in the battle.*

That was like Willie too. The man possessed a heart of gold.
Ash reached for Luke's much shorter note.

*It's certain that Willie's account of Sunday's battle will be more
interesting than mine.*

*Although he was raring to get to the battlefield, me found
meself thinking of Felicity and friends and neighbors back in Vicksburg. The city welcomed me family into its fold when I was but a
wee lad. It's my home. I love Mississippi, with its scorching
summers and mighty river that floods every spring. It was never
my desire to leave the people I've grown to love. Yet here we are, in
the midst of war.*

*Willie believes the conflict is over for good, a prevailing belief
among our company. For meself, me can't believe the ordeal will be
so easily resolved even if cessation of hostilities is what we all want.*

*Please make certain that Felicity has received my latest letters
and knows I am unharmed.*

*We've been told that we will camp at Manassas for some time,
though, with the army, things can change with the drop of a hat.*

Ash reread both letters. Jim might like to know that the
First Battalion Mississippi Volunteers were currently camped at
Manassas. Somehow it seemed a direct betrayal of his friends
to pass along information they'd shared in their correspondence.

No, he'd not take another ride to the tanner's home.
Instead, he'd take the buggy to Julia's house later and see if
she'd like to call on Felicity and Savannah.

They'd enjoy Willie's account of the retreat. Then he'd write
both men about how their girls fared.

~

*A*s they sat in the Adairs' family parlor that evening, Julia's heart lightened at Savannah's giggles over Willie's letter. Though Julia was relieved to learn of her friends' safety, the Union loss weighed on her. Did they have a fighting force that could win? Her neighbors surely didn't think so.

"Oh, this is so like Willie." Savannah's brown eyes sparkled as she studied the page. "Why, it's almost as if he were right here with us, telling us what happened. My own letter from him told more of the train ride and the sights." She traced a sentence. "He wrote of his disappointment at not fighting."

"As he did in mine."

"I simply must show Mother." Savannah stood. "Will you pardon me? I will return in but a moment. I'll send Josie in with blackberry shrub."

"Thank you. A cold drink will be welcome." Julia settled against the cushioned chair.

Savannah hurried from the room, her pink hoopskirt gliding over the blue rug. Cherry wood sofas and chairs contained cushions that matched the rug. Blue forget-me-nots dotted cream-colored wallpaper in the elegant parlor. It seemed a different room when not set up for dancing.

Ash turned to Julia. "I'm glad we brought his letter."

Julia had only to imagine Ash in danger for her to understand Savannah's distress. "Her anxiety didn't cease until his letter came yesterday."

"Pardon me, Miss Julia. Mr. Ash." A pretty black girl wearing a white apron over a gray skirt carried in a glass pitcher filled with purple liquid and four glasses on a tray. "I brought you refreshment."

"Thank you, Josie." Julia smiled at her. After all these years in Vicksburg, Julia had never grown comfortable with the men and women—and children—who served against their will. She had every reason to believe they were treated well in this home, yet that didn't alter the fact that they'd been given no choice. If the North won this war, surely, that would change Josie's life forever.

"Yes, miss." She set the tray on a table between Julia's chair and the sofa recently vacated by Savannah. "Is there anything else you be needing?"

"No, this will do very well. Thank you." Julia gave Ash a glass before sipping her own as the girl left the room.

"Delicious." Half the drink was gone in one long gulp. "Let's invite Savannah to go with us to Felicity's home."

"That's a wonderful idea."

"What's a wonderful idea?" Savannah glided gracefully through the open door in front of her mother, whose brown eyes and peaches-and-cream complexion had clearly been passed down to her daughter. Her blond hair, twisted in a bun at her nape, showed no signs of gray.

Ash rose. "Good evening, Mrs. Adair."

Savannah's mother gave her daughter a glass of shrub and then helped herself before sitting beside Savannah. "Thank you for sharing Willie's letter. Savannah's spirits have been understandably depressed this week. You've brought the first bit of laughter to our home since the news of Manassas."

"My pleasure." Reseated, Ash grinned. "I figured you'd enjoy Willie's sense of humor."

"Always." Mrs. Adair laughed and then sipped her drink.

Julia's smile wavered. "What was this wonderful idea you had, Julia?"

"Ash and I want to visit Felicity this evening. Will you join us?"

"The very thing I needed to revive my spirits. Perhaps we might ask Felicity to take a drive with us?"

"What a lovely suggestion." Mrs. Adair clasped her hands. "I'll ask Ollie to drive you in the landau, shall I?"

"In that case, may I leave my horse and buggy in your stable?" Ash scooted to the edge of his seat.

"Of course." Mrs. Adair gave a dismissive wave.

"I'll see to it. Thank you for the hospitality, Mrs. Adair." Ash rose and placed his empty glass on the tray. "Ladies, I'll see you momentarily."

~

*S*eated beside Julia, Ash let the cadence of the girls' chatter wash over him as the landau meandered the city streets. The women held dainty parasols that shaded them from the sun's heat, still strong at eight o'clock.

Julia tugged on his sleeve. "Do you want to?"

As they plodded along the smoothly graveled Washington Street, the city's main thoroughfare which ran parallel to the river, all eyes were on him. The last topic he'd heard was a steamer excursion they'd all attended last summer. Best own up to his inattention. "I fear you have the best of me. You were saying…"

"You weren't listening." Julia crossed her arms over the bodice of her peach-colored dress.

"Guilty." He grinned.

The ladies giggled.

"I asked if you wanted Ollie to drive us to the Sky Parlor." Savannah raised her eyebrows.

Ash ignored the ache in his leg, worse for the long rides he'd taken in the past two months. Being driven up the winding drive to the hilltop beat walking up its long wooden stairs by a long shot. "An excellent suggestion."

Savannah made her request to their driver. Ollie coaxed his team to a greater speed.

Two scores of well-dressed couples were already strolling on the hill when they arrived.

Ash helped each lady from the carriage as the sun sank toward the horizon. Then, with Julia's hand resting on his arm, they walked up the hill, stopping every few yards to exchange greetings and celebrate their army's victory.

Admiring the red, orange and pink horizon, Julia rested the tip of her cream-colored parasol on the grass. "I love watching dusk fall on the Mississippi. Such a beautiful river."

In that case, their next buggy ride would include a stop here. Ash peered at the wharves. Not as many steamers came in these days. Northern boats from upriver points along the Ohio River such as Cincinnati had nearly stopped. This week's battle might halt the arrival of northern goods altogether.

"I always think of Willie when I come here." Savannah's pensive tone shifted the mood. "You accompanied Willie and Luke here after my party, didn't you, Ash?"

"We ended here." Why had she mentioned it?

"He seemed happy that evening." Savannah studied the darkening river. "But the more I consider it, the more I believe he had something on his mind. Something deeper." She turned to Ash. "Did he tell you?"

Luke had told him after Willie's and Ash's rift, but Ash couldn't share his secret. What was safe to say? "A man preparing for a possible war has many things on his mind."

"Such as...?" Savannah studied his face.

"One thing for certain is that you are on his mind. He asks me to watch out for you in every letter." He peered around her at Felicity. "Luke does the same for you." Although, with the responsibilities of work and spying for the North, he hadn't done as a good job of keeping an eye on his friends' girls as he would have liked. "If either of you requires my help, you have only to ask." He meant it. It was the only way he could convince his friends that he respected their decisions even if he couldn't support them.

# CHAPTER 11

$\mathcal{N}$early three weeks later, Julia awoke before dawn on the first Tuesday in August. The Union hadn't shown signs of surrendering as her neighbors had assured her they would, for which she was profoundly thankful. One big battle wasn't going to decide the matter, after all.

It was Hester's and Daisy's day off. Julia didn't plan anything else on Tuesdays, for she cooked the meals and washed dishes all day. Mama made the beds and sometimes baked bread or desserts.

Eddie came to the dining room before their mother made an appearance, so Julia ate a breakfast of sausage, biscuits, and gravy with him.

"I want you to stay in our square today," she said.

It was a foregone conclusion that Eddie would play with his friends unless inclement weather threatened. An overcast sky again promised rain. Indeed, it had rained nearly every day for two weeks.

"Oh, Julia, that's not fair. If it does rain, it won't last long. We can't go to our hideout at the City Hospital?"

"Choose one closer to home." Julia steeled herself against

his pleas. If he stayed on their property or in their square, Julia wouldn't worry. As it was, Mama didn't care that he only came home for meals.

"We looked. There's no good place on our square."

He had a point. Homes, not businesses, surrounded them on every side, and her neighbors wouldn't thank her if Eddie built a stick structure on their property. "There are too many strangers in the city these days."

"How about if we go straight to our hideout and nowhere else? That is, after I fetch George and Tom." Gravy dripped from the fork he shoved in his mouth.

Her heart melted. He *was* a good boy, just adventurous. With far too much freedom. "Don't talk to strangers. And come right home when leaving your hideout."

"Thanks, Julia." He swiped his mouth with a napkin and then bolted for the door.

"Be home for lunch by noon," she called after him.

"I will." The front door slammed.

She would head over to his hideout before lunch to make certain he followed her rules.

She carried their empty plates to the kitchen, planning to make peach jelly they could eat with leftover biscuits and stuffed cabbage for lunch. Mama was in the kitchen. "Good morning, Mama. Did you want breakfast?"

"I'll eat a biscuit in here." She selected one from the basket. "I'll bake a marble cake for supper."

"That sounds lovely. Thank you." Julia began heating water in a large pan to wash dishes. "Have you given any thought to when we can invite the Mitchells over for supper?" She'd brought up the topic several times only to be brushed off. On the other hand, they'd hosted Carlton's family monthly.

"How about we invite the Bradleys instead? Molly's brother-in-law is visiting from New Orleans."

"Mama, he's over forty—and a widower with eight children." She tamped down her irritation. "Besides, Ash is my beau. Let's invite his family. We need to get to know them better."

Mama tilted her head, studying her. "Are you in love with him?"

Ash hadn't declared his love, though surely he would soon. She loved him but was unwilling to tell Mama when she was still pushing her toward other men. Gathering both families for an evening should go a long way to fostering love and friendship. "I want to continue our courtship. We have such fun together." And she trusted him, faith that she'd lost in her mother.

"If I invite Louisa and her family over here, she'll reciprocate, and then we'll have to go there."

"That's a good thing. She's very pleasant. I like all of them." After all, Mama owed her something after neglecting to care for her future.

"I suppose we must." Mama heaved a sigh as she placed her empty plate on the table beside the sink. "How about this Saturday?"

"That will do nicely." She didn't have plans with Ash for that day.

"I'll prepare the invitation and send it over with Silas today," she said, although she looked more resigned than pleased.

"Thank you, Mama." The invitation would be two months overdue, but Julia had nearly despaired of it happening at all.

Finally. Some good news.

~

*A*sh was as thrilled as his mama last night to receive Mrs. Dodd's invitation for supper. The two families would finally socialize at a gathering alone. Surely, it was a sign that Mrs. Dodd's attitude toward his suit was softening. Perhaps she'd learned that business at his saddle shop was picking up due his newspaper advertisements with new customers in the community outside Vicksburg. He'd worked until sundown every weekday that he wasn't traveling to Bolton or spying on Vicksburg streets.

He unlocked his shop before dawn on Wednesday, reveling in the early-morning chill from an overnight rain. Summer heat would dispel that after sunup.

Keeping the door open wide to allow in the coolness, Ash began to stitch where he'd left off the night before. He yawned. This schedule taxed his leg, but it was worth it. He'd nearly made up all he lost on the exorbitant dressmaker bill.

Something thumped on his wall. Didn't sound like a dog or a cat. A fist?

No one stood at the door. It had come from the back of the shop.

Another thump—as though a wooden club struck the rear wall. Such force could dent the shop.

Ash strode to the door. "Who's there?" Vigilantes? His heartbeat sped.

No answer. Nothing moved in the darkness.

His father's musket was inside the house. Ash grabbed a mallet and stepped outside. "Who's there?"

Booted footsteps struck the gravel behind his shop. Two feet of a gravel path around the building led to grass. Someone was close.

"Watch yerself." A gruff voice, vaguely familiar.

Had someone discovered his spying for Jim?

Running footsteps took the stranger from the area.

Who was it?

Did he want to know?

~

*T*hree days later, Ash was still troubled by his early-morning visitor when his family lounged in the Dodds' parlor after a delicious supper of baked fish, roasted vegetables, and bread pudding with plum sauce.

The wooden wall of his shop had indeed been dented when he inspected it at first light, so he hadn't dreamed the incident. He'd taken his pa's musket to the shop in the predawn hours the next morning. That didn't feel right, and given that the weapon would scare his mama if she caught him toting it around in the dark, he moved a cot inside the shop. That way, he didn't have to walk outside when working before first light. It hadn't been too difficult to explain to his family. So far, he hadn't heard so much as a footstep that couldn't be accounted for, yet he determined to keep a keen eye on his surroundings going forward.

Whooping, Eddie claimed victory over Daphne in the latest game of draughts in the corner of the elegantly furnished parlor, snapping Ash's attention to the gathering. Julia looked lovelier than usual in a pink gown that accentuated the color in her cheeks. Daphne was behaving. Mrs. Dodd had been gracious, introducing new topics with ease when the conversation faltered. His mother's Southern charm matched their hostess's—perhaps surpassed it because she was genuinely pleased to enjoy the evening at the Dodds' home.

Caroline, his quiet, studious sister, had been drawn to speak of her needlepoint by Julia. "My latest scene is of the river from the courthouse cupola. It's one I sketched before the war took its toll on the number of steamboats at our wharves, so it's quite intricate."

Ash stared at her. He'd had no notion what she'd been doing lately. He was so seldom free to do more than dine with his family.

"You create your own needlepoint designs?" Julia's brown eyes widened.

"How extraordinary." Tilting her head, Mrs. Dodd studied her guest. "Have you ever sketched a person to stitch in your designs?"

Her cheeks flushed. "No. I might try that. Perhaps I'll begin with Daphne." She looked at her sister, whose brown braids slid across the shoulders of her elbow-length green dress as she leaned over the board game. Caroline was slender and of medium height, whereas Daphne was short and slightly plump.

"An excellent plan." Mama gave Caroline a proud smile. "Her creations are above the normal."

"I enjoy tatting. Creating intricate lace patterns is one of my joys." Julia shook her head in wonder. "But I'd love to see your needlepoint."

"And so you shall." Mama beamed at her. "We shall have you over for supper before the month is out."

"Why, that would be lovely." Julia spoke quickly, without looking at her mother. "We'd love that above all things."

"I'd like that too." Ash smiled.

She blushed.

With a glance at the mantel clock, Mama arose. "My, how the evening has flown. Thank you for that delicious meal and stimulating conversation."

Her restraint was admirable, for she'd been anxious to impress Martha Dodd. Their hostess had held herself gracious yet aloof all evening, much as she had been with him throughout his courtship with Julia.

He kissed Julia's hand at the door. Her eyes sparkled up at him. She seemed to share his happiness about their gathering.

He drove his chattering family home, praying this evening meant that Mrs. Dodd was beginning to accept him as her daughter's suitor.

~

*M*ama hadn't mentioned any new bachelors' names to Julia since the evening with Ash and his family nearly two weeks ago that was be reciprocated at his own home this Saturday. Ash was taking her to the Washington Hotel for supper the day before without Felicity and Savannah —a rarity since the battle. She hummed as she polished a silver tray in the formal dining room.

"I fear Ash is further away than ever from supporting you in the manner you're accustomed." Mama's mouth pursed as if she'd eaten an unripe persimmon.

This again? "I don't care." Julia's euphoria evaporated as she wiped polish from the tray with a soft cloth. Mama had taken so much from her. Couldn't her mother allow her to enjoy falling in love with her handsome beau, who was more a true Southern gentleman than Carlton ever hoped to be?

"I ran into Louise at the market yesterday." Mama examined a spoon in the sunrays beaming through the open curtains. "She let it slip that Ash worries about money."

"He doesn't discuss such matters with me, naturally, but I can't help but feel Mrs. Mitchell exaggerated the situation." Mrs. Mitchell's only vice, as far as Julia could ascertain, was her tendency toward gossip. Such hints didn't help anyone since Mama's demands created a situation nearly impossible for Ash to overcome. "He's been busier at the shop than ever."

"Louise also said he's making multiple trips to the tanner's and only buying one or two skins each trip."

Julia frowned. That *was* strange. Why not buy several? "There's an increase in orders."

"Then where's the extra income?" Mama looked up from her grimy work.

Julia's chest squeezed as another troubling question rushed into her mind. How did Ash seem to know all the war news before she did? Both sides were reportedly strengthening their armies, but Ash often had information she hadn't read in the city's newspapers. She'd learned from him on Sunday that the Confederacy was to construct an ironclad in Memphis—the *C.S.S. Arkansas*. Where was this knowledge coming from?

There were explanations for all of this. Time alone with Ash was just what she needed. She hadn't told him about Papa's will either. Should she? If he thought he was courting a rich heiress, he needed the truth.

~

*F*riday promised to be another scorcher. No matter. Ash looked forward to this evening with Julia. He was taking her to her favorite restaurant and then for a drive into the country. Between recovering from his mother's expensive dress bill and three of his customers ordering and then not paying for their saddles in August, he hadn't been able to treat her to supper. Those saddles were still in his shop, ready for delivery. One of the customers who was also a merchant had told Ash that shortages of supplies that used to come in on Northern steamers had adversely affected his business.

Unfortunate. He'd hold onto it for a month in case the man changed his mind. The other two customers hadn't been by. Too busy? Mitch O'Flanagan, the blacksmith, didn't live far. He rarely delivered saddles unless requested to do so because it could appear he was pressuring the person for payment. But this time...

He rubbed his jaw. He *did* need the money.

Ash toted the saddle down Grove Street to the blacksmith's. He greeted the few idle men who smoked cigars just outside the entrance before stepping inside the barn. "Mr. O'Flanagan, I brought your saddle."

The burly man in his thirties didn't look up from pounding a horseshoe. "Didn't order no saddle."

"You did. Over two weeks ago." The same day someone had dented his shop's exterior wall.

The blacksmith raised a grimy face. "And I say I didn't."

The back of Ash's neck stiffened. Mitch hadn't forgotten. This was deliberate. Why?

Conversation stopped at the double-wide barn door.

"Watch yerself." Mitch's eyes narrowed.

The same words, the same Irish inflection, as that predawn visitor. He wanted Ash to know it was him. Another vigilante? "If you don't want the saddle, I'll sell it to someone else."

"You do that." The horseshoe sizzled as Mitch lowered it into a bucket of water with red-hot tongs.

Nothing to be gained from staying. He strode out, between the crowd that parted for him.

"And mind what I said." Mitch roared the words after him.

Ash continued his pace. What had he done to rile a man he rarely spoke to, unless he was still suspected of being a Unionist? Had the other customer, a wharf worker, ordered with no intention of paying too? Wasn't worth the confrontation to find out.

Too much of such shenanigans would destroy his business. He'd require a deposit for new customers from now on.

One thing was certain. He was being watched.

# CHAPTER 12

It was not quite eight o'clock when Ash guided the team past the congestion of town, away from the setting sun and toward smaller businesses, homes, and farms. "It feels as though we haven't enjoyed an evening alone for weeks."

"Seems that either Savannah or Felicity are always with us. Mind you, I love their company, but it's nice to speak with you alone sometimes."

"I thought you worried about them." Had he neglected his own girl to watch over his friends' girls?

"I do." Julia sat rigidly at his side.

"Have I done something to upset you?" He glanced at her.

Her feet tapped a staccato rhythm on the floorboard of the buggy. "There's something I've not spoken of to anyone."

He understood how secrets ate at one's gut. "You can tell me anything."

"Ash, Mama explained some family history that affects me. It's not pretty."

The sorrow in her eyes made him want to champion her even more. "Please. Tell me."

"I found out in June that Mama went to great lengths to ensure that Eddie inherited the land left to her by her father in South Carolina and her allowance from him should she die before he reaches his majority with no thought for me. My father didn't even provide for me in his will."

Ash couldn't blame her for the bitter tone. "Not even your father…"

"No." Her eyes shimmered with unshed tears.

"I'm so sorry." His heart sank. At last, he understood Mrs. Dodd's standoffish attitude toward him. Her arrangements had given her daughter nothing. Apparently, she'd assumed Julia would marry someone wealthy. "I'm building my business."

"I'm proud of your hard work." She swiped her finger across her cheeks.

He fought his longing to clasp her hand. Hold her close to comfort her. Instead, he braced himself for the end of their courtship should Julia desire it. "I'm not the wealthy suitor your mama wants for you." The words tasted bitter on his lips.

"No," she whispered. "Not until your shop is able to support your mom, your sisters, and a family in Mama's style. I'm sorry."

The loss from those unsold saddles slashed deeper. Their future shifted further into the distance than the war had already moved it. "What about you?" He hated to ask, but he had to.

"I want you as my beau." She tucked her hand around his rigid arm, gazing at him squarely. "I thought you should understand my situation. We should have honesty between us."

He halted beside a field of thriving corn. "Then know this— it matters not to me if you have thousands of dollars or not a penny to your name."

"Thank you for that, Ash." She leaned her cheek against his arm.

He breathed deeply. The fragrance of lilacs would forevermore remind him of this moment. Her vulnerability. Her honesty that he needed though it stung. He caressed her cheek. "This isn't the time to speak of our feelings for one another." She was too upset with her mother. "Just know mine for you are deep and true—and strong enough to wait—"

"You're right. I can't..." She shook her head. "Can we simply enjoy our drive?"

"Of course." He started the buggy again.

"I feel better for having told you." Her hand tightened on his arm. "There's so much against us already. If we don't have honesty between us, our courtship doesn't have a chance."

It was as if a chunk of ice formed in his belly. What if she discovered he was a spy?

Yet he'd sworn to keep his spying a secret. It wasn't an oath he took lightly.

~

*W*hen Ash flinched, Julia knew she'd struck a nerve.

Mama had kept a wagonload of secrets from her for three years. She couldn't stand the thought that Ash was doing the same. "Your mama says that you've got more saddle orders but you're worried about money, that you only buy a couple of skins at a time." Julia would figure out a way to earn money. She'd need an income whether she married Ash or not. But the only thing she excelled at was tatting lace.

Ash's brow furrowed. "She told you that?"

"She told Mama." Her hand slid from his arm. She pushed on to what concerned her more. "You always know war news before anyone else."

"I read all of our city's newspapers." He shrugged. "Join folks talking on the streets."

That could account for it. Of the city's six newspapers, she only read the *Daily Whig*. But she had a hunch there was more to it. "Is there something you need to tell me?"

"There's nothing I can tell you."

"What does that mean? Don't you trust me?"

"With my life." His jaw tightened. "You're making it difficult for me."

That pulled her up short. "Making what difficult? Does it affect me?"

"No." He held her gaze.

Mama's secret had affected both Eddie and herself and had been decided for years before Julia learned of it. She stared at the reins wrapped around his fingers.

"Can't you trust that I'd tell you if I could?"

His secret must have something to do with supporting the Union. Secret meetings with Unionists outside the city? She sighed. "I will trust you. But come to me if I can help."

"I promise." He stopped the buggy again. The forest surrounded the country lane. Putting an arm around her shoulders, he pulled her against his side. "You are precious to me." He kissed her temple.

Her heart leaped. She rested her cheek against his fast-beating heart. *He's falling in love with me.* The realization filled her with wonder. Yet, if he loved her, why keep secrets?

Julia met his anxious gaze. His words deserved a response. "You're becoming quite important to me as well." With so much uncertainty about their future together, she should say no more at the moment.

He kissed her, a chaste yet fervent kiss. Giving comfort rather than taking. She felt more cherished than she had since learning of her father's neglect. She cuddled against him, grateful for his strength.

Wheels creaked behind a trotting horse. It was as dark as twilight under the trees. Julia pulled away, hoping the driver of the approaching wagon hadn't noticed their embrace.

"Evenin', folks." A gray-haired gentleman halted his loaded wagon beside their buggy. "Your horse throw a shoe?"

"No, sir." Ash flushed. "We stopped to admire the view."

There was nothing to see except trees and brush. Julia's face felt like it was afire.

"We're heading back to Vicksburg now," Ash hurried to say.

The stranger nodded. "All for the best, son. There's danger a'plenty all around."

Julia stared at the man with eyes the color of the Mississippi River. He was clothed like a farmer.

Ash's gaze darted in every direction.

"Bears and such."

"Yes, sir." Ash didn't seem convinced that had been the man's meaning.

"Good evening to you." The stranger touched the brim of his hat.

"Good evening." Ash waited until he passed and then turned the buggy toward Vicksburg.

Julia figured they'd drive through dust stirred by the stranger's wagon, but there was no sign of him or the wagon. No dust stirred on the dirt road. "Do you know that man?"

"Never seen him before." His eyes darted to either side of the road as he drove. The stranger had warned of danger. Was Ash afraid for her...or himself?

~

*M*ama had outdone herself with the supper for the Dodds. Ash had been proud of Caroline's samplers, which she shyly displayed for the guests. Daphne played board games with Eddie, and Mrs. Dodd complimented the fragrant floral arrangements throughout the dining room and parlor.

Ash drove them home in his carriage. Though there hadn't

been a private moment with Julia the whole evening, the radiant smile she gave him at her doorstep made everything worth the effort.

The first few days of September had Ash on the lookout for the farmer he and Julia had encountered. The stranger had been headed into the city with filled sacks. Were the stranger's words a warning that he'd discovered Ash's spying? Did the man have something to do with the blacksmith, who as much as admitted he was Ash's predawn visitor? There'd been no more warnings at his shop, but Ash kept his musket handy and slept in the shop when he had to work in the dark hours.

The belligerent blacksmith had given Ash another reason to watch his back, day and night. Had his former Unionist talks on street corners brought this about, or did Mitch suspect him of spying? Impossible to know, but it troubled him.

As he rode the morning train to Bolton, Ash mulled over the physical attacks from the vigilantes, the early-morning thumps from the club-bearing blacksmith, the saddle orders that had gone unclaimed, and the strange words of danger from the farmer.

Julia had been with him. Was courting her putting her in danger?

Should he reconsider his spying?

He was the last one off at his stop and took the forest path rather than the open road to Jim's homestead. Too many folks watched him in Vicksburg. What about in Bolton? No one at the station had seemed to pay him any mind.

It was nearly noon when he arrived. Muted voices from the house silenced as he approached.

Ash ducked into the barn. Was Jim with a spy? Should Ash hide in the woods?

Footsteps on the cobblestone walk sent Ash scurrying to the stack of hides, trying to appear as if he'd been examining them for purchase.

"Ash? That you?" Jim's voice from the entrance.

He looked over his shoulder. "Yes, just looking to buy a skin or two."

"Come inside. Want you to meet a friend."

Ash frowned. He had always taken pains *not* to be seen at Jim's house, but he followed as instructed.

A balding man of medium height stood by the table.

"Ash, I'd like you meet Cal Jones, a blacksmith from Warrenton. Cal, this here's Ashburn Mitchell, saddle maker from Vicksburg."

"Pleased to meet you." Ash shook the man's callused hand. He was taller than the blacksmith who lived a few miles downriver from Vicksburg, but the man probably was a score Ash's senior.

"Pleasure's mine." He gave Jim a firm nod.

"Ash, you have something in common with Cal. While you report the goings-on in Vicksburg, Cal reports about the river and Warrenton."

Ash looked at the man with renewed respect.

"I'm a family man," Cal said. "It's difficult to find excuses to come to Bolton. Being down on the river, I hear stuff."

"My customers like to chew the fat with me too." When the older man sat, Ash straddled a chair.

"Cal's asking for a man in Vicksburg to deliver messages to." Jim rubbed his hands together. "You're the best man for the job."

Cal stroked his whiskered jaw. "It'd probably be twice a month, though there's no tellin' about such things."

Folks were in and out of his shop often enough that two visits a month shouldn't be noticed. He looked at Jim. "Then I'd be responsible for getting his information and mine to you."

Jim nodded.

"I'll do it." It'd help a fellow spy without adding more

responsibility than Ash could handle. Anything to speed this war to completion.

They planned for Cal to come to the shop during daylight hours. He'd order a saddle sometime in the fall, and Ash would buy tools from the blacksmith when necessary. The men shook hands, and the blacksmith rose to take his leave.

Cal stopped at the door and turned back. "I spotted you on the train here. Act as though we're strangers on the ride home."

Failure. Ash managed to nod. He'd been so careful trying to notice folks noticing him. He hadn't seen Cal at the depot.

That must not happen again.

# CHAPTER 13

*A*sh's letters from his friends in Virginia had grown sporadic. Willie's last correspondence had arrived on September second. He'd complained about the lack of another big battle. Since the North hadn't surrendered and skirmishes continued, he figured the conflict would continue a few more months. He commented that George was becoming a better cook, but Willie lacked appetite, which he blamed on the heat.

Luke's letter came a few days later. The single page was his shortest correspondence by far.

> *Drills and camp duties keep us busy. Sometimes me finds meself too weary to write Felicity before nodding off at night. Not to worry about us, though prayers will be most welcome, especially for Willie. He isn't taking to our increased camp duties with his normal vigor. He does not ask George to help with army duties, which is commendable, because a few others do. All Willie requires is for George to cook his meals, launder his clothes, and pitch his tent. Since we haven't moved for weeks, the last task isn't arduous. (In truth, all soldiers have become adept with putting up our tent homes in a matter of minutes.) Because we're in the army together,*

*me has observed the interactions between the two men more than previously and found Willie fairer than most slave owners. Quite a few officers brought a servant with them without giving them a choice in the matter. It has burned a fire in me soul. Willie has been fussing over trifling matters of late. Me avoids him when he's in such moods. George tells him to go to bed when he complains of headaches, yet there is always some duty to be done. Rest is not always possible. Willie is as brave as they come. Though me senses some inner struggle in our friend, he has not told me of it.*

Willie fussing? Luke avoiding him? That wasn't like either man. Willie's relaxed attitude was part of his charm. What of the headaches?

Ash hated that Willie's twenty-first birthday had passed without the celebration they'd planned. How he wished things were different.

He prayed for Willie, Luke, and George and then turned his attention to his business. His new requirement of a fifty percent deposit had lost him three sales in the past week—all from townsfolk he barely recognized. He couldn't help thinking that they wouldn't have paid him at all.

Was this, too, the work of the vigilantes? If so, it was far more effective than fists or hard shoves into lampposts because this blow affected his family's livelihood—and delayed his future with Julia.

~

*J*ulia ate supper with her brother and mother in the dining room the second Tuesday in September. "Eddie, are you excited to see your friends again at school?" Thank goodness, classes were resuming for her rambunctious little brother.

"Nope." His blond hair always stood up at the crown unless

covered by a hat, which it wasn't at the dining table. "George and Tom aren't neither."

"George and Tom aren't *either*," Julia corrected absently.

"Julia, grammar lessons begin tomorrow." He leaned on his elbow with a sigh. "Do I have to hear it tonight?"

"No." She well remembered the disappointment of losing relaxed summer days. "George and Tom will be at school with you."

"It ain't the same."

Mama's lips quirked.

"We've been everywhere this summer, fishing in the river—"

"You're not to fish in the river without an adult." Julia shuddered to imagine what would happen if one fell in and the current took them downstream, something that had nearly happened to Willie when he was not much older than Eddie.

"George's big brother took us."

"Paul is twelve. I hardly consider him an adult." Julia glanced at her mother, who ate a forkful of peas as if she had not a care in the world. "Someone at least fourteen, please. And always ask me or Mama first." Preferably herself.

"We also went to the post office, the market, the shops on Washington Street."

Washington Street? Just up the hill from the river? "That's too far for you to wander." She should have kept a better eye on him. Besides sewing for the soldiers, she'd been tatting every spare minute. As soon as she had several yards of lace, she'd sell them to the notions shop or maybe to seamstresses. It was a step toward her future. Still, she mustn't neglect Eddie.

"We played on the sidewalk." He speared a fried potato. "And you know what? Everywhere we went, we heard folks talk about the war. We want the South to win, right?"

Stricken, Julia looked at her mother. Had they not

explained to Eddie that they were Unionists back in the spring? She tried to recall a conversation.

"We don't wish anything bad to happen to Willie or Luke," Mama said, "or any of our friends and neighbors."

"Right." Eddie grinned. "I knew we were for Mississippi. I told that man."

"What man?" Just where had her brother been?

"The one who came to our house when I was out chasing fireflies after supper one night."

Julia gripped her fork. Had someone from the vigilante committee come to their home? Her thoughts flew back to the farmer she and Ash had met while on a country drive. The one who warned of danger.

Mama's face paled. "When did he come, Eddie? I didn't talk to him."

"'Bout a month ago." He ate another potato. "It was fine that you didn't see him. He said I told him what he needed to know."

Julia's heartbeat quickened. Someone had suspected their loyalties lay elsewhere. Perhaps it was a *very* good thing that she and Mama neglected to tell him. "Was he a farmer?"

"Didn't look like one."

"Eddie." Mama folded her hands. "I want you to come right home after school every day."

"I'm not allowed to play with George and Tom?" His jaw slackened.

"You may bring them here to play in the yard." Mama's voice remained firm. "I'll ask Hester to bake little oatmeal cakes for each of you tomorrow."

"Yes, Mama."

Julia's eyes widened. Mama acted like a parent, a rarity since her father's death.

As for the stranger, Julia would ask Silas to keep an eye out for him. Silas had a spacious room adjacent to their stable as part of his pay. He was a good man and protective of her family, especially Eddie.

She wouldn't worry Ash with the incident...unless it happened again.

~

Orders had slowed considerably in September. Steamers from St. Louis, Cincinnati, and Louisville no longer came to Vicksburg. Supplies in the city dwindled. No doubt, the shortages adversely affected Ash's customers.

He broached the subject with his mother at lunch on a Friday in mid-September. Daphne was at school, but it didn't hurt for Caroline to learn he wasn't making as much money.

Mama twisted her handkerchief. "Should I be concerned?"

"Yes...for now." Ash didn't intend to tell her about the three customers who'd refused to pick up their saddles—or the blacksmith's threats. Certainly not the visits from the vigilantes. No need to worry her more than he must. Papa had protected her. He'd do the same. "No one knows how long this will last. I might receive five orders next week. Or none."

"Oh, dear." Mama's hands fluttered. "This never happened when your father was alive."

Pa never had to support them while their country was at war with itself.

"What can we do to help, Ash?" Caroline turned to him.

This was more like it. "Curtail your shopping to necessities. Keep food and pantry items in stock. No new clothing."

"B-but we need new dresses each season," Mama sputtered.

"I have plenty." Caroline gave him a nod.

"Buy what you *need*." He hated adding that slight emphasis, for he loved their excitement over new gowns. Yet fabric bills and her seamstress were their highest expenditures.

"Your sister is still growing. She must have new clothes." Mama's mouth set in a mutinous line.

"By all means, purchase what Daphne requires."

Mama studied him. "My daughters will wear new dresses for the Adairs' annual Christmas Eve dance."

Ash's jaw tightened. His mother wasn't hearing him. Unnecessary expenditures hampered his goal of proving his saddle shop worthy of supporting his mother and sisters as well as a wife and children. And every day, he was more certain he wanted Julia to be his future wife. She may not be ready to speak of her feelings, but love for her blossomed in his heart.

~

Caroline brought mail to Ash's shop later that afternoon. "I went to the post office. This was the only letter."

"Thank you." Willie's handwriting. "And thanks for your willingness to wear older clothes."

"We all must sacrifice." Caroline gave a sad smile. "Mama's a shrewd woman, but she doesn't want to acknowledge that the conflict between our countries has already affected Vicksburg."

*Between our countries.* It rankled to hear his sister refer to the Northern half and the Southern half as two countries. It had happened with lightning speed. But he was a small part of the fight toward restoration.

"Mama only reads advertisements and society news. She skims over war news."

"What about you?" Ash studied her. Her brown braids were pinned in a coil. When had she begun to wear her hair up?

"I stay alert for changes. I read all the news." She ran her fingers over one of the rejected saddles he'd have to sell. "Mama turned over shopping for groceries six months ago. I'll stock the pantry. It will help to know how much I can spend since it's never been a concern."

"It's been a concern of mine," he corrected, "not Mama's."

"Keep me informed. I'll support you." Soft footsteps took her to the shop's door, where she turned back to him. "I have a bad feeling that the situation in Vicksburg will get a whole lot worse."

"Based on?" Had she learned something he should pass on?

"Nothing but intuition." With that, she was gone.

His gut said the same thing.

His gaze fell on Willie's letter, dated a week earlier. Ash had prayed for his friend daily, uncertain of the problem. Surly disposition. Headaches. Loss of appetite. Surely, he'd recovered now that the worst of the summer heat was behind them.

*Don't feel like doing much. I've been feeling peaked for a couple of weeks. My stomach's been a mite uncomfortable of late, and tonight in particular. Forehead's burning hot. It's probably the heat. The band's playing. Lots of fellows dream of home as they listen. Reckon that includes me.*

*Thanks for watching over Savannah. I guess you've got picket duty of a different kind, right? What with keeping watch over Savannah and Felicity for me and Luke. Wish you were here, though. Remember that last night we walked all over town? Darkened shops, starry sky, moonlight casting shadows on the muddy Mississippi? Something tells me...no, never mind. I'm being fanciful because I feel poorly. I'll explain when next I see you.*

*Sure do have a hankering to see Savannah's pretty face. Hearing her laughter would be a tonic to me, but I reckon some of my mother's broths and remedies would do me more good.*

Uneasiness overtook Ash. He regretted the hard feelings from that last evening. A kind of unspoken pact remained between him and Willie not to broach the topic again.

That rift tied his stomach in knots harder than his fumbling fingers managed to create when stitching his saddle, all the while praying for his friend.

～

That evening, Julia sensed Ash's concern for Willie after he asked her to ride with him to Savannah's house. They had planned to stroll about town after supper, but he'd brought his buggy. Another change in plans. No matter. She'd be with her beau, something denied Savannah and Felicity.

"Can I go?" Eddie tugged on his sleeve.

Ash shook his head as if his thoughts were miles away. "Not this time, little buddy. We'll go somewhere soon."

Julia and Ash had only taken Eddie to church with them that summer. There'd been none of the picnics, fishing, rides into the country, or fruit-picking jaunts with her five friends that had marked last year—before she'd begun courting Carlton—and Eddie had gone along on nearly all of them. Her neglect smote her.

"We haven't gone fishing all summer." Eddie's brown eyes pleaded for Ash's attention.

"What's that? Oh, yes. You're right." Ash squatted to his level. "I miss that, don't you?"

Eddie nodded.

"Shall we go on Sunday, after church?" He looked up at Mama and Julia for permission.

"We can pack a picnic luncheon." Mama's face brightened at the prospect.

"Sounds lovely." At least the picnic did. Julia didn't find it enjoyable to hold a line in the river in hopes of catching a fish. Yet Ash and Eddie enjoyed it.

"Oh, boy! I get to fish."

"Let's invite your family, Ash." Mama gave him a coaxing smile. "Tell them not to bring a dish. We'll supply what's needed."

Julia's spirits lifted, despite her worry for Willie. The two families had last spent the evening together at Ash's three weeks prior. Perhaps Mama's attitude toward Ash was thawing.

"They'll love that. Thanks, Mrs. Dodd." Ash ran a finger down Eddie's freckled nose. "How about you, little buddy? Does that suit you?"

His face puckered in thought. "It'd suit me better if my friends George and Tom came with us."

Ash laughed. "I'll leave that decision to your mother and sister, but"—he straightened— "it's fine with me. We need a couple more men in this passel of women." He winked at Julia.

Eddie turned to Julia. "Can they come with us, please?"

She ruffled his hair—unfortunately, causing tufts at his crown to stand up straighter. "Mama, what do you say?"

"They can come." She gave him an indulgent look.

Eddie bounced up and down. "Can I go ask them now?"

"Go on with you." Mama waved him on.

Running footsteps took him out the front door.

"Thank you, Ash. He's been at a loose end of late." Mama studied him. "You seem restless to get to Savannah's home."

"My apologies. I'd feel easier to know she's received a more recent letter."

"Then I won't keep you." She walked with them to the door. "My prayers are with Willie."

"Do you have the letter with you?" Julia waited until the buggy had started down the hill before asking.

He extracted it from his pocket. "You may read it. I don't believe it's wise for Savannah to do so."

She scanned the page with growing agitation. "Such melancholy isn't like Willie. Wonder what his ailment might be." Could be any of a number of sicknesses.

"Wish we could consult your father."

That stirred a pang of grief. "Me too." As a druggist, her father might have ascertained the cause of Willie's illness from the few lines. Yet she couldn't forgive his lack of fatherly concern for her. It hardened like a stone in her chest. "Willie's certain to be back to his old shenanigans as we speak."

"No doubt."

But the tension didn't ease from Ash's face.

Julia fell silent. Better to wait on further news than to speculate.

He didn't drive around to the stables as he usually did when visiting the Adairs. Instead, he looped the reins around an intricate pattern in the black iron fence. The two of them ascended the stone steps to the portico. Julia pulled on the bell rope.

"Evenin', Mr. Mitchell. Miss Dodd." A broad-shouldered man wearing a brown coat almost the color of his complexion opened the door.

"Good evening, Samuel." Ash removed his bowler hat. "We stopped by to see Miss Savannah."

"The whole family is out for the evening."

Julia glanced at Ash before addressing Samuel. "Do you know if there is recent news from Mr. Willie?"

"Yes, miss. A letter came for Miss Savannah. The family traveled to the Sanderson plantation to learn more." Samuel scratched his head. "Seems Mr. Willie is in the hospital out in Virginia."

*Hospital?* Julia slipped her hand into Ash's. His fingers tightened around hers.

"Been there since Sunday, so they say."

"He hasn't been shot or wounded in battle, right?" Ash stood ramrod straight. "It's an illness?"

"Yes, sir, typhoid fever."

A tremor ran down Julia's back. Most folks recovered when

care was started early, yet the ailment was fatal for some. *Please, God, don't take Willie too.*

~

*A*sh sat on the edge of a cushioned chair in Julia's parlor. Mrs. Dodd and Eddie, who gave them the good news that both his friends planned to fish with them on Sunday, had been waiting in the parlor for them. As Ash shared what they'd learned, Eddie played with a cup and ball in the corner.

"It's worrisome that Savannah's family went to visit Willie's family." Ash rubbed his hands over his knees.

Julia exchanged a look with her mother. "Savannah can become fretful."

Swiping sweat from his forehead, Ash stood. "The army may send him home for a period of convalescence after the worst is over."

"Hey, we might see Willie soon?" Eddie's stringed ball struck the rug as he ran over to Ash.

What a blessing that would be to all of them. "We'd like that, wouldn't we?" Ash hadn't thought the boy was listening.

"I liked it when you, me, Luke, and Willie tossed a ball in the yard at one of Mama's parties." Eddie grinned.

"I remember." A fond memory. What a difference a year made.

"Remember us boys went fishing while the girls walked by the river?"

"I do, indeed. We'll do it again."

The doorbell rang. Mrs. Dodd left the parlor. A moment later, her voice carried to them. "Why, Caroline, what is it? What's wrong?"

Alarmed, Ash strode toward the wide oak front door.

"Mrs. Dodd, is my brother here?"

A catch in her voice alerted Ash of her tears before he reached her side, the others following. "Caroline?" He put his arm around his sister. She wouldn't come unless the matter was urgent. "Has something happened to Mama? Daphne?"

A tear slid down her face, chased by another. "A telegram came for you. Mama read it." She handed him a crumpled page.

A terrible premonition washed over him. No one sent him telegrams. Ever.

He opened the page. Read the dreaded message.

*Please, God...no.*

Grief for his young-at-heart friend who'd now never grow old slammed into his soul.

"It's from Luke. It's as you all fear." He forced himself to speak past the cannonball-sized obstruction in his throat. "Willie is...dead."

# CHAPTER 14

*A*nother death of a loved one. Sorrow tumbled in waves through Julia at the grief on Ash's face. *Why didn't you save Willie, God?*

"No! It's not true." Eddie backed into the wall, hands splayed over the floral wallpaper. "Everyone said it would be over in one battle."

His violent reaction shook her from her shock, but why shouldn't he react this way? Her brother had experienced the death of their pa, four grandparents, and though he hadn't been alive for the death of his siblings, he surely felt their loss. Just as she did, even now. "Eddie, Willie didn't die in battle. He got sick."

"But he wouldn't be dead if he didn't go to Virginia." Freckles stood out on his pale face.

"We can't be certain of that." Kneeling, Ash placed his hands on her brother's shoulders. "Folks get sick and die even in Vicksburg."

"They said the Yankees would lose. That we'd win and everyone would come home to the biggest celebration ever." Tears spilled down his face.

"Who said that, Eddie?" Julia spoke softly. She'd never seen him so distraught, not even at Papa's funeral.

"Men at the street corner, and the post office, and the brickyard, and the wharves." He shook his head. "They told me and George and Tom not to worry about our soldiers."

"Those strangers can't predict the future. No one can." Though appalled to learn Eddie and his friends frequented the wharves, Julia hugged her brother, stymied that he'd believed the talk around town. But what else could he think? She'd never told him differently, never warned him that soldiers can die in war, no matter which side won.

~

*A*sh turned away, unable to focus on the boy's grief.

"Dearest Eddie." As Mrs. Dodd folded him against her side, Julia's arm fell to her side. "I'm sorry we didn't prepare you for the possibility. It's my responsibility. The fault is mine."

Willie was gone. That infectious sense of humor, the side-splitting laughter that invited everyone to join in, the impish grin. All were gone forever.

Ash couldn't take it in.

A soft hand clasped his callused one. "I was going to suggest that we all drive out to the plantation." Julia looked nearly as agitated as her brother. "I no longer feel that's wise."

"No." Ash's face stiffened as his fingers tightened around hers. "I'll ride out in case Luke's telegram is the first... Willie's family must learn..."

She rested his hand against her wet cheek. "I'm as sorry as I—"

"No, please don't say it." He brought her hand to his lips, tasting her tears. "This is a tragedy for us all." His gaze fell on Eddie.

"Yes."

Ash clasped Julia close to his heart, finding a modicum of comfort in shared grief. Sounds of gentle weeping drew his eyes to Caroline, who stood apart. He reached his other hand to his sister. She accepted it, and as he was loathe to release Julia, he drew both of them close. "My family will feel the void as well."

After a minute, Julia stepped away from Ash, as did Caroline.

"I'd best get to the plantation." Ash ran a hand through his hair.

"Savannah will need her friends." Julia's brown eyes glistened with tears. "But I fear in the first throes of grief..."

"You must stay back tonight, Julia." Mrs. Dodd spoke softly. "Not only for the reason that it will be appallingly late for your return but also that Savannah will long first for comfort from her family. I imagine the Adairs will spend the night at the plantation. We'll visit early tomorrow."

Ash had to drop Caroline off at home and check on his mother. It would be ten o'clock before he'd reach the plantation.

Mrs. Dodd extended her hand. "There's abundant grief in this tragic news for you as well, Ash. My condolences."

Clasping her hand, he sucked in his breath. "Many thanks." Releasing her, he knelt before the devastated boy. Reached out his arms. Eddie ran into them and buried his face in Ash's shoulder. Tears pricked the back of his eyes at the intensity of the boy's grief.

Willie had teased Eddie unmercifully, but they'd formed a deeper bond than anyone realized. Ash allowed the boy to keep his face against his chest until he was ready to move away. "I'll see you in the morning, little buddy."

Mrs. Dodd placed her arm around her son.

Julia's expressive face reflected her sorrow as she met Ash's searching gaze. He held her against him another moment.

"My prayers are with you, Savannah, and the whole family," she whispered against his ear.

"Thank you." He fought for control. That she'd pray for him when so many others with closer connections grieved comforted him beyond words.

~

*L*anterns hanging on either side of Ash's buggy did little to light the way as he drove toward the plantation.

No one on the lane tonight. That was fine with him, for he needed an hour alone.

Willie had only twenty-one years on the earth. Ash couldn't take in the terrible truth that was all Willy would ever receive.

Memories flooded over him. Fishing in the creek on the plantation. Hayrides in the fall as kids. Willie had attended a private school in Charleston beginning at eight years old. Ash only saw him in the summer and during Christmas holidays back then.

He remembered when Willie told him that his and Savannah's parents had decided they should wed when they were older. Willie didn't mind. Savannah was a beauty, even as a child, but truly, the pair had acted more like siblings, arguing over trifles one minute and climbing trees together the next.

Ash never envied Willie's relationship with Savannah, only that he already knew his future mate. At ten, Willie knew he'd inherit and run the plantation someday.

Ash turned right into the long drive leading to the columned portico of the three-story stone mansion, an impressive sight during the day. Two rooms were lit on the main floor, several more on the upper floors, meaning someone was up, though it had to be after ten.

A boy not much older than Eddie met the buggy as Ash

halted beside the wide stone steps leading to the home. "Want me to stable your team, suh?"

"I'm not certain." Ash hesitated. Under normal circumstances, he'd stay for the night rather than drive home to Vicksburg at such a late hour. "Please tie them to the hitching post. If I'm longer than half an hour, stable them."

"Yes, suh."

Sudden light poured from the massive double front door. "Who's there?"

"It's Ash Mitchell, Mr. Sanderson." He mounted the steps with a sense of dread. How he hated what he was about to do.

The senior William Sanderson stepped onto the wide portico, Savannah's father, Mr. Adair, right behind him. "You're always welcome, son—you know that. But is there a reason for this late call?"

Dread filled his stomach. They hadn't heard.

"I fear so." Ash reached the top step. "I think you're aware that Willie had typhoid fever."

"*Had* the fever?" Mr. Sanderson, a heavyset version of his son, crept closer. His voice was lower when he said, "Tell me, quickly."

"Luke sent me a telegram, sir." He extracted it from his pocket. "I'm sorry to deliver this terrible news." He extended it.

Shock held the father immobile.

"It's Willie, sir." Ash looked beyond the grieving mask of the man normally as jovial as his namesake to Mr. Adair. "He didn't survive the illness."

"No. It can't be. " Mr. Sanderson closed his eyes and covered his face with his hands.

"I'll take that, son." Mr. Adair perused the few words, his face set. "It's true, Will. This comes from young Shea."

He allowed the man a moment of grief, then said, "Come inside, Will." Mr. Adair put a firm hand on his friend's shoulder. "We must tell the womenfolk."

"He should have been home by now. One battle..." Mr. Sanderson allowed his friend to guide him inside.

Mr. Adair turned to Ash. "I can't understand how you learned the news first."

"I didn't know I did. I rode out here to make certain you knew." Ash felt smaller than Eddie to deliver the tragic news. "Luke sent it. He watched out for Willie."

"Come inside, son, and tell us what you know." Mr. Sanderson turned to him. "Then perhaps you won't mind heading back to the city so we can tell our families."

"Of course." Ash didn't even take a seat in the parlor as he told of Willie's letters. The brokenhearted father requested that he bring the letters tomorrow. Ash agreed, and Mr. Adair showed him out.

The little boy slept by the hitching post.

Ash touched his shoulder. "Thanks for minding my team."

"No!" The anguished shout rent the air from an open second-story window. Mrs. Sanderson?

The boy jumped.

Ash shuddered. The mournful sound pierced his soul.

"Suh, if you don't mind my asking, what did you say to them?"

Household staff would all know within an hour, if not sooner. "I had to tell them tragic news. Mr. Willie is dead."

His face crumpled. "Oh, no! Didn't nobody not like Willie Junior."

Ash's heart squeezed, as if from a giant hand. It was true. Willie had been nearly universally liked. They'd all miss him.

As he turned down the drive, a long scream pierced the night.

Savannah.

# CHAPTER 15

*J*ulia forced herself to concentrate on Savannah's sorrow as she sat with Savannah and Felicity in a corner of the Adairs' front parlor the next afternoon. The crowds of neighbors seeking to offer comfort, the subdued atmosphere, and the preponderance of black mourning clothes threatened to stifle her. It took her back to her own parlor, her own black dress, and mourning her dear papa, who never came home from a weekend hunting trip.

"I expected most people to drive to the plantation this afternoon." Savannah stared at the quiet groups of people scattered about. "The Sandersons need comforting."

"I'm certain of it." She'd needed comforting, too, at Papa's funeral. But Mama's weeping had shifted attention from her grieving children. Not even little Eddie's sobs had shaken Mama from her dark abyss of suffering.

Little wonder that Eddie lost control last night. He'd stuck like a burr to Ash's side until Mama took her son home an hour ago. But Savannah wished Julia to remain, and she must focus on her friend. People stood near the corner where their three cushioned chairs had been pushed together to allow them to talk. That arrangement had been Savannah's choice.

Julia sought Ash's gaze across the room, near the doorway. As if feeling her gaze, he looked up from his conversation with a couple from their church. He moved as if ready to come to her if she needed him. That look was enough to steady her. She gave a slight shake of her head.

"I believe those families are waiting to speak with you." Felicity inclined her head toward a white-haired couple leaning on canes.

"Let them talk to Mother and Father." Savannah arranged her black silk grenadine dress over her lap without looking up.

"I believe they already did," Felicity whispered. "They likely plan to go to the plantation upon leaving here."

"One hopes." Standing, Savannah took a few steps toward them and stopped.

Relief marked the couples' features.

"I'm glad she's talking to them," Felicity continued in hushed tones. "I hate to feel we're monopolizing her when so many want to extend comfort."

"I want to do whatever will comfort Savannah." Julia watched as her friend spoke graciously to several folks in quick succession who left immediately afterward. "Our presence seems to help." They'd sat with her for the past three hours. Three long, torturous hours when every mourner reminded Julia of her own losses in addition to her sorrow for Willie.

"Agreed." Felicity shook her head. "I still can't believe he's gone. Seems wrong."

"It *is* wrong." Savannah returned to her chair. The parlor was half empty. "I could stand it better if he died in battle...I think. But to die of illness..." She stared at the lacy handkerchief in her hand. "He should have remained in Vicksburg. Like Ash."

Julia went still. *Please don't ridicule my beau*—who bore his own grief for Willie.

Savannah dabbed at her cheeks. "I never imagined for one moment that the next time my brave soldier would come home would be...to be buried."

"He was in a Richmond hospital?" Felicity pressed a clean handkerchief into her hand.

Swiping at her cheeks, she nodded. "He so wanted to visit the Confederate capitol back in the spring."

And he'd died there. The unspoken words hung in the air.

"I know Luke will wish he could be here." Felicity spoke wistfully.

"No doubt." Savannah's face hardened.

Julia exchanged a glance with Felicity. She understood why Savannah was angry with Ash—she'd made that abundantly clear. Why was Savannah angry with Luke? He'd mustered into the army with Willie.

"The funeral is planned for Tuesday at the church. It will be a long procession back to the plantation."

Julia's mother would come. It might be best if Eddie went to school instead. The poor boy had been too heartbroken to eat breakfast.

"They will have a special service on Monday for everyone on the plantation." Deep sadness darkened Savannah's eyes. "Everyone loved him."

"I'm glad everyone will have an opportunity to mourn." Julia patted her hand.

"It's what W-Willie would have wanted."

Other mourners pressed close.

Savannah stood. "Pardon me a moment. Please don't leave." She stepped away to greet them, accepting condolences graciously.

"I do miss Luke something terrible, Julia. Do you think he's sick too?" Felicity asked.

Julia leaned closer. "There's no reason to imagine Luke is ill."

"Though it's possible." Felicity tugged on the handkerchief she held. "He hasn't written regularly of late. He did say they're all working hard."

"There's your answer." Julia gave a nod. "He's too tired to write. That's all it is."

Savannah returned to them. "That's how it started with Willie."

The sudden fear in Felicity's eyes struck Julia like a brick.

~

*A*sh was pleased Sunday's picnic and fishing expedition had expanded to include Savannah, Felicity, and her uncle and aunt, the Beltzers. Julia told him that Savannah, upon learning the day's plans, had begged her parents to be excused from another day of receiving guests in order to attend the picnic. Mrs. Dodd seemed happy for the additions.

They went downriver toward Warrenton for the picnic and ate a delicious lunch that included cold fried chicken, peach turnovers, and lemonade.

"Come on, Ash." Eddie tugged his arm. "We've been patient."

"Yes, you have." Ash grinned, but it felt artificial in the wake of Willie's death. How many afternoons had they passed, jerking one fish after another from the river? "Mr. Beltzer, these boys want to go fishing. Shall we take them?"

"Don't mind if we do." The thin, balding man patted Eddie's shoulder. "Between us, we ought to catch a whole string of bass."

"Ladies"—Ash tipped his hat at the women—"the men are going to fish. We will return in a couple of hours." He and Mr. Beltzer carried the poles he'd brought.

After a few minutes of scouting, the group agreed on a fishing spot along the Mississippi River bank. George, a redhead, was the tallest of the three boys and tended toward bossiness. Tom was the shortest, and his green eyes bespoke an adventurous spirit. Mr. Beltzer, who asked Ash to refer to him as Charles, turned out to be an excellent fisherman. He gave the boys some pointers. Soon, their lines were bobbing with catches. By the end of two hours, the five of them had caught seventeen fish.

Ash started to divide them, his mind leapfrogging back to the last summer when he and Willie and Luke had last fished in this spot. Grief almost paralyzed him.

When war loomed only as a threat. Now Willie had been the first of his friends to die. The first...now why had he thought of it like that?

~

*A*sh stared down at the mound of dirt covering his friend in the now-quiet cemetery. At this spot, two hours earlier, sobs had accompanied old hymns in lieu of an organ. The pastor's brief graveside message remained a blur. When Ash couldn't bear to share another memory with neighbors, he had asked Julia to pardon him from the lunch reception at the plantation house so he could steal a quiet moment in the cemetery. Because it was on Sanderson property, Ash wouldn't often return.

That nightly jaunt through the city was the last that he, Willie, and Luke would take together this side of heaven. If he only had known, he'd have pushed harder for Willie to stay home.

Yet that would only have dug a deeper wedge between them, one that had been plenty deep enough.

Willie's death somehow seemed more gut-wrenching—

senseless, perhaps—because he died from an illness rather than a battle wound. How many more must die before the country decided to reunite or stand divided forever?

There must be a way to hurry the ending of the war and save lives. Had his spying served a purpose?

He could do more. Though it was dangerous, he *must* do more.

But Luke was still in the army, and vulnerable. What if Ash passed on a message that led to Luke marching into an ambush? Most of what Ash learned pertained to this area, where a clash could affect his city, his fellow Mississippians.

His temples throbbed. There were no easy answers. What if Ash's small contribution helped the North win the war sooner? End slavery?

Luke believed in that cause. So did Julia.

Ash rubbed his aching temples. *God, please, show me the way.*

He bent down. Touched the fresh mound of dirt. Clods slid down to the ground. "Willie, your death won't be in vain. I'll do all within my power toward resolution and ending this terrible war. I promise you." A tear slipped down his cheek. "I'll miss you, buddy."

He'd do whatever he could to prevent men like Willie from traveling home in pine boxes.

A footstep at the gate told him his time with his friend had ended. Someone else wished to grieve alone for Willie.

Ash straightened. Swiped at his face with a handkerchief. Turning away from the grave, he sucked in a breath. A score of slaves lined the fence. Each held a single, freshly picked daisy.

# CHAPTER 16

"Julia, let's celebrate your birthday this coming Saturday."

Mama's suggestion came as a surprise because not a soul had mentioned her twentieth birthday. It had been such an emotional week that Julia hadn't even given it much thought. Her gaze darted at Ash, who'd sat quietly beside her on the veranda since lunch that Sunday afternoon.

"It's your birthday?" He straightened.

"Tomorrow." Her cheeks heated up. "I thought you knew."

"I only knew it was in the fall. What with all that has happened lately, I didn't think to ask. Please forgive me."

"Think nothing of it." The hurt she'd felt melted away. Since the funeral, he'd been working every daylight hour at his shop. He'd even sent a note around that he couldn't escort her to church Wednesday. Many men had been laid off from city businesses, and Ash had to work whenever orders came in. Reading's and Paxton's foundries, which produced cannons and such, were among the few establishments remaining at full staff.

"I think a smaller celebration is more in order this year."

Mama waved a fan over her face as they sat in the shade on the pleasantly warm afternoon. "Savannah wasn't betrothed to Willie but will no doubt observe a period of mourning."

"She'll still sew with Felicia now and then. Beyond church attendance, we probably won't see her." Julia glanced at Ash, who seemed upset at his blunder. "I'd like your family to come, of course."

"We'd be delighted."

"And Felicity and the Beltzers."

"Yes, Charles and Mae are quite good company." Mama nodded. "Will that be enough?"

"A small celebration suits me. Eddie needs something else to think about."

"That he does." Mama leaned back in her chair. "I'm glad he's with his friends today."

"Poor fellow is taking the news hard." Ash's hazel eyes darkened. "I'll take him fishing again soon."

"That will be lovely." Julia smiled at him.

"May I escort you to supper on Friday to celebrate your birthday? We can go to the Sky Parlor afterwards." Ash gave a half shrug. "I really am sorry that I didn't—"

"No apology is necessary." The man had been through enough without her adding any berating. "Supper and a stroll at the Sky Parlor sound perfect."

⁓

"*L*ovely." Julia rested her hand on her handsome beau's arm at the Sky Parlor while staring across the river at a pink and purple sunset on Friday.

"Agreed." Ash turned to her. "Although no sunset could match the beauty I see before me."

Her cheeks heated at his intense regard. "Why, thank you, kind sir." She'd enjoyed his complete attention at supper, and though there were a dozen groups scattered about the hilltop, she'd wager he wasn't thinking about them.

"Good." His hazel eyes brightened. "I want you to be happy."

She searched those eyes that had known so much sorrow the past two weeks. "I want that for you as well."

"Julia, I..."

"Yes?" She was ready for him to speak of his feelings, if that was his intention.

He reached for her hand. Sandwiched it between his own. "You're the most compassionate, kind, and loving woman I've ever met. Do you realize how much you mean to me?"

She stared up at him in the twilight, willing him to continue.

"I love you, Julia."

"Oh, Ash." Joy bubbled up, releasing the uncertainty that had plagued her since her mother suggested she see other men. "I love you too." This birthday celebration alone with him was the perfect moment for the declaration.

"You do?" His eyes danced with happiness. He leaned to kiss her, his lips soft yet firm.

When she didn't draw away, he gave her a lingering kiss that curled her toes. None of her other beaus had ever touched her heart like Ash. In this moment, it seemed she had always known they'd be together someday and had been waiting for him.

Someone cleared their throat. Julia's eyes flew open. Over Ash's shoulder, she saw an elderly couple stroll by.

They broke apart. Julia's face flamed.

"Shall we take a drive around the city?" Ash seemed as embarrassed as she to be caught in an embrace.

"Let's take the long way back to my house." She wasn't ready for the evening to end. And she had another birthday celebration tomorrow.

It couldn't top this one.

~

*C*al brought news from New Orleans early Monday morning. Ash memorized the note about treaties the Confederacy signed with the Shawnee and the Seneca tribes. More interesting was information about Mrs. Wanda Lakin, a Vicksburg widow unfamiliar to Ash. She and two female companions had left on a third trip to unspecified destinations since April. Cal suspected her of spying but didn't know for which side. Interesting. Ash burned the paper in the grate. Taking the train, he delivered Cal's message verbatim by half-past ten over coffee and biscuits.

"She's not one of my spies. Look into it." Jim scribbled Cal's message.

"I will." It was best to identify friends—and enemies.

"Your family know what you're doing??"

Ash shook his head. When he shoved the last bite of biscuit into his mouth, crumbs fell down his striped cotton shirt.

"You didn't tell your girl?"

That was a sore topic. "I promised you secrecy, but I'd appreciate permission to tell her a bit of what I'm doing."

Jim drew back against the hard-backed chair. "She's Unionist?"

He nodded.

"I'm sorry, but I still think it's best you keep it under your hat. I've got bad news. One of our riders is missing. Been gone a week."

Ash sat up straight. "What happened?"

"He didn't return home from a delivery. Confederates probably got him."

"Think he's alive?"

"Hope so. Might be held in prison. Probably being questioned. Maybe hung. Nobody's heard anything."

Not good news for any spy. Ash gripped the table. "You worried he'll give out your name?"

"Who knows what a spy will say under threat of a noose?" Eying him, Jim swiped at his sweaty brow. "This might not be a good time to ask, but this whole situation got me to thinking. Lots of folks are in and out of my homestead at all hours. It's bound to get noticed."

Jim's was a dangerous job, especially in light of this recent news.

"Will you take on a few of my Vicksburg contacts?" He drummed his fingers. "Information will come through your shop. Or you can arrange to meet at different places around town. Set a place and time. If they don't show, they don't have anything for you."

Jim's question bespoke trust. And added danger. "How many people?"

"Let's start with five, including Cal. Might grow."

A daunting task. "From Vicksburg?" Ash's temples throbbed. It was surprising to learn so many in the city supported the Union.

"From Vicksburg or a short distance from it."

Ash studied the older man. "Just how many folks report to you?"

"Best you don't know. I had no idea my simple plan would grow as it did. I prayed for guidance"—Jim spread his hands—"and this is what happened. You'll absorb some danger that fell on me, if you're willing."

It was risky, especially after the vigilantes' visits, the warning from the blacksmith who refused his saddle. But he'd made that vow at Willie's grave.

"There's a caveat." Jim leaned callused hands on the table. "The more you do, the more notice folks will take of you. My neighbors have commented that business must be very good with so many new customers that have come this summer."

A cold shiver ran through Ash's middle. Jim took greater risks than he'd realized. "There's danger a'plenty all around."

Jim stiffened. "What?"

"An old farmer said that to me in passing." He explained the strange encounter.

Jim's expression was grave. "An old farmer? He's not one of my spies. That was a warning, Ash. Should we reconsider expanding your tasks?"

Ash rubbed his jaw. "I'll do it. But I'll stop if it puts my family or Julia in danger."

"Then don't have spies meet you at your shop."

"Agreed. The first meeting will be at my shop, but then I'll arrange different places with each spy." He took a deep breath. "Now, tell me about these other four men."

～

*J*ulia looped delicate thread over and under the tatting needle, pleased that she had nearly four yards in this pattern. Ash had driven her family to church for Wednesday services in the carriage and left in the pouring rain after dropping them off.

Mama entered the parlor and sat in the chair beside Julia's. "Eddie was nearly asleep before his prayers were done. I won't be long behind him. Something so comforting about rain pelting the roof while one is tucked cozily under the blankets."

"Indeed. Or tatting lace." Julia didn't want to move from the fire's warmth on the chilly October evening.

"Tatting has occupied your evenings more of late. Concentrating on repeating those patterns over and over makes my head ache." Mama picked up the long strip. "I can't deny your ability, but why so much? Do you intend it for one of your gowns?"

"Not really." It was to be sold, if a notions shop or a seamstress would buy it.

"I suppose it matters little, as long as you use your quarterly allowance on the supplies." She yawned. "I'm off to bed. Don't be up too late. Our 'at home' is tomorrow."

Listening to Mama's footsteps ascend the stairs, Julia's rhythmic tatting increased a notch. She'd saved as much of her summer's allowance as she could and intended to use this quarter's sum on Christmas gifts. The rest she'd save.

Mama's unexpected praise of her talent had bolstered her courage to sell her work, though Mama would be angry to learn she'd even considered selling her lace.

But she needed to break her dependence on the allowance that would not survive her mother's passing.

~

A husky stranger in his thirties stopped in Ash's shop on Friday afternoon. "You a friend of the tanner's?"

"Yep." That was the phrase for Jim's spies. "Nate Miller?" The man fit Jim's description for the wharf worker.

"The same." Nate studied him. "Just got back from Bolton, so no messages. But there's news of one of ours getting picked up by Rebel pickets. He carried a message about Tennessee troops that they surely found."

Ash's heartbeat skittered. "They know about the rest of us?"

"Not if he kept his mouth shut. He's being held in Tennessee."

Not good news. Ash prayed those soldiers couldn't read the ciphered message. "Thanks. Where do you want to meet next time?"

"The oak grove near the City Hospital from now on."

"I know the spot. What day can you get away?"

"Not much work these days. Wednesday at two if I got something to say."

"Fair enough."

Nate left without another word, but he'd told him the most important thing—Jim's spy had indeed been caught.

Had he succumbed to questioning?

~

*E*arly in the next week, Julia pushed open the door of a seamstress shop on Lynn Street. "Miss Wind?"

"Miss Dodd?" A slender brunette in her late twenties pushed up her spectacles as she stood. "How lovely to see you. What may I do for you?"

Julia had walked past the shop five times before working up the courage to enter. "It's what I might do for you that I've come to see you about."

"I can't pay an assistant, but, of course, that's not why you're here." Scarlet stained her cheeks.

"Actually, I wondered if you need some lace." Julia fingered the delicate roll in her basket. "I've five yards to sell."

"My time has been spent on soldiers' uniforms. I don't believe—"

"Oh, please. Just take a look." Julia barely knew the woman. More importantly, neither did Mama, making it less likely she'd learn of her daughter debasing herself with trade. She unrolled several inches. "What do you think?"

Miss Wind's gaze fastened on the gauzy strand.

Julia held her breath while the seamstress bent close to the lace. Touched it.

"Why, this is exquisite. My first dress order for Christmas has already come. If I use this lace for her gown, someone else may see it and request it. If so, may I purchase more?"

Julia's heart sang. She'd written the "exquisite" lace pattern down so she could easily repeat it. "Under one condition."

She frowned. "What's your condition?"

"That you keep my name a secret."

"An intrigue." Her face relaxed. "My customers will love that in their lacemaker. How soon can you tatt another five—no, six yards?"

"Two weeks." It would push her, but she'd be earning money. Maybe she'd get faster with the extra practice.

Becoming independent from Mama made it worth the effort.

∼

"Any news of our rider?" Ash could barely wait until the door closed behind him at Jim's homestead to ask. It was the eighteenth of October. The spy had been missing nearly a month.

"He escaped."

"Thank the Lord. Did he keep our secret?"

"Let me tell the story. Rebel pickets took him to their sergeant, who found a page of messages folded up in his sock."

Ash's stomach tensed. "What did they do?"

"They couldn't read it, which made them angry." Jim poured two cups of coffee from a coffeepot on the stove. "They eventually took him to Tennessee, where a major questioned him."

Ash straddled a chair, his chest tight.

"They held him for two weeks while various officers tried to wear him down. Then they put him in jail with a guard. Four days passed before our spy saw his chance to escape when his guard fell asleep one night. He kept to the woods and made it back here yesterday."

Ash's icy fingers encircled the hot tin cup. "Is he done spying?"

"He's taking a couple of weeks to recover. I'll buy him a horse since he lost his."

"I have an unclaimed saddle if you'd like to purchase it." Ash wished he could donate it, but money had been tight with dwindling orders coming in. He'd try another newspaper advertisement.

"I was about to order one from you. I'll be happy to buy it." They agreed on a price. "Bring it next time."

"Thanks." That sale helped.

None of them could afford to relax their guard. Prison. Questioning. Could Ash withstand it as bravely as his fellow Unionist had?

$\sim$

On the last Monday in October, Julia stopped at a street corner beside Mrs. Cummings's seamstress shop and peered toward the center of the city. Servants carrying baskets walked quickly down the sidewalks. Soldiers in gray, joined by men from town, congregated in groups outside shops and the courthouse. Regiments from Louisiana and Texas often stopped in Vicksburg for hours or overnight before mounting eastbound trains taking them toward the fighting.

Julia pushed open the shop door. "Good morning."

Savannah sewed a white wool blouse at the window table where Julia was accustomed to sitting. She set the basket containing a lunch large enough for all of them on a side table along an inner wall.

"Good morning." Felicity looked up from the sewing machine where she stitched a gray jacket seam. "Yes, that's a good spot to work. That wall lantern shines directly on the table. You'll sew trousers again, if that's all right?"

"Whatever you want." Julia had sewn everything from underclothes to jackets to towels and bedding.

"Those soldiers in town will leave this morning. They have no idea what they face." Savannah's tone crackled with bitterness.

"True." Julia cringed at the change in Savannah. Even her laughter had grown brittle. Julia's little brother had changed too. The formerly adventurous boy came home right after school without complaint. Without saying much of anything, really. "Eddie believed the talk that the Confederacy will whoop up on the Yankees and win this war in a matter of months."

"And so they shall." Savannah's face was a set mask as she turned to face them. "Don't you believe that?"

Julia's breath quickened. Had her tone betrayed her Unionist support? "Battles continue six months after Fort Sumter. I *want* a quick resolution as much as anyone, but I'm not convinced we're going to have one."

"Not more than Felicity or me." Savannah looked at her. "Right? We're the ones with beaus who went to the army."

Julia was tired of insinuations against Ash's courage. She turned to Felicity. "What news do you have from Luke? Ash has received but one letter this month, and November is nearly upon us."

The whirr of the sewing machine halted. "He's ill, in a Richmond hospital."

Julia gasped. "What?"

Felicity's gaze locked on Savannah's. "Typhoid fever. Lots of soldiers in their company have suffered from it. His letter dated October twenty-first came Friday. He'd been there two days. I'm so afraid, Julia."

"You still don't understand how I feel. You could only do that if he died." Savannah dropped the white cloth. "And Julia will never know, because her beau stays where it's safe." She grabbed a shawl off a wall hook and marched to the door, slamming it behind her.

"I shouldn't have said anything." Felicity's chin trembled.

Appalled at Savannah's cruelty, Julia knelt beside Felicity. "I'm glad you told me." Did Ash know? She took her friend's hand. "Let's pray for him."

$\sim$

*A*sh's head reeled from the news about Luke that Julia and Eddie delivered to him at his saddle shop after the boy got off from school. Most folks recovered from typhoid, yet coming on the heels of Willie's death, Ash's fear was natural.

"Savannah didn't take it well." Julia explained what happened at the seamstress shop.

"That's unfortunate." Ash rubbed the back of his neck. "Are you all right?" He couldn't tell whether Julia was more upset about Luke or Savannah's cruel words.

She jerked her head toward her brother.

Ash caught Eddie's apprehensive look. He squatted until he was eye level with him. "How about you, buddy?"

"I don't want Luke to die." His expression miserable, he raised his eyes to meet Ash's.

Ash's heart broke. He gathered the boy in his arms. "Luke will get better."

"You sure?" Eddie's voice was muffled against Ash's chest.

"Pretty certain." The boy needed a distraction. "Say, this is your first time in my saddle shop, right?"

Eddie nodded and stepped back.

"Want me to show you what I do all day?"

"Oh, boy." His face brightened.

Julia waited while Ash spent the rest of their visit showing them around his shop. Eddie's genuine interest made the next hour enjoyable for all of them as he tried out the tools. They refused Ash's offer of a ride home and left in a happier frame of mind.

Ash's gaze traveled to the floorboard covered with hay that he'd avoided on the tour. There was so much news coming in from his five spies that Ash wrote scanty information down— just enough to remind himself of numbers and locations—and kept it hidden under a loose board. He'd arranged specific places and days to meet each contact. So far, all those transfers had gone well. He then memorized the messages and burned the pages in the grate.

All he'd learned about Mrs. Wanda Lakin was that she was the widow of saloon owner Oliver Lakin. The saloon near the wharves had been sold the year before. He'd ask Nate Miller, one of his spies, if he knew about the widow's trips.

It was almost a blessing that saddle orders continued to dwindle because he now reported to Jim twice weekly.

～

*F*our days later, Ash had just returned to his shop from meeting one of his spies on Locust Street near the old brickyard and was scribbling information concerning Confederate troops in Tennessee when footsteps approached. Dropping the pencil, he shoved the pages in his coat.

"What's that?" Caroline pointed to his bulging pocket.

"Just notes for my business. What brings you out here?"

"You mean to your inner sanctum?" Smirking, she rolled her eyes.

"Right." He forced a chuckle, tense from nearly being caught. It had only been his sister, yet it could have been anyone in town. Perhaps he should close his door. No, it was his practice to keep it open except in bitter cold, and everyone knew it. Jim had warned him to change as little of his daily routine as possible.

"I brought a letter from Luke." She handed it to him. "Thought you'd want to read it immediately."

"I do." It had been an agonizing week of waiting for news. "If you'll excuse me, I'll pass on any news at lunch."

Her face fell. "See that you do."

As soon as her footsteps faded on the stone, he extracted the sheets from his pocket and completed the secret message.

He peeked outside. No one approached. Going to the corner behind the saddle display divider, he pushed aside some hay to reveal the floorboards. Lifting the corner, he tucked the letter inside. Once the hay had been carefully arranged, he returned to his bench to read Luke's letter.

*Me hated to put the fear of God into all of you, what with falling ill with the same malady that took dear Willie's life. It was bound to happen, yet me regrets it. Mine is a milder case, nor did me allow it to worsen before reporting to the surgeon. He sent me on to this Richmond hospital. Hours pass slowly here, an emptiness filled with sadness for our friend who now rests beneath the clay.*

*The inactivity has surely replenished months of little sleep, for it seems all I do is catch forty winks throughout each endless day. Today is the first day me has felt up to penning a note. I've written Felicity already, and both letters will be given to the nurse before sleep claims me once more.*

*A few soldiers have been sent home to finish recuperating. There's been no talk of that for me, likely because mine is a mild case.*

With praise and thankfulness for God's answer, Ash strode to his house to share the good news. He trusted Savannah's better nature would allow her to rejoice too.

# CHAPTER 17

*A*sh waited in the oak grove near the hospital, scant shelter from the early-November rain. He'd give Nate Miller five more minutes.

Fallen leaves rustled behind him. He spun around. "Nate. I'd nearly given up on you."

"Mrs. Lakin is back."

The man never minced words. "The widow who hides her destinations has returned. Any idea where she's been?"

He guffawed. "That woman answers to no one. But your spy was right to wonder about her. She delivers letters that folks don't want crossing the mail by normal means."

Ash whistled. "A letter carrier. She *is* spying."

"Charges one-and-a-half dollars per letter."

"That's how she pays for her trips."

"No doubt." Nate shook rain from his hat. "And don't think of asking her to join us, for it's certain she's on the side of the South."

It had been a long shot, anyway. "Keep an eye on her. Maybe we'll learn something."

⁓

"Mama, are you still worried about Eddie?" Julia was on a ladder taking down the summer curtains in the middle of November.

She and Ash had taken her brother fishing twice since the news of Luke's recovery came, but they'd had few private moments since her birthday when they'd declared their love for one another. She'd been busy with Eddie, volunteering at the seamstress shop, and tatting. She'd sold two more rolls of lace and tucked the money away in a chest with Mama none the wiser. Ash had been busy, too, but it wasn't because of the saddle shop, to hear his mother talk. Trips to obtain supplies came more frequently. He'd received two letters from Luke, who was back with his regiment, a relief to them all.

"Eddie's too quiet." Mama, wearing one her oldest dresses for the dusty job, put her hands on her hips as she watched Julia work.

Julia agreed. "It's not like him to docilely submit to coming home directly from school."

"He asks permission to go places too." Mama accepted the floral fabric Julia handed down. "Also strange. Julia?"

After repositioning the ladder, she turned. "What is it?"

Mama stepped close and lowered her voice. "Do you feel we should talk to him about our Union loyalties?"

"Careful." Julia's gaze darted to the open parlor door. Couldn't be too cautious these days.

"Close the door." Mama mouthed the words.

Julia crossed the room and peered down the long hall leading to the kitchen, up the curved staircase, and across the entry hall to the dining room before closing the door. No one.

"Let's continue to whisper," Mama said when she returned.

"Please." Julia nodded toward the several windows open to allow a breeze in the mild weather. "Don't you recall the man who questioned Eddie about our loyalties?" Mama's attitude had grown more protective after learning of it, easing a bit of Julia's worry.

"That still concerns me, though the vigilantes have stopped their nightly visits to Unionists."

"Some weeks ago, as far as one knows. Probably because no one openly supports the Union." Steps creaked as Julia climbed the ladder with a heavy curtain panel.

"Eddie is like a rudderless vessel." Mama spoke with conviction. "Searching for answers. He needs to know our views. If we don't teach him what we believe, he will find someone else willing to speak. Who knows what lies people will pour into his tender ears?"

Julia blinked. "Mama, that's profound." It was more like something she'd have said before Papa died. Had Eddie's unhappiness finally shaken Mama from the grief that had clouded every action since her husband's funeral? Curtains hung, Julia descended the ladder.

"I've prayed about it." Emotion intensified her hushed tones. "You were right about the number of strangers in our city. One must wonder why they chose wartime to come."

"Vicksburg's location beside the mighty Mississippi makes us too interesting to both sides." The way he scampered around town, Eddie likely heard more news than any of them. "Let's tell him, though we must advise him to pretend to support the Confederacy."

"Agreed. We'll tell him the next time Ash takes him fishing. Only the four of us will go." Mama had been showing more parental concern toward Eddie. Yet Julia couldn't stem her resentment that Mama's only worry for her was that Julia marry well.

"*A*sh, I must ask you to deliver these messages to the next stop on the line. I've added your own information about the location of the *C.S.S. General Polk.*" Jim sanded the ink on the page he'd just written. "Are you up for the task?"

"What do you mean?" It was past one on that mid-November Friday, and he was to dine with Julia's family that evening.

"The fellow who carries the mail to the next junction is ill." Jim eyed him as he shook the paper. "Just this once is all I'm asking."

"How far?" Ash didn't want to overtax his horse.

"About eight miles. It's this side of Brownsville."

"Brownsville?" Northeast. Vicksburg was to the west.

"I give my riders five dollars each run." Jim sat back in his chair at the table where they'd both eaten a sandwich while Ash shared the messages. "Hefty sums from donors who believe in our cause allow me to offer this."

He *paid* his riders? Business had been poor. Ash had sold only five saddles that month with prospects for only one more. "I'll do it."

"You can take Stardust and leave your horse to rest in the stable."

"Thanks." That helped.

"Follow the main road to Brownsville until you get to a fork in the road. Veer left. The next road you come to will be on the right. There's a century-old knotty magnolia on the corner. Take that lane. After a mile, you'll see Harvey's Mill on the left. Harv's the one you want to talk to." He leaned closer. "The *only* one."

"Got it."

"Wait until he's alone. Ask for a five-pound sack of corn-meal. While you're making conversation, tell him you saw a blue jay on the way there. Then Harv will know he can trust you."

"Understood." Ash repeated the directions to ensure he'd memorized each detail correctly.

"That's it," Jim said. "If he says, 'Might have,' everything is fine. Give him the letter wrapped in your money—it's one dollar—and go on your way."

"What if someone's watching or another customer walks in?"

"He'll say, "Doubtful.' Then buy the cornmeal without delivering the messages and get out of there."

Sounded dangerous. Ash rubbed his jaw. Something must be done to end the bloodshed.

Jim extracted a purse from his pocket. "I'll even buy the cornmeal for your family." He laid six dollars of Confederate bills on the table and folded the letter inside one of bills. "Stardust is fresh. You can be back in ninety minutes."

If he hurried, no one would know. He could still make it to Julia's for supper.

～

*A*sh found the mill easily. Sacks filled a wagon in the yard. A red-headed boy of about twelve hitched a team of horses to it. "Can I he'p you, mister?"

"I'm looking to buy a sack of cornmeal."

"Pa's in the mill." He pointed.

Not overly friendly. Ash didn't blame him for not trusting a stranger in the current environment.

Ash strode into the mill, his stomach in knots. A long tray on table legs ran nearly the length of the mill. No customers, only a red-haired man filling a twenty-pound grain sack. "Mr. Harvey? My name is Ash Mitchell."

"Folks call me Harv." The bright-eyed man gave him the same considered look as his son. "What can I do for you?"

"I need a five-pound sack of cornmeal."

"Fair enough." Harv reached for a scoop. "Where you from?"

"Vicksburg. Born and raised there. I own a saddle shop."

Harv looked up from his work. "I'll remember you when I need a saddle."

Not a talkative sort. Ash had best state the phrase quickly or Harv would have the sack filled. "Pleasant day."

"Sure enough."

"I saw a blue jay on the way here."

Harv flashed him an intense look. "Might have. They've been seen near here." He went back to his work.

"Lots of illness going around."

Harv eyed him as he tied the sack closed. "Good to know. That'll be one dollar."

Ash gave him the bill with the letter hidden inside and hefted the sack to his shoulder. "Pleasure doing business with you."

Harv nodded. "Until next time."

Ash rode back to the Routeledge homestead, his relief at completing the task growing with each mile. It was risky, but this war must end with a Union victory. In such hard times, the provision for his family was a blessing too. He'd do it again if necessary.

~

Two days later, Julia asked Ash to take her and her family to a private fishing spot after church. He raised an eyebrow at the request but readily agreed. The weather was pleasantly mild for autumn. Eddie sat in back of the buggy beside Mama, his chin resting on his overlapped hands on the seat rail. A few trees still had rust and yellow leaves. Julia was happy to spend the day with her favorite people, even though a difficult conversation awaited.

Ash drove them north of the city to a secluded spot on the river. "I sometimes fished here with my pa as a boy."

"It's perfect." Tall trees shaded the area. The forest started about fifty yards from the river with a velvety grassy area between that likely flooded every spring. "I wonder that you never brought me."

"It's a better spot for families or boys wanting to fish." He untied the food basket and fishing rods.

"Agreed." Mama gave her a look.

Heat rose in her cheeks. Yes, it was too secluded for courting couples.

Julia had prepared roasted beef sandwiches for lunch. There was also cheese and crackers and Eddie's favorite oatmeal cakes, which he munched with gusto.

"Before you men go off to fish," Mama said, and Eddie preened at her description, "Julia and I wanted to discuss something with you."

Ash's brow furrowed.

"Eddie." Mama maneuvered to face him on the large quilt. "You once asked us which side of the country's conflict we support."

"I already know. We're for the Confederacy."

"We allowed you to believe that to protect you." Julia shot a glance at Ash.

Cake crumbs tumbled down Eddie's checked shirt. "Does someone want to hurt me?"

"Not you. Us." Mama frowned.

He leaped to his feet. "Nobody's gonna hurt you while I'm around, Mama."

"It's not like that." Reaching for his hand, she tugged until he sat beside her. "You see, lots of folks in Vicksburg are for the

Confederacy. They don't like anyone saying they're for the Union."

"What's wrong with the Union?"

"Our country divided after President Abraham Lincoln was elected," Julia explained.

"I know that." Eddie rolled his eyes. "The Northern states are in the Union. Southern states like Mississippi are in the Confederacy."

"When we first divided, most Vicksburg folks wanted to remain in the Union. That changed when Mississippi joined the Confederacy." Mama tilted Eddie's face up so he looked directly in her eyes. "Your sister and I didn't change our minds. We still support the Union."

"We do?" His brow furrowed.

"We never wanted our country to divide." It was a relief for Julia to speak openly to her brother. There shouldn't be secrets within families. "And now we want to be unified again as one country. That's where our loyalties lie."

"Ash?" Eddie looked up at him with shock-filled eyes. "Do you want the North and South to unite again?"

"More than almost anything. I think it was a mistake to divide. Most folks didn't think that secession would lead to war." Ash's eyes darkened as his hand clenched. "By and large, Southerners thought becoming a separate country was a peaceful way to escape what they considered tyranny. Federal leaders kept taking away rights they felt should remain with the states."

"Don't we like rights?" Eddie's face puckered in confusion.

"We do. Some laws need to change for the whole country —North and South—and some laws are for the states to decide. I agree with that. Let's just say I disagree on some laws that our more vocal townspeople want to remain with the states."

Julia frowned at him. Ash was confusing her brother.

"There are lots of reasons folks are mad enough to fight," Ash said. "I fear more soldiers will die before this war ends."

"Like Willie?"

"Willie became a soldier, sure enough, but illness claimed his life." Pain crossed Ash's face. "The sooner we become unified, the sooner our soldiers come home to go about their lives."

Julia hadn't intended to explain all those details, but Eddie had listened intently. Maybe Ash was right to touch on the divisiveness.

"Me and George and Tom talked about the war with some fellas at the brickyard. They talked about states' rights and stuff they said we didn't need to understand. I'll be ten in two months. That's old enough to hear things. Thanks for explaining. But what should I tell that stranger who comes to the house?"

"What stranger?" Ash's back stiffened. His gaze darted to Julia's and back to Eddie.

"The short red-haired man that comes to the yard and asks if we support Mississippians."

Mama gasped. "How many times has he been to our house?"

"Twice." Eddie pulled at tufts of grass.

"When was the last time?" Julia felt chilled as if a bitter wind had swept across the meadow.

Eddie scratched his chin. "Maybe two weeks ago."

"Don't tell him we support the Union." Mama held his gaze. "Not ever."

"What if he asks about our state?" A fearful look crossed his boyish face.

"Tell him we love Mississippi with a love that's deep and strong."

"Is that the truth, Mama?"

"Oh, Eddie, my son. That is most assuredly the truth."

"Good. Because I love Mississippi too."

After the conversation, Ash walked with Eddie to the shore, fishing poles and a bucket in tow.

"Do you think he understands?" Mama's troubled gaze followed them.

"I hope so. Regardless, he's happy we told him."

And Julia was glad Ash had been there for their discussion. However, she couldn't shake her worry. He'd said he couldn't tell her more but something felt wrong. Multiple trips to the tanner's and returning with one skin. His distraction. His mama's complaints that he was often absent from the shop. She intended to whisk him away from her family today and ask him directly. Carlton, thinking she was too simple to understand, had kept things from her. She couldn't bear to think that Ash was like him in any way.

~

*A*sh drove Julia and her family home later that afternoon. Eddie had stuck to his side all afternoon, asking all kinds of questions about the war, the Union, the Confederacy, and the presidents of both countries.

Ash answered what he could. It was as if a tidal wave of questions spewed from the boy now that he'd been given permission to speak of it. Ash warned him to only talk about supporting the Union to him, his mother, and his sister, and only when they were alone.

Once inside Julia's home, Eddie followed his mother and sister up the stairs.

Julia returned a few minutes later. "Mama's going to fill the bathtub for him."

Ash chuckled. "He'll need to scrub." The boy had stepped into shallow river water while snaring a catfish.

"Why don't we take a turn about the garden while they're busy?"

"I'd like nothing more." A quiet stroll with her sounded exactly right. They stepped onto the veranda. Julia's hand was tucked onto his arm, bespeaking trust and love that nourished his very soul.

The sloped yard, half the size of the Adairs', had a long flower garden by the sidewalk and rows of fruit trees on the other side. Embedded stones on a dirt path provided a pleasant stroll even in damp weather.

"Let's walk in the flower garden," she suggested. "Silas has done a beautiful job with the chrysanthemums, hyacinths, and jasmine. He's taken the day off."

The scent of jasmine wafted over. "The whole garden is beautiful."

"Thank you."

"But its beauty doesn't hold a candle to yours." He touched a soft golden curl that had been brushed back and gathered with combs, her customary style.

She leaned closer, bringing the scent of her lilac perfume.

Ash couldn't resist. He stopped to face her, kissing her soft lips.

Her arms crept around his neck, and she tilted her face, inviting another.

He gave her a lingering kiss, unable to believe how much his love for her grew, especially with her support following Willie's death, which had struck her nearly as hard.

Mindful of the potential for watchful eyes from the street and surrounding homes, he stepped back reluctantly and extended his hand.

She tucked her tiny hand into his, and they continued their stroll.

"I'm proud of the way you and your mother talked to Eddie today."

"That lost look has left him." Her cheeks were still deliciously rosy from their kiss.

"Agreed." His chest expanded with pride and love for the boy. "He won't be afraid to approach you with questions now."

"Good." She looked up at him. "Ash, I think you're keeping something from me."

"No, Eddie asked plenty of questions—"

"Not about Eddie," she whispered. "Let's sit."

She already knew he kept a secret from her. Did she suspect him of spying? He gestured a bench beside the white chrysanthemums. Once they were settled, he shifted toward her so that his knees brushed her wool dress. "What's on your mind?"

"You are." Her brow furrowed. "Your mama said you've been traveling every week. That quite a lot of hours pass when you're not in your shop."

His heartbeat quickened. His meeting with his spies most often happened in the evenings, but a lot depended on the other men's schedules. Mama, one of the biggest gossips in town, had noticed. "There's a lot in my shop"—and otherwise —"to keep me busy."

Brown eyes studied him. "I think there's more to it. You're distracted, as if with many worries."

He looked away. His secret involved too many people. He didn't have permission to tell her. And with that recent incident with the captured spy, the less she knew, the better.

"Ash?"

"There are things I'm not at liberty to say."

Her chin tilted. "Because I'm too simple to understand complicated matters?"

His head shot around at the hurt and anger in her voice. "You're the most intelligent woman I know." It was true. He valued her counsel, her opinions. "This has nothing to do with that."

"Then what?" Folding her arms, she gave him a direct look.

"Why do you travel to the tanner's weekly for only one skin? Why are you often absent from your shop?"

"I'd tell you if I could." Sweat poured down his brow. Julia's family was already being watched, as Eddie had revealed. It was safer for her and her family to remain in ignorance of his spying.

"Remember your promise to tell me if you face imminent danger." She pressed her lips together.

"I remember." If that came about and there was time, he'd tell her.

She lowered her shoulders as if tension eased away, though worry lines lingered on her face. "I couldn't stand the thought of you placing yourself in danger. I've lost too many loved ones. I can't lose you."

"You won't lose me." Ash sandwiched her icy hands between his.

"I'll hold you to that." Taking a deep breath, she rose to her feet. "Let's get back to Mama. There's a chill in the air."

His chest tightened as he escorted her to the parlor, where her mother and brother sat in front of a cozy fire. As much as he wanted nothing standing between them, Ash must keep his secret to Jim to protect Julia and her family from danger.

# CHAPTER 18

"*H*ave you heard about the Benevolent Society?" Julia had just finished asking a blessing over the meal she'd share with Felicity at the seamstress shop the last Friday of November. Mrs. Cummings had eaten an early lunch and was out on a delivery, so Julia and Felicity had the kitchen to themselves.

Felicity looked up from her bowl of chicken stew. "My family has no need for such charity. My uncle has kept his job at the foundry."

"Oh, no, I didn't mean to suggest..." Heat surged up Julia's face. "No, it's just that a society has been established to provide food for families of men who recently lost their jobs."

"I know that families are going hungry." Felicity tore a piece of crusty bread. "It isn't that food isn't available, thank goodness. Eggs were fifteen cents a dozen at the grocer's yesterday. Venison and pork were a dime per pound. And Mrs. Cummings said the chickens she bought for the stew were twenty cents each."

"Reasonable prices, if one has a job." Julia wanted to do something for her neighbors. For months, she'd been sewing for soldiers she'd never meet. This was different because it aided Vicksburg citizens.

"What does this Benevolent Society propose to do?"

"They have a 'Free Market.' Society members donate food, prepare baskets to give to families in need, and deliver them. I suppose one could simply donate."

"Could I help you prepare and deliver baskets on a Saturday?" Felicity's eyes sparkled.

"That will be perfect. I'll shop this week. Can you come over in the morning?" Julia tried to save her Saturday afternoons and evenings for Ash, though he was often too busy to see her. More of that something he wasn't *at liberty* to say. She was willing to trust him for now.

"It will be good to see you outside the seamstress shop."

Was Felicity lonely? Luke would not be home for a few months. "Have you seen Savannah?" Savannah hadn't been back to the seamstress shop since her cruel statement.

"No." She sighed. "And you and Ash haven't stopped by to take me for a drive lately."

"Ash has been busy."

"Oh, it's good that the saddle shop is doing well considering the businesses that have closed."

The stew churned in Julia's stomach. Ash was only moderately busy in the shop. Reason enough for her to sell as much lace as possible for those Christmas gowns Miss Wind was making.

❦

On Wednesday afternoon, Ash strode toward the heart of town for a potential message from Christopher Sparks, one of his spies who worked at the cigar shop around the corner. The family man in his mid-thirties sold a variety of cigars in a variety of prices so that both wealthy and poor frequented his store. Christopher often overheard conversations both inside and outside his business.

Ash meandered past Sparks's shop at two o'clock. Inside, Christopher was serving two gentlemen but glanced up at Ash.

If Christopher had any messages, he'd come to their meeting place on Jackson Street between Monroe and Walnut, where Ash would be waiting.

A group of men had gathered nearby. Ash would linger near enough to listen without joining the conversation.

Around the corner on Jackson Street, Ash leaned a shoulder against the brick wall of a milliner shop, where four hats were displayed in the window. An odd place to rest his leg, perhaps, yet it had the advantage of being close enough to the men to learn that the Confederate Navy had received a new shipment of armor that they would use to plate to the new ironclad C.S.S *Virginia*, the former U.S.S. *Merrimack*. He'd pass that on up the line.

Lots of folks strolled by that he didn't know. That suited him just fine. He didn't want to get caught in a conversation and miss his opportunity to talk with Christopher.

He checked the clock on the corner. Ten minutes past two. He'd give him five more minutes and then return to his saddle shop.

Closer to the bluff, a familiar, much beloved figure with basket in tow caught Ash's eye as Julia exchanged greetings with an acquaintance from church. She was already suspicious of his movements. Best not let her see him with Christopher.

Long strides took him around the corner, out of Julia's sight. He bumped into Christopher.

"Well met, Ash." Christopher stuck out his hand.

"Afternoon." A folded scrap of paper scratched his palm as they shook hands. He shoved his hands into his pockets and dropped the scrap inside. "Business good?"

"My customers are partial to their cigars." Frown lines deepened on his forehead.

"Good to hear." Ash gave him a nod and then continued on in the same direction.

Away from Julia, who was too intelligent by far. He didn't want her to see him with any of his spies.

That had been close.

~

$\mathcal{M}$rs. Carrie Holmberg, the grocer's wife, helped Julia with purchases for the Benevolent Society. The friendly blonde some ten years Julia's senior minded the store while her young children were at school.

"You'll want to stay away from items already purchased by other members, right?" Her green print skirt brushed against the lowest shelf as they perused the selection.

"Yes, so you know what's already been purchased for this week?"

"Well, let's see if I can remember. Deborah Sprinkle bought twenty pounds of cornmeal. Sallie Ayers toted three sacks of potatoes to her buggy just yesterday." The slender woman tapped a different finger for each purchase. "Linda Dindzans bought the fresh beef required for the baskets. Don't worry about meat."

It pleased Julia to learn of the provisions furnished by friends. "Is everything else on the list available?"

"There are plenty of choices. Wait. Come to think of it, April Riley bought cabbage and turnips." She started on her left hand. "Oh, and Mrs. Sprinkle also purchased a mess of peas."

How she loved the generous hearts of her fellow Mississippians, but... "Did they leave anything for Mama and me to purchase?"

"My goodness, yes." She tapped her cheek. "How about molasses? That's on the list."

Julia hid a grimace. The jars would grow heavy on the long climb up the hill. Nevertheless, someone had to tote them to the Society. "I'll take six jars of molasses, but I want to take something else."

"Soap." Mrs. Holmberg gave a decisive nod. "That's what I'd do."

"Perfect. Ten bars?"

She frowned. "That's nearly my whole stock. How about six?" She rapped Julia's arm with the back of her fingertips. "You might want to purchase soap for your own home. I'm not certain when we'll get the next batch."

"I'll buy eight and take two home."

"Good choice." She tallied the total, which Julia paid. "Is Ash waiting for you outside?"

"What?" Julia peered out the window.

"Ash Mitchell. I saw him a few minutes ago. He's your beau, right?"

Julia couldn't keep the smile off her face.

"I knew it." Mrs. Holmberg tilted her head. "My husband was always impressed with how that young man accepted the responsibility of taking care of his family and the saddle shop after his pa's accident. He's a good one, if you don't mind my saying so."

"I agree." How refreshing to hear praise instead of criticism of the man she loved.

Finished with her purchases, Julia took the heavy basket and hurried outside, hoping to find Ash so he could help her carry her things.

Men in wool coats, slaves with full baskets, and women holding the hands of young children crowded the streets and congregated outside open businesses.

Julia looked in both directions. No Ash. She plopped the

basket on a bench. Where could he be? Not at the milliner's. She'd just left the grocers. The other shops on this side of the street were closed.

Maybe she'd pass him on the way home. Next time, she'd ask Silas to drive her...or purchase less.

Julia lifted her basket with a grimace. Though she stopped often to rest her aching arm and kept a watchful eye for Ash, she never spotted him on the crowded streets.

~

"Ash, what took you to town today?" Julia barely waited until they started their stroll to church services that evening to ask. He hadn't dined with them on Wednesdays for the past month and often didn't escort her to church. Just what was occupying so much of his time?

"A simple errand." His arm tensed beneath her hand. "A good thing too. I met Curtis McManus while out. I got another saddle order."

Eddie scampered ahead of them. Mama, nursing a cough, had stayed home.

"Good. Mrs. Holmberg spotted you from the grocery. I hoped you could carry my purchases."

"My apologies." He flushed. "I wish I'd known you needed assistance. Eddie, watch where you kick that rock."

Julia followed his gaze. Her little brother kicked a penny-sized pebble precariously close to pedestrians on the sidewalk ahead. "Don't kick rocks at all when anyone is on the sidewalk with us."

"All right." Squatting, Eddie picked up the stone. "I'll save it for later."

Ash laughed, and Julia couldn't help joining in. Eddie ran back to walk between them. Ringing church bells hastened their step.

As they settled on the pew, Julia still mulled over Ash's errand. There'd been many of them lately. Had he seen her and not sought her out to speak with her? A troubling possibility.

~

*A*sh left his horse at home and rode the train to Bolton the next day. It didn't matter if he was gone all day because he only had one saddle order, which wasn't due until next Friday. Plenty of time. His last newspaper advertisement hadn't borne any fruit. He'd change the wording and buy another for Monday.

He took the forest trail on the nippy fall day to Jim's homestead. A strange horse was tied to the corral.

Tugging his collar up around his neck, Ash hunkered down behind a bush to wait.

A man wearing a wool checked shirt and gray trousers strode from the house a quarter of an hour later. The stranger's wide-brimmed hat hid his face on the cloudy day.

Ash shifted his own hat down his forehead as the farmer rode toward the east. Was he another spy or one of those funding Jim's spies?

Ash was in the yard before Jim made it to the barn. "Jim, I came after another skin."

"You came to the right place." Jim grinned. "Let's have a cup of coffee first."

"Much obliged." Ash followed him inside.

"What do you have for me?" Jim poured coffee into a tin cup and set it on the table.

Ash told him about the Confederate ironclad in Norfolk and then downed a long swallow of the hot beverage.

"I need you to ride again, if you're up for it." Jim added the news to a list of ciphered messages. "My rider is still feeling poorly."

"If I can take your horse."

"Sure thing. Any chance I can order three saddles from you? I'll need the first one by next Friday."

"That's no problem. I'm obliged for the order." Relief flooded over him.

"I like to help people who help me." Jim sprinkled sand on the ink so it wouldn't smear.

"Business hasn't been so good lately." It hurt his pride to admit it.

"I'll see if I can send you more business."

"Thanks." Word of mouth was the best advertising. He'd wait a week or two on the newspaper ad.

Jim gave him the note with some bills. Ash thanked him as he accepted it. The danger didn't matter as much as purchasing food the family needed.

~

*M*ama marched into the kitchen where Julia was preparing lunch. "We haven't received an invitation to the Adairs' Christmas Eve ball. Is there a problem between you and Savannah that I'm unaware of?"

It was December tenth. The invitation should have come already. Mama wouldn't do anything to jeopardize her relationship with the wealthier Adairs—and Julia had better not either.

"She stopped volunteering at the seamstress shop when Luke was in the hospital."

"That doesn't make sense. Lila told me Savannah's sewing for the soldiers twice a week, the only social engagement she's kept regularly during her half-mourning. Certainly, they haven't been coming to our Thursday 'at-homes' because they've curtailed their social engagements to give Savannah time to recover."

"Maybe they're not hosting a ball this year." Julia added a jar of canned tomatoes to a pot of vegetable soup.

"Nellie Rhodes received her invitation yesterday. She stopped by this morning on her way to the dressmaker."

Julia wished their neighbor had resisted the opportunity to discover if she'd received her coveted invitation before the Dodds. "Perhaps it will come today."

"Is there some problem between you and Savannah?" Mama put her hands on her hips.

Sighing, Julia explained about Savannah's outburst at the dressmaker's.

"She's in mourning, Julia. Savannah must be forgiven such a lapse." Mama's brown eyes turned steely. "Since the ball is definitely planned, the family must be receiving again. You and I will visit them this afternoon, and you will smooth over whatever is wrong between you. Understood?"

"Yes, Mama." Julia wouldn't tolerate any more slurs against Ash. Yet if Mama got a hint that Savannah—and therefore the Adairs—weren't pleased with him refusing to join the army, she'd have more ammunition against him to hurl at Julia.

≈

"How have you been, Savannah?" Her friend had consented rather ungraciously to take a turn about the garden when Julia suggested it that afternoon and then led the way silently up to the terraced hillside.

"A lot you care." Savannah snapped at her. "You didn't even bother to tell me Luke's illness wasn't severe."

Julia blinked at the attack. It had sounded as though Savannah wanted him to die that day. "That was wrong of me. Forgive me."

"And then to ignore me for weeks. Why, I'd quite looked forward to you and Ash taking me for drives."

"When you didn't return to sew at the shop, I thought you'd prefer some time alone." Perhaps Mama was right. It had been Savannah's bitter grief that lashed out at Felicity. And Julia, too, for she'd not been subtle about her resentment that Ash was safe at home.

"You were wrong."

They strolled all around the garden in silence before Julia spoke. "We've been friends a long time, Savannah. Can't we mend what's wrong between us?"

"I want to." Savannah halted. "I feel so alone. Every time I step away from the crowd, eyes follow me to ascertain if I'm holding up or ready to cry."

Julia's resentment melted. She hugged Savannah close. "I can understand how that grates on you."

"That's the perfect way to say it." There were tears in Savannah's eyes as she pulled away. "I'll ask Mama to send your family and Ash's family an invitation to our Christmas ball."

"Thank you. We'd love to come."

"And Felicity's family as well."

So Savannah had harbored resentment toward all of them.

"I shall love spending time with friends." Tears spilled over. Savannah brushed them away. "Mama and Mrs. Sanderson won't dance on Willie's grave. I've decided to dance only a few dances so there will be plenty of time for visiting."

"We'll treasure talking with you as much as you like." Compassion filled her heart at her friend's sadness. The ball would be an ordeal for her. Understandably so. But she and Felicity could make it endurable.

She vowed to do just that for her childhood friend.

# CHAPTER 19

*A*sh sat between Julia, who was breathtaking in a white satin gown with a red sash, and Caroline. Christmas Eve at the Adair mansion had become a tradition. Close friends and family were always invited with additional guests arriving for the ball afterward. Yet it was difficult not to look around for Willie, even with Julia and his family here.

Caroline had turned sixteen last month. Daphne, who'd turned fourteen in October, attended the supper for the first time. Ash's mother always bought a new dress for herself and her daughters for the holiday. When she learned that several women didn't order new gowns in support of their soldiers at war, she likewise refrained. Ash also wanted to think that Mama was cutting back on expenditures, as he'd requested.

In addition to Jim's order, five more had come from nearby plantations this month. Income from his now-weekly runs to Harvey's Mill had allowed Ash to buy Christmas gifts and restock the family pantry.

Mama had noticed he was now gone every Thursday. As long as he left the horses, she didn't complain.

"You're quiet tonight." Julia, spooning a bite of charlotte russe, looked at him with compassionate brown eyes.

"My apologies." Ash's heart remained as heavy as a stone. He tried not to look at Savannah, beautiful in her green gown, because of the man sitting next to her.

Not Willie.

"No need to apologize." Julia squeezed his arm with a gloved hand. "I share your sadness."

Savannah hadn't been betrothed to Willie, so she didn't wear mourning black. Ash was glad for Willie's sake that she hadn't encouraged anyone to court her. Everyone was seated between people of the opposite sex, a feat made easier for the hostess because the Hill City Cadets were home on furlough. Only four had been invited to dine with the family—one of them sat between Caroline and his mother—to round out the numbers. More soldiers would arrive for the dance.

Mrs. Adair stood, signaling the end of the meal. Guests followed her to the ballroom.

Julia tugged on Ash's arm to pull him away before they joined their families. "Don't talk about Willie unless Savannah mentions him first," she whispered. "We'll spend as much of the evening with her as she desires."

"Excellent. I will dance with her and Felicity this evening." Despite the opportunity to waltz with Julia, the most beautiful woman at the Christmas party—and indeed, all of Vicksburg— the dancing was what Ash most dreaded. He'd especially miss Willie in the refreshment room and on the veranda, where men tended to gather. Undoubtedly, Savannah felt the same melancholy, for different reasons.

Julia smiled as her friend joined them. "Felicity, you look lovely in that gown the color of spring grass. That white trim sets it off beautifully. Good evening, Mr. Beltzer. Mrs. Beltzer. It's lovely to see you."

Ash shook hands with Charles Beltzer and exchanged

greetings with his petite wife. He hadn't seen the couple since the fall picnic.

"Mama has already selected a group of seats for us, ladies." Julia gave Felicity a smiling nod across the area cleared for dancing. "Shall we?"

Julia had inherited her mother's gracious manners, for she had set the Beltzers at ease by including them. Savannah, Mrs. Adair, and Willie's mother and three sisters were sitting with his own family and Mrs. Dodd.

Those who hadn't seen one another earlier exchanged greetings of the season. Couples, groups of soldiers, and families arrived, and soon the band began to play a waltz.

Ash inclined his head at Julia, but she was looking at Savannah, who stood alone. It was as if no one knew who should approach her to dance.

*Watch over her.* Willie's plea in every letter returned to him.

He bent to speak in Julia's ear. "Will you mind if I waltz first with Savannah?"

"It's what I want." She beamed up at him. "Quickly, for I see sadness overtaking her."

Ash squeezed her hand before hurrying to his friend's girl. "Savannah?"

She looked up, her complexion ashen.

"Will you do me the honor of dancing this first waltz with me?" He bowed formally, something he had never done when they'd danced in the past. Everything had been done in fun back then.

"Oh, Ash." Tears shone in her brown eyes but didn't spill. "I think Willie would have wanted it that way."

Her grief scratched at his own. Brought it to the forefront. "Agreed." He took her gloved hand and led her to the dance floor.

Other dancers watched them as they waited for the music

to begin. Caroline's partner was the schoolteacher, Peter Higgins.

"I dearly wish everyone would stop watching me." Savannah's tormented gaze met his. "It's as if they expect me to cry all evening. Well, I won't give them the satisfaction. I'll dance when asked, even if I'd rather sob alone in my room."

"I regret this is a trial for you." Ash's gaze dropped to the polished wood floor. "I know it's not the same but I miss him too."

"That's what I most needed to hear." Her smile was tremulous.

The music began. He clasped her hand. With his other hand on her waist, he led her around the room. His limp kept them from looking as graceful as he wished.

"You dance elegantly." He smiled as he complimented her.

"Thank you, my friend. Will you give me a twirl?"

"Gladly."

As she held lightly to his hand, Savannah's green hoopskirt swirled about her. Other dancers shifted to the side, watching the beautiful woman cast aside her grief for a moment. Her looped braids lifted off her shoulders as she spun a second time before returning to his arms.

"Thank you for that." Her eyes sparkled.

It was what Willie would have done. "My pleasure."

"I feel their gaze again." Her smile faltered.

Probably aghast at his limping performance. No, they were looking at Savannah.

Ash smiled. "You're a lovely woman enjoying a dance. They're happy for you."

Her face radiated her joy in the moment.

The last strains of the dance gave Ash a pang of regret. In this moment, their shared grief bonded them together.

Ash released her. "Savannah, I hope you will come to me if

you have need of my help. I will do whatever is in my power to do."

"Thank you, Ash." Her laugh sounded forced. "If you see me without a dance partner..."

"We will stick so close, you'll wish to be rid of us." He bowed and led her back to her mother.

Julia and Felicity waited with Mrs. Adair. They immediately engaged Savannah in conversation.

Ash stayed close to Julia as much as possible, remaining at her side while she and Felicity chatted with Savannah. When Savannah consented to dances, the other two also danced.

Savannah's acceptance of him and, more importantly, the healing of Julia's friendship with her, eased his heartache. This evening was a step in the right direction toward reunifying everyone, even with Willie and Luke missing.

～

The ball couldn't be going better. Julia had enjoyed a nice talk with Savannah and Felicity after Ash and Savannah waltzed. It wasn't long before she and her two friends were dancing with soldiers. Ash had fetched her a glass of punch in the dining room before being pulled into a conversation with Mr. Adair. She sipped the cold drink, glad to give her much-trodden-upon feet a rest.

"Merry Christmas, Julia."

Julia turned toward the vaguely familiar voice. "Merry Christmas, Mrs. Bradley." She rarely crossed paths with the gray-haired widow with a reputation for gossip.

"I was pleased Lila decided to host this ball again this year. The family has suffered so."

"Indeed." Julia had no intention of gossiping about her friend. "It's a lovely party."

"Agreed. Speaking of lovely, did you notice how well Ash and Savannah look together?" Bright blue eyes studied her.

Julia's euphoria brought on by the ball and multiple waltzes with Ash crumbled at the inference. "Why, no. I didn't. They are friends, after all. Willie was Ash's closest friend."

"All the better. I thought I detected a romantic spark."

The back of Julia's neck burned like a smoldering coal. "You're mistaken. Ash has courted me these past months." Setting her cup on a tray, she flounced from the dining room.

The nerve. Why, Ash might even give her a ring for Christmas. That would end any lingering speculation about his interest in Savannah, the undisputed beauty in Vicksburg.

~

*J*ulia's anger at Mrs. Bradley still simmered Christmas morning. The need to prepare for guests stopping by that afternoon, an annual tradition, pushed that aside. After she and Eddie had finished decorating the parlor and formal dining room with branches of holly, she gathered hyacinths and chrysanthemums.

Silas helped her cut the stems. "Miss Julia, it feels more like springtime than Christmas."

"It does, indeed." She wore the lightest of shawls. "No complaints from me."

"Me neither." The tall black man with a muscular frame studied the growing pile of flowers. "Want me to carry some of these inside?"

"Yes, the hyacinths. Mama's waiting to arrange them." She tapped a finger on her cheek. "Is that enough to fill two vases?"

"Sure enough. Might have some left over." He loaded them in his arms.

"If so, put the third vase in the family dining room."

"Be glad to. That puts me back near Miss Hester's cooking." He grinned. "Might coax a cookie or two out of her."

The family would eat a big meal at noon with Ash and his family and then serve light refreshments. "Save some for the guests," she teased.

"If I steal too many, Miss Hester knows how to apply a wooden spoon to advantage."

Julia laughed, then turned her attention to cutting chrysanthemums. Their staff received their gifts from the family and then ate breakfast with them on Christmas morning before each scattered to continue preparations for visitors.

Julia's parents had long adopted a custom of opening their home for neighbors who wanted to celebrate a portion of Christmas Day with them, often receiving as many as thirty guests. It was unlikely she'd enjoy any private moments with Ash. Unfortunately.

She'd been pleased that Ash invited Savannah to the first dance. She'd been less pleased when other couples stopped to watch them...as if Savannah was the belle of the ball and Ash her handsome escort.

That all diminished with Julia's first dance with Ash. His hand clasping hers while he gazed at her as if she were the only woman in the room reminded her yet again of his love for her. Her joy had lingered even when she danced with countless soldiers. In fact, all the ladies in their party were in high demand.

Then Mrs. Bradley spoiled it. Ash had done as Julia had asked him to do—comfort a grieving friend. There was no romantic spark between Savannah and Ash, yet might she come to rely on him *too* much in the hole left by Willie's loss?

∾

*a*sh brought his family over after lunch, happy that they were the first guests to arrive. Julia, stunning in a green dress with a white sash ribbon, took them to the parlor where her mother and Eddie greeted them.

"Mama, let's exchange our gifts before other guests begin arriving," Julia said, her gaze on the packages Ash placed near the hearth where orange flames licked the wood.

"Of course." She gave Mrs. Mitchell an indulgent smile. "Julia has long been this way at Christmas."

Eddie was first. He tore the brown paper, exclaiming over his new game, The Checkered Game of Life. Mrs. Dodd fingered the folds of her new blue woolen shawl. In addition, Caroline had stitched the family a beautiful scene of a steamer on the Mississippi River that had required hours every evening for three months. Mrs. Dodd proclaimed it a work of art. Daphne, Caroline, and Ash's mother received soft silk sashes.

"You've been very patient, my dear." Ash leaned to kiss Julia's cheek, which turned a delicious shade of rose. "Happy Christmas to you." He gave her a small brown package tied with string.

"Thank you." Her smile grew radiant. "May I open it now?"

"Please." He'd splurged on her gift. Caroline had assured him Julia would love it.

"Kid gloves?" She held the soft white gloves against her cheek, but did he imagine that the light in her eyes dimmed a bit? "Ash, they're lovely. Thank you." She stood on tiptoe to kiss his cheek, even with all eyes on them. He *was* imagining things. She seemed delighted.

His heart melted like butter on a Vicksburg summer afternoon. "I'm happy you like them."

"I have a gift for you." She laid a stringed package onto his palm.

Whatever it was, he was prepared to love it on their first

Christmas together. He broke the string. Nestled inside were three large white handkerchiefs. Useful, indeed. "Thank you, Julia."

"Look at the embroidery. Caroline demonstrated, but I did all the stitches." Julia peeked over his shoulder.

Mystified, he shook one to open the folds. "A saddle? You embroidered a saddle on each one?" What a thoughtful present to a saddler, all the more precious because it came from her.

Everyone drew close to admire the handiwork.

Ash looked into Julia's eyes, trying to convey his pleasure. Perhaps she understood, for she gave him a brilliant smile in return.

A knock on the door halted the family celebration. Multiple neighbors stayed for short visits, including Felicia's family and the Adairs. Mrs. Dodd played Christmas carols on the rarely used piano in the parlor. Everyone nibbled on generous refreshments displayed in the formal dining room.

Ash talked with Mr. Adair on the veranda until a bitterly cold wind banished spring-like weather.

By six o'clock, all guests had left except Ash's family.

"I'd love some lemonade." Julia rose from the sofa and gave Ash a look.

He followed her into the dining room. "I'd begun to imagine we'd not have a private moment together."

"Me too." Taking his hand, she drew him toward the low blaze on the room's hearth. "I must ask you about Savannah." She released his hand.

"My heart goes out to her." He'd tried to push his own grief aside to celebrate the birth of his Savior, the one unchanging rock in a world where everything else was in chaos. "Her sorrow is to be expected."

"But a romantic interest in her deceased beau's dearest friend isn't." Julia held his gaze, her eyes questioning.

He blinked. "What are you talking about? There are no

such feelings between Savannah and me, nor have there ever been. Nothing Savannah and I ever said to one another shames any of us. What's wrong, Julia? Please tell me and I'll make it right."

"Last night, Mrs. Bradley suggested there was a romantic spark between you."

That woman was a busybody. "There's not a *spark* of truth in it. Mrs. Bradley is a gossip."

Two circles blazed bright red on her cheeks. "It's not just that. The way you smiled at each other...others stopped to watch."

"We were remembering Willie." He raised her chin. "You're the only woman for me."

She rubbed the glove on her left hand. His gift.

He bent to kiss her. "You have a hold on my heart, Miss Julia Dodd." Taking her into his arms, he kissed her again. "In case you didn't know."

She nestled against his chest. "A woman likes to hear such things now and again."

"I love you, Julia."

"I love you." She raised glowing eyes to his. "Oh, Ash. It's wonderful to hear it again."

"Our first Christmas together." He kissed her rosy cheeks before claiming her lips for a longer kiss. "I've a hankering to dance with you. Think we can convince your mother to play a waltz?"

"I believe so." Her radiant smile enhanced her beauty.

He released her to offer his arm. "Prepare to twirl."

She giggled. "I shall become quite dizzy."

He laughed with her, dizzy himself—dizzy with happiness that the most precious woman in the world loved him.

# CHAPTER 20

*J*ulia tatted lace in the parlor alone after Ash's family left. She shouldn't feel such disappointment this Christmas night. He had expressed his love for her, not only in words but in his attentiveness to her slightest wish. She shouldn't be so downtrodden over not receiving a marriage proposal—except it signaled that his finances weren't up to Mama's standards. She studied the lacy ring she just completed, the only one she'd have this Christmas.

"Tatting again?" Mama wandered into the parlor and sat before the glowing embers on the hearth. She yawned. "I wouldn't imagine you possessed the energy."

"It relaxes me." And gave her time to think. She still hadn't told anyone about selling the lace—to supplement Ash's income or support herself if Ash didn't propose—especially Mama.

"Expensive leather." Mama fingered the gloves resting on the square table between their armchairs. "Perhaps business in Ash's saddle shop has improved."

Julia held her breath. Dare she hope...

"I've given him a chance, though it's doubtful he'll attain the income necessary to marry—at least not while war rages in our country." Closing her eyes, Mama leaned her head against the cushion. "Your life will be a drudgery if you marry a saddler."

Julia's fist closed around the delicate lace, destroying the fabric that could tip the scales in favor of her dream of marrying the very saddler her mama scorned.

~

*J*n early January, Julia braved the long walk to Miss Wind's shop in blustery breezes that whipped at her cloak. After greeting the seamstress, she set her basket on a barren work table. "I've brought the lace you requested. Six yards, I believe you said." She held her hands toward the warmth emanating from the stove.

"I'm sorry, Miss Dodd." The seamstress put her hands on her red cheeks. "I asked for it before Christmas. If you had delivered it before all the Christmas balls..."

Julia's smile died. "What are you saying?"

"No one has ordered *any* clothing since Christmas." Miss Wind bit her lip. "I've no means of support without them."

"I'm so sorry. What will you do?" Besides reject the lace she'd *not* stipulated must be delivered in December.

"I'm moving to my sister's home in Kentucky. She needs help running the homestead while her husband fights in the war."

Julia didn't ask which side he fought for as she wished her Godspeed with as much grace as she could muster.

She scarcely noticed the cold on her walk home. The rejection was a blow. Earning money for the first time in her life had given her a sense of purpose, renewed her spirit.

Must she give up that independence? If no one was ordering dresses, blouses, or jackets, lace trim was certainly not in demand.

No. She'd not quit.

Lace would eventually be needed.

~

When Julia learned that the foundries in Vicksburg allowed women to visit, she took Eddie with her on a tour of both the Reading Foundry and the Paxton Foundry. The shells they'd seen manufactured and the cannon they'd seen casted were all Eddie could talk about at his birthday celebration a week later. Ash seemed just as interested, even asking Julia extra questions after dinner.

Winter weather didn't stop the strengthening of fortifications in Vicksburg. Most citizens seemed unconcerned by an increase of soldiers about town.

Julia broached the subject while knitting socks for the soldiers at the seamstress shop on a Friday late in January. "Felicity, what do you think about the fortifications going up around our city?"

Felicity sewed a pillow case, the whirr of the sewing machine a familiar sound. "Are you asking if I feel safer with soldiers here?"

She nodded. "Along with the military preparations for some future battle."

"I'm torn." The machine stopped. "If there's to be a battle here, surely, the artillery will make us safer. But might those very preparations invite a battle?"

"That's it exactly." Julia poked her needle in the blanket and set it aside. There are fewer and fewer boats in the wharves. A Federal naval blockade had stopped ships from bringing goods to Southern ports. Commonplace supplies would soon become scarce. "You've struck upon the very core of what's robbed me of sleep."

"Those fortifications aren't so far from our city that we'd

escape destructive shells." Felicity's brow furrowed. "I want Luke's regiment to return and protect us. I miss him so."

"I'd feel safer if Vicksburg soldiers protected us also." Julia studied Felicity's brooding expression. "He's still in Virginia, isn't he? That's where Luke's last letter to Ash was from."

"Yes." She fidgeted with the high collar of her red print dress. "At least his regiment hasn't been in any big battles."

"I'm glad of it." And thankful for Ash's presence in the city —when he was here. Julia hadn't seen him on Wednesdays since Christmas. According to his mother, saddle orders had dropped this month again, yet Ash's visits to Bolton to replenish supplies continued twice a week. Curious.

Ash had told Julia there were things he couldn't tell her. Was he meeting with Unionists away from the city? If so, to what purpose?

~

*A*sh looked up as someone opened his shop's door. The first week of February was too nippy to keep it open. "Jack, good to see you." He stepped forward to shake the hand of a short, stocky man of about twenty-five who had been a customer for years.

"Good morning to you, Ash." Jack Edwards shook his hand firmly. "Your family good?"

"Yep." Ash settled in for a chat. Some men liked to chew the fat before placing an order. "Peter Higgins has called on Caroline the past two Sundays."

"The schoolteacher?"

Ash nodded. Both Caroline and his mama were pleased about the potential courtship. He wasn't certain whether the man supported the Confederacy. He'd warned Caroline to mind her words with him.

"Annabelle's a mite upset about a decision I made."

"Oh? What's that?" Ash's ears perked up. These days, it behooved him to learn what he could, even about with a spat between married couples. Anything that might help the Union was worth passing on.

"I was laid off at the wharf. Not as many steamboats to load and unload." His face tightened. "Just so happens, the army needs soldiers, so I've mustered in. We're starting another Vicksburg company. Maybe three of them."

Ash's stomach tightened. This was news the Union wanted to know.

"I've joined the King Cotton Guards." He stuck out his hand to receive Ash's congratulatory handshake.

Ash obliged. "Good man. Lots of brave men fight for the South." Including Luke.

"How's business for you?"

"Slower than last summer." Most of his orders came from farms and plantations near the city. It left more time for his twice-weekly rides to the mill. *That* steady income provided for his family. Some of the extra cornmeal went to the Free Market for families like Jack's.

"Then join the King Cotton Guards with me."

That didn't take long. "This bum leg won't allow it."

Jack gave a disgusted snort. "Ain't you gonna defend your own state? Your own city?"

Ash's face burned at the scorn. "I do what I can."

"You ain't worth my time." Jack flapped his hand in dismissal, then stalked away.

Nausea rose like bile at Jack's scorn. Would he spread rumors about Ash?

～

*T*he next morning, Ash took the morning train to Bolton with a page of messages tucked in his boot. His five spies reported something nearly weekly—sometimes at great risk, one Ash shared because his meetings were all over the city. There were too many details about action around Tennessee forts for him to remember everything. While recording the information increased the risk, his written details were scanty. Anyone reading them would need to know the whole picture to understand. It was the most he could do to protect himself.

He pulled his hat down low over his eyes as he watched out the window. They passed a number of Confederate soldiers digging fortifications just outside Vicksburg and standing guard. Ash had spotted pickets in the trees near the road on Monday. Mississippi had decided Vicksburg was worth protecting. Unfortunately, that probably meant the soldiers were here to stay. If these Confederates left, others would come to man the artillery. He turned his face away from the window.

If the same men noticed his comings and goings, they might get too curious about his business outside town. Ash deemed it wiser to take the train for the time being. He wore different hats, trousers, and scarves every time, but his boots were his only pair. Same with his winter coat.

Folks along the road to Harv's must be familiar with him. He'd study the maps to vary his route. It could save his life.

He exited the train in Bolton and strode to the Routeledge homestead. At least the Confederate soldiers didn't stop citizens leaving the city, though that might change.

There was an unfamiliar horse tied to a bush outside Mr. Jim's house. Ash ducked into the forest to wait for the guest to leave. Could be a customer *or* a spy. Maybe both, like Ash.

A man wearing a burgundy frock coat exited the house, tapping a cane on the walk. No skins, so he likely wasn't a customer. He rode off toward Jackson, the state's capital. His beaver hat slanted low over his eyes, making it impossible for Ash to identify him.

Ash waited until the hoof beats faded to step from his hiding place. Jim surely had spies from all walks of life because the stranger's coat had been of a more expensive cut than Ash's wool frock coat.

"Morning, Ash." Waving toward the barn, Jim crossed the yard. "Come into my workshop, will you?"

"Happy to." Ash wasn't buying a pig skin today—and probably wouldn't on his next visit. He had ample supply to make two months of saddles under normal circumstances, which these days definitely weren't. He peered in every direction as casually as possible before following his host inside the barn.

"You've got more messages?" Jim spoke in low tones.

Ash extracted the note from his boot and elaborated on the sketchy details concerning Confederate troop movements in the area of Tennessee's Fort Henry and Fort Donelson.

"Good job, Ash. I appreciate the risks you are taking." Jim sighed. "Union armies press toward us from the north. I fear times will get worse before they get better." The wrinkles on his forehead deepened.

"Agreed." They'd all participate in the suffering. Ash prayed he wouldn't participate from a prison cell.

"Our other rider for your route quit two days ago. His wife discovered what he's been doing. Threatened to tell their neighbors if he didn't stop."

A chill crawled up Ash's back. More reason to hide his spy activities from his gossiping mama, who wasn't pleased he was gone so often. And now Jim had even more work for him.

≈

*J*ulia, who had tatted enough lace to adorn one hooped skirt in the first two weeks of February alone, had put that task aside and spent the morning preparing to host an 'at-home' visit. Mama wasn't feeling well. Despite her elixir, her illness had returned, confining her to her bed. She had stayed home all week but wasn't better.

Mama planned to greet her guests from her comfortable armchair. Julia would serve tea and refreshments. It should work out, unless one of the coughing spells overtook Mama.

Julia hurried to the kitchen to check if refreshments were ready. The aroma of freshly baked cakes wafted to meet her.

"Hester, those oatmeal cakes smell divine."

"Good to hear." The servant wiped her hands on the blue-checked bib apron that protected her brown dress. "Tea cakes are in the oven."

"I hope you made extra." Julia grinned. The half-cake, half-cookie desserts were Hester's special recipe.

"I did." A smile touched her lips as she pointed to a bowl of dough. "This is the second batch. Silas is most partial to them too."

Julia tilted her head. "Are you and Silas courting?"

"Not so's you'd notice."

"But Silas wants to be more than friends?" How had this gotten past her? She'd be thrilled if the two of them married. She considered them all part of the family. Daisy, Hester's daughter, had been twelve when Hester came to work for them.

She laughed. "The way to that man's heart is his stomach."

"Then I expect his heart is already yours," Julia teased.

"Don't know about that." Hester removed a pan of tea cakes from the oven. "Is Miss Martha feeling better?"

"No." She sighed. "Mama was coughing when I took her a cup of tea about an hour ago."

"Shame about that bronchitis coming back. Thought she'd licked it."

"I wish that were true." Julia tried to push aside her worry. She and Eddie both needed Mama, especially now that she had resumed some parental duties. Julia couldn't imagine life without her.

∼

The following Monday morning, Ash wrapped his cold hands around a hot cup of coffee at Jim's homestead. It had been a brisk walk in the rain from the Bolton depot, not unexpected for the third week of February, and he now warmed himself in front of a blazing fire in the hearth.

"News of my spies has reached a prominent gentleman living in the capital." Jim stared at steam rising from his cup. "Good thing he supports our cause."

Jackson was less than twenty-five miles from Bolton.

"If one man in Jackson has heard what I'm doing, others may also." Jim raked his hand through his red hair. "I've been careful. But have *all* my spies watched what they said and did? I don't know."

Ash digested that worry with his coffee. It didn't set well. One person's carelessness heightened the danger for all of them. "What are you going to do?"

"I can't have our work stop if I end up in prison. You've accepted a portion of my risk."

"I'm still willing to have your spies report to me." Those five men kept him busy.

"Things are about to heat up, especially with Confederate soldiers building up defenses at Vicksburg as you reported today. I have a new contact outside Yazoo City. This man will take another route north toward Tennessee, where the Union has an eye on Confederate forts and cities. They need to know where Confederate troops are camped, what kind of weaponry they have."

Ash gave a low whistle. "Good work."

"You'll take your messages directly to Yazoo City once a week."

His admiration took a swift turn. "Me? Why, that's nearly fifty miles from Vicksburg." No trains to shorten the journey. He'd have to ride, but his leg ached just imagining it.

"My contact lives about a mile from the city." His brow furrowed. "Think your leg can handle it?"

"Don't know. That's a good half day's ride." Ash rubbed his clean-shaven jaw. "And I'll have to rest my horse before returning."

"Remain at the grocer's shop—he lives in the same building —only long enough to deliver your messages. Rest in the forest on the way back."

A grocer. Always something he could buy there as an excuse for stopping if there were other customers.

"Here's another task for you." Jim showed Ash a page with columns and rows of alphabetical letters and indicated he take a seat at the table. "I've been coding our messages using this cipher. Harv coded those you took directly to him. I hated to ask you to do more when you were already doing so much." He explained how it worked and watched as Ash gave it a try. "That's good. You'll get faster with practice."

Letters followed a grid so that resulting words were nonsense. Ash should have been doing this all along. No one between Bolton and Vicksburg had searched him...but they might have.

"From now on, use this cipher to write coded messages before starting out." Mr. Jim's serious gaze intensified. "I have another copy. Burn that cipher as soon as you have it memorized."

"That'll take some doing." Didn't seem to be rhyme nor reason to the arrangement of letters.

"You're up for the task."

Was he? If he was caught, arrested, would he be able to keep his mouth shut? Hold Mr. Jim's confidences?

Cold sweat trickled down his brow. Determination and resignation battled one another. But he wasn't going to give up now. "You have my word."

"Nor will I betray you."

Ash believed him. What of the spies who reported to Ash back in Vicksburg, though? One might break under pressure—a frightening possibility. "What about Harv?"

"You'll ride that only once a week now. Harv's getting skittish." Mr. Jim pulled his purse from his pocket. "Fifty dollars a month for the weekly trip to Yazoo City."

Ash stared at him. Where did a tanner get that kind of money?

As if guessing what Ash was thinking, he said, "I've got folks who pay me to get the messages through the lines. The man who just left donated a hefty sum toward paying my riders." He sighed. "I'll give you three months in advance for agreeing to the plan today. After that, I'll pay monthly until...well, until I'm caught, or I think I might be."

"How will I know to quit coming?"

Jim stared into the fire. "If I have an inkling I'm being watched, I'll paint my corral fence white. I may not have time to finish, so I'll start by the road. If you see a white fence, hightail it out of here. And never come back."

A chill formed in Ash's stomach and spread to his chest. Would the pressure and risk never cease escalating?

∾

*O*n Friday three days later, Julia received a note from Ash, delivered by Caroline, that he would see her the following day for supper and take her to their favorite restaurant.

She'd been expecting him that night, and though the prospect of dinner out sounded wonderful, disappointment swirled within.

"Did he say why he can't come tonight?" Julia asked.

Caroline shrugged. "He didn't tell me what was in the note."

"Oh. It's nothing of consequence." She'd ask him directly. "Is Peter still calling on you?"

Caroline blushed. "He's escorting me to church. Mama has invited him to lunch Sunday and would like for you and your family to come. I'd be pleased to learn your opinion of him."

"Mama's still feeling poorly, but Eddie and I would love to join you."

"I'll say a prayer for her." Caroline promised to let Ash know they'd attend the luncheon and headed away with a smile of anticipation.

Mama had left their 'at home' gathering yesterday during a coughing spell that alarmed their guests. She wouldn't risk going out in public until she was better.

∾

*A*sh, who'd uttered a considerable number of prayers on his journey, felt thoroughly chilled when he reached the grocery shop outside Yazoo City. It was located at a country crossroad. Horseback riders and drivers of wagons along the route had provided more risks for him to be noticed. He'd dressed in a workman's clothes, the same as he wore in his saddle shop. Nondescript brown trousers. A brown frock coat. Black boots he wore daily. Nothing to attract attention. Not the way the expensively dressed gentleman leaving the Routeledge home had caught Ash's eye. He'd learned a lesson from that man's carelessness.

A wagon with its team harnessed stood outside the two-story white clapboard store. The family likely lived in the second story. *Spencer's Groceries* had been painted on a sign hanging from chains over the door. Ash took his time dismounting to allow the customer inside to finish and leave. Good thing, for his left leg buckled before he caught himself on the hitching post. On the next trip, he'd get off a few miles before arriving to give his leg an opportunity to recover.

"You did a good job, girl." He rubbed Rosebud's neck. They'd both need a rest before riding back. After looping her reins over the post by the water trough, Ash pushed his hat over his forehead.

A boy of about twelve carried a loaded box toward the door as Ash stepped inside. "Howdy, mister."

Ash touched the brim of his hat but didn't respond.

Shrugging, the boy went outside.

"Elijah Spencer." A tall, broad-shouldered man stepped from behind the counter, hand extended. "I don't believe we've met."

"Ashburn Mitchell." Ash shook his callused hand. Not a streak of gray in the grocer's blond hair or beard. He guessed him to be in his early thirties.

Recognition flickered in the man's eyes, and he stopped Ash before he could speak. "Not yet. Joey will return."

With a nod, Ash turned to study the half-filled shelves.

The door opened, letting in a blast of cold air on the cloudy day.

"Here's the last box, Joey." The grocer handed him a filled crate. "You tell your mama hello from me and the missus."

"I surely will." The boy gave a nod and headed out the door.

Ash waited until wagon wheels creaked away from the

shop. "Got plenty of flour?" That was code to ask if it was safe to deliver the message. A positive answer meant everything was fine to proceed. A negative response meant to leave immediately.

"I can spare a pound."

Affirmative. "Good. That'll be all I require."

"Call me Eli. Most do." Eli put a small burlap sack on the counter between them.

"Friends call me Ash." He extracted a dollar from his pocket with a page folded inside. "This is what I owe you."

"Very good." His large hand closed over the bill. "Lots of customers in the morning. Not so many in the afternoon."

Afternoons in the future. "Much obliged." They stared at one another, taking one another's measure in this dangerous venture. "I'll likely return to this area a week from today."

"Good Lord willing, I'll be here." They shook hands.

Ash tried to control his limp as he stalked out. That had gone smoothly. He just had to get past the Confederate soldiers on picket duty outside Vicksburg without raising suspicions. And pretend that he'd worked late in the shop so his mother didn't realize he'd been gone all day. He'd slept in the shop and left at dawn, long before she arose, and it was not quite eleven o'clock.

First, he'd find a quiet spot on the Yazoo River to eat the sandwich he'd brought and feed his horse. Then he'd walk a couple a miles to extend Rosebud's rest...maybe work out the stiffness in his leg. There'd be frequent stops for the mare on the trip back. Next week, maybe he should make it a two-day trip. Stopping over at one of the ramshackle barns along his route was a sight better than running his horse too long. This first trip taught him what not to do.

Looping Rosebud's reins in his hand, he led the horse on the soft grass beside the dirt road for the next two miles, stopping when she grazed.

After remounting, he kept a keen eye out for potential shelter away from farms and homes and found a barn a stone's throw from the Yazoo River. Mature trees hid it from view from the road. Missing boards in a few places, but the roof seemed intact. Not ten miles from the grocer's.

After taking a long swig from his canteen, Ash released a long sigh. Explaining weekly overnight absences to his mother was his greatest challenge. Caroline could keep his secret hidden from Mama. If she knew. Did he dare chance telling her what Julia didn't even know?

No, that would hurt Julia.

He'd tell his family he must work late and arise easy so he'd sleep on his shop's cot. For Mama *couldn't* keep a secret. She didn't even realize Ash's allegiance was to the North.

If Mama discovered his spying, he'd have to quit. And he couldn't quit. Too many spies depended on him.

Gloomy clouds hid what little sun there was that afternoon when Ash dismounted to lead Rosebud to get a drink and rest. His leg wobbled. Bitter wind swept across the river. He shivered. Another twenty miles to Vicksburg, and Rosebud's steps slowed. He'd best walk a good portion of it. Although, if he did, his leg wouldn't be worth much tomorrow. He'd already postponed his evening with Julia. If he showed up late and limping, she'd be sure to demand answers he couldn't give.

# CHAPTER 21

"*H*ester made you a cup of chamomile tea." Julia brought the tray into the second-floor family parlor where Mama had spent most of that Friday before the fire.

"Set it on the table." She tugged at a quilt arranged over her lap. "Such a brisk day. I'm glad you're home from the seamstress shop."

"I've been knitting socks for them here. Fabric is growing scarce. Folks wear more clothes made from homespun."

"If that's the worst circumstance of this war, we have no cause to complain." She coughed. "Seems I do better when I don't talk."

"Perhaps a sip of tea?" Once bronchitis took a good hold on her, Mama usually felt poorly about three weeks. She was halfway through. There was always a niggling fear that, one of these days, it could develop into a serious lung ailment.

She picked up the cup and saucer and sipped obediently. "That does help."

"How about some elixir?"

"I'll take it at five o'clock." She glanced at the mantel clock with a sigh. "Another hour."

Julia wandered restlessly to peer out the window at the dreary winter's day. Ash was considerate of her feelings always. A gentleman. He didn't often alter their plans. What was he doing?

Regardless, it didn't hurt to pray for him.

～

*A*sh pushed himself to his feet, aided by the rough bark of a mighty oak. He glanced at his pocket watch. Half past five. He'd fallen asleep an hour before. There'd been no sun to mark the afternoon shadows. Foggy haze covered the tops of trees, descending toward the river.

He gave Rosebud a handful of oats. "I'll not ask you to carry my weight. Let's get back to the road. Perhaps a wagon will come by." Rosebud tossed her head. Ash took that as an agreement. If no one stopped to help, they'd walk as far as they were able, then rest again. Walk and rest until total darkness fell.

He hadn't spotted any soldiers earlier along his route, nor did he have any incriminating evidence on him. Still, he kept watch as they ambled along the road.

They'd walked over a mile when the sound of wagon wheels cheered him. It was hard to say if dusk had fallen in the fog. Perhaps he'd be in luck that the traveler headed to Vicksburg.

"Ho, there." Ash held up his hand to hail the driver.

"Evenin' to you." The wagon rumbled to a stop. "Did your horse go lame?"

It was the gray-haired farmer that he and Julia had encountered on their romantic buggy ride outside Vicksburg, the man with piercing eyes under a wide-brimmed hat. He wore the same red wool shirt and gray trousers, with the addition of a long wool coat.

"No, just needs a good rest."

"I don't believe we've been introduced." They'd spoken briefly before but hadn't exchanged names.

"I deliver produce for me and my neighbors all around these parts." The farmer studied him as if with recognition. "You need a ride?"

"I'm bound for Vicksburg."

"I can get you within three miles. That suit you?"

Relief flooded him. "Much obliged." Not far from Confederate pickets who'd be more suspicious after dark. He'd take a forest path to avoid them.

"Let's get that mare of yours tied to the back." He jumped down with the energy of a man half his age. Streaks of brown in his gray beard suggested him to be at least in his mid-forties.

Ash led Rosebud to the back of the wagon.

"That limp looks pretty bad. You need to stretch out in the back?"

That sounded like heaven. It seemed rude not to sit and chat with the stranger, but his leg wouldn't hold him up much longer. "If it's not too much trouble." Ash secured his horse to the wagon.

"No trouble." He extracted a burlap sack. "Your horse need oats?"

"Fed her a while back." Ash's leg throbbed. He stared longingly at an empty spot among the crates and sacks just about long enough for him to stretch his leg.

"Here's something to hold you off until supper. It'll restore you." The farmer handed Ash a strip of jerky. He placed a handful in Ash's saddlebag. "Got more than I need. Keep this with you on journeys. Might help."

"Thanks." The man was as neighborly as any Ash had met in Mississippi. He was grateful for his matter-of-fact manner. "I am a mite hungry." He took a big bite. Either he was hungrier than normal or this man knew secrets for preparing jerky that his grocer didn't.

"Plenty of water in your canteen." The farmer tossed it to him. "Take a drink."

Ash eyed the stranger as he took a swig. His own father couldn't have anticipated his every need so well. "What did you say your name was?"

"Call me Michael."

"I'm Ash." If the stranger wasn't sharing his surname, he'd keep his own to himself too.

"I don't talk much, so it won't bother me none if you want to rest a spell. Need help getting in?"

He'd crawl before letting someone help him into that wagon. He sat and scooted until his back was against the seat. Blessed relief.

~

"Ash?"

A hand shook his shoulder.

Ash awoke refreshed from a deep sleep. He'd felt safer than he had since taking on spying responsibilities. "How long was I asleep? Where are we?"

"About three miles outside of Vicksburg."

"What?" Ash sat up and climbed over the side of the wagon. When his leg hit the ground, it buckled. He gripped the side of the wagon to steady himself. "How did we get here so quickly?"

"Old Nell may not look like much"—Michael chuckled—"but she can still pull a wagon with the best of them."

Ash glanced in every direction. No Confederate soldiers standing picket, but he'd take the forest path to be certain. "I'm obliged for the ride."

"If you ever need to rent a horse while on that stretch of

road, I know a couple who live twenty miles from Yazoo City. Dave Metzger is a blacksmith. Wife's name is Nancy. They've got two little boys."

That might be Ash's answer. "How do I find him?" Ash untied Rosebud.

Michael explained how to find the Metzger home. "He runs his blacksmith shop out of his barn. They have all the usual farm outbuildings. You can't miss it."

"Will they rent to a stranger?" Lots of folks didn't trust strangers these days...for good reason.

"Tell them Michael sent you." The farmer climbed onto the wagon seat. "Give them five dollars for their trouble each time. They're struggling same as most." The wheels creaked forward and picked up speed.

"Will do." Generous yet fair. "Thanks for your help," he called.

A sideways wave was his only response.

Shaking his head at the potential answer to his prayers, he turned to Rosebud. "You look rested. You didn't sleep as you ambled behind the wagon, did you, girl?"

The mare tossed her head.

"Let's get on home." Ash's leg protested, but he was able to mount. He guided Rosebud to the dark forested path, grateful beyond words for the kindness of a stranger.

~

*J*ulia studied Ash's pained expression as he drove the buggy away from Washington Hotel on Saturday evening. Despite the nip in the night air, he'd suggested a drive around the city. "Not too long." She hated to disappoint him. "Mama's still feeling poorly."

Mama hadn't felt well enough to greet Ash when he picked

up Julia but might be downstairs waiting when they returned. Ash had promised Eddie a game of draughts.

"I know." He sighed. "A short drive, then."

"Why didn't you come last night?"

"Let's talk in a few minutes." He kissed her gloved hand. "It's too dark for a drive outside the city—my first choice."

Not Julia's. Not since the soldiers had come. The loud laughter from two tables of them had made it difficult to concentrate on her own conversation.

"We'll drive up to the Sky Parlor."

"Sounds perfect." The stars shone clear and bright. She didn't mind the cold when she was with Ash.

He stopped the buggy at the top of the drive. There were only two carriages and a wagon already there. This boded well for finding a secluded area for their conversation.

He lifted her from the buggy and kept his hands on her waist. The love in his eyes made her gasp a moment before he lowered his mouth to hers, warming her lips. He had read her mind so completely that when he raised his lips a fraction, she smiled at him. He kissed her once more in the buggy's shadow.

He loved her. The knowledge was heady.

With his crutch for support, he held her hand as he limped. It was a slow stroll along the top of the hill, and they exchanged cordial greetings with neighbors and two other couples Julia didn't recognize.

Once they passed the others admiring the starry sky, Julia's curiosity got the best of her. "Can you tell me what happened?"

A sigh escaped as he stared out over murky waters and the wharves. "I took Rosebud for a ride, and I had to walk a good bit."

"How far?"

He grunted. "Reckon it doesn't take long to make this old leg of mine demand attention."

"That explains nothing." She placed her hands on her hips.

He turned away. "Not much more to say."

"You're keeping something from me."

He turned to face her. His hazel eyes smoldered. "We're at war."

"Not with each other!"

He said nothing, and anxiety swirled in her middle. "I will keep your secrets, Ash." She lowered her voice.

He rubbed his clean-shaven jaw. "I trust you. But I can't say anything more."

Where was he going when he left the city? She'd thought it was the tanner's house.

Julia glanced over her shoulder. Five soldiers, one of them holding a whiskey bottle, staggered across the hill toward them. "We need to get back to Mama. Eddie's waiting for you."

"Quite right." Ash offered his arm, veering them away from the soldiers.

"Eddie so loves the game you gave him." Julia prattled on about the gift, sensing Ash's tension. When they passed the soldiers, she kept gazing ahead.

Ash gave them a cordial nod. His crutch thumped against the grass. Finally, they reached the open buggy, and he aided her inside before climbing up next to her.

She spread a blanket over their knees. Was he so nervous because the soldiers were drinking?

Julia's thoughts were in turmoil on the drive back. His reaction to the soldiers was more than that of a Unionist toward the enemy. The soldiers had been a constant presence for months. As a resident of Vicksburg, Ash should be accustomed to their presence.

Something wasn't right.

# CHAPTER 22

*O*n his ride to Yazoo City the next Thursday, Ash was still troubled by Julia's need to know his activities. Just last week, he'd learned from Cal, one of his contacts, that a spy's wife had been jailed overnight because they suspected her husband of passing information. He'd broken her out of prison upon returning from a mission and moved the whole family to parts unknown.

For Julia's own safety, the less she knew, the better. Someday, he'd tell her everything. If they could get to someday.

By the end of the morning, he'd arranged to rent a horse every Friday from David Metzger, the blacksmith Michael suggested. Mr. Metzger would also stable and feed Rosebud. The whole thing would cost six dollars. A fair price, given the times.

The best thing was, he could accomplish the journey in one day.

Perhaps that would keep his overly curious mother from asking too many questions.

"*D*id you know Ash's birthday is March seventh?" Mrs. Mitchell drew Julia aside at her mother's "at home" on the last Thursday of February.

"He'll turn twenty-one." Julia had knitted him a red scarf that complemented his brown coat. He hadn't been free of late on Fridays, so she'd thought to invite him and his family over for supper on Saturday, the day after his birthday.

"I'm planning a small supper party for him the evening of his birthday. Of course, you and your family must come." Her eyes glowed as she spoke of inviting the Adairs, Felicity's family, and Caroline's beau, Peter Higgins. She'd also invite Matthew Boswell and John Pierce, foundry workers and casual friends of Ash's from church. "But mum's the word." Mrs. Mitchell wagged her finger. "This is to be a surprise."

Julia gave a smiling nod, though her mind swirled. Whatever Ash did on Fridays took a fair portion of the day. It wouldn't do to have a party for him when he walked in unsuspecting as guests waited, but she couldn't bear to spoil Mrs. Mitchell's joy in the occasion.

Sitting in her parlor with her family and Ash on Sunday afternoon, Julia was still torn about whether to tell him about the party. If he wasn't there at the start of the party, his mother would be humiliated. She didn't deserve that.

"Let me walk with you to the stable." Julia stepped onto the front porch after him and closed the door.

"I'd love that." He offered his arm, which she took.

She waited until they reached the sidewalk. "Ash, there's something I must warn you about."

His whole body stiffened. "What?"

"I hate to ruin your mother's surprise, but she's planned a party for your birthday on Friday. I know your plans sometimes take you away from home—"

"Julia, thank you." Relief washed over his features. "I'll pretend to be surprised. I promise."

~

*W*hile working on a saddle in his shop the following Thursday, Ash thanked God most fervently that Julia had warned him. If she hadn't, he would certainly have been late, and then everybody in attendance would know, or at least suspect, that he was keeping something from his mother. And all of them.

The party meant he couldn't take his weekly ride, nor could he get word to the blacksmith and grocer expecting him. He had the impression that the Metzgers welcomed his rental fee the past two weeks. When Ash explained what happened on his first journey to Yazoo City, Jim had added enough pay to cover the horse rental, making it worth Ash's aching leg once again.

Even without the funds, he'd have found a way to continue the rides. It was impossible to fathom what two separate countries would mean for future generations, a prospect that strengthened his resolve to continue this grueling and dangerous schedule.

"Ash?" Caroline pushed open his shop door. "Good. You're here today."

Her remark brought him up short. She was more observant than he'd realized. He'd decided that her best protection was ignorance of his activities, just as it was for Julia. "If I'm not out for supplies, I'm here, working hard."

"I reckon you have to go farther afield for supplies because so many items are growing scarce in the city." She sighed. "I can't find candles, so I'm after cottonseed oil for our lanterns today." She studied her clasped hands, but he caught her faint blush. "Among other things."

Ash smothered a grin. She was no doubt buying food for tomorrow's supper.

"Is there a limit to what I can spend?"

"How much do you figure on?"

"Most things cost more these days." She swallowed. "Thirty dollars?"

He blinked. That was nearly four times their weekly household expenses. "Costs have risen so much?" Thank heaven for his new route.

She nodded. "And we must restock the pantry..."

He rubbed his jaw. "This won't happen every week?"

"I should be able to keep weekly costs under ten dollars the rest of the month."

He stifled a groan. Just when he'd hoped he'd be able to save for the future...

He crossed to his cash box, hidden among his tools. "Here's thirty-five dollars. Make this last as long as you can." He regretted the birthday celebration already. "Don't put anything on credit. That's what hurts me most."

"I'll do my best. You coming in for lunch today? It's nearly ready."

He often ate a sandwich in his shop on busy days—and it helped mask his absences. "Yep." He slung his arm around her shoulder in a brief hug. "Thanks for working with me on the expenses." He opened the shop door and followed her out.

"Your limp seems more pronounced of late. And you've often used your crutch." She glanced at his leg. "Does it hurt?"

It ached fiercely after rides to Yazoo City. "Sometimes."

"I'll see if the druggist has liniment."

"If we have the money." His last bottle had been used up months hence.

"I'll make certain of it."

Their steps echoed on the cobblestone steps.

"When will Peter call again?"

Pink stained her cheeks. "I expect to see him soon."

Of course. Peter was invited to the party. Ash followed his sister inside the home and into the cozy parlor, where a fire burned low in the hearth.

"Ash, the most wonderful news." Mama waved a letter at him. "Caroline, you must hear this too."

"What is it?" He hadn't seen his mother this happy since... he couldn't remember. Before the war started.

"Your Uncle Clark is coming for a visit."

Caroline gasped. "Mama, that's wonderful. We haven't seen him since—"

"Our last visit to Texas was in 1854." Mama pointed to a line on the page. "Clark reminded me."

Eight years.

Ash knelt to build up the fire with a lighter heart. "I'll be pleased to see him again." His uncle was calmer, more level-headed than Mama. Ash's cousin Clark Junior had drowned attempting to cross a swollen river a year after their visit. According to Uncle Clark's letters, Aunt Agnes became a shell of her former self. Pneumonia took her in 1856. Since then, Uncle Clark had immersed himself into building up his ranch.

Fire roaring, Ash stood and regarded his excited mother, an elbow resting on the wood mantel.

"He's asked us to visit numerous times over the years." A smile touched Mama's lips as she scanned the page again. "Even asked me to bring my family out to live with him. I'd run his household. You know what a spacious home he's built."

Uncle Clark wanted them to move to Texas? This Ash hadn't heard. He met Caroline's shocked gaze before turning back to Mama. "When did this happen?"

"The first time was in 1858, after your father passed. I couldn't imagine such a thing, not back then. Now that soldiers prepare for battle in our very city..." Mama's hands fluttered. Her face crumpled. The letter fell to her lap.

Caroline knelt beside her and covered her shaking hands. "What is it, Mama?"

"I don't like what's happening. Store shelves nearly bare of necessities. Armed soldiers traipsing the streets. Saddle orders dwindling at Ash's shop." She raised dread-filled eyes to her daughter. "What's to become of us if we stay?"

Caroline turned a shocked face toward Ash.

He felt as if he'd been struck in the gut. "Mama, I didn't think those things bothered you."

"I thought my children could handle the changes better if I pretended everything was normal." She shook her head. "I can't pretend any more. Your uncle has offered the safety of his home. I think we should accept it."

Straightening, Caroline turned to face the fire, her expression anxious.

"I can't leave Vicksburg." Ash's head reeled. Julia, the saddle shop, his home...his spying. All that tied him here like an unbroken cord.

"I thought you might say that." Mama sighed. "And I don't blame you, what with Julia... What would you think if your sisters and I return with him?"

It certainly answered his dilemma about Mama's curiosity of his absences, but he'd not be so selfish to agree for that reason alone.

Yet they'd be safe with his uncle. Ash rubbed his jaw. "Let me pray about it."

# CHAPTER 23

*J*ulia sat before a crackling fire in the Mitchells' front parlor, surrounded by Savannah, Felicity, Caroline, and Daphne. Mama, Mrs. Mitchell, and the rest of the older women selected sheet music beside the piano at the back of the room. Thankfully, Mama had recovered her stamina days before, with no sign of recurrence.

Pride in her beau, so handsome in his brown coat and trousers and favorite red vest as he stood chatting with male guests near the doorway, swelled up in Julia. He'd done a credible job at feigning surprise, his grace and manners always that of a fine Southern gentleman. Supper had been delicious, all the more enjoyable because no one brought up the latest battle or war news.

Mrs. Mitchell lightly clapped her hands, and all conversation stopped. "We'll begin with two waltzes, and then Martha will favor us with some reels."

Ash crossed to Julia's side. No crutch, and his limp was less noticeable this evening. He bowed. "May I have this dance, Miss Dodd?"

"You may, Mr. Mitchell." She curtsied, enjoying his formality to begin the dancing.

Peter bowed before a blushing Caroline.

Charles led his wife, Mae, out onto the floor as if he accompanied royalty.

John Pierce approached Felicity while Matthew Boswell bowed before Savannah.

With so many Vicksburg men away at war—and another company of new recruits leaving for camp tomorrow—there was a shortage of young bachelors. Julia silently congratulated Mrs. Mitchell for evening out the numbers for dancing.

Matt had brought his fifteen-year-old brother, Stephen. The boy didn't seem to fit in with the older men, and Julia had worried he'd be too bashful to dance. However, he crossed the parlor toward fourteen-year-old Daphne. She gestured to the seat next to hers. When Stephen slumped into it as if he'd been saved from a fate worse than death, Julia held back a giggle.

Eddie summoned both of them to a corner table where puzzle pieces were spread.

Ash led her to the makeshift dance floor. The first few steps began hesitantly, as they usually did until some of the stiffness worked its way from Ash's leg. Julia didn't mind one whit, not with his hand clasping hers.

∼

It was after eleven when Ash went with John and Matt for refreshments. Dancing had ended, and the ladies were talking. Tea cakes, lemon cookies, and sliced sandwiches were arranged across the dining room table. The buffet held a beverage tray with a bowl of milk punch and a teapot with cups.

"Thanks for having a birthday today," Matt teased as he

shoved a whole cookie into his mouth. Crumbs slid down his brown beard.

"My pleasure." Ash chuckled.

John, a short man with prematurely thinning brown hair, helped himself to sandwiches.

"Didn't you eat supper?" Matt pointed to the heaping plate.

"I live in a boarding house. My landlady feeds us fellows as though our stomachs were the size of little Eddie's. I eat whenever given half a chance."

"Mama likes to see a man with a healthy appetite." Ash clapped John on the back.

"Sure was a shame about losing Fort Henry and Fort Donelson last month." Matt shook his head.

The Confederacy had sustained tough blows in February with the fall of Fort Henry on the Tennessee River on the sixth. Fort Donelson surrendered ten days later. It was a source of satisfaction that Ash had passed along information about Confederate troops around those Tennessee forts before they fell.

"It was." John spoke between bites. "Bigger shame was when we lost Nashville."

"Agreed." Confederate soldiers had surrendered the city on February twenty-third. Vicksburg was attracting too much Union attention to escape unscathed, and the possibility of battle here filled Ash with trepidation for his loved ones. Soldiers continued to strengthen their city's fortifications. Perhaps it was best his mother and sisters go to Texas with Uncle Clark.

Peter entered the dining room and filled a plate with sweets.

"What the Union did after Nashville fell was an affront." Matt's face darkened.

"How so?" John's forehead wrinkled.

"Them varmints marched into the city, right up to the

capitol building." Matt clenched a fist. "They set up camp on the grounds."

"I heard that." Peter licked sugar from his fingers. "Our Southern citizens watched, horrified, from the banks of the Cumberland River."

"Shameful," Ash lied. His heart sank at the disgust on Peter's face. Seemed as though he'd discovered where the man's loyalties lodged.

"They took Tennessee's capital." Scarlet spread up John's neck to his face. "But they're not taking any more of our capital cities."

Matt cheered. "That's right. We'll give 'em what for."

Ash forced a smile of agreement.

Groaning, John put down his plate.

"Think you finally got filled up?" Ash was glad to steer the conversation elsewhere. Their disgust about recent Union victories strengthened his resolve to continue facing danger. He and the other spies were making a difference.

~

"Your mother seems quite excited about the possibility of living in Texas." Julia studied Ash's face as they ate in a quaint restaurant away from the center of town a week later. Among the dozen tables, five were occupied by soldiers. One could not escape them these days.

"Yes. She's happier than she's been in years." He ate a bite of pork chop before continuing. "Our mayor worries that martial law in Memphis and New Orleans will drive thieves, swindlers, and the like to Vicksburg. Our population has swelled so that there are strangers everywhere. The militia has to help the police patrol the idle mobs."

"And they're moving all the cotton out of the city." The city council now prohibited cotton to be stored within the city. The intention was to burn the valuable commodity if necessary. Such as if the Union army attacked. Julia shivered at the possibility.

"Exactly." Ash spoke quietly in the midst of the loud soldiers' conversation. "Though it's good the mayor has made stores selling liquor close early every day. It's helped maintain the peace, but Mama will still feel safer elsewhere. I've had a letter from Uncle Clark. Whether simply for the duration of the war or as a permanent home, he wants all of us to come."

Julia nearly choked on a roasted carrot. The thought of Ash living in Texas struck with the force of a blade.

"I'm not going. I didn't mean to frighten you." He glanced around the room. "Have you and your mama considered staying at her family plantation for a few months?"

"No." Bitterness lodged in her heart. "My grandparents are dead, and I doubt my uncles would welcome us." They didn't want her any more than her grandfather had. Maybe they'd care about Eddie, who'd someday own land adjoining theirs.

Compassion and sorrow clouded Ash's hazel eyes, making them smoky. "I didn't mean to cause you pain."

"It's all right." By now, she was almost used to the fact that her grandfather and her parents had amply provided for Eddie with no thought for her.

He reached across the table.

"Papa's neglect hurts worse. I believed he thought more of me." She squeezed his hand and then let it go as soldiers from the next table glanced their way.

"He adored you. I remember the pride in his face when he looked at you."

Tears pricked her eyes. She'd thought the same. It was comforting to know she hadn't been wrong about his love for her. "Mama still thinks my only option is to marry a wealthy man."

~

*A*sh's heart plummeted. All of Julia's former suitors had fit that requirement. Not him. Apparently, it would still take years to build his shop to the level her mother wanted. His chair squeaked as he drew back. "Tell me plainly. Is that what you want?"

"No." She held his troubled gaze.

"I'm working for our future." They loved each other. He'd find a way to satisfy Mrs. Dodd. He must.

"I believe you." Looking into his eyes, she clasped his hand.

Silence descended as they resumed their meal. Julia picked at hers.

He hated that her family hadn't provided for her, but he planned to see she had everything she needed after their marriage.

"Did your uncle say when he'd be here?" Julia asked.

"Next month. And there was good news." He'd initially intended to see if Julia's family could leave Vicksburg and escape the fight he was now certain was coming. That had only hurt her. He was glad to change the topic. "Uncle Clark has given me my biggest saddle order yet. I'm to make saddles for him and all his ranch hands." He'd provided the height and stature of each man. "He's also asked for side saddles for Mama and my sisters."

"A bit premature on that one, right?" Julia pushed her half-full plate away.

"Mama's nearly ready to agree. Daphne wants to wait until summer to leave." He ate the last bite of pork.

"Does Caroline want to stay for Peter's sake?"

He shook his head. "Peter joined a Louisiana regiment that was stopping through the city early this week. He left with them yesterday."

By the surprise on her face, she hadn't heard. "Is Caroline devastated?"

"She's unhappy. I hope a potential move to Texas will distract her." The reasons mounted for his family to leave for the remainder of the war. Uncle Clark's arrival in early April was most welcome, indeed.

He'd rest even easier if Julia could head to her family in South Carolina. But that door was closed. Her safety remained on his shoulders.

~

*O*n the following Sunday, Julia sat in her family's formal dining room between Ash and Caroline. Hers and Ash's families had attended church together.

"Louise, have you made a decision about moving to Texas?" Mama studied her expression as she sliced a piece of steaming chicken pie.

"I believe so." She looked at her daughters. "I'm increasingly anxious about the atmosphere in our city."

Daphne shifted in her seat.

Caroline eyed the peas as if they'd roll off her plate without her supervision. Were her thoughts on Peter?

"Yes, there is tension in the air." Mama sighed. "I can't like all the soldiers about town...though we most assuredly are safer for their presence."

"That's it exactly. There haven't been any soldiers near my brother's ranch." Mrs. Mitchell's shoulders relaxed. "Clark will arrive next Tuesday, April first. We'll have a family supper that evening we hope you'll attend." Mrs. Mitchell sipped her coffee. "You'll want to meet him. He's a jovial soul."

"We'd love to come."

Hester and Daisy entered to clear the table for dessert, a cherry cobbler made from canned fruit.

After the meal ended, Eddie and Ash went outside. Her mama and Mrs. Mitchell settled in the parlor with a cup of tea.

Julia turned to Ash's sisters. "Sit with me on the veranda?"

They went outside to enjoy the pleasantly warm sunshine. Ash and Eddie tossed a ball in the orchard, out of earshot.

"How do you feel about moving?" Julia asked.

"I don't remember much about the ranch." Daphne played with the lace trim around the sleeve of her yellow print dress. "Ash told me I'll probably ride horses daily. That's what he remembers most."

"I'm torn." Caroline pushed the brim of her straw hat down her forehead so that it shaded her eyes. "I love Mississippi. My home. I'd miss Ash something fierce."

"Will the cook stay?" Ash was so busy with other tasks, he'd likely starve otherwise.

"Jolene's a widow and Lucy, our maid, is a spinster. Lucy asked to go with us. Mama's considering it. She'll have to ask Uncle Clark, of course."

Two unmarried women couldn't live in the same house with just Ash. This was a problem.

"Jolene said Joseph Hutchins has been courting her for nigh a year." Daphne settled back against the metal seat. "He works at the Reading Foundry."

"If they marry, he'll share her room off the kitchen." Caroline sighed. "Otherwise, she must find another place to live while working for us. Or Ash will hire a woman whose husband is off at war to cook for him five days a week."

"I want to know about our rooms and what we'll do each day." Daphne's gaze settled on pedestrians strolling down the sidewalk as if she didn't see them. "Mama will manage my uncle's household. Will he expect us to be maids?"

Good questions. They needed to know what was expected of them. "Will you miss Peter very much, Caroline?"

"It was pleasant to receive his attentions. If he wants to write me, I will reply. But I think the correspondence won't last."

A very mature attitude. Julia was impressed with both sisters.

"Everything's changing. Too quickly." Caroline rose restlessly. "A year ago, I wouldn't have imagined our city would ever consider burning its store of precious cotton."

"I didn't think we'd ever live two states away." Daphne frowned. "But I don't believe I shall mind it."

Julia didn't think she'd ever be penniless. Caroline was right. Everything had changed.

~

*A*sh made his run to Harvey's Mill in Brownsville on Monday, the day before Uncle Clark's train was due, and was back that evening for his first patrol of the city with a newly formed squad with Matt and John. Men not members of a company were encouraged to form into squads to assist police efforts. For Ash, helping to maintain order gave him an opportunity to serve the community he loved.

He awoke the next morning with a stiff leg from yesterday's ride and last night's street patrol duty. Looked as though he'd meet his uncle sporting a crutch.

Ash waited on the wharf for the man's arrival. The Mississippi River divided the railroad tracks between Louisiana and Mississippi. Cars and passengers were transported by ferries across the river. A broad-shouldered man of medium height scanned the crowd, waving when he spotted Ash.

"Uncle Clark." His crutch thumped on the gravel as he strode to his uncle, palm extended.

Dropping a stuffed carpet bag to the gravel, Clark Farmer shook his hand in a firm, strong grasp. "Ash. I'd know you anywhere. You have the look of your pa."

That observation choked him up. He didn't often hear anyone speak of his father. "I'm proud to know it."

"Your mama and sisters here?" The brown-haired man with a smattering of gray at the temples peered over his shoulder.

"Everyone's waiting at home. My buggy's tied to that hitching post." He pointed. "Where's your trunk?"

"I brought a small one. Figured the womenfolk would have lots of trunks on the return journey. I'll fetch it."

Ash stowed the surprisingly heavy carpetbag in his buggy. The Texan was back within five minutes, and the horses were soon climbing the cobblestone street.

"Your mama wrote that you had some questions. Might as well get them out of the way."

"Let's wait on that. The girls and Mama want to hear everything." Although Ash liked Uncle Clark's direct manner. "How was your trip?"

"The train journey wasn't a problem. I got on it in Monroe, Louisiana. That's where the tracks begin."

"How'd you get from your ranch on the Neebes River to Monroe?"

"My foreman drove me in my wagon to Marion. I took a stagecoach from there."

"Is that how you'll return?"

"Yep. We'll need two wagons, maybe three. I suspect Louise will want to bring half the furnishings in her house." He grinned.

Ash laughed. The man knew his sister.

"My ranch hands will meet us in Marion. I'll send a telegram when I know what we'll need."

"You sound like a man who knows how to take charge." Ash admired the kind authority in his voice.

"Ranch owners gotta know how to be the boss. If you don't, you learn fast. How long before my saddles are done?"

"Most will be ready to leave with you after Easter. I'll ship the rest by the first week of May."

Clark gave a satisfied nod. "That suits me fine. I'll pay for everything before I leave."

"I'm obliged for the orders. Mama said the ranch has grown."

"Five thousand acres."

Ash whistled.

"Not as big as most, but big enough for me to feel good about it. Seven hundred fifty-six longhorns. That's enough for my foremen's crew to handle. Might need to hire another ranch hand next year."

"Impressive."

"Thank you, son. Sure you won't come with us?"

Tempting. A real job, a chance to be a ranch hand. Yet he couldn't go, nor could he explain that he was serving the Union as a spy. That was too important to stop midstream. Ash shook his head. "Too much keeping me here."

~

"You said you wanted me to manage your staff." Mama took a dainty bite from her ham sandwich, her gaze riveted on her brother sitting at the foot of the dining table, with Ash at his habitual chair at the head. "How many maids do you have?"

"One maid. One housekeeper." Uncle Clark stuffed the last bite of his sandwich in his mouth and then picked up a spoon for his vegetable soup. "A cook and a scullery maid."

"I can manage that many."

Uncle Clark nodded. "My housekeeper is more a follower than a leader. She wants me to give her daily jobs each morning, which I hate."

"I prefer it that way."

Indeed, that should be easy for Ash's mother. She'd enjoy the challenge of a new place.

"What will Caroline and I do all day?" Daphne asked, blunt and to the point.

"I'll hire a tutor for your schooling. We do a lot of riding. Do you like horses?"

"Oh, yes."

"I got a corral full of them. Of course, the ranch hands have their favorites." He grinned. "We'll pick out a couple of gentle mounts to get you girls started."

Daphne bounced in her chair. "What else?"

"We ride into town for supplies once a week."

"Do you have neighbors?"

"Yep. Two families within ten miles of my place."

Caroline paled. "Ten miles?"

"I knew you'd be happy they live so close." His plate empty, he started on his coffee. "There's a church in town. We'll go every Sunday it's not storming. We can eat at a restaurant while we're there, or else you'll be mighty hungry by the time we get home."

"How long is the drive?" Caroline tilted her head.

"Just over an hour." He rubbed his cleanly shaven chin. "More like an hour and a half, I reckon, if we take it leisure-like in the wagon."

"Quite a change from what they're used to." Ash wanted this to be a considered—and he hoped a unanimous—decision. "What about shops?"

"There's at least a general store in every town. Post offices, restaurants, dry goods stores, feed stores...oh, a millinery shop opened in Sumpter last year. And there's a woman who does seamstress work."

"I remember riding good distances everywhere we went." Mama nodded. "We stayed a month, and I grew accustomed to the routine."

Mama wasn't scared away by the lonely picture Uncle Clark had painted. Daphne looked intrigued. Caroline was harder to read.

"We have church picnics and potluck suppers and dances almost every month." Uncle Clark's smile dimmed. "And you'll be safe there." He studied his empty plate. "A man gets lonely without seeing family. Even if other folks you care about are around."

Ash's breath hitched. This then was the crux of the matter.

He was satisfied they'd be cared for. Cherished. They had his blessing to go.

# CHAPTER 24

"A few more bites." Julia coaxed a young soldier with a bandaged arm to finish the cup of nourishing beef broth. It was the second of April and her first day volunteering at the Ladies' Hospital Association.

"That's enough, Miss Dodd." The man's eyes glazed in his feverish face. "Think I'll sleep now. Thank you kindly."

"My pleasure." She carried the cup to a private room off the ward, where Mrs. Ebbing measured powders into a spoon. "Zechariah ate half a cup of broth."

"Good work, Julia. That's more than he ate all of yesterday." The pretty mother of two gestured a bucket. "Please take the water bucket around both wards."

Julia stopped to speak with each patient as they drank from the dipper. She went home tired but pleased to help.

She was unprepared for the wounded arriving a few days later from a battle at Shiloh, some three hundred miles from Vicksburg. She learned that Ash and his uncle were among those who carried wounded from cars in the pouring rain to wagons bound for hospitals and homes.

At the hospital, Julia washed hands and faces, rinsed bloodied rags, and offered water from a dipper to groaning—sometimes dying—men.

"I brought your medicine, Mr. Hoover." Julia knelt beside a soldier about her age with a bloodied bandage wrapped around his head. "It should relieve your headache."

"Thank you, Miss Dodd." He swallowed the morphine. "If it's not too much trouble, will you pray for me?"

"It will be my privilege." The surgeon couldn't remove shrapnel from his head. He wasn't expected to live. Julia knelt and prayed. The soldier was asleep when she stood.

"That was a mighty powerful prayer."

Julia, fighting waves of sorrow, turned. "Mr. Farmer, I didn't expect to see you here." What was Ash's uncle doing here?

"I've a bit of experience dressing wounds, administering medicine. Need help?"

"We'll accept whatever aid you can give." She placed a hand on her throat, suddenly tight with gratitude.

"Let's get to it, then."

～

*J*ulia, exhausted from too many days with little rest, helped her mother host a party on Easter for the Mitchell women's last day in Vicksburg.

Mrs. Mitchell's closest friends had been invited to luncheon, and Hester outdid herself for the occasion. The rest of the many guests came and went throughout the afternoon to bid the Mitchells farewell. Several hinted that they'd not be long behind in leaving Vicksburg.

After seeing so many wounded soldiers at the hospital, Julia couldn't fault their decision to leave. She had worked long hours for several days and then dreamed that no matter what she did, it was never enough. For a few days, that nightmare was a reality.

Shiloh was far too close for comfort. And a bombardment on New Orleans by Union gunboats had begun on April eighteenth. Good Friday hadn't been a good day for either side. It was reported that a chain of soldiers had stretched between Fort Jackson and Fort St. Philip on either side of the Mississippi River, effectively halting the Union's advance.

The whole situation was frightening. Thank goodness, Ash's family was going to a safer place. Mama's refusal to approach her brothers for help made things more difficult for their own family. Yet they'd spoken ill of Julia's father before her parents' marriage, words that stood between the siblings to this day.

Caroline became emotional as she stood alone in the parlor after saying goodbye to a neighbor. "Let's go out on the veranda. I believe our brothers are outside."

Ash joined them, patting his sister's shoulder. "Are you all right?"

"Most of my friends came today." Caroline dabbed her eyes with a handkerchief. "I didn't talk to anyone long enough."

"We shall write to one another faithfully." This goodbye was going to be difficult for Julia as well. "You must tell me of ranch life."

"I promise." As Caroline stood and greeted approaching guests, Ash bent closer to Julia.

"How are you?"

"Fine." Though in truth, she had not recovered from long days at the hospital. Her fingers entwined with his. Thank heavens he wasn't moving to Texas. She relied on his strength now more than ever.

~

227

*A*sh rode the eastbound train to Bolton on Monday morning at the same time his family rode the westbound train. Tearful hugs from his sisters and his mother had wrenched his heart. The goodbyes were all the more difficult for not knowing when he'd see them again.

Now, Uncle Clark wasn't the one without family around, Ash was.

He had Julia and her family. God willing, they'd be his family someday soon. The war left him precious few hours to contemplate the future.

Mama's most expensive items, including half the silver and all her wedding gifts smaller than a hatbox, were on their way to Texas. Daphne's and Caroline's rooms contained little more than a bed. Income from his deliveries had covered his family's journey and given his mother funds to prevent a total dependency on her brother.

Uncle Clark had hired Lucy to work at the ranch. Three new additions to the household warranted another maid.

Mama had hired a soldier's wife, Mrs. Anthony, to clean Ash's home two days a week. Ash didn't know her and hoped she wasn't the nosy type who'd be curious about him being away from his shop. His cipher had been burned weeks ago. Ciphered messages stowed in his room needed a new hiding place. He'd tell the maid to come on Tuesdays and Thursdays so she wouldn't discover his weekly trips.

Surprisingly, their cook, Jolene, was now Mrs. Hutchins. Joseph Hutchins moved into her bedroom off the kitchen immediately following the ceremony. Joseph worked long hours at the foundry, so he wouldn't witness the comings and goings at Ash's shop. A man who made artillery to supply the Confederacy probably supported the South.

Best keep an eye on that situation as well and replace one or both employees if necessary.

The Battle of Shiloh had been a terrible tragedy all around, but it had solved one of Ash's biggest worries during his uncle's visit. Uncle Clark had spent hours caring for the wounded at the hospital, allowing Ash the freedom to make his runs. Unfortunately, there were more Confederate soldiers surrounding Vicksburg. They'd stopped him once, and his explanation of obtaining supplies for his business satisfied them.

The ciphered messages in his boot dealt with the number of Confederate troops now in Vicksburg and Southern regiments defending the continued bombardment of Fort Jackson and Fort St. Philip in New Orleans by Union gunboats, so it was imperative he deliver them today.

Ash wanted a Union victory, of course, but the thought of the Union fleet heading up the Mississippi toward Vicksburg tied his stomach in knots.

◦

*J*ulia walked to the seamstress shop on Monday morning, her heart aching for Ash. His mother and sisters were even now on a westbound train in Louisiana. Her beau had some adjustments to make in his daily life.

A little bell rang when Julia pushed open the door. "Good morning, Felicity."

"Good morning." Felicity sewed a dress from homespun fabric at a table by the window.

Heavy footsteps clumped down the stairs and then across the kitchen at the back of the shop before Mrs. Cummings appeared through the rear door. "Julia, how lovely to see you." The plump woman clasped her hands. "I'll never forget how you sewed all those months for our brave soldiers. Volunteered your services. Great is your reward in heaven, dear child."

Julia flushed at the effusive praise. "I apologize for not helping—"

"You've done plenty, child. Plenty." Mrs. Cummings beamed at her. "Now, did you come to order a dress for you or your mama? Trousers for Eddie? Little boys do go through the clothes, don't they?"

"Yes, ma'am, that's true of Eddie." Did she have the courage to try and sell her lace in front of Felicity? "No, I came to sew."

"No need of that, my dear." Mrs. Cummings waved a dismissive hand. "We're almost out of fabric. I'm weaving homespun on my loom upstairs while Felicity sews the few orders we can fill. If there's nothing else, I'll get myself back to my loom. That cloth won't weave itself."

"Mrs. Cummings?"

She halted at the doorway to the kitchen. "Yes?"

"I have six yards of lace I'd be happy to sell you." She reached into her basket for the delicate roll. "I have another six yards in another pattern—"

"No one's trimming homespun with lace." The seamstress barely glanced at it. "Best hold onto it until folks get back to work or the war ends, whichever comes first."

All that work for nothing. Julia's heart sank. Miss Wind now lived in Kentucky. Mama knew all the other seamstresses, and they were sure to tell her if Julia attempted to sell to them. "Thank you." She waited until the seamstress left and then sat opposite Felicity.

"When did you begin selling lace?" Felicity quirked an eyebrow.

"A few months ago." Sighing, Julia told her about Miss Wind.

"Is this income for your future with Ash?" Felicity pushed a needle into the indigo fabric and set it aside.

Julia nodded. "Mama doesn't believe his shop will support

us. Making lace could help us—if only there were a market for it."

"No doubt." Felicity slumped back in her seat. "Mrs. Cummings is right about the homespun. She has little money to spend on lace and trim, I'd wager."

"I won't stop. Times *will* change." Julia squared her shoulders. "One thing—please don't tell anyone. If word got back to Mama..."

"I understand. She won't hear it from me."

"Thank you. And if you hear of someone who needs lace, please tell me."

"Count on it."

"Any news from Luke?"

"They've had another reorganization. The Twenty-first Mississippi mustered in over six hundred men for it." She sighed. "The army rejected his request for a month's furlough."

Julia comforted her friend the best she could before she left, determined to use the time for tatting. When jobs returned, she'd have a supply in several patterns ready.

~

*J*ulia headed toward the heart of the city on the last Friday of April to purchase items for the food baskets.

Pedestrians crowded street corners, their attention toward the river. Soldiers in gray milled about, but not much was happening on the Mississippi that she could discern. No, folks were looking toward the depot. Why?

"Julia, did you hear?" The slender blond grocer's wife stepped from behind the counter.

"What is it?"

Carrie Holmberg waved her hands. "Sallie Ayers received a

telegram from her cousin in New Orleans. General Mansfield Lovell expects New Orleans to fall into enemy hands." A slight Swedish accent colored her tones.

Julia's heart skipped a beat. Was her family safe? Was Ash aware?

"General Lovell has started sending troops and supplies from New Orleans."

Julia gasped. "You're joking." The general must indeed believe her city to be the Union's next target.

"Linda Dindzans was in, and a telegram from her nephew confirmed it. She said to expect gunpowder, cannons, rifles, and ammunition."

Julia's head spun.

"Soldiers will likely take the cannons to the bluffs to protect the city."

An attack must be imminent. Julia's drumming heartbeat felt as loud as a military band.

Mrs. Holmberg wrung her hands. "I wish Einer wasn't off fighting the war. It's frightening to face this danger alone."

"If you're afraid with your husband gone, stay with my family until the threat passes."

"Thank you. Deborah Sprinkle already offered. She stopped by before lunch." She craned her neck to stare out the window. "I'll keep my children in our apartment above the shop as long as I can. Einer's parents live in Bovina."

A train stop ten miles from Vicksburg. "You should be safe there."

"I believe so. What can I get for you? Buy it while you can. Folks may panic when—if—New Orleans surrenders."

Julia made her selections, her mind in turmoil. She didn't like to disturb Ash at his saddle shop, but today's news warranted it.

∾

*L*ater that day, Ash waited for a young mother and her family, all dressed in homespun, to finish shopping at Elijah Spencer's store. He picked up a strip of jerky as if contemplating a purchase while Eli, carrying a full crate, followed them outside to their wagon.

Wheels creaked as the wagon picked up speed on the dirt road. The grocer stepped inside, closing the door after him.

"Got plenty of flour?" Ash questioned.

"I can spare a pound." Eli cleared his throat.

Ash regarded the man he'd learned to trust in past several weeks. "Something on your mind?"

"What news do you have of New Orleans?"

"Situation's getting hotter. They're taking fire from Union mortar boats." Ash handed him a bill wrapped around coded messages.

"Think they're coming for Vicksburg next?" Eli scooped flour onto a scale.

Ash's gut clenched to hear his fear spoken aloud. "I believe so."

"Will you continue deliveries?" Eli asked in a lower voice.

"As long as possible. I'm only assured of a fresh mount on Fridays." Ash rubbed his chin. "I'll ask if that's changed and let you know when I'm in next."

Because he had a terrible feeling news would soon come at a fevered pitch.

~

*T*he door to Ash's workshop was closed in the middle of the afternoon. Julia knocked, then pressed her ear to the wood. No sounds of pounding or stitching or stretching leather to fit over padding. The knob refused to budge.

Locked. Where was her beau?

Julia, her anxiety growing, returned to the sidewalk and surveyed Ash's home. She needed his strength. His mere presence calmed her agitation.

She turned at footsteps on the sidewalk behind her. "Good afternoon, Jolene."

"Miss Dodd." The cook patted the high neck of her plain blue dress. A snood covered brown hair fashioned into a bun. No apron, a nearly integral part of a cook's dress. "Mr. Ash didn't tell me to expect you."

"He didn't know I was coming. Is he here?"

"He's gone all day every Friday."

So it was every Friday. Julia's heart sank.

"I feed him breakfast and pack him a lunch. Since he doesn't want his supper ready before seven, I took the liberty of a day off, what with Mrs. Mitchell living in Texas now." Jolene's glance fell, pink staining her cheeks.

"Can't say as I blame you for taking some hours for your own needs." Perhaps she expected Julia to chastise her. "What's it like with the women of the house gone?"

"Well, I don't mind telling you, my job got a lot easier. Mr. Ash eats supper with you Saturdays and Sundays. The rest of the evenings, he eats alone in the family dining room."

Julia's heart went out to her beau. He must miss his family.

"Miss Caroline and Miss Daphne used to try their hand at cooking on Sundays, my day off, but I can't say they ever got good at it."

"I see." Julia rather liked the woman's blunt manner. "Do you like Mrs. Anthony?"

"Not so's you can tell it." Her lips thinned. "She demands a special menu for the days she works. Can't say I'm impressed with her cleaning job none either. She's taking advantage of a man who doesn't know she ain't doing it proper-like."

Julia sighed. Something else she'd need to discuss with Ash. Another was their city's safety. She prayed he'd tell her there was nothing to fret over—and mean it.

# CHAPTER 25

The next day, Ash still had four more saddles to make to complete Uncle Clark's order. It required every free moment he had if he was going to send them out on the train by May ninth. He'd already told Julia he'd only see her on Sundays the next two weeks.

Booted steps on the sidewalk drew his gaze to his open door. Four soldiers peered in at him. His heart nearly stopped before thundering against his ribs. Were they here to arrest him for spying?

He stood. "Afternoon, fellas. Pleasant day."

No one spoke, nor did they step inside.

Reminding himself to remain calm, Ash took a couple of strides closer. "Anything I can do for you?" He prayed the soldiers weren't here for saddles, for he'd not relish working with their unfriendly ways—although that would be a sight preferable to an arrest.

They merely looked around his shop without speaking. Ash stiffened. They meant to intimidate him. Why?

After what felt like a quarter hour but was likely mere seconds, they walked on. Slowly.

He waited until their footsteps faded and then sat. Who were they? Was that a warning? Or had they simply been new troops from New Orleans, curious about Vicksburg citizens?

~

*A*sh understood why all the talk at lunch after church the following Sunday was of the soldiers and supplies coming into Vicksburg. Everyone feared what it meant for their city.

"What do you think, Ash?" Julia asked.

There was nothing to be gained by masking the coming danger. "To send soldiers to us in the midst of their own battle, they must be certain New Orleans will fall." General Lovell had a force of around three thousand in New Orleans. Those soldiers outside his shop were likely part of those new troops in Vicksburg. They hadn't returned, nor were they at church, but someone must suspect something to treat a fellow Southerner in such a way. Ash focused on Eddie's worried expression. The boy deserved the full truth. "General Lovell sending artillery and soldiers to protect Vicksburg means he fears the Union navy is heading here soon."

"Don't we want Union soldiers to come rescue us?" The boy's freckled brow wrinkled.

"It's not that simple." He met the boy's confused gaze squarely. "There might be a battle here. I don't want anyone to get hurt."

"Don't worry." Eddie sat straighter in his seat. "I'll watch Mama and Julia while you work."

"Good man." Ash placed his linen napkin beside his empty dessert plate. "I regret leaving so soon, but I've yet to complete my uncle's order."

Julia stiffened. "I had thought to take a quiet stroll together."

"I'm sorry. I'll be working late into the evening as it is. Let me take you to supper on Saturday." Ash didn't want to let his uncle down, especially since he had to arrange for a wagon to meet the train in Louisiana.

"I suppose I must be content with that." She stood without looking at him.

It was impolite to leave so quickly. Ash vowed to make it up to her.

~

*W*hen Ash arrived at Jim's farm the next morning, his friend stalked across the yard, beckoning for him to follow. "The Confederates got another of our spies." They were barely inside the door.

"Where?"

"Tennessee. This one was missing three days before we figured out where she was."

Ash's jaw dropped. "You have a woman rider?"

"More than one. Two of our spies are trying to rescue her now."

"Think she talked?"

"No idea. Watch yourself." Jim handed him a page of coded messages. "Don't spend too much time with me or any of your spies." He opened the door for him.

Ash kept a keen eye out for strangers on the ride to Harv's. The mill owner sped him on his way as usual. A handful of riders and only one wagon passed him on the road, driven by a boy of perhaps twelve. Raising his hat, Ash gave him a friendly nod.

He was at the Bolton depot when he realized he forgot to buy leather. No help for it now. Every seat in the first car was filled with gray-clad soldiers staring straight ahead, as if they'd endured an ordeal.

Pushing his hat lower on his forehead, he made his way down the aisle. Some military men gave him a nod that Ash returned with a casual "How do you do?"

His smile might have looked as forced as it felt. He was supposed to be happy more Confederates were coming to defend his city. Truth was, the more troops that came, the more unlikely the city was to surrender without a fight.

Surrender meant no one would be killed, citizen or soldier. It sped the end of war, always his goal.

Troops occupied the first few seats of the next car. Ash meandered past them to where the townspeople and farmers sat. He chose a seat upwind of the goat that stood in the back aisle.

Wheels clanking across the tracks smothered a whispered conversation between a middle-aged couple. Soldiers exchanged a few words now and then that Ash was too far away to overhear.

The train chugged into Vicksburg before five. Ash respectfully waited for soldiers to exit. Wagons, crates, boxes, and barrels were stacked in the station yard. Even the cows were driven from the stock car before he rose from his seat. He allowed the farmer to pass with his goat in tow and ended up as the last person off in a continuing, slow exit. What was the delay?

A soldier of average height stopped him after he disembarked. "Got a military pass?"

"No, sir." First time he'd been asked for one. Nor had he been questioned at the Bolton depot.

"What's your name, fella?"

"Ashburn Mitchell." His gut churned.

"What's your business in Vicksburg?" The steely-eyed bearded man in his late twenties held his gaze.

"I've lived here all my life."

"Occupation?"

"Saddler. I own a saddle shop."

"Why did you travel today?"

"I needed supplies for my shop."

"Where are they?"

Sweat beaded on Ash's forehead. "Everything's getting scarce. I'll have to go back."

The soldier rubbed his chin without taking his eyes off Ash.

He forced himself not to look away while his heart hammered against his ribs. What a terrible day to forget his purchase.

"Apply to the provost marshal for a pass to travel in and out of Vicksburg. Move along." The soldier crossed the bustling yard and disappeared into the crowd.

Ash wasted no time striding from the train yard to the provost marshal's office. Obtaining business supplies was an acceptable reason to travel, and Ash left with a pass in his pocket.

He'd never forget to make a purchase again.

~

*J*ulia ran into Felicity outside the courthouse on her way to volunteer at the hospital on the first of May. "Aren't you working today?"

"No, I'm grateful to work three days a week." Felicity shrugged. "Mrs. Cummings talks of going to her sister's home until the battle is over. Will you stay?"

Julia nodded. "Mama's not leaving." Now that New Orleans had surrendered, there was every reason to believe a Union fleet wound its way up the Mississippi River. City leaders expected them within a week or two. "She's not budging from the home Daddy had built for her and the only home my little sister knew." And thanks to Mama's ongoing rift with her brothers.

"My uncle's trying to decide what's best. If they leave, I will go with them."

Julia nodded. "It's probably wisest to go." She felt safer with Ash being in the city.

A caisson wagon pulled by a mule team struggled up the cobblestone hill, likely on its way to the bluffs above the city. Soldiers and enslaved men dug to reinforce fortifications.

"So much happening around the city. And not only here. It's a shame about that Union spy they hung in Richmond." Felicity's face turned grave.

Most citizens would rejoice at the news that filled Julia with dread. She looked in every direction. Thankfully, there was too much happening on the streets for anyone to pay attention to them. "It is," she whispered.

Julia's skin tingled. Felicity was for the *Union*? They stared at one another as if each realized their blunder.

"I-I'm working at the hospital today. Will you join me?" Julia spoke in a rush.

"No, I'm on an errand for my aunt." Felicity twisted the strings of her reticule. "Another time, perhaps?"

Julia assured her she was welcome any time and then watched her scurry toward the river, where batteries of heavy guns were being moved to guard against approaching enemy ships.

Ash's mother and sisters were safe in Texas. Felicity had an opportunity to flee the danger. Savannah's family would likely take refuge at Willie's plantation while Julia's family would face whatever came head on.

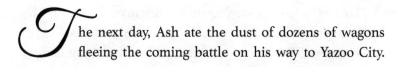

The next day, Ash ate the dust of dozens of wagons fleeing the coming battle on his way to Yazoo City.

There'd been riders and wagons along this dirt road every trip, but not like this.

Never like this.

Factory workers had been dismantling machinery. Some machinery headed toward Jackson on the train, and others was carted out of the city on wagons like a few Ash had ridden around.

Shop owners had boxed up merchandise to prevent the enemy from plundering it. Businesses all around the city closed. Much of those goods went to Jackson. Others chose to cart their products to farther parts of Mississippi.

Ash was torn between relief and sadness that a few families had already packed their belongings and left to stay with friends or extended family. Those women and children were safer out of the city. Yet the reason they left wrenched at his heart.

And he must accept his share of the blame. His spying against his neighbors carried repercussions. If they only affected himself, he could accept it. But Julia and her family would also pay the price of his spying.

He'd helped the Union by passing along information about troops, fortifications, weaponry *in his own city*. And placed his friends, his neighbors in harm's way as a consequence. Soldiers would be killed because he didn't remain silent.

The weight was too much on his conscience. Yet he must not stop.

It was half past noon when he rode into the blacksmith's yard.

"I about gave up on you." David Metzger placed a glowing iron into a bucket of water.

"Lots of wagons today." Ash led his mare inside the big barn. "You might receive new customers from the traffic."

"Hope so. They came yesterday too. And the day before."

David removed his thick leather gloves. "Got your horse saddled for you."

"Much obliged." Ash transferred his canteen and saddlebag to the fresh mount.

Sad news from Richmond weighed on his mind as rode on. Union spies had been imprisoned in the Confederate capital last month. One of them, Timothy Webster, had been hanged on April twenty-ninth.

Jim's female spy in Tennessee had been rescued. He prayed that it had been without exposing her comrades.

Would the two armies colliding here produce so much danger and pressure that someone here in Vicksburg would slip up? Maybe him?

# CHAPTER 26

"*H*alt."

The voice jarred Ash from his sleepy state.

A sergeant held up his hand and waited for Rosebud to stop before reaching up for her bridle.

What was this? "Good evening, sergeant." Ash was fully awake in an instant. He'd dozed on a return trip from Yazoo when he should have taken a little-known forested trail the last three miles.

"Dismount." The officer waited until Ash complied.

A half dozen soldiers, holding muskets leveled at Ash's knees, stepped into the dirt road a mile outside Vicksburg that evening at dusk, darker here in the woods.

Ash's heart skittered. These men surely knew of the female spy who had been caught and then escaped. "Pleasant evening."

"What's your business in Vicksburg?"

"I've lived there all my life." Despite his racing pulse, he answered calmly. "I'm a saddler."

Silence stretched while the sergeant lit a cigar. "Where have you been?"

He folded his arms, as if settling in for a long chat. "Some neighbors left to stay with friends for a spell. I tagged along." It was true. He *had* accompanied wagons a few miles.

"You plan on leaving Vicksburg for good?"

"No, sir."

"Everyone's heading out of the city." He looked at Ash expectantly.

"Some are mighty scared." In the growing shadows, Ash's glance skimmed the group. Recognized two of them as having been in his shop. His breath hitched.

"You ain't?"

"A man would be a fool not to keep an eye on the river."

The sergeant grunted. "Such a thing brings out the spies."

Ash stiffened. "Reckon it could." He'd delivered messages that very day about new troops and artillery in Vicksburg.

"Show me your pass." The sergeant extended his hand.

Ash retrieved it from his pocket.

The man tilted it toward the waning light. "Anything else in those pockets?"

"No, sir." How thankful he was that his ciphered message had been delivered. He turned them inside out to prove it.

"Check his boots." The sergeant's eyes narrowed.

One of the soldiers raised his rifle toward Ash's chest while one of the men who'd been in his shop stepped forward. There was nothing for it but to comply. Ash sat on a log and removed his boots, which were thoroughly examined.

"Nothing." Seeming disappointed, the man gave them back.

"Might as well search his hat." The sergeant spat. "And his saddlebag."

Ash handed over his hat and then put on his boots while the items were searched.

"Just some jerky and a sack of flour in the saddlebag, Sarge." The soldier looked at the officer.

Ash stood.

"Give him his hat." The sergeant studied Ash as his pass and his property were returned. "Be on your way."

The soldier holding a rifle on him hesitated, then lowered it.

Did they treat everyone entering the city like this? Or did they suspect him specifically? The soldiers who'd visited his shop two days before might have been a warning. Ash mounted, his leg protesting the movement.

The soldiers stepped back into the woods.

Unwilling to betray his fear by galloping away, Ash held his mare to a walk for a quarter mile and then increased to a trot. Jim had come mighty close to having another of his spies captured tonight.

Ash's heart finally settled to its normal rhythm when sighting his home. He dismounted carefully on his bad leg. It wasn't going to be good for much tonight. Or tomorrow.

He led his tired horse around the back of his shop to the red barn.

The wide door stood open. He was certain he'd closed it. Were soldiers waiting inside?

"I'll get you and Apple Blossom some oats and water." Looking in every direction, he stroked Rosebud's neck as they walked inside the dark, dank barn smelling of hay.

Good. No soldiers hiding inside.

Wait. Where was his other mare?

Ash dropped the reins to check the open stall in the corner. No Apple Blossom.

One of his neighbors could have borrowed her. Or Jolene's husband...Joseph. Ash would appreciate being asked first, but it might have been an emergency.

Tamping down his uneasiness, he tended Rosebud. Then he went to the kitchen.

"Mr. Ash." The cook looked up from stirring a bubbling

stew. "I've kept your supper hot." She looked down at his muddy boots.

"Thank you, Jolene." She might well be surprised because he never came to supper without cleaning up. His mama had demanded it, and he'd not stray from it now. "I'll change and be down to eat in a few minutes. Who borrowed Apple Blossom?"

"The army took her." Shoulders hunched, Jolene raked one hand over the other.

Ash gave his head a little shake. "Wh-what?"

"Soldiers knocked on the front door after lunch." With a shrug, she removed the stew from the stove. "Said the army needs horses, if we had any to spare. I told them we didn't and you were out. They said they'd just have a look around. I couldn't stop them."

The hair stood up on the back of his neck. Had those soldiers been the same ones who came Saturday? Had they been after his horse then and waited until he was gone to approach his cook?

"They brought back a piece of paper a few minutes later. Said it was a receipt for the horse and your country is grateful to you."

A worthless page for an animal taken without his agreement. No payment. Outrageous.

"It's a good thing you had Rosebud, else you might be missing two horses." Jolene gave a decisive nod.

Long strides took Ash from the kitchen to his saddle shop, where another lock was stored. He secured it to the barn door.

He'd loved that horse, the weaker of his team. Everyone with spare horses had donated them to the army, so there was no opportunity to replace her.

What other atrocities awaited citizens?

One thing was for certain—soldiers suspected Union spies would come to Vicksburg since the fall of New Orleans.

Little did they know, they'd allowed one to ride away free this very evening.

~

"*Where* do you go every Friday?" Julia waited until they'd left the restaurant and were in Ash's buggy to confront him. It was May tenth, and his uncle's saddles had been on yesterday's westbound train. She wasn't going to be put off again.

His gaze darted to the soldiers on the street corner. "Let me get past the congestion."

She folded her arms and waited until he was climbing the bluff the city was built upon. "Well?"

"Let's sit in your garden to talk."

"Very well." There was a sad resignation on his face that frightened her as much as the soldiers all about town.

She maintained her silence until they were strolling on her mother's terraced hillside.

"I see you're set on knowing." He sighed. "I'll tell you, but you must promise it will go no further. Not your Mama. Not Eddie. No one."

"Agreed."

"I'm a Union spy," he whispered.

"You can't be." Her hands covered her face. Deep inside, in a place where there were no words, she'd feared this very thing.

"I had to find a way to serve the Union without fighting." His face was ashen.

"Ash, this is just as dangerous as becoming a soldier." He could be caught and hanged, just like that spy in Richmond.

"It is dangerous. That's why I didn't tell you—to protect you." He reached for her.

She stepped back from him, and his hand fell away. "That makes no sense. Why, you've put me and my family in danger.

248

Should Union gunboats bombard the city, my Unionist family isn't any safer than hundreds of Confederate supporters remaining in the city."

"I never intended to put anyone I love in danger."

"So it's fine to pass on secrets that hurt someone you don't know?" Julia shot at him.

"Julia, my love, think what you're saying." He crossed his arms. "Shall I only support the Union in principle but not in action?"

Her cheeks burned. "I thought losing Willie was difficult. I couldn't bear it if..."

"I know. I'm careful."

"Do you work alone?"

He shook his head.

"Who else?"

"That I cannot say."

Likely, the tanner was in on it. Or at least someone in the Bolton area. Spies were imprisoned. Shot. Hanged. She understood why he couldn't tell her more. "I can't believe you kept me in the dark all these months after I *asked* you to tell me."

"I was sworn to secrecy. With our city in turmoil, I can no longer hide it from you." His hazel eyes smoldered with pain. "I didn't mean to hurt you. I'm doing this for my country."

She shook her head. "I need time to think. Don't escort me to church tomorrow."

~

*a*sh drove himself to his lonely home. Julia had been right to blast him for putting her city at risk, for that was what he and his fellow spies had done. There was little doubt that sharing what the Confederates had done in various places had allowed the Union army to prepare. Surprise attacks had become anticipated battles because of advance warnings.

Yes, he was as guilty as she said, though it stabbed at his heart that she didn't support him. Perhaps her zeal for the Union wasn't as strong as his.

Still, he must not stop. This war had gone on too long. Too many had died.

~

"Is Ash sick?"

Julia had anticipated Eddie's question. They walked to church on the pleasantly warm spring morning. Mama had stayed home. "No, he just can't come today."

Eddie's face puckered. "He's busy all the time."

"Yes." Now she understood why.

"I see him sometimes in the city. I run but I never catch up with him because he's always so far away."

"He's in a hurry." The same had happened to her.

"Sometimes he talks to a man by the oak grove across from my hideout."

Julia's heart raced. Had her brother witnessed Ash's meeting with other spies? She must warn Ash that since Eddie had seen him, someone else probably had too. "I expect he likes to pass the time of day with his friends the same as you." Church bells rang. "Let's hurry."

Once inside, she couldn't concentrate on the hymns or the sermon. Her courage failed her at the possible battle ahead on her very doorstep. Ash had supplied the Union with information that would affect everyone in this church, this city on the bluff. It proved his Union loyalty, his valor.

What if her neighbors discovered that he'd not only spied on the South but on their city specifically? They'd imprison him at the very least—or run him out of town. Some hotheads might grab a noose or a rifle and pursue him.

He had more strength of character than she. Her fears had

made her act irrationally. His resolve to stand on his beliefs, even in adversity, strengthened her own. She'd support him even as it terrified her to do so.

~

*J*ulia walked over to Ash's house the next day. It was locked. Was he out meeting a spy, or had he left town again?

She now knew better than to raise suspicions by talking to his staff. Instead, she spent the day at the Ladies' Hospital and then tatted lace all evening. She and Ash would need the income more than ever soon.

The next day, she returned after preparing lunch for her and her mother. This time, the door was open.

"Julia? Is that you?" He stood from his bench, both hope and apprehension fighting for dominance on his face.

"Good afternoon, Ash." She stepped inside. "We ended our time on Saturday rather abruptly. I'm sorry."

He held up his hand. He shut every window and the door. "Soldiers were on this street earlier. As for Saturday, it was my fault entirely. My apologies for keeping—"

"No, I understand your reasons." Speaking softly, she moved closer. "It still terrifies me, but I understand."

"Thank you." The apprehension on his face didn't lessen.

"You're such a brave man. Kind. Compassionate. You're so good for Eddie." She waited until he looked at her. "For me."

Hope sparked in his eyes.

"Can you tell me where you go on these missions?" It might ease her worry.

He shook his head. "I've already said more than I should."

"All right. Then please tell me if the danger escalates."

"I promise." He held out his arms.

She snuggled against his chest. Tightened her arms around him. She mustn't lose this man.

"Folks will notice if I leave my door closed." Releasing her, he strode across the room.

"One moment."

He halted with his hand on the knob.

She explained what Eddie told her about spotting him near his hangout.

"Oh, boy. I was so careful." He released a long breath. "Thanks. It won't happen again." He opened the door.

His new maid stood outside. She peeked in at Julia but spoke to Ash. "Jolene sent me. You forgot to eat your lunch." She gave him a plate with a napkin covering it.

"Thank you, Mrs. Anthony." He nodded to her.

She left after another long look at Julia.

Ash held a finger to his lips. His head cocked to one side until her footsteps faded. "She's never delivered my lunch before."

Sneaking about? Was the wife of a Confederate soldier spying on him? "I'll go."

He nodded. "Thanks for coming. I'll see you Saturday, if I may?"

"Yes." Julia left with a greater understanding of what Ash faced daily. She resolved not to add to his troubles.

～

*A*sh leaned on his shop's door as Julia hurried down the street. Two of the soldiers who had been at his shop smoked a cigar under a tree across the street. Coincidence? Or were they watching him?

Mrs. Anthony definitely seemed mighty curious about her employer's activities. What had he done to make the Confederate soldier's wife suspicious of him? He didn't leave town on her workdays, though some meetings with his spies happened those days. Had she followed him?

He'd test that theory this afternoon. See if his maid or the two soldiers glancing his way followed him on a jaunt around town. If he spotted them, his "chance" meeting outside the hospital wouldn't happen.

Two hours later, Ash locked his shop. There were no soldiers in sight. He didn't set off up his own street to the hospital, a five-minute walk. Instead, he strolled toward town, stopping now and then to exchange greetings. A group of businessmen on a street corner shared that the Seventeenth, Twenty-sixth, Twenty-seventh, and Thirtieth Louisiana artillery regiments, recently evacuated from New Orleans, were now repositioned in Vicksburg. Exactly what the Union needed to know. He'd pass that on.

He glanced in every direction before moving on. There was no sign of the two soldiers who liked to loiter about his street.

But Mrs. Anthony stared at a window display across the street when she was supposed to be working.

She'd followed him. He had his proof. Was she the reason those soldiers visited his shop? Or that two of them he'd spotted walked on his street at least twice weekly? All that started around the time she began working for him. Coincidence?

He couldn't afford to ignore it. There was nothing in his home to find. The ciphered message hidden in his shop would be burned. He vowed not to write anything else at his shop.

How could he fire the maid without raising her suspicions, and therefore, that of the soldiers?

# CHAPTER 27

*S*o it was true.

Alerted by one of his spies, Ash had bought a newspaper to read the notice in the privacy of his parlor. The city had issued an order that all men between eighteen and fifty were to muster into the local militia. They were to bring their own guns to the courthouse on Saturday morning, May seventeenth.

He ran his hands back and forth through his thick hair. After avoiding this very thing for over a year, he'd be in an organized military company in two days, the city's Home Guard.

In Ash's mind, it was a clear response to the city of Natchez's surrender without a fight earlier in the week. This order was further proof that Vicksburg leaders would choose to stand their ground.

Ash mustered with Matt, John, and other members on their squad on Saturday morning. One of the city's grocers, Charles Smedes, took them through drills on courthouse grounds. Men with graying hair stood alongside boys with not enough whiskers to warrant a razor.

It was clear from the solemn faces that everyone understood the gravity of an approaching Union fleet. They were to protect their fellow citizens, their homes.

Trained soldiers patrolled the bluffs, the town, the riverbank.

And, if needed, a barely trained home guard would stand ready to augment their efforts in protecting the city.

When Ash thought about it that way, Papa's old musket didn't sit so heavy on his shoulder.

~

"*A* portion of the Union fleet has arrived." Julia's heartbeat escalated more from the dreaded words than Ash's kiss on her cheek on Sunday morning. She'd opened the door to his knock to find the worst had come.

"Since we've no way to know when they'll shell us, I suggest we pray from home instead of going to church." Ash's hazel eyes darkened.

As his words darkened her spirit.

As she stepped onto the porch, her gaze sought confirmation of Ash's news. Several tall sails cast shadows across the swollen Mississippi River.

He sandwiched her shaky hand, drawing it to his cheek.

Julia's fingers quaked within his warm clasp. She turned to call her mother.

Mama and Eddie came to the door. "What is it?" Mama asked.

Julia gave a nod toward the river.

"Are those the gunships?" Eddie's mouth dropped open.

Mama wrapped her arms around his shoulders and drew him close, so that he stood with his back to her while they all stared as if transfixed. "We'll pray for safety from our porch."

Silas, Hester, and Daisy drew up chairs with them on the sunny porch.

"Do you have to go to the Home Guard?" Julia's throat tightened on the words.

"Only if we're called to go." Ash covered her hand with his. "Some four thousand Confederate troops defend us. Doubtful we'll be needed."

She curled her fingers around his, thankful for his presence. Julia half expected one of the town's cannons on the bluffs to the north and along the river to begin the attack, so ready were the soldiers to guard the city, but nothing happened all morning.

At noon, a ship lowered a longboat, a white flag flapping in the breeze.

"The Union wants to talk." Ash wrapped an arm around a white porch pillar, gaze intent on the river.

A shot echoed from the Vicksburg shoreline over the bow of the approaching boat, a clear warning.

Julia gasped. The first shot at Vicksburg reverberated in her soul.

The Union boat, accepting the warning, stopped. A steamer from the shore met it and then returned to the wharves.

"I'll go see what I can discover." Ash strode down the stairs.

"Can I come too?" Eddie followed him to the walk.

Ash looked at Mama, who nodded. "Let's go, buddy."

Silas stood. "Believe I'll mosey along too."

Ash put his arm around Eddie. "We'd welcome your company."

~

The steamboat had been back to shore thirty minutes when Ash and the others reached the crowded wharves. A hundred men or more—and a few women—arrived with them.

Silas offered to find out what he could and disappeared.

Ash answered Eddie's questions about the Union ships while they waited along the riverbank. The boy's excitement was liberally sprinkled with fear.

Same as Ash's.

Silas sauntered back. "It's what we figured."

"A demand for surrender." Ash's heart sped at the very word. "Who signed the notice?"

"Captain S. Phillips Lee." Silas folded his arms. "We've agreed to give them an answer at three."

"We ain't surrendering." A man nearby raised his fist.

Cheers met his pronouncement. Ash's heart plummeted. Surrender was the only way to guarantee no one got hurt. The citizens weren't about to agree.

~

*J*ulia stayed on the porch all afternoon. Movement from the wharves testified to a crowd mingling there. What must Eddie think about this? Would they be able to protect her young brother?

Fear penetrated her soul. War had come to her city.

The white-flagged Union longboat returned to its former position halfway to the shoreline. No ship left the wharf.

The women waited. Nothing happened.

They'd all missed lunch. Mama asked Hester to start supper about four o'clock.

An hour later, just as a steamboat left the Mississippi shore, Ash limped up with Eddie. "The Union Navy demanded surrender. We stayed long enough to learn our answer. Silas remained behind to see if the Union responds immediately."

Julia stood slowly, her hand at her throat. "What's our answer?"

"Three rejections. One from Mayor Lindsay. One from Colonel Autry, our city's military governor. The last is from

Brigadier General Martin Luther Smith, the commander of the city's defenses."

"No surrender." Mama paled. "The Union will be very certain of our response."

They all turned toward the river. The exchange having been made, the two ships parted.

"What do we do now?" Julia couldn't tear her gaze from the river.

"We wait." Ash put his arm around her, tucking her against his side. "And pray."

~

*B*ecause the Union fleet hadn't responded to Vickburg's refusal of surrender with mortar shots by Monday at dawn, Ash left on the train for Bolton. He'd written nothing down since catching his maid following him. One of his messages was about Vicksburg's artillery, and another gave counts of soldiers in the city.

A loud whistle signaled his stop. He started down the aisle as soon it the train chugged to a halt.

"Mr. Mitchell?" A female voice. Vaguely familiar.

He looked over at a woman wearing homespun, seated against an open window. His new maid. "Mrs. Anthony?" A large, fully packed basket on the seat beside her reached her shoulders.

"I reckon you might as well know I'm moving to Jackson to live with my in-laws." The tall blonde gave a crisp nod.

"I didn't see a note informing me of this." Not that he was disappointed. No more looking over his shoulder—for his maid, at least.

"That's because I didn't leave one. The sight of those gunboats decided me." She squared her shoulders. "I got my pay through Saturday, so you don't owe me anything."

Through the coming Saturday? What presumption. But no reason to quibble over two days of pay, not when it relieved him of her suspicious presence. Most likely, she'd nosed about his home. "I wish you all the best in Jackson." He tipped his hat.

"Why are you stopping in Bolton?" Her green eyes narrowed.

An impertinent question. "Buying supplies for my shop." He moved away.

He'd be more selective when hiring his next maid.

∼

*J*ulia kept Eddie close to the house on Monday and Tuesday. She wanted him where she could protect him if the battle began. Mama agreed.

After supper on Tuesday, a Union ship fired a shot toward the bluffs, sending smoke billowing toward a blue sky. Julia dropped the broom she was using to beat a rug on the veranda.

"Julia, did you see that?" Eddie's voice squeaked. "That boat sent a cannonball toward soldiers on the bluff."

"I saw the smoke." Her lips trembled. "Let's pray that's all there is to it."

As Eddie ran back to watch the boats from the street corner, she knew it wasn't the end.

It was the beginning.

∼

"*J*ulia! Mama!" Eddie ran inside their home on Wednesday afternoon.

"In the parlor." Julia, her hands a sooty mess, emptied ashes from the fireplace.

"What's wrong?" Mama placed the bird figurine she'd been polishing onto a side table.

"M-mayor L-Lindsay got another m-message from the boats." He was breathing hard. "Women and children have twenty-four hours to leave Vicksburg. Then he'll attack."

Mama gasped.

Julia, in the act of rising, fell back against the brick fireplace.

"You hurt?" Eddie helped her to her feet.

"Just embarrassed." The brick had left a scratch mark on her dress. There were bigger problems.

"The nerve. The very nerve of them." Mama's face turned the color of a ripe cherry.

Julia wiped soot from Eddie's hands using her apron and then cleaned her own while Mama paced.

"Those soldiers know some families lack the means to travel...or even a family member to flee to, like us." Her pace increased. "Yet they will fire at the city, anyway."

"Mama, Savannah's at the Sandersons' place. I'm certain they would host us too." Julia didn't like the idea of being frightened from her home, but it was better than facing a siege.

"We're staying. Those boats aren't running me from my home." She stopped at the front parlor window with its view of the river. "Don't ask again."

"Yippee." Eddie hugged his mama's waist. "I won't miss the battle."

"Son." Mama raised his chin so that he looked squarely in her eye. "You'll not be allowed to play outside. There will be new rules. I don't yet know what they will be, but you must obey them."

"I will, Mama."

Julia crossed to the window to view the menacing ships on the river. Mama's mind was made up. They'd experience whatever hardships awaited them. She'd pray fervently for them, Ash, and all her friends.

The next day, the gunboats opened fire on the city and bluffs.

Cannonballs fell short of the bluffs where soldiers manned artillery. Shells exploded in the city. Julia kept Eddie inside, where he watched from upstairs windows, running from bedroom to bedroom in his effort not to miss anything.

She glanced out the window. Another cannonball flew high overhead, as most did. The ground trembled when it exploded. Screams of terror came from farther up the hill. She prayed flying shrapnel hadn't struck anyone.

A rush of air overhead warned another shot had been fired. A loud boom signaled it found a destination. More cries.

Answering booms from cannons on the bluffs brought hope of stopping the attack.

Silence for five minutes. Ten.

Then a cannonball whooshed to the right, in the direction of Ash's house. But how long before she learned if it had been struck? Few ventured from the relative safety of their homes.

She fell to her knees before the parlor window. *Lord, protect us, all of us. Protect Ash, who always feels a need to act ever more courageously. He's proven himself, over and over. Convince him he doesn't have to die to prove his bravery.*

~

*A*sh ran to Julia's home from his shop as soon as there was a lull in the cannon fire. He jumped over the fence along the sidewalk and knocked on the door. A surprised Hester let him in and took him to the parlor, where Julia and her mother sat near the window.

"Ash?" Julia stood as he rushed to her side. "Is all well?"

"That's what I came to ask you." Sandwiching her hands between his, he kissed Julia's cheek. "The trains are running. We can get you all out of the city in the morning."

"We're not leaving." Mrs. Dodd spoke harshly.

He exchanged a concerned glance with Julia. "I can take you to the Sanderson plantation."

"No one's running us away from our home." Mrs. Dodd turned away.

Ash's frustration escalated. "I'll take you to Jackson, then. You'll be safe in the capital."

"No." Mrs. Dodd's lips tightened.

Julia laid her hand on his arm. "Let it go, Ash."

He pressed his lips tight to contain further protest. Mrs. Dodd's determination to hold onto the feud with her brothers might cost her children's safety. If they survived this war, Ash would never allow such a fracture in the family he and Julia created. Wasn't this war proof enough of the Scripture that a house divided would fall?

∼

*J*ulia disliked confinement to the house, but not as badly as Eddie. Considering that a cannonball blasted a hole in the Methodist church's roof and another bored a hole into a neighbor's kitchen, it wasn't safe inside either.

After a few days of shelling, most of the Union fleet floated south, leaving only a portion of the former gunboats in sight of Vicksburg. Those continued the attack at a slower pace.

Felicity stopped by the first Tuesday in June.

Julia hugged her, truly happy that her friend was back. "Will you mind sitting on the rear veranda?"

"Not at all. I've noticed the gunboats haven't struck this far up the bluff."

"My family attended church with Ash on Sunday after spending several days inside. The gunboats shoot a cannon at us every now and then to remind us they're here." On the way to the back of the house, Julia paused to ask Hester to serve refreshments. They arranged metal chairs inside the scanty shade.

"As if we could forget." Felicity spread her blue print dress about her ankles. "How is your family?"

"Exploding cannons stirred the dust. Mama's suffered from it, or she'd be here to greet you. Eddie is interested in what's happening about the city."

"We were at the Sandersons' for a week."

A boom from the river spurred both of them to look up. The cannon exploded to the left of the city. No screams.

"Frightening, isn't it?" Felicity gazed toward the gray cloud caused by the exploding shell.

Julia's heartbeat slowed...until the next one came, heightening the smell of gunpowder. She walked to the edge of the veranda to peer at the river. "Did you ever have a premonition? A feeling that something is about to happen?"

"Like what?" Felicity joined her.

"I don't know." It was more than a niggling of worry as yet undefined. She feared it had something to do with Ash.

~

*A*sh accompanied Julia and Eddie to church on June eighth. Mrs. Dodd was feeling poorly and stayed home. Ash studied the river on their stroll home. The fall of Memphis two days before had opened the Mississippi for Union ships to approach Vicksburg from the north. The city could now be attacked from the river on the north and south. "No matter what you're doing, listen for a whooshing sound," Ash warned Eddie. "Watch for puffs of smoke on the boats and keep your eyes on where the cannon is coming."

"I will." Eddie's promise brought only a modicum of

comfort. "George and Tom are back, and we all watch or we're not allowed to play outside."

"Good man." Ash clapped him on the shoulder as he met Julia's concerned gaze.

"They're not allowed to go more than two streets away in any direction." Julia gave her brother a look. "Right?"

"It's not fair." His face scrunched.

"None of that." Ash admonished, though he sympathized. There was nothing fair about war. "Your sister said to stay within two squares of your home."

"Sorry, Julia." Eddie stopped in front of his house.

"Just as long as you follow the rules." She tilted her head at him.

"I will." He ran up the stairs and inside.

"I can't stay for lunch. I have to get back to the shop." No new orders were coming in, but he had two saddles to complete that were taking longer than normal because he spent a portion of each day with Julia to make certain of their safety.

"I have to check on Mama, anyway. She wore herself out coughing yesterday." She glanced up at her home.

"I'll pray for her. Keep an eye on Eddie."

"What if things get worse and I can't allow him outside at all?" Julia's tense face showed her strain.

"It will get worse." He gathered her close to his chest. "Without a doubt, the Union Navy will send more boats. The only question is when."

～

*A*sh took the forest trail out of Vicksburg on the second Friday of June. Avoiding the sheer number of soldiers in the city made it tricky to ride to Yazoo City, causing him to get a late start. He requested to keep Mr. Metzger's horse overnight for double the cost so Ash could rest. He'd spent less money since his family moved to Texas, and it was obvious the Metzgers needed it.

After leaving the blacksmith's, he rode to a forest trail where he ciphered his memorized messages. Dismounting, he walked Moonbeam to a mature magnolia tree with low-hanging branches. It hid both rider and animal from the trail, and he'd never encountered anyone on it.

This would be an excellent spot to conceal money, pencil, and paper. Confederates were getting mighty nosy. If soldiers searched him again, they'd want to know why he carried writing supplies. Because he was now doing two trips weekly to Yazoo City, it was doubly risky. Next week, he'd bring a trowel to bury a stash of supplies.

Ash continued his ride and reached the closed store after six. He knocked.

A minute later, Eli opened the door. "I gave up on you, Ash." He waved him inside.

"I was delayed leaving Vicksburg." The smell of frying chicken wafted from the upstairs living quarters. "Would you let me in if I came even later than this?"

Eli closed the door leading upstairs. "Something wrong?"

"Hard to avoid soldiers, so I'm taking backroads." Ash lowered his voice to match the grocer's. "It's longer."

"I'll answer if it's before midnight. Hide your mount behind my home and knock on the back door so I'll hear you."

"Thank you." Ash handed over a bill covering his ciphered note.

"You'd best watch yourself around here." Eli pocketed the note. "The Confederate Navy moved an ironclad they're building to Yazoo City. Sailors are mighty interested in keeping their secrets."

"Shall I investigate?"

"No, we've got it covered. You're taking enough chances as it is."

Ash couldn't argue.

"Don't want my family seeing you, but I can send you off with a chicken leg for your supper."

"Much obliged." A little while later, food in his saddlebag, Ash rode away, pondering where to spend the night.

That familiar magnolia tree offered a canopy of protection not far from the blacksmith's home. He'd stay there.

~

*A*mid sporadic attacks, a few neighbors returned and opened their boarded-up homes. The number of soldiers arriving in Vicksburg far outnumbered them.

Six bearded men dressed in gray knocked on Julia's front door a week later. Silas was out back, and Julia hesitated to open it. Finally, she cracked it about a foot.

A tall soldier with a bushy auburn beard stepped forward. "We've got no place to sleep, miss. We wondered if we might bed down on the veranda."

She'd heard that, with so many troops in the city, the Confederate army was having difficulty finding a place to sleep. Yet if she agreed, they'd return tomorrow night and the next... until they left the city, most likely.

The men waited, hats in hands, in respectful silence. One of them looked about eighteen. The rest were older, maybe married with children. Some women's husbands. Some children's papas.

Julia's throat tightened. Southern hospitality ran deep. It was hard to refuse...but men sleeping on the veranda with only Silas for protection?

Mama was in bed from a coughing spell. Best not disturb her sleep.

"Miss Julia?" Silas came around the house and climbed up on the porch, eyeing the men as he passed.

Relief washed over her. She needn't deal with this problem alone. "May I have a word with you?" At least the soldiers understood that women in the house weren't without protection.

"Yes, Miss Julia."

"You gentlemen will excuse us for a moment."

The auburn-haired man spoke again. "Of course."

Julia stepped inside, Silas following and closing the door. They retreated to the stairs where the men wouldn't overhear.

"I figure them soldiers is already sleeping in the yards of folks who left and can't refuse 'em." Silas spoke softly. "No guarantee others won't ask if we refuse."

"What should we do?"

"I don't feel good about them sleeping so close to the house. I can keep my eye on 'em if they bed down by the flower garden in plain view of the street."

"Do that. Will you show them where to lay their bedrolls?"

"Sure will."

Julia crossed the hall to open the door. The men were gone. Confused, she turned back to Silas.

"Reckon they moved on to an empty house. Lots of those around. Hope folks don't have a hard time shooing them off their land when they return."

That was the best reason she'd heard to stay put in Vicksburg.

Thank goodness they'd left. With so many husbands and fathers gone from Vicksburg, it was difficult to know if these new soldiers would treat the women and children honorably.

A chill spread through her. Certainly not if they knew her family were Unionists.

# CHAPTER 28

*W*here was Eddie? Julia crept to the center of town in search of him, her attention riveted on tall sails in the river. There were more Union ships in the fleet today, June twenty-fourth. Why, they seemed to fill the Mississippi from bank to bank. What did Union naval leaders plan for her beloved city?

She shuddered thinking about the deadly force of the cannons they'd already experienced. Looked like the boats intended a bombardment this time.

Soldiers milled about the streets, their attention on the river. Julia's uneasiness mounted. Concern for her brother was the only thing strong enough to prompt her to leave her home's safety.

"Julia? What are you doing out here?" Ash rushed up to her.

"Eddie sneaked out."

Groaning, he clasped her hand. "Let's begin at the wharf. He'd want to see the boats."

Her fingers tightened around his strong hand. They searched all the wharfs. No Eddie.

"Let's try the brickyard." Ash tugged on her hand.

"All right." She shaded her eyes to scan the city. Where was he?

Not at the brickyard.

"Do you know where his hideout is?" Ash surveyed the nearly empty streets.

"Yes." Relief flooded over her. She led the way and found her brother cowering in his makeshift shed. "Eddie, why aren't you home?"

"Soldiers won't find my hangout." There were traces of tears within smudges on his face. "I'm safe here."

Her heart breaking at his fear, Julia gathered him into her arms.

"You're a lot safer at your house, buddy." Ash knelt and put his arms around both of them.

"If you say so." He rubbed his eyes.

Julia stepped back to put her hands on his shoulders. "You're not to leave the house. Understood?"

He nodded.

"Let's get you home." Ash put an arm around them and kept a hold on them until they reached the porch, where Julia released a sigh of relief.

~

*A*sh ate supper with them. No church for them that day even though there'd been little shelling. Not with the threat in plain sight of Julia's front porch.

Eddie tugged on Ash's arm. "Ash, let's go outside while we can."

"An excellent idea." Julia followed them as far as the veranda.

Ash tossed a ball with Eddie. When the boy quit to chase fireflies across the yard, Ash sat with Julia on the veranda.

"Mama and I have been busy boxing valuables." Julia rested

her back against the chair. "Most things that break have been packed in sawdust and stored in barrels in the cellar."

"Good idea." He was proud of her foresight. "I don't like what might be coming at us. Bury anything worth stealing."

"Where?"

"In the flowerbeds when the soldiers aren't around. The ash pile. If there's a hidden compartment in the house or a place to dig in the cellar, so much the better. No witnesses there. Be certain to pack down the dirt so no one can see it's been dug."

"I'll see to it."

"Don't let anyone but your mama and Eddie know what you're doing." No telling what hard times they'd face in days ahead. The fewer people to know about hidden valuables, the better. "I'd do it for you, but Hester and Daisy would notice."

"Have you buried things?" she whispered.

He couldn't tell her about the writing supplies and two hundred dollars he'd buried under a tree along his trail. "I've a supply of leather that I'll wrap in oilskin and bury among the ashes. A few other things too. Mama took most of our valuables to Texas."

"Maybe that was wise. Have you heard from them?"

"Letters can't get across the Mississippi with the fleet in the harbor, but two letters from Daphne and three from Mama and Caroline came last month. They're settling into ranch life. The girls are learning to ride."

"And your mother?"

"She feels safe. Content. That makes it worth uprooting the family. Packing up the house." He shrugged. "Doing without a maid."

"Mrs. Anthony quit?" She straightened.

"Moved away last month before the trouble started, but honestly, it hasn't seen a good cleaning since Mama left."

"Why didn't you tell me? Felicity needs a job."

"You want your closest friend cleaning my house?"

"If she's agreeable." She frowned. "You're always in the shop or gone during the day. Your mama complained often enough about that."

"True. I usually eat lunch in the shop too." This could work. Jolene had taken on shopping for food when Mama left. She didn't have time for cleaning. "Will you ask her?"

"I will."

"How about a stroll in the garden?" Twilight had fallen.

"I thought you'd never ask." Accepting the arm he offered, she smiled into his eyes.

He leaned to kiss her. "Did I ever mention how blessed I am that you're my girl?" When the danger passed, he'd propose. The money he'd saved from deliveries might be just enough to satisfy Mrs. Dodd's expectations, especially in war times. Unless they needed it to survive after the shelling ended.

Eddie ran down the sloping yard toward them. "Will you come help me chase fireflies?"

"Sure thing." Ash grinned at Julia. Their stroll wasn't going to happen this evening. Instead, they'd spend a carefree hour with his future brother-in-law.

~

*A*sh rode up a side trail to the back of Eli's store at dusk on Friday. He'd already transferred the ciphered message from his boot to his pocket, as was his custom.

A sense of not being alone alerted him. He looked around but saw no one in any direction.

Something felt off. It wasn't simply the heat on the late-June evening. An oppressive stillness in the air warned him to leave —and quickly.

He turned Moonbeam's head around just as he caught movement from the main road. A man in butternut. Another in gray. Were there more soldiers?

"Where's the fire?" One of the soldiers raised an eyebrow at him. "You're in a mighty big hurry to take off."

Ash's heart skittered. He'd been seen. Should he run for it or talk to them?

"No fire." Although the page in his pocket burned like a blaze. Ash coaxed Moonbeam toward them. Only two men. No stripes or bars. Pickets on patrol? Or simply enjoying a few hours off? "Just realized it's later than I figured. The grocer ain't open."

"Nope. Sure ain't." The older one was about Ash's age and had a full brown beard. The other looked sixteen but might've been older. "Reckon you'll have to come back tomorrow."

"Reckon so." Ash guided his horse onto the road. "You all have a good evening."

"You do the same."

Not pickets. Who, then? Sailors from the ironclad in Yazoo City? Seemed likely.

Ash took off at a slow trot and then increased his speed. After a mile, he looked around. No one followed.

His heartbeat returned to normal rhythm.

Too risky to ride on the open road. Dismounting, he walked Moonbeam into the forest. It was as dark as midnight a few paces in. He paused to allow his eyes to adjust.

Horses approached on the road, riding at a canter. When he spotted them, his throat ran dry.

The two soldiers from the store had followed him, after all.

No way was he going to Eli's store in the morning. *Lord, protect Eli and his family. Let all the suspicion rest on me.*

Those soldiers would come back in search of him if they didn't tire of the game.

Questions that led to prison were not a game to Ash. He delved farther into the woods and then walked parallel to the road for an hour. Once he found a creek, he heaved a sigh of relief. He'd follow it to his trail, which flanked the creek for a couple of miles.

He refilled his canteen. While Moonbeam drank her fill, he rubbed his throbbing leg.

No lights in any direction. No smell of wood burning from a chimney. An owl hooted from a branch overhead.

Should he push on in the darkness or get some rest? *Lord, guide my steps.*

The coded message in his pocket must be destroyed because he'd been spotted. He must protect not only himself but his fellow spies. Darkness was pitch black under a canopy of trees. Should the soldiers be close, even a tiny fire to burn it exposed his position.

Riskier still to keep the message.

Ash fished a match from the saddlebag. Kneeling, he shielded the flames engulfing the printed page. Then his boot ground the ashes back and forth to ensure no word survived.

That done, he led Moonbeam to the open trail. He'd continue on. With Providence on his side, he'd be at the blacksmith's by breakfast.

# CHAPTER 29

$\mathcal{N}$ ightmares awoke Julia after midnight. Something was wrong.

She hadn't been asleep long because the gunboats had sent fire upon the city until ten o'clock. The attack was escalating.

Donning her robe, she crept down the hallway to see if her mother had suffered a relapse from all the canning they'd done. But she was breathing evenly. No coughing.

Julia closed the door and then crossed to Eddie's door. Moonlight streamed across the bed through the open window. Her brother lay crossways, the sheet flung about the bed.

Everything normal there. She returned to peer out her bedroom window toward the river. All silent.

Her agitation escalated. Something was amiss with Ash. Some danger, perhaps. He'd never explained details, though she'd guessed his involvement ran deeply.

She tried to assure herself Ash was in his bed, sound asleep. What if he wasn't?

Kneeling beside the window, she stared out over the dark waters. *Lord, please watch over Ash. Guide his steps. If he's in danger, lead him to safety.*

*I*t felt as if she'd only been asleep a few minutes when her bed began shaking.

A tumultuous roar catapulted Julia from her bed.

The floor shook as streaks of cannonballs shot across the sky. A deafening attack from the river disoriented her. Terrified screams erupted from every direction.

Julia threw a robe over her shoulders and ran toward Eddie's room. He stumbled out of it, eyes wide and frightened. She wrapped her arms around him, and they both ran to Mama's room, where Mama already had a robe secured over her nightgown.

"Get Silas inside where it's safe." Mama gathered her weeping son close. "I'll see to Hester and Daisy."

Exploding cannons rained down fire on the city. Julia ran onto the veranda. Silas was already there.

"Get inside!" She tugged on his muscular arm.

He resisted. "Look there."

She followed his gaze.

Her neighbors, some dressed and others wearing night-clothes and robes, ran up the street toward the safety of the bluffs.

Hester and Daisy were among them.

"They're running for their lives." Silas raised his voice, or she wouldn't have heard him over the roar.

Julia's heartbeat pounded in her ears. Were they all going to die tonight?

"Think we should head for the hills?" Silas's gaze was fixed on the shouting people in the streets.

She forced herself to think rationally. Those running folks were out in the open, in greater danger from cannons and flying shrapnel. "We'll stay."

~

*A*n hour past dawn, Ash was astride Moonbeam on the blacksmith's country road. He'd walked for hours and then ridden the last two miles. "Rough night. Almost there, girl." Ash leaned to pat the tired horse's neck. "You were worth your weight in gold this trip."

The smell of sizzling bacon and coffee stirred his senses, reminding him supper had been a meager jerky strip. He hated to arrive at breakfast, but Moonbeam needed sleep. Ash did, too, but he needed to reach Vicksburg more. He'd raised suspicions by riding to the grocery store via a back trail.

Twenty miles between him and those soldiers might be enough. Or they might have gone back to enlist help. His shiver wasn't caused by the early-morning chill.

He rode through the empty yard and into the barn. Dismounting was a struggle on his stiff leg. He led Moonbeam to her stall and attended her needs before the blacksmith entered.

"Ash? Didn't expect you until midmorning." A delicious scent of coffee wafted over from Mr. Metzger's cup.

"Hope it's not a problem." He tried to insert a heartiness to his voice to mask his exhaustion.

"Not at all. Will you want a refund for one day?"

"Keep it." The least of his worries. Ash fed Rosebud from a feedbag.

"Want some coffee? I think there's a biscuit left from breakfast."

"I'm much obliged to you."

The blacksmith strode to the house while Ash saddled Rosebud. He was ready to ride when his host returned.

Ash ate the biscuit in four bites and downed the scalding coffee as quickly as possible. "Thanks for everything." It was too dangerous to return. For both of them.

"My pleasure."

Ash touched the brim of his hat and rode toward the side road, an old wagon trail. Rosebud was fresh enough to canter, so he relaxed the reins. His horse knew the way.

Some time later, distant mortar blasts roused him from a stupor.

Rosebud needed a rest. He led her to a stream and dismounted. He'd expected sounds of exploding cannons to diminish. They had not. The Union fleet must be employing its entire force with a full Confederate response to create such a racket.

Julia must be terrified.

He mounted his faithful horse and rode toward the onslaught.

~

The tumultuous attacks slackened around breakfast and then began again. Julia and her family cowered on the main hall's floor while shells exploded from seemingly every direction.

Mama clasped Eddie close and kept a hand on Julia's shoulder. They'd sat there all morning, quaking at every explosion.

"I don't feel safe in the house." Julia's courage nearly failed her in the onslaught.

"They can't keep up the fever pitch." Mama's grip on her shoulder tightened.

"Mama, you're hurting me."

Her mother released her instantly.

Julia looked up as the floorboards creaked from the back of the house. Silas's heavy booted steps weren't alone.

"Look who just rode up." Silas stepped aside.

"Ash." Julia stood and ran into his arms.

He clasped her to his chest. "Is anyone hurt?"

"No." She rested her cheek against his fast-beating heart. "Are you?"

"Had to dodge mortar shells to reach you." He held out a hand to Eddie, who crashed against his side. "How are you, buddy?"

"Scared." The boy's voice was muffled against Ash's shirt.

Perhaps her beau could calm her brother, a task she was too shaken to accomplish.

"I understand." Ash looked into Julia's eyes, a mixture of concern and reassurance shining in his. Dark shadows under his bloodshot eyes accompanied a stubble of whiskers foreign to his usual clean-shaven face. He looked as if he'd endured an ordeal.

Something inside her stopped shaking. They were in this together.

He kissed her cheek, then released her and knelt until he was eye level with Eddie. "Do you feel safer in the hall?"

"There's no windows." Eddie swiped at his face.

Ash nodded. "Then I'll move chairs from the parlor." He straightened and raised Mama to her feet before limping from the hall.

A cannonball whistled in the air and struck a structure below them. The sound of splintering wood could signal the destruction of a house, a stable, a shop—she had no way of knowing.

Julia held her breath while Ash carried two sofas and four chairs into the hall from the front room. Those nearly floor-to-ceiling windows lining the porch had kept them from entering the parlor all morning.

"Thank you, Ash." Mama's tone was subdued, yet her eyes showed her gratitude.

Julia looked up as footsteps approached.

"Miss Martha, I've rustled us up some lunch since everyone missed breakfast." An explosion in the city below halted Silas's words. He waited for a break in the roar from the river. "Do you want to eat in the kitchen or in here?"

"Kitchen." Julia decided for her. The hall was the farthest from any windows and therefore safer, but they needed some degree of normalcy. They'd all eat together, staff and family. No, not staff. Simply family.

~

"*W*ill you help Silas dig us a cave in our hillside?" Julia asked Ash when he returned the following morning with his crutch. The shelling that had lasted all day yesterday continued today.

"I saw him digging. Others have the same idea for shelter from the bombing. I'll start now if you've got another shovel."

"Check the stable." Her conscience smote her as he limped away. Exhaustion was etched in his face. He never used his crutch unless the pain in his leg was severe. He was a true hero in her eyes.

She and Eddie watched them work from the back window. Digging halted whenever the shelling got bad or when fog from cannon fire got too thick to see shells in the sky. The shelter wasn't large enough to stand in by Sunday night.

"I'll return about supper time to dig again." Ash's face and shirt was covered in dirt. "Remain watchful tomorrow."

"You too." Her heart quaked that he was leaving the city. Maybe on the train? Dr. Emanuel, who owned the railroad, was still running his train, but the loading area was now two miles outside Vicksburg. "Be careful."

Hester came back shortly after Ash left. "Daisy's scared of the shells. She stayed at my son's place along the Big Black River."

"Are you staying?"

"I don't know as I won't join my children sometime."

Julia understood. Both staying and going held its dangers.

⁓

"*I* can't go back to Yazoo."

Jim whistled. "You had a time of it, didn't you?"

Ash couldn't argue.

"We must assume those fellas told their comrades about you." He heaved a sigh. "They might suspect they allowed a spy to sneak past."

"I pray I didn't put Eli and his family in danger."

"I'll send someone to see how they fare. We'd best bypass Eli's place for a few months."

That comforted Ash. He'd developed a friendship with the grocer. "Hate losing the extra money."

Jim sat back. "How do you feel about riding to Yazoo City from my house? It's a different route. Fewer miles."

"They're watching for me in Yazoo City." The coffee he'd drunk formed a hard knot in his gut. "Those fellows got a good enough look to recognize me. And we just agreed to bypass Eli's place to let suspicions die down."

"I've got another contact in the city. Those soldiers likely set up pickets at the crossroads by the grocer. I'd arrange to rent a fresh horse halfway on the other route."

The idea filled Ash with dread.

"I'll let you pray on it." The tanner stood. "It'll take a couple of weeks to figure it out. Maybe more. Just plan on your runs to the mill for now. I'll pay you for July when you get back."

Five dollars a week was still a decent wage, especially with so many men laid off.

Riding to Yazoo City kept information flowing North. Was it worth the risk?

# CHAPTER 30

*T*he assault from the river continued. Julia's family stayed huddled inside.

They felt only slightly safer when the large shelter was completed on July first. A narrow entrance opened into a room roughly ten feet by twelve feet. The ceiling was seven feet high, a perfect height for both Silas and Ash, who stood at the back, awaiting her verdict.

"Thank you both for creating this shelter." Hands on hips, Julia surveyed the sanctuary. Two lanterns lent sufficient light. She'd bring her tatting. "It's perfect."

"Yes, my thanks to you both. We'll sleep in the house after the daily barrage stops." Mama coughed into a handkerchief. "A few chairs and blankets will give us comforts from home."

"I've never lived in a cave before." Eddie stared at mud caked on his shoes. His trousers from the knees down were the color of the loamy soil.

"Let's bring a side table from the parlor." The ground shook under Julia's feet as a mortar shell struck the ground. The cave absorbed some of the sound.

"I think two will fit." Mama spoke as if the world wasn't exploding, accustomed to the sound.

"I'll get the blankets." Julia stooped to leave the shelter.

"Show us which chairs you want." Ash followed with Eddie.

Whooshing noises overhead drew their eyes. Julia gasped at a round cannonball over her home.

"Run!" Ash took their hands and pulled them into the house.

A mortar shell exploded behind the bluff. "When will it end?" She trembled.

"Hard to say." Ash drew her into his arms. "You've got a shelter now."

"Julia?" Eddie tugged on her sleeve.

She reluctantly left Ash's arms, the only place she felt truly safe in this madness. "Yes, Eddie?"

"We can take my game of droughts to our cave. That'll make you happy."

"Yes, very happy."

Eddie ran to the parlor.

"You're a strong woman, Julia." Ash held both her hands. "And that's what Eddie needs to see."

An explosion in town made her flinch.

He was right. Her ten-year-old-brother needed her strength. Doubt and weakness she'd save for private moments. And for Ash, who understood her as well as her own mother.

Julia raised her chin. "Then that's what he shall see."

Ash kissed her. "That's my girl."

◇

*I*ndependence Day passed with plenty of fireworks... courtesy of the Union fleet lopping mortar their way. Not the way anyone wanted to pass the day once celebrated with picnics and fishing as the Southerners had done before the war. It was a Friday, normally the day Ash would head to Yazoo City. Instead, he waved away the smell of gunpowder on his walk to Julia's, the odor stronger than the aroma of cigar smoke at a party.

Julia beckoned him into the shelter, where Silas was the only one missing. "Silas has been hired by three families to dig each one a single-room cave. He's charging fifty dollars for each."

Quite a boon for the hard-working man. Ash was happy for him.

"I've got our game set up." Eddie beckoned him to a table of draughts.

"I hoped you would." Ash grinned at him. It passed the hours of enforced confinement.

"Is Jolene's husband still working at the foundry?" Choosing a chair near the entrance where daylight gave more light than the lanterns, Julia picked up her tatting.

"He works as he can during the shelling." Another fact the Union knew about because of him and his spies.

"They're welcome to share our shelter." Mrs. Dodd embroidered a handkerchief.

"I took the liberty of inviting them. They'll join us if they get scared." There was no room on his property to dig a cave like this one.

Ash couldn't meet with his spies during the shelling. Folks ventured out only when they must. He couldn't prevent his city from digging in its heels and fighting.

Nor could he prevent families from being caught in the mortar fire.

Like this family he loved. If called upon to do so, he'd die protecting them.

*a*sh headed to the train station early Monday morning, accompanied by a couple of mortar shots on the two-mile walk. The post office and telegraph station had been moved outside the city with the depot. He'd check for mail from Luke on the way back and send him one he'd write later in the week, something he could do from the shelter.

No mail had crossed the Mississippi River since the shelling began. Hopefully, Mama wasn't too worried about them, though he coveted her prayers. Mama would have been undone by the attack still underway. In his nightly prayers, Ash thanked God for Uncle Clark's foresight.

More freight than passengers traveled toward Jackson. Ash had no trouble reaching the tanner's home by midmorning.

"Ash, got anything for me?" Jim shut the door.

He told what he knew about troops and cannon placement in his city and then sat to cipher it.

"Add them to the page I started." The widower brought him some coffee, then straddled a chair. "Got things figured for you to resume the Yazoo City trips."

Ash's heart leaped, then thudded. "So soon?"

"Can you come back Wednesday?"

"Two days?" Ash put his pencil down. The battle hadn't shown signs of letting up. "What have you planned?"

"Ride one of my mares on a country road toward Yazoo City. I've got a map you can memorize." He laid it flat and traced the route with his finger, stopping at a farmer's house where Ash would rent a horse for the continuing journey. His contact in Yazoo, Josh Allen, ran a newspaper office with living quarters upstairs.

"Is he in the heart of the city?"

"On the edge of town. Always a bit of risk involved. He'll have information for me. If he's afraid soldiers are pressing in, he'll mention how bad the mosquitos are this summer. If all is well, he'll recognize your name and slip you a paper. Leave immediately because there are soldiers in the area."

"I prefer to memorize everything."

"No time. Too many folks in and out of his office."

Sweat beaded on his forehead. "Then send me to someone less visible."

"The very fact so many visit means you won't be noticed. Best time to get there is between one and two. Shouldn't be a problem."

Unless those two soldiers happened to be in the city.

~

*J*ulia didn't like the sound of Mama's cough. Spending hours daily in a damp cave wasn't helping, but Mama waved away her concern. With the continued shelling, what choice did they have, after all?

Ash was with them Tuesday evening, but he was tense, his mind far from the board game he played with Eddie. He accompanied them inside at dusk. Mama excused herself and took Eddie upstairs to bed.

"Julia, do you have a minute?" Ash touched her shoulder.

"Of course."

Ash's eyes held a troubled look as he followed her into the parlor. "I'll make this brief." Holding her hand, he sat beside her on a sofa facing the window. "I have an errand outside the city tomorrow that worries me."

Her body went still. A delivery. He never discussed the particulars. "Is it dangerous?"

He kissed her hand. "Not if all goes well."

"You're...concerned it won't." Her fingers tightened around his.

He looked away.

"Then don't go." Last month's premonition returned full

force, when he'd come to them during a terrible attack with bloodshot eyes and a day's stubble on his chin.

"If it doesn't go well, I won't do this particular route again."

"How many routes do you..." Her heart thudded at the danger he faced to end the war.

"Two. Only two." He cradled her against his chest.

Julia clung to him. She wanted to ask him to reconsider. To send someone else. But she must allow him the freedom to face the danger if he considered it important. "I will pray for you."

"That's all I ask." He kissed her once and then deepened his kiss. She clung to him with all her strength, never wanting the kiss to end. Fearful of what was to come.

"My sweet Julia." He caressed her face. "I must go." And he strode from the house without another word.

She ran to the window. He walked into the night, his back ramrod straight despite the limp that seemed more trouble-some these days.

"God go with you."

# CHAPTER 31

*B*efore one o'clock on Wednesday, Ash had rented a fresh horse from a farmer who asked no questions on the way to Yazoo City. He'd delayed his lunch until after the delivery in order to be early.

Too early. He'd reached his destination. He slowed his mount to a walk as he entered the outskirts of town. He pushed his wide-brimmed hat over his eyebrows as his gaze darted in every direction, searching for sailors or soldiers. Specifically, the two who could identify him by sight.

No military at all. Children played inside white picket fences. A woman shook dust from a rug. Another hung clothes on a line.

Seemed peaceful enough.

He made it to the last white building on the right with a red door. This was it.

Ash dismounted and checked his pocket watch. Three minutes to one. If this was Mr. Allen's lunch hour, hopefully, he'd returned early.

He took three steps to the porch and then opened the door.

"Howdy." A curly-haired man in his thirties looked up from a desk. "Can I do something for you?" He stood.

"Howdy. Name's Ash Mitchell."

"Good to meet you." His green eyes darted to the right and left as Ash crossed the room. He held out his hand as if to shake. A piece of paper was inside.

Ash shook his hand and then slipped the paper into the lining of his hat. From his pocket, he extracted a bill wrapped around his note. "Can I buy a newspaper?"

"Sure thing." He handed him a single folded page.

Ash gave him the bulky dollar, certain Mr. Allen understood what was inside. "Obliged."

Mr. Allen's money disappeared up his long sleeve. He looked beyond Ash's shoulder. "Best be heading on. The mosquitos are getting bad."

Ash's heart skipped a beat. That was the code *not* to make the exchange. Turning on his heel, he opened the door to leave.

An armed man in butternut jacket and trousers stood on the other side. Brown hair, full beard. The man from outside the grocer's.

There was nowhere to run.

"Where's the fire?" The soldier grinned.

"Couldn't tell you. Pardon me." Ash started to go around him.

"Not getting away from me twice." A hand clamped down on his arm. "You know this fella, Josh?" He peered into the room.

"Never seen him before, Clem. Stopped in for a paper."

The soldier grunted. "Much obliged, Josh."

The newspaperman waved without looking up from his work. His calm exterior was admirable. Ash schooled his own features while searching in every direction for escape and finding none.

"Petty officer sent me for a paper. I'll give him yours." Clem dragged Ash down the steps. "My friends and I made a bet on you. And here you are to clear it up."

"I can't imagine that I'm so interesting." He managed not to wince when Clem's grip tightened.

"Well, you weren't. Until my comrade and me couldn't catch up with you on the road that evening. Did you get lost?"

"As a matter of fact, I did."

Peering at them, a shopkeeper across the dusty road paused in sweeping the walk outside his store.

"Don't believe ya." Clem pointed toward the hitching post. "That your horse?"

"Yep." Near enough. It wouldn't do to mention the poor farmer who'd rented it to him.

"Good. Let's go. I'll ride. You walk. I think my sergeant might like to talk with you."

Panic sped through Ash's veins. He had to get rid of the coded message in his hat that he could only guess had something to do with the Confederate Navy's ironclad in the area.

Clem mounted the horse. "Don't get no ideas about running away." He laid his musket in front of him.

"I'm not here to stir up any trouble." Ash tried to keep a casual tone. His heart threatened to thump right on out of his chest.

A hundred yards out of town, Clem relaxed enough to drink from Ash's canteen.

Ash managed to extract the note while scratching his head. He dropped it in the tall weeds beside the road.

"Don't think that limp makes me feel sorry for you." The canteen hung again by his saddlebag. Which contained his lunch. He carried nothing that would identify him.

Ash's main goal was to keep himself out of prison and not implicate anyone.

Why hadn't he listened to his gut and stayed in Vicksburg?

*Julia, pray for me.*

~

*S*helling continued, though not as heavy as it had been. Dust stirred up by exploding cannons throughout the city crept into the cave shelter. Mama's cough had grown worse all day.

"Let's go inside this afternoon, Mama." Julia maneuvered around the small room where Silas played draughts with Eddie to sit beside her. "The shells aren't coming at such a pace today."

"Counted five the last hour." Hester knitted a shawl near the lantern light. "Been thinking about starting supper."

"That would be lovely, thanks, Hester. Just be mindful as you cross the yard." Julia turned back to Mama. "I think you'll feel better in your own bed."

"Perhaps I will lounge on the hall sofa." A coughing spell overtook her.

"I'll write to Caroline while you rest." And pray for Ash. Writing to his family somehow bonded Julia with them.

Mama stood when the cough subsided. "Eddie, Silas, be careful when you come inside."

"We'll finish our game first."

In the house, Julia got Mama settled with a pillow and blanket. While Hester made a pot of soup for supper, Julia tried to write her letter, but she couldn't concentrate.

How had Ash's delivery gone?

While Mama napped, Julia prayed for his protection.

~

*C*lem took Ash to a camp of tents with a few wooden buildings on the Yazoo River. The *Arkansas,* as Ash had learned the Confederate ironclad was called, had a number of men at work on the top deck where a tall cylindrical smokestack sat in the center. Slanted sides with openings for cannons led to a main deck a foot or so off the waterline. Ash gave a low whistle.

"Pretty, ain't she?" Clem dismounted.

"Impressive. Good to learn we've got a ship worthy to combat Yankee ironclads."

"Surprised to hear you feel that way." Clem gripped Ash's upper arm. "Iffen you do."

A few men on the shore gave him a curious glance.

Clem stopped in front of a tent tall enough for Ash's six-foot frame to stand erect. "Sarge, you in there?"

A husky man in gray pushed back the tent's fly entrance. "Who you got there, Clem?"

"You recall that feller what disappeared on the road 'bout two weeks ago?" His grip tightened on Ash's arm.

He tried not to wince. Did the fellow think he'd run now, when he hadn't during their ride out?

"That him?" The clean-shaven sergeant eyed Ash.

"One and the same."

"Where'd you find him?"

Clem explained and was dismissed.

"I'm Sergeant Bradford. And you?"

"Ash Williams." He'd use his middle name and omit his surname. A fake name might protect him.

"Come inside, Mr. Williams."

He stepped into the confined space that held a cot, folding chair, and table covered with documents. Ash wasn't invited to sit.

"Clem's suspicious of you." Sergeant Bradford stacked pages and turned them over, hiding what was written there. "Can you account for that?"

"Not at all, sir. I stopped to buy a newspaper." Ash clasped his hands behind his back.

The officer's eyes turned steely. "What's your business in Yazoo City?"

"No more than passing through. Got acquaintances on the Big Black River."

"Name?"

What was Hester and Daisy's last name? "Maple, sir."

"Never heard of them." He crossed his arms. "Clem thinks you're a spy ferreting out information about work on the *Arkansas*."

"Not at all, sir."

"Empty your pockets."

Thank God he'd discarded Josh's ciphered message.

When his pockets turned up only a piece of jerky and Julia's embroidered handkerchief, his hat was inspected. Then his boots and the lining of his jacket. When the Confederate wanted to examine his trousers and stockings, Ash started to protest but quickly realized it made him seem guilty.

Once nothing incriminating was found, he was allowed to don his clothes again. Would they let him go?

"I'm not going to bother the lieutenant with you. He's got more important matters to contend with." Sergeant Bradford rubbed his jaw. His whiskers sounded like sandpaper. "Clem's certain there's something fishy about you. He's usually a good judge of character."

"You've discovered nothing. Now, please release me to go about my business."

"Can't do that. You've seen the *Arkansas*."

"I won't tell anyone." The thought of being locked up made his skin crawl.

"Nope. You'll stay here." He widened his stance. "Didn't find proof that you're spying, but we'll just keep you here for a while. That way, I'll know you can't tell the wrong people about our ship."

Prison. His courage nearly failed him.

# CHAPTER 32

Out in the middle of the wilderness, Ash's prison had no bars. No windows. The four-by-six-foot building was nothing more than an outbuilding for storage. With a lock fastened on the outside.

He'd been locked up only a few hours and sweat poured down his face that had nothing to do with sweltering July heat. It reminded him of his panic in being locked in the saddle shop by his father as a four-year-old boy.

This ill-constructed outbuilding was a waking nightmare.

At least lines of daylight streamed across the hay-covered dirt floor. Two boards on one wall weren't flush together. Ash pressed his face against the half-inch opening. It allowed a glimpse of tents close to the river and the ship's bow. Not much connection with soldiers and sailors walking in freedom, but it brought Ash a modicum of comfort.

He fished the handkerchief Julia had given him for Christmas from his pocket. Held it up to the sunrays. Kissed the beautifully stitched saddle. "Julia," he whispered. "Keep praying."

Footsteps approached.

Ash folded the handkerchief and stuffed it back in his pocket.

The lock clanked against the door and then it opened. "Figured you might need to visit the sinks." Clem held a musket.

"Much obliged." One long stride took Ash outside, where he bent, hands on knees, gasping for air. Sunlight.

"Ain't that hot in there, is it?" Clem stuck his hand inside.

"Can't stand to be locked up." Ash gulped fresh air.

"Don't try to run." He patted his musket. "This thing's loaded."

Ash's stiff leg needed a long walk, but the camp was small. Less than two hundred people called it a temporary home. Most men were on the ship, pounding nails, fastening metal plates to the side. One soldier built up a campfire as they passed. Others led horses toward the river for a drink.

Once back at the shed, Clem gave him a canteen of water and two large square crackers. Ash downed a long swallow with an eye to his torture chamber. This was his punishment for betraying his city even as mortar rained down on it. Clem couldn't know just how completely it destroyed him to step inside.

"Get in. We'll visit the sinks once more before I hit the hay, then you won't see me until breakfast." Clem locked the door.

His shoulders against the wall, Ash sank to the floor. It could be worse. Had they found a cipher or message on him, he'd likely be hanged.

Hanging would have been preferable to this sweltering prison...except he might survive to return to Julia.

∾

*J*ulia acquiesced to Mama's wishes to return to the shelter on Thursday morning. Mortar fire wasn't as intense, so they all ate lunch inside. Then a coughing spell convinced Mama to lie down on the hall sofa.

"Let me fetch your medicine." Julia hurried to the stairs.

"I'm out of pills and elixir." Mama coughed into a linen handkerchief.

The blood drained from Julia's face, leaving her dizzy. "You didn't tell me you were low on medicine when I asked you last week." Dr. Alison lived three squares away. Was he hunkered down in the city? "How long have you been out?"

"Monday."

No wonder Mama was worse. "I'll fetch you some." Her heart quaked at the thought of being vulnerable on the streets.

"Send Silas or Ash." Her voice wobbled.

"Silas is digging a shelter. Ash isn't here. I'll hurry." Ash would come for supper. If nothing had happened.

"I'll come with you." Eddie ran to the front door.

"No." Julia and Mama spoke in unison.

"Sit with me while we wait for her." Mama held out a hand to her son. Dragging steps took him to her. "Be careful, Julia."

"I will." Julia stepped onto the street, looking up for cannonballs flying toward her. None. She squared her shoulders. If Ash could ride into danger in service of his country, she could walk into it on a mission of mercy for her mama.

～

*T*he shadows lengthened Thursday evening. Ash had been in this prison over thirty-six hours, time he counted by the pounding hammers on the ship. Men shouted orders after sundown. The low hum of voices just out of earshot tortured him as much as the oven he was enduring because those conversations might give him something new to pass on to his contacts—if he made it out alive. Yet anything was better than silence.

Last night had been the worst—when his prison turned into a nightmarish blend of darkness and anxiety closing in on him, as it was doing now. Clem had already locked him in for the night. Ash spoke only when his guard wished to talk. Other than that, it seemed prudent to keep his mouth shut.

Ash gripped the handkerchief Julia had embroidered. He pictured her lovely, calm face. She knew something was wrong by now. There was no way to comfort her. He thanked God fervently that she couldn't see him being held by Confederates.

Why had he ever agreed to spy for the Union? It had brought untold pain on his city, his neighbors, his loved ones, his sweet Julia.

Voices grew fainter. Lights extinguished. Darkness became complete.

He paced for several minutes. It didn't release his agitation. Leaning his shoulders against the wall, he began to pray...for Julia and her family, his neighbors, his city, his family. For himself. Then, speaking aloud, he quoted every Scripture he remembered.

He'd heard it said that no good deed ever went unpunished. Long hours in this sweltering box gave him time to wrestle with the cost of his actions and realize his contribution *had* made a difference in keeping the communication flowing northward. If it ended now, if his fate was to die for serving his country, he'd face it like a man.

But oh, how he wished to see Julia one last time.

How she'd clung to him, pleaded with him not to make this delivery.

"I'm sorry, Julia."

～

On Friday, Ash tried to walk inside his prison to prevent his leg from stiffening. Two short strides and he reached the wall. Two back. He stopped counting his steps upon reaching five hundred.

He'd learned to appreciate the boards overhead not meeting in two places. He sat there when the sun shone inside to feel it on his face. It took the edge off his panic.

A key turned in the lock. Bright sunshine blinded him.

"Thought you might want to sit outside to eat supper." Clem set two metal plates with bacon and a biscuit on the ground.

"Much obliged." A veritable feast. His best meal since his capture two days before. The jerky was long gone.

"You ain't looking so good." Clem waited until Ash sat and then joined him. "Mississippi sunshine might be better for you than the food."

It was hot, nearly airless, in the shed. He'd slept poorly since being captured. "Might be." Ash prayed silently for his meal and then made a sandwich of the meat and biscuit.

They ate in silence. When even the crumbs were gone, Clem stacked the plates. "I figure you were up to no good that night. Sneaking up on the grocer like you did wasn't right. Just ain't sure you were spying." The soldier met Ash's eyes squarely. "If I thought you were, I'd put a bullet between your eyes."

"I wasn't spying." He'd been a spy delivering a note.

"Mebbe not. Sarge didn't find nothing. Nothing in your saddlebags either."

Ash didn't trust himself to speak. Could barely breathe. Clem would kill him if he found proof.

"Spies have caused us no end of trouble. Your life ain't worth much if we find proof you did it." Clem rattled the plates together. "I'll be back to take you to the sinks at sundown."

Once he was locked inside the outbuilding again, sweat poured down Ash's face.

~

*S*aturday afternoon, July twelfth. Still no word from Ash. Julia touched her lips. He had kissed her goodbye on Tuesday evening.

While Eddie was playing a game with Silas in the back of the cave that afternoon, Mama leaned close to Julia. "Where's Ash?"

"I don't know. Just pray for him." Julia's voice quaked.

Mama stared at her, willing her to say more. "Be strong for your brother, then. You know how Eddie loves Ash."

"I know." *I do too.*

Eddie had been satisfied that Ash was working up to now. Soon he'd start asking questions.

Julia was nearly half crazy with worry. Where was her beau?

There'd been silence from artillery on both sides yesterday, but the bombardment was back today. Mortar blasts continued, though not at the same fever pitch as that first terrible day. Julia had made it to the doctor's house. He had given her a month's supply of pills but had no elixir. Mama improved somewhat after getting the medicine, but the gunpowder smoke was the culprit. She'd finally relented, and they now slept in the house again.

Julia prayed the Union boats would be long gone before the medicine ran out.

She spent every spare moment praying for God to protect Ash, to spare his life, to bring him back safely.

What if Ash didn't come back? Was she strong enough to lose him?

War had a way of reminding one that death was part of life.

But yes, she'd grown stronger. She'd struggle if Ash never returned, but God would take care of her. She'd remember the good times and be strong for her brother, as Ash had asked her to do.

"Ash, please come back to me," she whispered aloud. "But if you never return, I'll cling to the knowledge that you loved me. I'll love you to my last breath."

～

*C*lem unlocked the door of Ash's cell Sunday at twilight. The inactivity of the last five days had been nearly as hard as imprisonment. Increased activity around camp all day had warned him something was up. As he walked as slowly as possible back from the sinks, soldiers stuffed possessions into knapsacks. Men washed clothes in the river.

"Things will be different come tomorrow." The musket on Clem's shoulder was a constant companion on every walk. "You might as well know we're pulling out. You'll be locked in."

Ash's heartbeat thrashed in his ears. Locked up and no way out.

His worst nightmare.

Clem locked the door behind him.

Ash fought down his panic.

*Lord, help me find my way out of here.*

～

*S*houts woke Ash some time later. He pressed his face against the slits in the boards. Scant moonlight showed the ironclad leaving the riverbank. There was no movement in camp.

*God, please help me.*

Ash waited until the dark shape floated away. Then he

rammed the door with his shoulder as he'd longed to do for days. It didn't budge.

A rustle in the leaves snagged his attention. Then he heard the clip-clop of horse's hooves striking dirt.

Someone rode into the deserted camp on horseback.

Impossible to see who it was. Jim, maybe? He was the only one who knew Ash's route, the only one who knew he didn't return to Bolton as planned.

Wishful thinking.

The horseman picked his way through camp as if searching for something.

Was he friend or foe? Didn't matter. Ash must escape his prison.

"Over here," Ash called, keeping his voice as soft as possible but loud enough for the rider to hear, "in the outbuilding."

The rider's head whipped around. He galloped over. "Is it you, Ash?"

"Yes!" Something vaguely familiar about the voice. "Who are you?"

"Josh Allen. I've been waiting to free you."

The spy who'd sold him the newspaper. "They've locked me in here. The *Arkansas* is gone and everyone with it."

Josh dismounted. The lock jingled. "Give me a minute."

He disappeared from Ash's sight through the narrow slit. Footsteps sounded outside the prison. Then something smashed against the metal lock.

In less than a minute, the door opened wide.

Ash stumbled out. "Boy, am I grateful to see you."

"Did they find my message?"

He shook his head. "I dropped it in tall weeds along the roadside, maybe a hundred yards from your place."

"I'll find it. Your note was memorized and burned ten minutes after you left."

"Thank you." This spy was wise. "My horse may be here somewhere."

"I'll help you look and then you'll have to hightail it out of here. There are folks in town who'd do you harm even on suspicion of being a spy."

They might lynch him first and ask questions later. Energy shot through Ash. "Let's hurry."

They found the saddled mare tied to a bush beside the river. Josh gave a low whistle. "Clem must have had his doubts about you being a spy. He's not a bad sort."

The one supper Clem had shared with him proved he'd have killed Ash himself if he was certain he was a spy. The saddled horse showed Clem figured he'd escape his prison.

"I've filled your canteen. You'd best go before first light." Josh shoved strips of jerky into the saddlebag. "It won't take folks in town long to realize the ironclad is gone. Curiosity will drive them to look around camp."

"I've never been more ready." Ash forced his protesting leg over the saddled horse. He grasped Josh's hand. "My thanks is not enough."

"Your safe arrival home will be." He stepped back and Ash rode away.

He had miles to go before getting to Julia.

# CHAPTER 33

$\mathcal{A}$sh picked his way in the darkness until finding his original route's country lane. The mare began to slow about ten miles from Yazoo City, just seven miles from the farm where Jim's horse awaited.

Gray clouds delayed sunrise. After dismounting, he led the mare—couldn't recall her name—to a creek.

He washed his face, head, and arms in the bracing water. That so refreshed him that he took a quick bath while the mare munched on grass. He rinsed his none-too-clean green blouse, rung it out, and then donned the uncomfortably wet garment.

A strip of jerky combined with the bath revived him. Those clouds might bring rain, the kind that just made it hot and steamy afterward. He pulled out Papa's old pocket watch, grateful that he'd been allowed to keep it. Twenty-five minutes past six.

Julia must be frantic at his continued absence. Best get moving.

He pushed against a tree to stand. His right foot in the stirrup, he tried to swing his stiff, aching leg over the saddle. It didn't obey.

He tried to mount using his left foot first in the stirrup. It couldn't stand his weight.

Walking ought to ease the stiffness. As he led the horse by the reins, soft rain began to fall.

It took three hours to reach the farm where he'd left Jim's horse. The gray-haired farmer didn't demand extra fees for the six-day delay in returning the horse—a blessing, for the money that had been in Ash's saddlebag was missing. All the farmer cared was that the mare was in good health.

The farmer's wife fed him chicken stew and biscuits on the front porch. Although he managed to eat only half a bowl and one biscuit, the gracious woman seemed to sense he'd survived on far less for several days. She wrapped two biscuits in linen for when he got hungry on the trail.

Ash's leg had never hurt like this, even immediately after the original injury. He couldn't mount Polka Dot, so named for the white circles dotting its brown coat. The farmer helped him mount using the corral fence for a boost.

Twenty-five miles to the tanner's house. His next destination seemed as far away as the Gulf of Mexico.

He'd ride until Polka Dot required a break. No possibility of him getting back in the saddle again today. Probably not tomorrow.

*Lord, help me make it safely to Julia.*

~

*J*ulia's family was back in the shelter on Monday afternoon. Mama sat, eyes closed, with her head against the seat.

"I'm counting the explosions, Julia." Eddie sat on a blanket near the cave's entrance.

"How many so far?" Anxiety for Ash made it difficult to focus on her brother—or the letter she was writing to Caroline.

"Eighty-nine. Think we'll get to one hundred fifty like we did yesterday?"

"Hope not." Julia glanced at the cave's opening shrouded by wispy smoke.

Where was Ash?

*Lord, watch over Ash and keep him safe. Bring him home.*

∾

"*A*sh, wake up." A hand nudged his shoulder. "Ash? You hear me?"

His back grazed a tree's rough bark as he woke with a start. He was in the woods by a stream where Polka Dot grazed. Had the soldiers found him again?

"You're safe." A strong, callused hand rested on Ash's shoulder. "You look like you've endured a nightmare."

The farmer he'd met while riding with Julia? This had to be a dream. "Michael?"

"Yes, it's me. Eat this jerky."

Starving, Ash reached for it eagerly. Manna from heaven must have melted on the tongue like this. "Thanks." He leaned back against a tree as he ate. His eyes closed.

A hand shook his shoulder. "Ash, wake up. Eat another strip of jerky."

He did as he was told, more awake this time. "I have to get to Julia. But first to Jim Routeledge's place."

"I know of him."

"My leg won't make it. I'll rest here tonight."

Intense eyes the color of the Mississippi studied him. "I've got my wagon. You can stretch out in the back."

A sense of déjà vu washed over him. The farmer had helped him months ago. "I'm not sure I can get into the wagon." It shamed him to admit it.

"Where's the pain?"

"My entire left leg." Ash rested his head in defeat against the sturdy trunk.

Kneeling, Michael massaged the knee.

Ash grimaced but didn't speak. After a minute or two, the pain eased.

"Think you can stand now?"

His throbbing knee wasn't as stiff. "I'll try." He pushed himself to his feet. After standing a moment, he turned to fetch Polka Dot.

"I'll bring the mare. You get into the wagon."

The forest's horse trail had widened to fit a wagon about a mile before he collapsed by the stream. How had Michael found him?

Ash sat on the loaded bed and scooted on his backside until his boot rested against a barrel at the end.

Marveling at how the delicious jerky satisfied his appetite, he watched as Michael secured the mare to the wagon. "You out on a delivery?"

"Might say that." He laid a canteen within Ash's reach before climbing onto the seat. "We've got better than twenty miles to go. Might as well sleep."

Soldiers were miles away. He was safe. Ash slept.

~

Furious fighting from the north overshadowed the gunboats' attack from downriver on Tuesday. Julia's family watched a battered Confederate ironclad come to a rest on Vicksburg's wharves from their front porch. Citizens who ran to greet them turned away as if horrified.

What was on the boat to cause such a reaction? Dead men scattered about the deck? She'd seen some gruesome wounds as a volunteer at the hospital. She shuddered.

"It's the *Arkansas* we've been hearing about." Silas leaned on the porch rail, his gaze fixed on the river. "That ship must have endured a fierce battle. Surely took courage to steer toward what must have felt like certain death."

How courageous those men must be. The lone ironclad had fought several Union ironclads upriver and escaped only to take on the Union fleet downriver from Vicksburg. Julia's Unionist loyalties didn't stem an overwhelming admiration for the sheer bravery required to step up for such a daunting, almost suicidal mission.

Ash had showed the same courage, over and over. Would she have the chance to show him how proud she was of him?

~

*A*sh stared at his pocket watch. Five o'clock? He limped down the creaky stairs at the tanner's house. "I didn't sleep around the clock, surely."

"'Fraid so." Jim turned a chicken leg frying in a cast-iron skillet before looking up. "You missed three meals. I planned on waking you for supper."

"You never want me to stay above an hour." Ash yawned.

"You've never been six days late from a delivery."

"There are two biscuits in my saddlebag."

"Fetch them."

The men did justice to a meal of fried chicken, mashed potatoes, and biscuits before the tanner put down his red-checkered linen napkin. "I'm ready to hear all of it."

Ash told him everything...capture, prison, Josh's rescue, and the wagon ride from Michael. The master spy was more interested in the Confederate ironclad. Ash told him all he'd gleaned. Both men agreed his runs to Harv's would suffice henceforth. He'd never return to Yazoo City.

"I must get to Vicksburg." Ash folded his napkin and rose. "Julia must be worried sick."

"Imagine so, but you'll have to wait until tomorrow. The next train leaves Wednesday afternoon."

And his horse was in Vicksburg. Feeding and watering his mount wasn't Jolene's job, but he prayed she or her husband had taken care of Rosebud in his absence.

He'd stop in to feed Rosebud, bathe, shave, and then go to Julia's. *One more day, Julia.*

# CHAPTER 34

*W*ednesday passed slowly without word from Ash. The Union fleet seemed to take turns battering the city and the *Arkansas* with shells.

Julia waited with her family in the hall while Hester made yet another pot of vegetable soup from canned vegetables because they couldn't visit the market, even if stores were open. Too dangerous to walk the streets.

"Where's Ash, Julia?" Eddie bounced from one foot to the other.

"I don't know, Eddie." Ash had told Julia that Eddie needed her strength. Mama had warned her to shield her brother from worry. But the strain was growing too heavy to bear.

"Did a shell hit him?" He tugged on her arm, anxiety in his eyes.

His question shot terror into her soul. Was he dead? Lying wounded, in need of loving care?

"No, we'd have heard." From the sofa, Mama held out her arms to her son. He ran into them.

Julia stared at the front door, willing Ash to walk through it.

No, gunboats attacked the city right now. He'd come to the veranda, where he'd be less of a target.

"Miss Julia?" Silas's voice came from the back of the hall. "Someone's here to see you."

"Julia." The voice carried through the house, a phantom sound. For it couldn't be...

Ash?

Or did she dream it? She turned. Her heart wrenched.

"Ash!" Eddie ran to the tall, gaunt man who stared at Julia, his heart in his eyes. Eddie crashed into his legs.

"Hey, buddy." Ash winced. He bent and hugged him. "You all right?"

"Now you're here."

"I'm glad to be here too." He ruffled Eddie's hair. "I must talk to your sister."

Julia felt rooted to the spot, her gaze drinking in his dear face, the shadows under those magnificent hazel eyes. He was dressed in a blue print blouse and gray trousers as befitted a city under attack, not a beau coming for supper. Even so, he'd never looked more debonair. "Ash, are you really here?"

He held out his arms.

She ran into them, wrapping her arms around him, reveling in the strength he poured into her soul with the embrace.

"Are you all right?" His voice rumbled in her ear.

"So glad you're here." She looked up at him. "Where have you been?"

"Doesn't matter. All that matters is that I'm where I've dreamed to be the last eight days." He cradled her to his chest. "Please forgive the worry I've put you through."

She kept her voice low. "Can you tell me what happened?"

Glancing past her, he shook his head. "Someday." His arms slid away with seeming reluctance.

She stared up at him. "For now, it's enough that you're here. Safe."

"Ash, we've prayed for you." Mama had stood and approached. "You're a good man, the best man for my daughter."

Julia gasped, her gaze darting to Mama.

"Thank you, Mrs. Dodd." He sandwiched her hand between his. "That's what I've longed to hear." Releasing her hand, he turned back to Julia.

"Looking back, I see God's guidance upon me every step of the way." His fingers caressed her cheek. "I'm a blessed man."

Somehow, they were holding hands. Could this be *the* moment...

"Julia, this is not how I planned it." He brought her fingers to his lips and kissed them. "But nothing has proceeded as planned for anyone since the war began."

Julia couldn't speak as she stared up into his eyes. *Ask me.*

"If you want me to go down on one knee, we'll have to postpone—"

"No, of course not!"

He chuckled and then turned serious. "You are the kindest, most compassionate, loving woman I know, and I want you always in my life."

A sheen of her tears hid his dear face. She blinked them away.

"Miss Julia Dodd, will you do me the very high honor of becoming my wife?"

"Yes, yes." She threw her arms around his neck and kissed him. She was finally an engaged woman, betrothed to the man she loved more than her own life. His return kiss hinted at passion held in check and all the love she'd craved. "I love you," she whispered against his lips.

"I love you." He kissed her and then turned her around to the assembled family. "Folks, it's my great honor to announce to you all that Julia has agreed to become my wife."

Eddie and Silas cheered. Hester clapped. Mama cried.

"My heart is full." Mama clasped Julia's hand and Ash's. "I felt for my Harrison what Julia feels for you. I want that same happiness for her...and she's found it."

"Thank you, Mama." Tears streamed down Julia's cheeks. "You're right—Ash is the best man for me."

"I see that now." She smiled at Ash. "I look forward to the day I may call you my son."

∾

*A*sh took the train to Bolton the following Monday, July twenty-first. Jim planned to give his Yazoo City route to another rider sometime down the road. For now, Ash was only to make the runs to Harvey's Mill.

When he returned to Vicksburg late that afternoon, he learned that the *Arkansas* had faced significant direct attacks while moored at the city's wharfs but had sent two Union ships aground. Those boats righted themselves and skedaddled downstream.

A victory in a slew of victories for the crew of the *Arkansas* that came at a high cost. Ash learned that the crew of about one hundred was down to a tragic sixteen. The rest had been killed or wounded.

He hoped with all his heart that Clem was one of the survivors. The man had captured him, raised suspicions in his comrades, and threatened to kill him if he proved to be a spy. Even so, he didn't deserve this fate.

When the Union fleet sailed south on July twenty-seventh, ending the battle, Ash mourned the Union loss, knowing they'd return someday and attack the city again. It meant more death. More loss. More spying because the lone ironclad, coupled with Confederate cannons at Vicksburg, had succeeded in running off the Union fleet.

The city itself had lost two citizens in the sustained attack.

A young mother was killed by a shell while leading her little boy to safety. A little girl was killed when playing with an object that turned out to be an artillery shell. Ash mourned the deaths much as he had mourned Willie's—all tragedies.

Luke had been as sporadic in his communication as Ash in the last few months. But when he returned from his short stint at the Rebel camp, there had been a letter waiting for him at the post office. Luke's regiment had fought in battles around Richmond the last week of June. Thirty-two men in his regiment had been killed and one hundred nineteen wounded. It was the biggest action his friend had encountered, and he badly needed a furlough.

Ash's mother didn't know of the planned nuptials yet. Railroad service west had been stopped about two months before. His and Julia's letters should reach them any day.

No wedding date was set yet for Ash and Julia. If Luke got that furlough, they'd plan it then. How he wanted at least one of his buddies to stand up with him.

# CHAPTER 35

"*L*uke's coming?" Clutching Felicity's arm, Julia squealed. They were able to safely sit upon the veranda in the evening again in early August, though she doubted she'd ever forget the fear of those two months. "You said he hoped to come this month."

"Yes, he'll be here on the twenty-third. His letter came today." Felicity's blue eyes shone. "He wants to stay with Ash for the nearly four weeks he'll be here."

"Ash didn't mention it." Julia's excitement for Felicity mounted. Julia understood the terrible fear of not knowing what a loved one endured.

"I doubt he's received his letter yet. Will he mind?"

"He misses Luke something fierce. And now that you're cleaning Ash's house, you'll get to see him there too." Julia and Eddie stopped in at lunch on the days Felicity worked to dine with them at Ash's house. "Tell me truly, is the job to your liking?"

"Yes. It's very manageable. Most of the rooms are closed off with the rest of the family gone. Will you keep them closed once you're married?"

"Not all of them." Warmth rose in her cheeks just to imagine being married to Ash. "Eddie insists upon his own room for when he stays with us."

"Your dress is coming along nicely. It should be ready in about a week, then I'll add some of the lace you tatted to your mother's dress."

"Good." Though closed shops had reopened when many citizens returned to the city the last three weeks, who knew when satin or silk fabric would be available. Therefore, she'd hired Felicity to modify an old dress, a blue silk gown. What had been worn as a full hoopskirt would become a modified hoop dress trimmed with lace and silk bows. She could wear it for other celebrations later. "I hope that allows you to spend enough time with your beau."

"I'll work at night if necessary." Felicity laughed. "I'm not missing one moment with Luke. Aunt Mae's planning to cook all his favorite meals. You'll all be invited."

It would mean the world to Ash if Luke could attend the wedding. Julia intended to ask Mama if they could be ready within three weeks, and then approach Ash.

This would be perfect.

~

*A*sh and Luke had stayed up talking until the wee hours the day he returned. Ash would save news of his spying for later—if at all. The fewer who knew that secret, the better.

The next day, August twenty-fifth, his family arrived from Texas. The change in his mother astounded Ash. She'd found renewed purpose at the ranch. Uncle Clark bragged that his nieces had become accomplished riders.

Ash couldn't believe his happiness simply to have them all

near. He'd come so close to not surviving that he'd never take anything for granted again. His leg hadn't yet recovered its stamina, yet no one remarked on his crutch. It hadn't made him less of a man, as he'd always feared.

Uncle Clark came into the saddle shop, where Ash was measuring a piece of leather, the day after they arrived. "Love the smell of leather. Reminds me of your pa. Mind sitting a spell?"

"Not at all. My work bench suit you?" This was the first quiet moment for him and his uncle. His mother and sisters had been full of news, requiring only that the men listened.

"That'll be fine." Uncle Clark sat at one end. "I like having your family on my ranch. My invitation for you—and now Julia and her family—is still open. My hands could help you build a house. How'd you feel about living on a ranch?"

"I'm a saddler. I know nothing of that lifestyle." Even so, his interest was piqued.

"The closest saddler is fifty miles away." Uncle Clark leaned forward. "The quality of your work impressed my neighbors. If you lived closer, they'd be ordering from you. We'd build you a saddle shop."

Excitement tremored through Ash. A new shop. A chance to start a new life with Julia in Texas. "I'll talk to Julia." He didn't want to get too excited until he knew her thoughts.

"I'll speak bluntly. I want to name you my heir. I'd train you to run the ranch so when the time comes, you're ready to take over."

Ash's heart hammered against his chest. Mama, gossip that she was, had never hinted at this possibility. "I don't know what to say. Thank you."

"There's a condition. I've got another heir in mind...one of my wife's nephews, but my first choice is you. I want to leave my land to someone who will tend what I've built, keep it in the family. Pass it down to his own sons. In short, I want to know that you want it."

On his visit as a child, he and his cousin had ridden all over the ranch. Though it had been smaller in those days, it had seemed like heaven on earth. With Julia and his family close by, it would be. "I want it, Uncle Clark. Let me see how Julia feels about moving to Texas."

"This was on my mind in the spring. You were so set against moving. After that big battle here, I thought I'd try again."

The Union would attempt to take Vicksburg again. No doubt, another battle was coming. Maybe worse next time. He wanted Julia, Eddie, and Mrs. Dodd out of harm's way for this next one. "Julia is getting ready for the celebration supper they planned for tomorrow. I'll talk to her now." He shook his uncle's hand, his head reeling. He prayed Julia would be just as excited.

～

"Live in Texas?" An hour later, Julia and Ash sat on her veranda on the pleasantly warm fall day. "Are you considering it?"

"I want to move all of us—your mama and Eddie included —to the ranch."

"I couldn't leave them behind. Not with the war going on."

"The Union fleet will be back. Recall how your mother suffered with the smoke."

"I don't believe she wants to endure another battle. Eddie will love the ranch. You know how adventurous he is." She'd been envious of others who had family in whom to take refuge. Now that she could have it, the last of her resentment against her parents and grandparents melted away. God had planned something else for her all along.

"It'll require some forethought. We'd move within a few months of the wedding. Sooner if the war demands it."

"Perhaps we can send some possessions on ahead." She'd have to dig up everything she'd buried in the cellar in preparation for soldiers overrunning her city. Or have her future husband perform the task. She couldn't help smiling.

"I figure we'll leave by March. Julia, we're going to live in Texas. And I'm thrilled that I'll one day have a ranch to pass on to our sons." He gave her a lingering kiss that curled her toes, then gathered her close for a long embrace.

Julia laughed.

"What's so funny?" He quirked an eyebrow.

"Remember Mama's requirement that I marry a wealthy man? Looks like she got her way, after all." She nestled against his chest, which rumbled with laughter.

~

Julia stood at the back of the church with Eddie. Her brother was to give her away and then take his place next to Luke, dressed in his Confederate uniform, as Ash's best man.

Felicity, wearing a peach gown, was her maid of honor. Savannah, as beautiful as ever in pink, stood beside her.

Mrs. Mitchell, who'd been in town a week, confided to Julia she had been determined not to miss the ceremony she'd been praying into existence. That they'd soon live near one another again brought them all joy, even Mama, who was relieved not to have to endure another battle.

Ash's family. After today, that included Julia, Eddie, and Mama.

When the piano began to play, she smiled down at Eddie. Her brother was nervous about his role. Giving his sister away wasn't something he'd wanted to do until realizing it meant Ash would always be his big brother.

Julia placed her hand on his arm and started down the aisle

to her future. To the man beaming at her, his whole heart revealed in his hazel eyes.

To Ash.

Did you enjoy this book? We hope so!
**Would you take a quick minute to leave a review where you purchased the book?**
It doesn't have to be long. Just a sentence or two telling what you liked about the story!

Receive a FREE ebook and get updates when new Wild Heart books release: https://wildheartbooks.org/newsletter

*Book 1: Avenue of Betrayal*

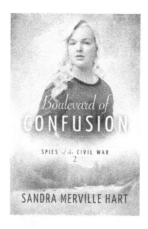

*Book 2: Boulevard of Confusion*

**Book 3: Byway to Danger**

# ABOUT THE AUTHOR

**Sandra Merville Hart,** award-winning and Amazon bestselling author of inspirational historical romances, loves to discover little-known yet fascinating facts from American history to include in her stories. Her desire is to transport her readers back in time. She is also a blogger, speaker, and conference teacher. Connect with Sandra on her blog, https:// sandramervillehart.wordpress.com/.

# ACKNOWLEDGMENTS

I've learned much through the patience of Robin Patchen, Denise Weimer, and Erin Taylor Young, three amazing editors. Misty Beller is such a blessing, as is the whole team at Wild Heart Books, who have been both professional and gracious to me. I look forward to working with them on the next book in this series.

Historical novels require much careful study to add authenticity. Months of Civil War research continues as I write the book. My research trip to Vicksburg reaped many benefits. The battlefield has been beautifully preserved to mimic conditions, as much as possible, during the 1863 battle and siege of Vicksburg. I invite you to check it out.

My husband and I toured the Vicksburg Military Battlefield with Michael Logue, author and licensed battlefield guide. We exchanged many texts in advance of our meeting, enabling Michael to tailor the tour to my needs. I was then near the beginning of my research. That Michael's family history is entrenched in the area—his ancestors owned land on the battlefield!—was extremely beneficial. Michael also sent me an original map of the city. What beautiful details it provided for the story! Thank you, Michael.

I'd also like to thank Andrew Miller, one of the rangers at the Vicksburg Military Battlefield, who further explained what happened in specific areas of the battlefield. He was extremely helpful. Thanks to him and the whole staff.

Thanks to family and friends for their continued support, especially my husband, who is on this whirlwind journey with me.

Thank You, Lord, for giving me the story.

# AUTHOR'S NOTE

I learned that Vicksburg didn't celebrate our country's Independence Day for one hundred years. What tragedy did this city's citizens suffer that made this a difficult day a century later? I knew there had been a long siege before Vicksburg surrendered on July 4, 1863. A desire to learn what happened inspired this book and the next two in the series.

Surprisingly, most Vicksburg citizens wanted to stay in the Union when the South seceded. When Mississippi voted to join the Confederacy, the city supported the state's decision. They were Mississippians first. They worked to crush Unionist support in the city. A vigilante group harassed outspoken Unionists, and some were arrested in the first few months of the war.

Once Union supporters were publicly silenced, the vigilantes ended the harassment. A few Unionists continued to support them in other ways—such as spying. My battlefield guide told me there was plenty of spying going on in Vicksburg. I read many books about Civil War spies, but there were scanty details about Vicksburg spies. Philip Henson was the most famous Union spy from Mississippi. This fictional story portrays dangers faced by Union spies living in the South rather than being based off a specific spy's experiences.

The fall of New Orleans, the South's largest city, was a blow to the Confederacy. The surrender cleared a path on the Mississippi River to the city set on the bluffs. Confederate General Mansfield Lovell began sending troops and military supplies by railroad to Mississippi's capital and from Jackson on to Vicksburg when he realized the surrender of New Orleans was imminent. Both the military and citizens recognized Vicksburg was the Union Navy's next big target.

Confederate Naval Lieutenant Isaac Brown was given command of the *Arkansas* in May of 1862. The ship, at that time, was without an engine or armor to make it an ironclad and was docked in Greenwood, Mississippi. Brown got a crew together that also included soldiers and moved the ship to Yazoo City to finish it.

The Union Navy was understandably interested in work done on the *Arkansas*. Union spies would have been eager to discover progress made while it docked at Yazoo City. The Confederates would have been equally as eager to protect it, inspiring our hero's dilemma in the story.

The Union fleet was still in Vicksburg when the *Arkansas* left its dock on the Yazoo River before dawn on July fourteenth. The crew of the *Arkansas* proved their courage in fighting several Union ships before reaching the Union fleet in Vicksburg, where the battered ship arrived on July fifteenth. Reported numbers vary on how many men Brown had on the Confederate ironclad at the start of its journey, but it was at least one hundred. At the end of the battle, sixteen remained. The others were dead or wounded. Still, the *Arkansas* possessed enough gun power to convince the Union fleet to float south on July twenty-seventh. The Union bombardment had lasted sixty-seven days.

Citizens began digging simple one-room caves for shelter during the bombardment. Many families had left before it started. Others refused to be frightened away.

The main characters are fictional. The struggle Vicksburg's citizens faced isn't. A few historical figures who lived in Vicksburg grace the novel's pages. Mayor Lindsay was Vicksburg's mayor. Colonel Autry was the city's military governor. Brigadier

General Martin Luther Smith commanded the city's defenses. Dr. Alison was a Vicksburg physician. Dr. Morris Emanuel was a druggist and president of the Southern Railroad. Mademoiselle Cognaisse fashioned Parisian-style gowns in Vicksburg.

Charles Smedes was a Vicksburg citizen who owned a grocery shop. He drilled local citizens in the Home Guard before the attack. The Home Guard was to be available to fight if called upon to do so.

Mrs. I. O. Smith was a Vicksburg citizen during the war who took several trips that seemed suspicious to me, though I couldn't find historical confirmation of her spying. She inspired the character of Mrs. Wanda Lakin, the Confederate letter carrier in our story.

After all my research, I'm convinced that most of the spying never made it into the history books. Spies kept their activities hidden to protect themselves and their loved ones. Of course, Northern spies received praise after the war ended. Southern spies received scorn.

I hope you enjoyed this story set in Vicksburg from May of 1861 to September of 1862. There is much more to tell. Books 5 and 6 will continue to highlight the city's history. I invite you to read the whole series.

*Sandra Merville Hart*

## WANT MORE?

If you love historical romance, check out the other Wild Heart books!

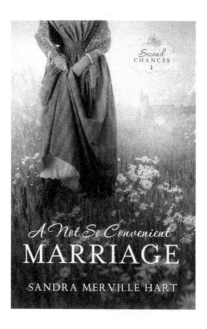

*A Not So Convenient Marriage by Sandra Merville Hart*

*A spinster teacher...a grieving widower...a marriage of convenience and a second chance with the man she's always loved.*

When Samuel Walker proposes a marriage of convenience to Rose Hatfieldso soon after the death of his wife, she knows he doesn't love her. *She's* loved *him* since their school days. Those long-suppressed feelings spring to life as she marries him. She must sell her childhood home, quit her teaching job, and move to a new city.

Marrying Rose is harder than Samuel expected, especially with the shadow of his deceased wife everywhere in his life. And he has two young children to consider. Peter and Emma need a mother's love, but they also need to hold close the memories of their real mother as they grieve her loss.

Life as Samuel's wife is nothing like Rose hoped, and even the townspeople, who loved his first wife, make Rose feel like an outsider. The work of the farm draws the two of them closer, giving hope that they might one day become a happy family. Until the dream shatters, and the life Rose craves tumbles down around them. Only God can put these pieces back together, but the outcome may not look anything like she planned.

*Jeanette's Gift by Blossom Turner*

**This life wasn't the one she dreamed of, but happily ever afters don't always come when and how we expect.**

At twenty-nine, Jeanette Williams has watched each one of her four sisters marry and start families of their own. It's hard not to believe God has forgotten the desires of her heart, especially when most people refer to her as Spinster Williams. Without the beautiful children she teaches, life would be unbearably lonely.

When the handsome widower, Theo Wallace, and his six children move into the Shenandoah Valley, every available woman is atwitter—except for Jeanette. She has no such aspirations that someone as plain as her could draw even a smattering of interest.

As life throws this unlikely couple together, Jeanette can't help but fall in love with Theo's children and their soul-wrenching plight. Before she knows it, her heart is far more invested than she could've ever imagined. And not just with the children, but with their handsome father as well. Is she headed for another heartbreak, or is it possible God had a beautiful plan in the works all along?

~

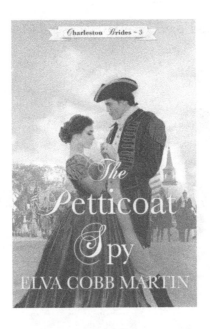

*The Petticoat Spy by Elva Cobb Martin*

*A Southern belle turned spy and a dashing blockade runner fight a hopeless battle against the British.*

When Anna Grace Laurens's parents are murdered by the British and her Charles Town plantation burned, she seizes her only option for escape—a desperate leap into the Cooper River. She'll do anything to survive...and get revenge.

John Cooper Vargas is used to danger as he sails his sloop upriver through war-torn colonies, but seeing a woman plunge into the river amidst Tory gunfire is something he wouldn't have thought possible. Until now.

Rescuing her draws him into a web of intrigue, but he can't let her fight the British on her own. As the American Revolution closes in around them, it may take a miracle for them—and their love—to survive.

Printed in the USA
CPSIA information can be obtained
at www.ICGtesting.com
JSHW011520070324
58222JS00013B/146